IRV SEGAL

SECRETS

OF THE

RABBI'S MAFIA

A Jake Cooper Novel

Dedication

To Sim.
Thanks for always having my back and being so supportive
throughout all my struggles.

Glossary

This story includes Hebrew and Yiddish words and phrases. I've tried to make their meaning obvious from the context. However, you may want to visit my website at irvsegal.com and request my free bonus content. It includes a glossary of these terms I think you'll find helpful and an extra "something" I think you'll really enjoy reading.

– Irv Segal

About the Author

Irv Segal graduated from *yeshiva*– Rabbinical College with a B.A. in Talmudic law and led an Ultra-Orthodox Jewish lifestyle as a young adult.

He earned a certification in computer programming and held a variety of positions in the software field before starting his own software services firm.

Secrets Of The Rabbi's Mafia was inspired by Irv's experiences living in an Ultra-Orthodox Jewish community. He also authored several nonfiction books including Small Business Success: *On Demand*, How to Cash in on the Phone Company's Biggest Mistake Ever and co-authored The Complete Guide to Property Tax Consulting.

Table of Contents

Chapter One

Autumn 1995, Chicago, IL USA

Grabbing his long beard, Jake Cooper slowly squeezed the scissors, feeling the snip of each coarse strand. As each follicle sailed off into the sink, he felt the agony relentlessly haunting him fade just a hair more. He repeated the process, shaved the rest, then sheared off his *payos*, the long curly sidelocks gracing either side of his head.

Gazing at the man in the mirror, now sans beard and *payos*, he recalled the happy young face that once stared back before fatefully devoting himself to an Ultra-Orthodox Jewish lifestyle. A face untouched by tragedy.

Jake's efforts to regain that youthful happiness was a bittersweet turning point, given the circumstances that ended in his recent divorce from Rachel, and the guilt that lingered from his tragic failure that led to it.

He chose this particular night for his facial transformation to venture out to his first Jewish single's event, something unheard of in Ultra-Orthodox circles. He donned his formal attire, optimistically descended the stairs, and marched out to the street to locate his car and begin his journey.

His old Chevy Nova's air conditioning hadn't worked in years and the three-block hike from the only legal parking spot he could find when he arrived, had him working up a sweat. Wiping his brow, he hoped his dark-blonde hair hadn't wilted into a wet blob.

He approached his destination, straightened his tie, tucked in his white shirt, and adjusted his navy-blue suit-jacket. He habitually reached for his *yarmulke*, but his barren head reminded him that he purposely left it in the car– to shed the very last remnant of that life. It was his first time out in public without it, and he felt like everyone was staring at him, wondering why he wasn't wearing it.

Jake tugged on the large glass door of Park West– the venue where the Society of Young Jewish Professionals was hosting their singles event. It was his first foray into the modern single world and he was nervous as hell about fitting in.

The door opened to a sparsely populated entrance-hall and he immediately realized his first two mistakes. He arrived amateurishly on time, and despite leaving his black hat at home and ditching his *Yarmulke*, he was terribly overdressed in the remainder of his *yeshiva* garb– a white shirt, dark suit, and a tie, all staples of Rabbinical College dress code.

He joined ranks with three other too-early bachelors and made a mental note of their assortment of dark slacks and open collared silk shirts. They may have arrived early, but at least their attire wouldn't give them away like his would as the evening wore on.

While waiting for the ticket booth to open, a tall muscular bachelor with curly blonde hair extended his palm.

"Hi, I'm Pinky." He pointed to the short, slim fellow to his right. "This is Big Al."

Jake placed the two of them at about his own age-- thirty-five, somewhat older than bachelor number three, moping silently behind them.

Jake introduced himself and listened intently as Pinky and Big Al argued the finer points of the modern Jewish singles scene. Although he mentally recorded every word to desperately update himself, he questioned the qualifications of his sources.

After the ticket booth opened, Jake forked over his fifteen-bucks and collected his S.Y.J.P. membership card.

"I'll be sure not to leave home without it," he quipped, as he pocketed the card.

Entering the main hall, he scouted the large, dark, and conspicuously empty room, like a presidential secret-service agent. There were several U-shaped cocktail booths sculpted in black fabric that continued upward, lining the walls. Several dark balconies edged with black track lights dropped from the ceiling. A thick black curtain hid the main stage and served as a backdrop for the small, wooden dance floor.

An assortment of thirty to forty-something bachelors trickled in, eventually followed by an equal array of women.

Putting off the inevitable, Jake hid in one of the empty booths. He watched one macho gut-sucking hunter after another approach their prey and break away from the crowd with their victim on their arm.

A scantily clad waitress's breasts suddenly appeared in his face. "And what can I get you?" she inquired.

I'll take two of those, he thought while struggling to recall the name of a drink he had at his cousin's Bar Mitzvah last summer-- the *only* drink he ever had.

"Got anything fruity?"

"I can get you a Daiquiri," she replied as her headlights flashed. "You want banana or strawberry?"

Opting for banana, Jake gazed longingly as she

gyrated back to the bar. Having never been in a bar or ordered a drink, he realized he had no clue what was expected of him upon her return.

"Do I pay for the drink now? Do I tip her? How much do I tip her? Do I tip now, or later before I leave?" He began to regret pushing himself to come here and felt as if he'd landed on another planet without so much as a road map.

Spotting Pinky, he dashed to the master and asked for directions.

"Haven't you been to a bar before?" Pinky mumbled from the side of his mouth, sizing up a tall redhead across the room.

"Actually, no."

Jake's response broke Pinky's concentration, causing him to lose sight of his mark.

"Damn Jake– where've you been? In the dark ages?"

Jake never considered the matter before, but the *dark ages* seemed a rather fitting description of his past life in the secluded Ultra-Orthodox community.

"It's a long story, but sort of."

After Pinky briefed him on barroom etiquette, Jake confidently returned to his booth. He was determined to learn the skills Pinky seemed to come by naturally.

He nodded to the occasional passer-by, while nursing his drink through the tiny swizzle-stick. Having blown most of his meager budget on the entrance fee, he wanted to make the one drink he could afford last the entire evening.

He felt safe in his little observatory-booth until Pinky approached. "Jake, you've gotta mingle. You'll never meet anyone sitting here like a lonely-heart. C'mon."

Reluctantly following the guru's instructions, Jake settled into a forced nonchalant stance amongst a group of bachelors lurking near the room's main entrance, hoping to preemptively strike, before the catch-of-the-day fell prey to one of the other sharks circling the room. Feeling a new camaraderie toward his fellow oglers, he once again felt confident he could make up for his sheltered life all in one night.

As the dance-music beat at an ear-deafening level, Jake tapped out impromptu dance-steps with his foot while continuing to nurse his drink.

Once again, his mentor came to his rescue. "Don't stand by the door. That's the *worst* thing you can do-- you look desperate. Follow me. I'll introduce you to some people."

Jake followed Pinky to a large booth, where he introduced Jake to several people.

Sitting nervously in the crowded booth, he listened to the conversation intently, trying to think of something clever to add. But his opportunity slipped away as everyone migrated to the dance floor, including Pinky who'd connected with a drop-dead gorgeous blonde.

Once again, Jake was alone.

"Hi there," a deep, raspy voice purred. "I'm Marsha. Can I join you?"

Her jade-green eyes staring down at Jake were set-off by jet-black shoulder-length hair.

Marsha's skin-tight, black, leather mini-skirt revealed slender shapely legs. Her youthful looks were betrayed only by her hands, which revealed an age somewhat older than her thirty-something appearance.

When he remembered to breathe, Jake fumbled a response, "Oh-- no, I mean yes-- *please*, have a seat."

"I'm Jake Cooper."

They chatted for a while, Marsha picking up most of the conversation. Jake basked in the warmth of her deep voice, barely recalling most of what she actually said. He did manage to glean a few vital nuggets: she was visiting Chicago, looking for a job, possibly moving here. She asked about his background and seemed fascinated as he described his former Rabbinical College life, recent divorce, and now-abandoned Ultra-Orthodox lifestyle.

Jake felt an inner warmth from the attention he was getting from this gorgeous woman and he didn't want it to stop. But an uncomfortable lull found its way into the conversation and Jake sheepishly reverted to nursing his Daiquiri.

Marsha finally broke the silence. "Wanna dance?"

Recognizing his cue, Jake shed his jacket and tie, rolled up his white sleeves and surrendered his hand to his new-found companion. Marsha led him through the crowd like a shepherd.

They made their way across the dance floor.

Jake's eyes fixated on the crowd's dance-steps.

Eventually, they carved out a spot and became one with the mass of human flesh jiggling to the pulsating music. Jake was so intent on moving his feet in the proper directions, he didn't notice that Marsha was staring deeply into his sky-blue eyes.

A slow dance tune mellowed out the crowd and Marsha ran her fingers through his thick hair, hugging his torso as he struggled not to crush her delicate feet.

Despite shedding half his wardrobe, Jake

overheated shortly thereafter.

"Mind if we take a break?"

They returned to the booth where Jake took a few swigs from his now slightly spiked ice water. Excusing himself, he dashed to the bathroom and splashed cold water on his sweaty face.

He returned to find Marsha swirling the ice around a Black-Russian with her index-finger.

She withdrew her finger from the intoxicating beverage, then seductively slid it deep into her mouth. She slowly extracted it, and wrapped her painted, ruby lips tightly around it.

"I bought a drink while you were away, but that's okay. You'll pay for the next one."

Jake was stunned at her expectation.

He didn't want the magic to end, so he simply smiled.

Marsha said she was ready for more dancing. Complying with her request, Jake gained confidence in his footwork with each dance. Eventually, she steered him towards the outer edge of the dance floor, near the narrow hallway leading to the washrooms. Leading Jake by the hand into the narrow corridor, Marsha leaned her perfectly shaped, firm breasts against him, forcing his back to the wall. Slithering up his chest, she half-closed her eyes and puckered her thin lips.

Inhaling her perfume, Jake abruptly turned his cheek.

Marsha jerked back. Her jaw dropped.

"I can't *believe* you just did that. Any guy here would kill to be with me and *you* blow me off when I show you some attention?"

Jake just stood there stunned, like a child caught red-handed. He knew it made no sense. But something wasn't right. She seemed like everything he'd ever dreamed of in a woman, physically. Yet something begged him not to get involved with Marsha.

He'd been a virgin before his marriage to Rachel and wondered if he was scared to be with a sexy modern woman.

Marsha shook her head.

"Haven't you got a damn thing to say? Maybe it's true. Are *all* you Talmudic scholars a bunch of homo's? That's what I hear."

Jake looked away.

"You don't know what you're missing. I'm going to find someone here who appreciates what I have to offer. Maybe you should go back to your secluded *yeshiva* world.

Next time, keep your little *yarmulke* on your head so we'll know who you *really* are, instead of coming here, pretending to be a *real* man."

It was gone in a flash. Jake felt like any hope he had of finding happiness, vanished in an instant. "Was this what all modern women offered? Was it all just sex and affection in exchange for free drinks?"

Jake made his way back to the still-empty booth to take refuge. He watched longingly as the crowd danced their cares away. There were more Jewish singles here than he'd ever seen before, yet he'd never felt more alone.

It confused and scared him.

A friendly tap on his shoulder revived him.

"What happened to the babe you were with? You didn't scare her off, did you?"

He recounted the episode for Pinky.

"Lots of women *are* just looking for money," Pinky admitted. "It takes dough to make things happen and they know they can get it."

"It just doesn't seem fair," Jake insisted. "I'm a big boy-- I learn fast. But on my limited budget, I can't see how I'll ever afford to wine and dine a woman long enough to get a relationship going."

Their conversation continued-- Jake was grateful for

the distraction. The topic turned from women to money, then to business, religion, and politics, then back to financing relationships.

Jake hesitated, then decided to share his money-making idea.

"I've got this how-to book I bought from an infomercial that explains how to win the lottery by charting and wheeling numbers."

"Does it work?" Pinky asked.

"It works on paper, although I can't figure out why," Jake admitted. "Certain numbers repeat in identifiable patterns. There's a software package that'll do most of the work. I've won on paper, usually on four numbers. Couple of times I hit five, which would've translated into a few thousand bucks. It's not fool-proof, but it is the *smart* way to lotto."

"So how come you're so broke, mister computer-whiz?" Pinky asked, skeptically.

"Because I can't afford to risk the forty bucks per drawing it takes to keep playing until you win. You have to buy enough tickets to cover all the combinations the software picks."

Pinky hesitated, then said, "I know people who are always looking for something to put a few bucks into. I'm *sure* I could raise that kind of cash. How about we get together on this?"

Before the evening ended Marsha cornered Jake one more time, offering him a second bite at the apple. Pinky's confidence assured him he'd have enough money to finance at least the rest of the evening buying Marsha drinks, so despite the warning signals screaming through his brain, he spent the rest of the evening, and all the cash in his pocket, flirting with her.

Chapter Two

Mindy Stein felt the blood drain from her face as she recalled Sender's reaction to her request for a divorce.

He sat with a cold, expressionless face. No yelling, no arguing-- nothing. As if he hadn't heard a word she'd said.

It took her by surprise.

After years of his irate tantrums, it was certainly not what she expected. He simply nodded at her request. She was treading thin-ice, trying not to trigger Sender into a rage that would whip the community into a frenzy against her, as she knew he could. That would be awful-- not only for herself, but more so for the children, her three sweethearts.

Mindy pulled her car out of the downtown Chicago parking structure near her work and made her way onto southbound Lake Shore Drive toward her West Rogers Park neighborhood.

The intense rush-hour traffic and the dreary overcast sky did little to lift her spirits as she mentally prepared to face what awaited her at home.

She picked up her children from the sitter, parked

the car, and unloaded the kids, ushering them into the red-bricked Georgian she shared with him.

When they entered the dimly lit front-room Sender was standing there, arms folded.

"Where's dinner?" he growled.

Mindy was smart enough not to reply. She silently returned his stare.

"Forget it-- I'll do it myself!"

He stormed out of the large room slamming the door to the den behind him.

That was fine with her.

She slowly let out a deep breath, lowered her head, eased the den door open. Sender was standing just inside. It had been a while since she'd been this close to him. The pungent odor turned her nose.

"We may as well just do this. Are you ready?" she asked.

Sender looked away. "What are *you* going to tell the kids?"

"Exactly what Dr. Bulinsky told *us* to."

At her request, they consulted a child psychologist before breaking the news to the children. She mistakenly took Sender's cooperation as a positive sign. His only request was that they see a Orthodox Jewish psychologist.

In an effort to expedite the process, she reluctantly agreed.

Dr. Bulinsky explained how important it was to tell the children that the divorce was not their fault and that it was crucial that this came equally from both parents.

Both parents.

"And what did he tell *you* to say?" Sender replied.

"You know very well!"

Mindy strained to keep her anger bottled up just a little while longer.

"It's supposed to come from *both* of us, remember?"

"*You* created this problem– *you* handle it." Sender insisted.

Sender summoned their three children into the den like a Sergeant's roll call.

"Your *mother* has something she wants to tell you."

Later that evening, she settled the kids into bed in her new apartment, just a few blocks away from their home-- what she now considered Sender's home. She asked a neighbor to stay with the children while she returned to the Georgian to gather the few last items she needed.

She opened the back door and came eye-to-eye with Sender, arms crossed, lips drawn tight.

"I spoke with a lawyer. I don't have to let you take

anything out of this house-- not a single thing."

He continued blocking the door.

Suddenly, Mindy missed the quiet Sender of the past few weeks. But this was the Sender she knew. They'd already agreed on a list of items she would take. She was determined not to let him bully her. She wanted to avoid provoking him, but this was more than she could bear. There was no way she was leaving without the photos of her children, some of their toys, and her jewelry.

"*Move!* Don't make me force you-- because I *will*."

"I could call the police and stop you." Sender threatened.

"Go ahead. Do what you have to. I'm not leaving without my things just because you're angry."

Classic Sender.

He hadn't objected to her taking the children-- it was her *possessions* that really got to him.

To her surprise Sender stepped aside. She marched inside and began picking up the items she'd planned to take. Figuring this might be her last opportunity, she rummaged through the file cabinet in the den, looking for any last-minute items she might want.

Chapter Three

Rabbi Miklin wiped his brow and took a sip of ice water.

"Oh, and please set up for the Janisburg case. They're coming in at two. The hearing should start at two-thirty."

Acknowledging the rabbi's instruction, the clerk sauntered off to the library mentally listing the many volumes of Jewish law-books and commentaries they'd require. He knew them by heart. In fact, he knew these books better than any of them. He despised his lowly position with the *Beis Din*-- the Jewish religious court. If not for his unfortunate circumstances, he surely would have been head judge by now, his rulings on the topic of every Talmudic lecture.

Slowly scaling the library walls, he retrieved the required texts. Placing them on a metal cart, he wheeled them to the courtroom. The wheels of the cart squeaked as he guided it along and he mentally noted to oil them. He was proud of this library. It was his baby. He was intimately familiar with each of the hundreds of books. He could instantly recall the location of any particular volume using the cataloging technique he had devised.

He neatly piled the books near the judge's microphone, then sat for a moment in the Judge's leather chair. This was where he *really* belonged– head judge of the *Beis Din*. Removing a small leather case from the inside breast pocket of his black suit-jacket, he slipped out the small hand-held mirror it contained. Sitting upright, he meticulously examined his appearance. Licking his fingers, he smoothed his eyebrows and ran his fingers through his neatly trimmed beard. He gazed into the little mirror, admiring the distinguished looking rabbi staring back at him.

Yes, he would make a fine head judge indeed.

As two-thirty approached, he begrudgingly extracted himself from the large leather chair and skulked to his little clerk's desk off to the side of the courtroom where he patiently waited during the entire session.

The case was a money-matter, nothing of particular interest-- at least not for his purposes.

After the session, he gathered the volumes and carefully returned each one to its place on the shelf.

Later that day, Sender sauntered into the building wearing a misshapen black fedora, and a wrinkled black suit jacket, peppered with dandruff.

"I'm Sender Stein. I'm here for my appointment,"

he announced as he approached the receptionist.

The elderly receptionist checked her appointment book and said, "Rabbi Miklin is just wrapping up an emergency session. He'll be with you shortly. Meanwhile, feel free to make yourself comfortable in his office."

Sender slithered down the narrow corridor, checking the name-plates on each office door until he came to one marked;

Rabbi Isaac Miklin, Chief Judge
Illinois Rabbinical Board

He lingered in the doorway of the tiny office for a moment, stroking his long oversized oily nose with his bony forefinger and thumb. He wiped his oily fingers on his black, wrinkled suit-jacket. He entered the room and sifted through a pile of papers on the rabbi's desk.

He opened several file cabinet drawers rifling through the neatly aligned folders.

Pulling out one of particular interest, he began reading it. Tilting back his misshapen black fedora, he furiously scratched his greasy hair adding even more snow to his suit jacket. He hated being kept waiting by anyone, but made good use of the opportunity. The secretary did tell him to make himself *comfortable*. And nothing made him more comfortable than conducting *research*, as he liked to think of it.

After perusing most of the file, he heard the clacking of steel taps emanating from the tiled hallway. He slipped the file back into the cabinet and quietly closed the drawer.

The steps drew closer.

"Mr. Stein, I apologize for the inconvenience."

The tall stately looking rabbi adorned by a long white beard and full-length black coat presented his open-palmed hand.

"I hope I haven't kept you waiting too long."

"That's okay. I've been making myself *comfortable*," Sender replied.

He noted the rabbi's freshly pressed suit, crisp starched white shirt and perfectly shaped jet-black Homburg perched on his head.

As the rabbi took his seat behind the large oak desk, he motioned to Sender to occupy one of the guest chairs opposite him. Sender promptly complied, slithering into the well-worn cracked-leather chair.

"I didn't know about our emergency session when I scheduled your appointment. But we are here about you now, so let's see how I can be of help. What is it that you need?"

"Recently my wife moved out of our home with our three children. She is demanding a divorce and I'm more than happy to give her one."

"I see. Have you tried counseling?"

"No. That's not the problem. My wife has decided to throw away her Orthodox Judaism and become like the *shiksa* women she sees walking the streets with their short skirts and low-cut blouses. If that's what she wants, good riddance I say. But she's subjecting our children to her new lifestyle. Already she's fed them non-kosher food and exposed them to television and movies. She tells my boys they don't have to wear their yarmulkes. Last night, she took them out to eat at a McDonald's."

He rested his pimple-ridden forehead in his hands and let out a deep forced sigh. He slowly lifted his head, drawing his hands down across his pockmarked face. He cocked one eye to gauge the rabbi's reaction.

"You see, Rabbi Miklin, I'm concerned about the upcoming *Shabbos*. I'm afraid– no I'm certain, she's going to desecrate the *Shabbos* day with them. Adam, my twelve-year-old, called me yesterday begging me to save him because she's planning to take them to the movies this Friday night."

"Mr. Stein. My heart goes out to you and your

children. This is terrible. Unfortunately, I cannot say it is the first time I've seen this sort of thing. How can I help?"

Sender tried to hide the smirk that reflexively flashed across his face.

"Well, since all of my children are over the age of six, I believe I should get custody. Which would be most appropriate under the circumstances."

"Are all your children boys?"

"The two oldest are boys. My youngest is a girl."

"Well, you're correct, but only about the boys. If they're both older than six you'd get custody if the *Beis Din* saw fit. But mothers usually get custody of their daughters unless there are extenuating circumstances. From what you say, there most certainly are."

Sender delivered his well-practiced look of desperation.

"Then you *can* help me."

"That all depends. Being that your wife turned away from Jewish traditions and laws, it's unlikely she'll come to a *Beis Din* hearing. Has she filed a petition with the civil court?"

"Yes."

"Well then, I'm afraid I have some bad news for you. You see, we will not take a case that is already pending in civil court."

Sender wasn't prepared for this. His eyes flared open. He leaned forward in his chair and slammed his open hand down on the rabbi's desk.

"Then I won't give her a *Get* until she turns my children over to me. Without that she won't be able to remarry. I'm sure that will motivate her."

"Mr. Stein, I would not advise that course of action. It can backfire on you. Especially under the circumstances you described."

"What do you mean?"

"You also cannot remarry until you give her the *Get*. I'd advise you to give her the *Get* right away-- before she strays so far from Orthodox tradition that she won't cooperate with that either."

Sender cursed himself for not having thought of this. His frustration caused beads of sweat to run from under his hat down his face and into his beard.

"Can you officiate the *Get* for us before the civil divorce is final?"

"I'll be more than happy to. But I cannot issue the certificate that proves you delivered a *Get* to her, which you'll need to remarry, until the civil divorce has been completed. We must follow the local laws of the land."

Sender suggested several other tactical proposals for coercing Mindy into relinquishing custody of the children, all to no avail. Rabbi Miklin insisted that any such action would push her further away from Orthodox Jewish tradition and certainly not serve to gain her cooperation.

His plan backfired, which made him even more determined to get his way, *somehow*.

Chapter Four

Marsha carefully placed her hot-chocolate mug on the counter and slid onto the overstuffed stool next to Laurie. The small Dunkin' Donuts diner was jammed with black-hatted worshippers pouring out of nearby synagogues after morning prayers. The Devon-Kedzie location was the area's only certified-kosher donut shop.

"Laurie, I've finally got you beat-- well, almost."

Marsha needed to convince her she was really playing the game she'd proposed to Laurie. They'd both been raised strictly Orthodox Jewish and they'd both grown to resent living that restrictive, secluded lifestyle.

As adults, they chose to lead secular lives, rebelliously violating every religious rule they knew.

Eventually, Laurie married back into the fold, but not until after she'd crossed Marsha in the worst way. Now that Laurie was getting divorced, Marsha had challenged Laurie to see who could be the first to seduce a strait-laced Orthodox man.

She knew that would make it easy to dupe Laurie into her revenge trap.

"From your description, and the dreamy look in

your eye, I take it this Jake guy is one hell of a catch— a real hunk, I told you molding a black-hat fanatic into a real man would be exciting-- like breaking in a new horse."

Laurie was taking the bait. After carefully sipping her hot chocolate, Marsha stared right into Laurie's eyes and continued the ruse of their rekindled friendship-- which was crucial to fulfilling her revenge for the pain she'd caused.

"Once again, you know exactly how I feel. It's like we're twins."

Laurie cracked a faint smile.

"Actually, it's *more* than that. I feel the same way about mine."

"Laurie Smilow, are you holding out on me?"

Laurie was Marsha's only long-term friend. Ever since leaving Chicago as a young girl, Marsha corresponded with her regularly. They shared everything about their lives-- until that one weekend. For a full year after Laurie had ruined her life, Marsha hadn't spoken to her. She'd waited, silently plotting her revenge. Now Laurie was falling right into the trap she'd waited years to set. This was almost too easy.

"I was planning to tell you soon. He's a special one. Not only is he a black-hatter, it gets *better*."

Marsha snapped her head to flip her long black hair out of her eyes.

"Oh, come on, don't tease me. Let's have it all."

"He's *married*," Laurie said.

"*Married*? That's *incredible*! How'd you snag him?"

"That part was easy. I met him at Glatt World, that little kosher grocery down the block. I work the register evenings for pocket money."

Pushing aside her untouched French Cruller, Marsha leaned her elbows on the counter, plopping her chin into the headrest formed by her hands, eagerly awaiting to hear more.

"I first met him on a Friday afternoon, right before *Shabbos*. The owner had already left-- he usually lets me lock up. I'd just finished pulling down the blinds when he walked in. I thought it was strange he didn't leave when he saw we'd be alone with the blinds drawn. He picked up a few items and brought them to the register. I figured this might be a guy I could work with."

"How did you get him to go out with you?" Marsha asked.

"I told him how scared I felt, closing up while being alone. I mentioned how it's really bad when we're open after *Shabbos*. On Saturday nights, I open the place after sundown and close up at midnight. There's no one else running the store and it's usually empty."

Laurie's tale had Marsha completely mesmerized. She downed the last drop of the now not-so-hot chocolate from the belly of her mug.

"So? Did he come back Saturday night after *Shabbos*?"

"It was already midnight and he still hadn't shown," Laurie explained. "I was about to lock up when he rapped on the window. That's when I *knew* I had him hooked."

"But he's married. How could he do that?"

"You know these guys. They can rationalize anything. If they really want something, they'll find a way to make it okay. Most of them are married to what we almost became-- fat, frumpy, hags with five babies on each arm. These guys get hard-ons just walking past women like us."

"How long has this been going on?"

Instead of responding, Laurie swiveled her stool toward the window. Nibbling her Cruller, she studied the Orthodox men milling around the tiny parking lot.

"*Laurie*! How long have you been keeping this from me?"

"Oh, it's been a few months now. I didn't want to say anything until I got him into bed."

Laurie placed the barely nicked donut on the counter and patted her lips with a napkin.

"That was the bad part."

"Why? Can't he perform?"

"Gosh, no-- nothing like that. But this guy *smelled* so baaad-- and his *skin*. Ugh! I wonder if he even bathes for *Shabbos*."

"How can you *stand* being with a guy like that? Our little game can't be worth *that* much to you?"

"Oh, I set the ground rules right away. He bathes before he comes to see me and wears fresh clothing. Otherwise, he knows he won't get anywhere with me."

"Besides, he's worth the effort."

Laurie fingered the heavy, braided gold chain around her neck.

"It's real."

Though she knew it would help perpetuate the ruse, Marsha couldn't give Laurie the satisfaction of a compliment. She'd beat her to the punch-- again. But this time it was okay. There was more on the table than the initial snag-- far more than Laurie knew.

Marsha smoothly slipped into her secret phase-two

agenda.

"So, what's his name?"

"No-- I can't. Maybe later. But for now, I can't tell anyone. It's not that I'm keeping secrets, it's just that, well-- he's married. You understand."

But she didn't.

Marsha missed the times when there had been no secrets between them. She used to cherish Laurie's friendship. It carried her through some tough times.

She toyed with her empty mug, silently wondering if Laurie was on to her scheme.

Laurie was the first to break the ugly silence.

"At least your guy doesn't seem to have any problems. What's the deal with him?"

Marsha jumped through the door Laurie opened.

"Oh, he's quite the hunk, like you said-- dresses a little stiff, but he's new at it. At first, he wouldn't even kiss me. You should've seen him. He looked like a lost sheep at that party, lost without a clue what to do. But he's a quick study."

The competing duo sat at the counter entertaining themselves with the parade of customers that continued to flow through the tiny shop. When the crowd finally dwindled, they paid their tab, put on their jackets, and headed out to the parking lot.

Laurie zipped her coat and pulled up her collar.

"So, tell me about your new job," Laurie insisted.

"It's not a job, just an interview. But it looks promising."

"It'll be great having you back in Chicago– like old times."

But Marsha knew it could never again be like *old times*.

What Laurie had done was unforgivable. But it was too soon to let on to that. Marsha had taken great pains to convince Laurie she'd put that behind them-- that their life-long friendship was stronger than that one, isolated incident.

"You can't imagine how long I've been looking forward to moving back. I should hear from them later this week," Marsha said.

"How did you hear about it?"

"My uncle's rabbi told him about it. It's the perfect job for me-- they're looking for someone with my specialty."

Chapter Five

Despite his best efforts, Sender was running a half-hour late. He'd gotten caught up preparing for the upcoming Jewish New Year— *Rosh Hashanah*, all the while dreading the year to come, expecting nothing but trouble from Mindy with the divorce.

He located *The Rav's* address on Francisco and entered the long narrow vestibule. He pressed the button beneath *The Rav's* mailbox until he heard the inner door rattle in response. He yanked the heavy wood and glass door open and raced up the first flight of stairs where he was greeted by a middle-aged woman, peering out from behind a half-closed door.

She squinted at him through thick bifocals and exposed her yellowed teeth.

"Stein?"

He nudged his black fedora off his sweaty pimpled brow and mopped it with his coat sleeve.

"Yes. I'm Sender Stein."

She adjusted the curly dishwater-blonde wig perched lopsided on her head, and swung the door open.

"They're waiting for you in the office."

She led him down a long narrow hallway lined with antique photos of long-bearded men and babushka-clad women. Sender followed her to the back of the flat.

She pointed to one of the bedroom doors.

"In there."

He pushed the door open without so much as a knock, revealing a tiny room crammed with books, files, and time worn furniture. The hot stuffy room was shaded by dusty half-closed blinds, resting just above atop an old gray air-conditioner precariously hanging out the window. A white-bearded man Sender gauged to be in his seventies sat behind an old mahogany desk facing the door.

He was instantly intrigued by the secrets he imagined the room held.

He closed the door behind him and discovered a pudgy balding man, sitting opposite *The Rav*. Several long strands of graying hair were draped across the fifty-something stranger's scalp, accentuating his conspicuously bare-head. His dark narrow-set eyes peered over the gold-rimmed reading glasses perched at the bottom of his bulbous nose.

Sender was irritated by his presence-- he didn't like surprises.

"Mr. Stein, this is Mr. Rudy Garbacz, an attorney

well versed in cases such as yours. He has graciously taken time from his busy schedule to advise us this afternoon."

The Rav pointed towards the empty seat beside Rudy.

Sender took the proffered seat and recounted his fictitious story about Mindy corrupting his children's religious beliefs.

The Rav shifted the large black *yarmulke* on his head, then pulled a stray hair from his beard. He twisted the white symbol of wisdom between his thumb and forefinger several times, then buried it between the pages of an old book.

"This is a delicate situation, my friend. We must coax your wife into giving up custody without traumatizing the children."

"I was thinking that I shouldn't give her a *Get* until she gives me custody. I'm sure she'll want to remarry. The pressure of withholding that will surely be enough to persuade her."

The Rav leaned forward and furrowed his brow.

"Let me assure you, Mr. Stein. This would be a *grave* mistake on your part. Withholding the *Get* can be a two-edged sword. Your wife needs to receive it to remarry. But she also must *accept* it for *you* to remarry. You need *her* cooperation as much as she needs *yours*."

The Rav slowly leaned back in his worn leather chair.

"No, my friend. Give her the *Get* as soon as possible. If your wife has truly left her Orthodox ways, as you say she has, she may not be that willing to cooperate. She may even, God forbid, feel that she is free to remarry without a *Get*. That would be most unfortunate."

The Rav sat upright and pulled his chair toward the desk. The short quick jerks forced several squawks from the chair's legs, dragging across the bare hardwood flooring, sending shivers up Sender's spine.

"Perhaps Mr. Garbacz can suggest another, less risky, method you could employ to obtain custody-- *after* you take care of the *Get*."

They discussed several possibilities, all of which Sender readily discarded. He bitterly opposed the compromising scent of joint custody, and he refused to *buy* her cooperation with financial sacrifices. They were *his* children-- he shouldn't have to buy them back. He began to feel *The Rav* lose patience with him as the hour grew even later.

Rudy fell silent for a moment while pondering the issue.

"Perhaps, the best way to approach this matter is head on. Currently, your wife has no more legal claim to custody than you do. You have no separation agreement and very little time has passed since you separated."

"You could simply take them from her."

The Rav stroked his beard several times.

"What about the children? We don't want to upset them with an ugly scene."

"Not necessary," Rudy assured him, as he patted the strands of hair draped across the bald part of his head. "You do see the children on a regular basis, don't you?" he asked Sender.

Sender nodded.

"Well then, next time you have the children-- *after* you give her the *Get, keep* them. You might be able to withhold visitation from her until the civil divorce is settled, or at least until she can get a court date for a temporary custody hearing."

Sender rubbed his oil-slicked forehead with his right hand, stopping to pop one of several zits.

"Won't that be like kidnapping?" Sender asked.

"Not at all. You said she doesn't keep *Shabbos*, and feeds them non-kosher food. We could file an emergency motion seeking temporary custody based on serious endangerment to the psychological, emotional, and religious wellbeing of the children. The court will order an evaluation and schedule a hearing. And you're in Cook County. I was just at the Daley Center yesterday, setting trial dates for another case. The calendars are booked solid for months. You probably won't get a hearing date until next summer."

"How would a *delay* help Mr. Stein?" *The Rav* asked.

"Well, first-off, in the interim, you might be able to prevent her from seeing the children at all. Even if that fails, you'll have temporary custody-- and we can argue that you were the primary caretaker of the children up until she removed them from your home."

"You were the primary caretaker, *weren't* you?" Rudy asked as he smiled at Sender and nodded his head up and down in an exaggerated fashion.

"No, mostly *she* took care of the kids."

"Mr. Stein, perhaps you didn't hear me." Rudy once again flashed his teeth at Sender and nodded. "*You* were the children's primary caretaker, *right*?"

"*Oh*-- right, right! Yes-- *of course* I was."

"Good. That plays a big part in determining custody-- even temporary custody."

"Meanwhile, you'll undeniably be the primary caretaker while you have temporary custody. That will bolster your petition for permanent custody when the case goes to trial-- if it goes that far. If she doesn't get any visitation, or very limited visitation in the interim, that would certainly put enough pressure on her to cooperate, assuming she really wants to see the children."

"Oh, she does. Believe me, she *really* does," Sender assured him.

A wide grin slowly spread across Sender's face. He slouched back comfortably in his chair, arms folded, legs crossed, staring at the ceiling.

He decided that he and Rudy would get along just fine after all.

Sender smiled uncontrollably, nearly breaking into giddy laughter.

He vigorously shook the two men's hands, thanking them both and wishing *The Rav* a good *Rosh Hashana*– a good Jewish New Year.

He couldn't have hoped for a better turn of luck.

This would be a wonderful New Year after all.

Chapter Six

Mindy answered the ringing phone.

Sender said he wanted to finalize their Jewish divorce by giving her a *Get*.

Although she was relieved to hear this, his unusual cooperation made her anxious.

Sender suggested the name of rabbi she'd never heard of to officiate.

She wanted her *Get* to be readily accepted by anyone without question. The Illinois Rabbinical Board was the logical choice, as everyone in the community accepted their stamp of approval.

She insisted that Rabbi Miklin officiate the *Get*.

Sender objected, but then quickly relented to her request.

They agreed to meet on the following Thursday.

After hanging up, her anxiety level *raised* several notches.

Sender seemed a little *too* easy to deal with.

When Thursday evening arrived, Mindy finally felt relieved and was eager to get it over with.

There would still be the civil divorce, but finalizing

the *Get* concerned her more. Orthodox Jewish men often used their powerful position in the Jewish divorce process to blackmail their ex's to-be, who were required to receive the divorce-decree document-- the *Get*-- before remarrying.

Without it, a woman was stuck in limbo.

Under Jewish law, the man has all the power. The husband must give the *Get* to the woman. She cannot initiate it, or force the matter.

Often, men demanded money or better settlement terms-- *that* she could deal with. It would be worth *any* price to be rid of Sender.

But sometimes they wanted more– much more, like custody of the children.

On rare occasions, they'd refuse to give the *Get* altogether.

Mindy recently heard about a woman in the community who was married to a man she despised, who refused to give her a *Get*. Rather than endure a lifelong sentence of loneliness, she abandoned her Orthodox traditions altogether, and waited only for her civil divorce before remarrying.

Knowing Sender's scheming nature, *this* was an opportunity she thought he'd be unable to pass up. She couldn't imagine him letting the opportunity pass unexercised.

Surely, he had *some* surprise waiting for her.

Whatever he had in store, she'd find out soon enough.

But after tonight, it would be over.

Once he gave her the *Get,* he would no longer have it to hold over her head.

After parking in the near-empty lot outside the tiny one-story building in Skokie, she rushed inside.

The receptionist's desk was unoccupied.

Wandering down the corridor, she looked for signs of life, until she heard voices emanating from a room at the far end of the hall.

She rushed to the only room sporting half-open doors.

A placard on the door read BEIS DIN, indicating the room was designated as the Jewish courtroom. Underneath the placard a sliding sign announced that the *Beis Din* was IN-SESSION. But a glance past the open doors proved otherwise.

Mindy entered the large, paneled room lined with polished mahogany bookcases. A matching wooden step ladder rested against one of the packed bookcases. A large oak desk on the carpeted stage at the front of the room bore a brass nameplate with Rabbi Miklin's moniker.

Sender was huddled in a corner at the back of the room, chatting with several bearded men. She wondered what lies he was telling them.

Here it comes.

She braced herself for the worst.

She slowly advanced toward the all-male crowd.

A tall, elderly man broke away from the group. He smiled warmly as he strode towards her, holding his hands intertwined behind his back, instead of extending a hand to shake.

Mindy immediately recognized the maneuver.

Orthodox Jewish law prohibits men from touching a woman outside their immediate family.

"Mrs. Stein? We spoke earlier."

He pressed his fingertips to his large chest.

"I'm Rabbi Miklin. I'll be presiding over your *Get* today."

She'd expected an older looking, shorter man. But the Rabbi's black Hamburg, heavy gold-rimmed bifocals, well-groomed white beard, and crisp long black coat gave him a stately aura. There was a warm sparkle in his eye, and his stride had an energetic spring to it.

Rabbi Miklin beckoned the group in the corner to

join them.

He introduced two other men as the official witnesses, and identified a younger man clutching a shop-worn brown leather briefcase as the *sofer*– the scribe who would write their *Get* document for them.

Sender lurked behind the group, hands behind his back, whispering to a bearded man whom Rabbi Miklin neglected to introduce.

Rabbi Miklin stretched one arm toward the front of the courtroom.

"Let us begin."

During the entire hour-long ceremony, Mindy fought the temptation to imagine what traps Sender had set for her.

She tried to focus on the closure tonight's event would bring, and for the first time since her childhood, she looked forward to her future.

She made a concerted effort to avoid looking in Sender's direction.

But a murmur at the witness table caught her attention, causing her to glance toward them, catching the wrath of Sender's *evil-eye* as she did.

Had he been staring at her all this time?

For a moment, her body tensed, the claustrophobic

feelings she thought she left behind the day she moved out momentarily returned, suffocating her.

The pit in her stomach grew larger, as if fed by the invisible fire emanating from his loathsome eyes. She jerked away, turning back to watch the *sofer* complete her long-awaited declaration of freedom.

After what seemed like an eternity, the *sofer* placed his quill on the table. He gently blew onto the wet letters he'd scratched onto the parchment until satisfied that the lettering on the *Get* was dry.

Finally, he announced that the *Get* was ready.

The *sofer* then ceremoniously read the contents of the *Get* aloud for all to hear.

Following Rabbi Miklin's commands, Mindy stood up and cupped her hands waiting to receive the *Get* from Sender.

Her arms formed goose bumps, and she felt every hair on the back of her neck.

Rabbi Miklin, the witnesses, the *sofer*, and even the rabbi's clerk, turned to watch her every movement.

Mindy felt cold and alone in the crowded room, like an outcast.

It was the first time she'd ever been alone in a room full of men, behind closed doors.

She fought her tears, choosing to focus instead on her imminent escape from the man who'd imprisoned her and her children in a living hell all these years.

It was time to step into *freedom.*

Mindy stood, quivering-chin up, proudly extending her cupped hands.

Sender stood and stepped purposefully toward Mindy, resuming his intimidating glare.

For the first time, Mindy *locked* eyes with him and returned the stare with fierce determination.

Her intensity sent Sender stumbling. His torso slammed into the corner of a table.

Rabbi Miklin shot up out of his chair.

"Mr. Stein– are you okay?"

"I'm fine."

Mindy held her stance as Sender once again locked eyes with her. He raised the *Get* up for all to see and dropped it into the human bucket formed by her cupped hands.

She accepted the *Get*, raising it up to demonstrate her full possession of it, and then clutched it to her chest.

Freedom.

The nightmare was over.

Unexpectedly, Rabbi Miklin immediately asked her

to surrender the *Get* to the *sofer* who took a razor knife to it and sliced a big "X" through the document, destroying it.

"This assures the *Get* cannot be used again for another couple with the same names. Each *Get* must be specifically drafted for the divorcing couple."

Rabbi Miklin filled out and signed two copies of a form certifying their religious divorce had been executed.

"We will not release these until your civil proceedings conclude. We must follow the laws of the land-- you cannot use these certificates as proof of your Jewish divorce to remarry until you obtain your civil divorce, as is the law of the land in the State of Illinois."

On her way out of the room, Mindy passed Sender.

Unable to resist repeating the look that almost toppled him earlier, she decided to give him one more shot of *her* evil-eye stare.

But as she turned to deliver the attack, she faced Sender's sly, overly confident grin staring back at her, sending shivers down her spine.

Chapter Seven

Jake thoroughly enjoyed spending time with Marsha, but it was time to make a decision about his future with her.

The High-Holiday season– the days commencing with the Jewish New Year, the *Rosh Hashanah* holiday, and concluding with *Yom Kippur*-- the Day of Atonement, was nearly ending.

The ominous *Yom Kippur* holiday seemed to force his hand.

He'd already put it off far too long.

He certainly did feel *something* for her.

But he wondered– was it his *heart*, or his *animal instinct*, doing the feeling?

He knew the answer– and knew what he needed to do. But he'd already displayed far too many signs of affection to easily extract himself from the relationship abruptly.

The red roses and card he sent her for the *Rosh Hashanah* holiday certainly weren't going to help matters.

There was now less than an hour to spare. *Yom Kippur* services would begin at dusk.

Jake showered and dressed in navy-blue slacks and a crisp white shirt. He topped that off by affixing a crocheted *yarmulke* to his hair with a bobby pin.

Marsha had sent it with an accompanying card that read, *"A new yarmulke for a New Year, Love, Marsha."*

Love. What a nice thought– or maybe what a frightening thought!

Jake supposed that Marsha spent hours crocheting this. It was beautiful. And so was she-- in most ways.

But there was something else.

Something deep within her that reared its ugly head, in only the slightest of ways.

Barely noticeable, yet undeniably there.

He hoped wearing the *yarmulke* she sent him would soften the blow.

Jake met Pinky at the *synagogue* and stayed until the evening services were over.

He headed home eager to sleep through the night– he'd need his strength to fast the entire 24-hour period, until the fast was over.

But he tossed and turned restlessly.

He couldn't stop worrying about how Marsha would react when he let her know it was over.

Those thoughts occupied his mind through most of

the *Yom Kippur* day services.

He barely noticed his hunger pangs and pounding headache– the result of refraining from food and drink since dusk the previous day. Even water was prohibited during the fast, according to Orthodox law.

But when the sun finally set and the fast ended, he set aside all thoughts of Marsha.

It was time for the single most important shopping mission of the year.

Physically dragging Pinky by his muscular arm-- a feat not easily accomplished, Jake led his friend south on California, ignoring Pinky's pleas to stop for a bite first.

Jake reached into the brown paper sack he'd grabbed from the synagogue's cloakroom on their way out, he retrieved two of a dozen oatmeal-raisin cookies and tossed the rest to Pinky.

The two of them wolfed down the sustenance while race-walking to the shopping frenzy that immediately commences after the *Yom Kippur* fast breaks.

Sukkos, the festival when Orthodox Jews build huts to dwell in, would begin in a matter of days.

Every male over *Bar-Mitzvah* age is not only required to dwell in the hut, but also to acquire their own *lulav* and *esrog*. The palm-like branch and citrus fruit were required to use ritually during *Sukkos* services

These scarce ceremonial items can only be obtained from a few individuals and the Hebrew Book Store, and they first went on sale immediately after *Yom Kippur*.

There was always a mad rush to get the best of the crop.

Marching through the crisp night air, Jake and Pinky passed many backyards and driveways lit-up with work lights to enable construction of *sukkahs*– the small huts.

Most of the *sukkahs* were fashioned from wood or canvas and covered with evergreen branches, or bamboo mats.

Jake wasn't building his own hut this year-- Pinky and he made arrangements to use the synagogue's communal *sukkah*.

Right now, Jake's attention was focused on scoring the best *esrog*– the semi-tropical lemon-like fruit, which commanded a handsome sum from the seasonal entrepreneurs who imported them from Israel.

The experience was a bit like Macy's on Christmas Eve, only the patrons were all half-crazed men who hadn't shaved, bathed, or barely eaten in the last twenty-four hours, each determined to leave with nothing less than the very best *esrog*.

Pinky struggled to keep pace with Jake as he hustled down California.

"Just a few more blocks. I promise," Jake assured him.

It would be the most expensive produce purchase of the year. Fifty, seventy-five, even hundred-dollar price tags and higher are common for these imported jewels.

Fortunately, Jake cultivated a relationship with Rabbi Joseph Skumansky, an older man who studied at the same *yeshiva* Jake attended. The rabbi supplemented his income with a seasonal *lulav* and *esrog* importing sideline.

As they crossed Pratt, single-family homes turned into two and three-flats and an occasional multi-unit building. Pinky stopped for a moment, raised one leg slightly and coughed loudly. A foul odor briefly permeated the air, compromising his camouflaged maneuver.

When they reached Devon, they veered right, passing a grubby unshaven middle-aged man in a wheelchair who held out an expectant grease-stained hand mumbling something Russian sounding.

Jake ignored the beggar, and pushed Pinky's arm away as he was handing the man a dollar. "Don't contribute to that fraud. I've seen him walk just fine when he thought no one was looking. Plus, the first time I saw him, I gave him five bucks only to watch him cross the street and buy cigarettes."

Picking up the pace, Jake burst into a sprint. "If we don't hustle there won't be much left to pick from."

They turned south on Francisco and jogged the rest of the way.

Not recalling the exact address, Jake identified their destination by the backyard clamor.

It was a large brick three-flat, with a small front-yard and tiny porch leading to the vestibule.

Motioning to Pinky to follow his lead, Jake raced along the narrow brick-paved path between buildings that led to the backyard.

Flood-lights cast a yellow glow over the clamoring crowd.

A swarm of black-hatted men dressed in disheveled dark suits and ties were already busy making their selections from crates laid out on folding tables stretched across the backyard.

The crate-lids were all propped open, exposing hundreds of the fragrant yellow *esrogim*, each cradled in horsehair wadding, like a freshly laid egg in a nest.

A single large plastic garbage bin stuffed with the

lulavim– the palm-like branches, was parked next to each table.

Their entrance caused a lull in the group's clamor, as the Ultra-Orthodox crowd gauged their modern dress-slacks, open collar white shirts, and colorful crocheted *yarmulkes*.

One man, wearing a long black coat, a black fedora, and narrow wire-rimmed glasses, perched on the edge of his nose, stared directly at them like a child in awe of a circus act.

Jake returned the stare with a quick smile and flash of teeth.

The gawker quickly looked away and whispered to his neighbor who gave an understanding nod.

No one uttered a word directly to either of them.

Eventually the awkward moment passed and each man resumed his quest.

Jake and Pinky merged into the crowd.

This community used to consider Jake somewhat of a prodigy, though he'd never understood why.

He'd been regarded as the best student at the *yeshiva–* the Rabbinical College. His friends, teachers-- the entire community all had high expectations of him.

He was their pride and joy-- *until now.*

Now they seemed ashamed of him-- he'd left their fold to join modern society.

As Jake approached one of the long tables, the crowd quickly dissipated as if backing away from a horrible disease. A spot miraculously cleared for him as his ex-fans shuffled away from the heathen who'd re-entered their world.

Plucking a bundled *esrog* from one of the open crates, Jake delicately unraveled its horsehair womb, drawing it upward to inhale its unique citrusy aroma. The blend of lemon, lime and sweet flowery scents breathed life into his soul.

Pinky held up a *lulav* branch for Jake's approval.

"How's this look?"

Jake's mouth widened to a grin.

"At least *someone's* still interested in my opinion."

A long line of men waiting to ask Jake's opinion of their *lulav* and *esrog* used to greet him at these events.

"Is the tip straight enough?"

"Do you think this blemish is a problem?"

He'd always smile, wish them a good year, and give them a thumbs up or down.

But now they *shunned* him, ashamed of the traitor garbed in modern dress.

Jake gently extracted the *lulav* from Pinky's tight grip.

"Let's have a look."

Locating the spine of the branch, Jake ran his thumb upward, checking for split leaves and eyeing the overall straightness.

"Pretty good-- for an *amateur*."

They made their selections quickly and were ready to pay.

As they passed through the crowd of despising gawkers, Jake was greeted by the friendly smile of Rabbi Skumansky, the proprietor of this seasonal sale.

He was a stout elderly man with a long white beard.

The rabbi extended his arms with both palms-up

"Reb Yankel, it's good to see you."

Jake graciously returned the smile and introduced Pinky, who seemed unusually fidgety.

"It's so *kind* of you to bring me new business."

He pointed a finger up in the air.

"For *you*, I have a *very special* price."

The old man scribbled on a pad of sales-receipts with a grease pencil. Crossing out the first number, he jotted down a second, crossed that out as well, and then finally underscored a third.

Jake patiently waited for the rabbi to complete this annual ritual.

They gladly paid the standard *for-you-my-friend* price and left.

As they made their way home, Jake thought about Rabbi Skumansky's overly friendly demeanor.

It was as if nothing had changed.

That left Jake with an *uneasy* feeling.

Chapter Eight

Other than the cookies they'd devoured earlier, Jake and Pinky hadn't eaten in over twenty-four hours.

Pinky placed his hand on his rumbling tummy.

"I'm starving. How about joining me for a real meal?" Pinky asked.

"Sounds like a plan, but let's go to my place, I got something special for the occasion," Jake replied.

They retraced their steps up California toward Jake's apartment. When they entered the vestibule, Jake flipped the keys on his ring, retrieved his mail and scooped up the Sun Times laying on the chipped gray and black triangle tile floor.

Jake opened the stairway door.

Pinky rushed past him, flying up the stairs two at a time, while Jake climbed slowly, sifting through his mail. Jake approached his second-floor apartment's door. He glanced up to see his impatient friend tapping his foot on the threadbare gray wool Berber carpeting.

"Sorry. I get a little crazy when I'm hungry."

Jake opened the door and entered the small one-bedroom apartment.

Pinky followed.

Jake motioned to the couch.

"Have a seat. it'll take a few minutes to warm up the food."

Jake tossed the stack of envelopes and the Sun Times on the couch next to Pinky.

"Try not to eat the mail."

Jake dropped his keys into an ashtray on the black-lacquer entertainment center lining his front-room wall and disappeared into the kitchen. He retrieved a large brown paper bag from the humming refrigerator, removed two take-out containers, and carefully placed them in the oven. He checked his watch, and returned to the front room to join Pinky, who was buried in the Sun Times.

"Twenty minutes to food. It'll be worth the wait."

But Pinky was too engrossed in the paper to hear a word.

Jake cupped his hands over his mouth forming a megaphone.

"Hellooo, Earth to Pinky-- anyone home?"

Pinky looked up, startled.

"Jake, did you see this? It's about a rabbi named Fogal. Says he's been charged with federal tax fraud. There's even a picture of the guy. It made the front page."

He turned the paper toward Jake, displaying the mugshot and headline for his review.

Jake snatched the paper from his hands and read the article, shaking his head.

"You'd think they had better things to do than focus on one *so-called* rabbi. A guy like that has no business cheating on his taxes-- it reflects poorly on the entire community. He may *call* himself a rabbi, but no truly Orthodox Jew would do such a thing."

"Oh, buddy, you've got a *lot* to learn," Pinky said. "You don't know half of what goes on. These black-hatters do whatever they please. They always find some way to excuse it according to Jewish law-- to *hell* with secular laws. Talk about *scofflaws*! There are black-hat drug-dealers, thieves, adulterers-- *you name it*. They've got the same bad seeds as any other segment of society. The only difference is they walk around with a *holier than thou* attitude and use religion to justify their actions. Do you have *any* idea how many of these guys sneak out of the hood and do whatever they please? There are even specialty-hookers that *cater* to these guys. Some of the wealthy ones keep mistresses on the side. It's all supposed to be hush-hush. But people find out, and people talk.

"In fact, I hear there's a married guy here in Rogers

Park-- a black-hatter, sleeping with Laurie Smilow. Claims his wife left the fold and feeds his kids non-kosher food. Meanwhile he's been running around with another woman– a *married* woman no less. Her husband refuses to give her a *Get*."

"That's just a *rumor*. You don't know that for a *fact*," Jake insisted.

"Well, I *personally* saw her at O'Hare Airport, off to the side of one of the concession stands. She was smooching with a guy that was *definitely* a black-hatter. *That* I saw with my own eyes," Pinky said. "Put that together with the rumor and I say where there's smoke there's fire."

Jake knew that Pinky had a way of exaggerating things, especially negative things about the right-wing Orthodox community-- as if he had a *personal* vendetta with them. Still, he couldn't ignore the Sun-Times article, especially when combined with Pinky's first-hand account.

Jake glanced at the faux-granite pendulum clock gracing his front-room wall. "*Damn!* I forgot about the food!"

He raced to the kitchen, spun the black oven knob to *off* and ripped open the oven door.

"I think we saved the patient," Jake announced.

He set two place mats on his black-laminate dining table and set out some utensils. The two friends feasted on the take-out dinners Jake had picked up before the fast from Blind Faith-- a vegetarian cafe in nearby Evanston. Pinky maintained a strict vegetarian diet and although Jake didn't, he found the cuisine more than satisfying.

They filled their bellies with brown rice and pan-fried tempeh burgers on toasted whole-wheat buns with alfalfa-sprouts, red onion, and just the right mix of stone-ground mustard and mayo.

A tall glass of carrot-juice washed down the feast and granola fig-bars rounded out the meal.

After clearing the table, they slumped onto the couch to watch The Late Show.

Pinky lifted one leg and began coughing, prompting Jake to run and open a window while holding his nose.

"Oh, before I forget," Pinky said, "I got a bunch of blank lottery cards in the trunk of my car. When can you start filling them out? My money guys are anxious to get started."

"I'm done loading the Illinois winning numbers onto my hard-drive," Jake replied. "But I still need about an hour to figure out how to get the software to pick our numbers. How about coming over here tomorrow night to get started– say seven-thirty?"

"Great. I'll grab a pizza on the way over."

Chapter Nine

Mindy entered the crowded synagogue's large rectangular social hall, filled with dozens of twenty to forty-something Jewish singles. The crowd's dressy-casual *modern* attire made her feel like she'd dressed as an old lady.

Despite feeling that the crowd was judging her attire, she was determined to meet people.

Most of the singles milled around a buffet of fresh-baked goods and liquid refreshments. A dozen round banquet tables surrounded by metal folding chairs filled the center of the room. Multicolored plastic tablecloths were coordinated with the plates and cups retrieved from the buffet by the occasional couple who, locked in conversation, had moved to the tables.

She made her way to the buffet.

A short, balding, twenty-something man clad in a green sport jacket and faded blue jeans introduced himself as Ralph Ginzberg.

He began boasting about his limo business when Mindy's ear caught a nearby discussion.

She intended to glance toward the group *briefly*, not

wanting to be rude to Ralph. But her eyes locked on a tall, slim, clean-shaven man in his mid-thirties.

His chiseled, muscular features and youthful face were complemented by his wavy dark-blonde hair.

He stood tall and straight, wearing an open-collared button-down yellow Polo branded shirt and black pleated trousers.

A thin, green-eyed woman, wearing a white skin-tight pullover, hip-hugger jeans, and red pumps, hung on his arm as he seemed to eloquently address the small group surrounding him.

Mindy looked up, attempting to engage his sky-blue eyes, but he didn't seem to notice. She felt a sudden connection to this man.

Suddenly, he turned toward Mindy and seemed to give her ultra-conservative outfit elevator eyes.

"Am I right?" he asked.

Blood rushed to her cheeks, making her feel as red as her hair and even smaller than her five-foot height.

She'd been so intent on getting his attention that she hadn't heard what he'd asked.

She fumbled for a response.

"I think that's...*very interesting*."

"Which part?"

"How you seem to be judging the way I'm *dressed.*"

Damn! Where did that come from?

It certainly wasn't what she wanted to say.

She'd lost control.

Her mouth, brain, and heart were completely taken with this fascinating man.

"Sorry about that. I'm a recently reformed black-hatter myself– I graduated from the *Yeshiva.* I meant no offense to you."

Mindy slowly regained her composure.

"None taken."

Turning away from the crowd that had now grown by several dozen, he let go of the woman on his arm, stepped toward Mindy, and extended his hand.

"I'm Jake– Jake Cooper."

Mindy panicked.

She wanted to reach out and shake his hand. But her body wouldn't cooperate. She'd been trained to shun physical contact with men.

Now she was expected to do the opposite spontaneously.

She balked.

But Jake gracefully manipulated his extended hand

and reached to adjust his hair.

"And *your* name is...?"

"Mindy."

She didn't want to use Sender's sir-name, even though legally she was still a Stein.

The two continued chatting for several minutes until the skin-tight pullover tugged at Jake's arm.

Jake took the pullover's hand in his.

"Mindy, this is Marsha Rein. Marsha, Mindy."

Marsha slipped her arm into Jake's and pulled him close, but Jake didn't pick up on the hint.

"I'd really love to continue our conversation sometime."

"Me too!"

Marsha whisked him off into the crowd.

Mindy watched longingly as the she-devil held tight to Jake's extended arm, leading him across the room.

She was certain Jake had mistakenly labeled her an Ultra-Orthodox, right-winger. It was the *last* thing she wanted.

She cursed her decision to dress in her old garb. How could she please everyone? If she dressed modernly, the community she wanted no part of would say she was corrupting her children. But dressing this way wasn't what she wanted– it made her feel old and ugly and gave the people she *did* want to meet the wrong impression of her.

Once again, she felt trapped.

Cradling a wedge of seven-layer-cake and nursing a Diet-Coke, she wandered the room. Several suitors made their way to her side, advertising their wares and requesting her number. But she paid little attention to their pitches.

Her eyes followed Jake's *every* move...

Her mind and her *heart* were with *him*.

She *had* to see him again.

Did he really want to continue our conversation? Why didn't he ask for my number?

As yet another bachelor serenaded her, she watched Jake slip on a leather jacket.

He was leaving-- with *her*.

Mindy summoned an unknown strength.

Boldly excusing herself, she hastily scribbled her number on a slip of paper she retrieved from the depths of her purse and rushed through the crowd toward Jake, who was now being whisked out the door by Marsha.

She ran after them, waving the paper scrap in the air with one hand.

"Excuse me!"

Jake turned abruptly and raised his eyebrows.

Marsha shot her a *stay-away-from-my-guy, bitch* look as Mindy handed the paper to Jake.

"I forgot to give you my phone number."

Chapter Ten

Visitation was working out surprisingly well.
Sender was unusually punctual and consistent about
picking up and dropping off the kids.

As much as Mindy loathed him, he *was* the father of
her children and they needed his attention.

Between his cooperation with the *Get* and visitation,
she wondered if he wasn't trying to demonstrate he'd
changed in the hopes of winning her back. That was
definitely out of the question, but it would still be
something.

But that hopeful thought quickly vanished when she
recalled his chilling grin following the *Get*.

She was sure the old dog was up to *something*.

Mindy rose early Sunday morning, dressed the kids,
and saw them off to spend the day with Sender.

After deciding to dress as she pleased when the
children were not around, she slipped into a black wool
skirt and a hot-pink Angora sweater and headed out for a
relaxing day of shopping at the Old Orchard Shopping
Center, in Skokie.

At four-thirty, she begrudgingly ended the day and

headed home to greet the children who were due to be dropped off by Sender at five.

The fierce storm that developed on her way home delivered driving rains and an occasional whiplash of light followed by a thunderous clap.

She arrived home with seconds to spare.

She tossed her packages on the couch of her second-floor apartment just as she heard Sender's horn wail through the pelting rain.

She grabbed a raincoat and dashed downstairs to greet her children, who would no doubt be running up the path to the front door, arms open.

She eagerly anticipated their loving hugs.

But she was greeted only by bouncing rain as she looked down the cement path that led from the front door toward Sender's car.

She flipped up her raincoat collar, drew the open lapels tightly across her chest, and sprinted toward the rusty brown Chevy wagon.

As he approached the car, she peered inside, looking for her children.

"Where are they?"

Sender leaned over, cranked the passenger window down, and yelled through the downpour, "I stopped by to let you know, they're staying with me."

The shock sent blood coursing through her veins.

"What do you mean they're *staying* with you?"

"They're not coming back now."

The building's plate-glass windows rattled behind her in response to a crash of light immediately followed by a clap of thunder.

Mindy shielded her eyes from the rain with one hand.

"Our *agreement* is Sundays till *five*. If you want to keep them longer, I need advance warning-- I've already made dinner plans."

Sender cracked an all too familiar smile. "They won't be coming back-- and I *don't* mean just for a few hours."

Another flash of light followed by booming thunder caused the ground to rumble beneath her feet.

Mindy's dark red freckles faded to pink whispers as the blood drained from her usually ruddy complexion, turning her face ash-white.

"What are you *talking* about? Where are my children!"

Sender chuckled.

"They don't want to live with you anymore."

"What? Says who?"

"Says the kids. They begged me not to make them come back here."

"How dare you– you little *creep*! There's no *way* they'd ever say that!"

Sender smirked.

"Well, they *said* it to *me*. They don't feel comfortable with you. It's no wonder-- you're not even home for them anymore, being so *busy* and all, gallivanting around to singles parties and shopping sprees, playing quite the bachelorette. They're *much* more comfortable with me– and *I'm there* for them."

The veins in Mindy's neck throbbed against the matted wet hairs of her sweater.

"You were *never* home-- never gave a *damn* about the kids. *Now* you come up with this crap? That's *ridiculous*"

"It's not what *I* say, it's what the *kids* say. The divorce is hard enough on them. Why make it any harder? Let them live where they want to. It's in *their* best interest. I'm sure you'll agree once you calm down."

Mindy wanted to crumple his jalopy into a metal ball, shove it down his throat and wait for a bolt of lightning to fry him.

The *bastard*-- how *could* he? How dare he use her children like this!

No *wonder* he'd been so cooperative-- making damn sure to get regular visitation until he was ready to lower the boom.

It all made perfect sense now.

She slammed her tight fist on top of the wagon's roof so hard that she slightly dented it.

She pried her clenched teeth open and growled in a frightful tone that even she didn't recognize. "How *dare* you, you manipulative *bastard*!"

But Sender just mocked her and rolled the window up.

Mindy met the rising glass with both her hands, forcing the window down.

"If you don't bring them back here, and I mean right now– *I'll kill you!*"

She couldn't believe those last words had spewed from her mouth.

Sender sped off.

Mindy turned to face an audience of eavesdropping neighbors.

Chapter Eleven

Marsha should have been on her way back to Cleveland on Sunday. She wanted to save the few vacation days she had left for interviewing.

But now, there was an unexpected complication.

She only planned to snag an Orthodox man to make her challenge with Laurie seem real in every way. But she hadn't expected meeting a man like Jake Cooper. He had the looks she desired in a man, to be sure. But there had been dozens like him in that regard-- all *pigs* underneath it all.

But Jake was *different*– he was genuine.

Jake had it all-- character, kindness, passion, and he was clearly interested in her too. She could sense his physical yearning for her– the way he hesitated to leave her side, the way he leaned in toward her when they spoke, and that deep passionate kiss he could deliver with nothing but his intense, beautiful eyes.

She hadn't told him how wet he made her just with that one look.

Going home now meant risking losing Jake to that frumpy redhead, Mindy. Marsha knew precisely what

Mindy was after.

She could see it in her eyes.

Once was enough.

She wasn't losing the man of her dreams twice.

Taking no chances, she postponed her return trip until Tuesday morning and called Jake. He hinted there was something important he wanted to tell her and arranged to meet her.

Jake met her in the lobby of the Hyatt Regency on East Wacker, where she was staying.

He arrived in a wide-striped, blue and white button-down shirt, and dark-blue pleated slacks. Marsha wore her favorite red silk blouse, a black leather miniskirt, and matching pumps.

After meeting in the lobby, they hoofed their way together over to Michigan Avenue.

Marsha's black hair trailed behind her in the brisk Lake Michigan breeze. They strolled south on Michigan, people-watching, and window-shopping.

They approached the entrance of the Congress Hotel.

Marsha pointed to the hotel's gift-shop window.

"Let's stop here."

Jake opened the heavy hotel door for her.

They made their way inside, squeezed into the tiny shop and stood in line by the counter. Marsha opened her black leather Gucci purse and fished out a small, round, flat bonbon tin with raspberry clusters and French writing on the lid.

She twisted open the empty tin.

"I had the last one last night. They're my favorite and they're so *hard* to find. I hope they carry them here. I've had luck finding them at hotel gift shops."

Marsha was in luck.

The clerk offered her an array of flavors to choose from.

"Raspberry– it's my favorite."

The clerk rang up the sale, announced the price and smiled expectantly at Marsha with his hand on the counter, palm up.

Marsha turned, gazed into Jake's eyes, and put on her puppy-dog face.

Jake paid the clerk and they left.

They continued strolling up and down Magnificent Mile until the rumble of rain-clouds cut the day short.

They stood in the now slight drizzle and hailed a cab.

Jake hadn't revealed the matter he alluded to earlier.

Marsha was bursting with excitement, anticipating the good news which was *surely* something that would further their relationship.

But the best things in her life had come to her slowly. *Patience* was her best virtue.

"I really enjoyed our day."

Jake said nothing other than to direct their rescuing cabby to Marsha's hotel.

When the cab pulled up to the hotel curb, Marsha blew Jake a kiss and invited him up.

She wasn't prepared for his devastating response.

Chapter Twelve

Jake returned to his apartment after dropping Marsha at the hotel. By the time he made it upstairs, his stomach was in one big knot. Marsha's response to the breakup was *far* worse than he'd anticipated.

The slap she delivered to his cheek still stung– the image of her heaving at the side of the cab still burned in his eyes.

He lay awake till four in the morning wondering why he'd dumped her. Marsha was a looker-- his body had certainly said *yes*.

But she was controlling and manipulative.

She seemed *peeved*, when he told her, to say the least.

He dragged himself out of bed the next morning to get ready for work, but his brain needed more sleep.

Ever since his employer downsized and generously offered him a deep pay-cut to keep his job, things had gotten ugly.

He dreaded going into the office every morning.

He called in sick and slipped back into bed.

He finally rolled out of bed at eleven-thirty, then

shaved and showered.

Slowly sipping a fresh-squeezed glass of orange juice near the open kitchen window, he enjoyed a taste of his favorite Chicago-weather-- chilled air, blue skies, and a slight breeze.

He decided a brisk walk through nearby Indian Boundary Park would do him good.

He grabbed his leather jacket and was halfway out the door when the phone rang.

At first, he ignored it, but then thought it might be some emergency at work. Until his lottery deal with Pinky panned out, he still needed a paycheck.

Jake grabbed the phone.

"Hi Jake. It's Mindy."

The name didn't ring a bell.

"Mindy Bloom. We met at the singles party Saturday night, remember? I introduced myself as Mindy *Stein*. But Bloom is my *maiden* name."

"Oh yes. Sure. I remember you."

"I didn't think you'd be home," Mindy admitted, "I was gonna leave you a message."

"Oh. Okay-- what about?"

"I'd really like to continue the conversation we started at the party. Also, I could really use your advice."

"I was just about to go out for a walk," Jake explained. "Why don't you join me? We can take advantage of the weather and talk at the same time."

"I wish I could, but I've got to cook for the *Succos* holiday. Why not come to my place? We can talk while I cook. I'm on Sacramento and Albion."

"That's not far from here. I could walk over now," Jake said.

"Great."

She gave him the address.

* * * * *

Jake arrived at the light-brown, brick, four-story, eight-unit building.

He made his way up to Mindy's second-level flat.

The door was wide open.

"Hello? Mindy?"

"I'm back here, in the kitchen. Come on in."

He followed a small hallway off her large front-room past a bathroom and two bedrooms that eventually led to a large kitchen at the back of the unit.

Jake sat at the kitchen table taking in his surroundings and the mouth-watering aroma of Mindy's kitchen.

The kitchen's decor lent a cheerful air to the tired old room-- matching yellow polka dot curtains adorned the window above the cracked porcelain sink and the back-door window. An over-sized smiley-face clock hung above the yellowed-enamel gas range. A dazzling collection of magnets hid the discolored door of the old Frigidaire. Gaps between warped peel-and-stick linoleum floor-tiles exposed the old wood flooring.

Something about her kitchen felt more like home than his own.

He watched her juggle several pots on the range while he sipped iced-tea from a tumbler.

"My friend-- my *so-called* friend told me she was appalled to hear I was getting divorced," Mindy said. "She completely cut me off when I started dressing more modern."

Jake listened intently to Mindy, slouching in the soft, padded, kitchen chair, enjoying a cool breeze from the open back door.

An untrained eye might not have given the front and rear open doors a second thought, attributing it to the cool cross-breeze sweeping through the hot kitchen.

But Jake was familiar with the procedure, intended

to allow open access to the apartment so they wouldn't technically be considered *alone*.

Jake was perplexed and intrigued.

Mindy definitely acted Ultra-Orthodox in some ways, but seemed so very modern in others. Like the way she was dressed today-- yellow T-shirt over black stretch pants.

He'd never met anyone quite like her and wasn't sure what to make of it.

He watched as she bounced from cooking at the stove to washing dirty dishes at the sink.

Facing Jake while drying the last dish with a white flour-sack dish towel, she said, "Losing my friends turned out to be the *least* of my problems."

She put the clean, dry dish on the counter but held onto the damp towel. "But that isn't really what I wanted to talk to you about."

Jake put down his tumbler and sat upright with arms folded.

"What is it then?"

She took a deep breath, then slowly exhaled.

"Sender, my ex-- well, he will be after our civil divorce is final-- had visitation with the kids and was supposed to drop them back here."

Her rate of speech accelerated as she continued.

"But instead of returning them, he came by and announced that he's *keeping* them. Just like *that*, he took them from me."

She twisted the towel tightly around her hand.

He sensed she was holding back tears.

"I can't even *speak* to them. I called last night and again today. But he won't even let me speak to them. He says they're busy or away at a friend's house, no matter when I call."

"I don't know what to say. God– that's *awful*."

"I appreciate that. But I was hoping for more," Mindy said.

Here it comes. Why do they always want something from me?

He tried hard to avoid dealing with his *own* conflicts. The last thing he wanted was to get involved in someone else's.

"What else can *I* do?"

"Well, I remember you said that you studied at the *yeshiva*. So, I figured you must be an expert in the Jewish laws that apply to this situation. I was hoping you'd have some *advice* for me."

Having thought she wanted him to talk to Sender or

get involved *personally*, Jake was relieved.

Advice was something he could handle.

"I don't know that I'm an *expert*. But I'm familiar with the laws. What exactly do you want to know?"

"Is there anything I can do, short of hiring a lawyer and taking Sender to civil court over visitation rights? I'd hate to let it go that far unless I *absolutely* have to."

Jake thought for a moment.

"Well, you *could* approach the *Beis Din* and ask them to summon him to a hearing."

"Actually, I'm not sure I'd get an unbiased hearing at the *Beis Din*. Sender has spent a lot of time and effort strategically planting *filthy* rumors about me."

Jake kept one eye on the towel, now wrapped so tightly around her hand that he could see her fingertips turning blue.

"Have you petitioned the civil court yet?"

"For the divorce, yes, but not for visitation."

He absently stroked his missing beard and considered her alternatives.

"You could go to the *Beis Din* and request *Zabla*."

She scrunched her freckled face into a puzzled expression.

"*Zabla?*"

"*Zabla* means a *Beis Din* consisting of three rabbis, who hear both sides of the case and issue a ruling. You can request a court composed of one person of your choosing, one of Sender's, and a third chosen by those two."

Mindy stared at the ceiling, as if pondering what Jake was saying.

"I'd still be concerned about the third man."

She slowly unraveled the tourniquet-towel.

"Can I pick the third man?"

"No, but you can tell your representative your preference. But hear me out before getting your hopes up. First of all, the *Beis Din* might not even take your case while you have a civil divorce petition pending. You might have to withdraw that first. Also, Sender could easily delay the hearing by taking his time selecting a representative or by instructing his representative to reject all of your representative's choices for a third man. It could drag on for years. Meanwhile, the *Beis Din* will require you to refrain from petitioning a civil court while the case is pending with them, leaving you with no way to get any resolution. You wouldn't see your kids, and you wouldn't be able to finalize your divorce. But even if you *don't* request *Zabla*, Sender might, if he can find a *Beis Din* willing to take it on while your divorce is pending in civil court. That would block you from petitioning the civil family court about the visitation."

"Oh, I think Sender already *knows* who he'd pick. He was adamant about using a particular rabbi for the *Get*. I can't recall the name-- I'd never heard of him. I insisted on using the Illinois Rabbinical Board, of course. I wanted the *Get* to be from someone widely recognized. Rabbi Miklin's the Chief Judge there. He's well regarded, even outside Chicago. I was lucky Sender agreed to that. But he really seemed to want this other rabbi."

"I'm impressed-- that was a smart move, Mindy. It could save you problems down the road. But getting back to my point, even if Sender knows who he wants, he can still delay everything. He can wait to officially announce his selection, and like I said, he can instruct his representative to reject all of your representative's choices for the third man."

Mindy resumed the towel twisting, suffocating her fingers.

"So basically, if I want to see my kids anytime soon, I have to get an attorney and take him to civil court."

"Looks that way."

They continued talking about divorce, lawyers, and courts,

Mindy put away the dry dishes piled up on the counter. She pulled an unlabeled spray-bottle from under the sink and spritzed the counter-top.

Jake contorted his nose.

"Is that vinegar?"

She held up the spray-bottle.

"This? It's water with the smallest drop of vinegar in it. I'm surprised you can smell it."

Jake pointed to his bloodhound.

"I've got a sensitive snout."

He enjoyed a sampling of her cooking for a make-shift lunch and listened to more tales of her divorce war-story.

Their conversation continued well into the afternoon.

Her vivacious personality and petite, yet entertaining, spitfire body held him captive while she rambled on about her ex-to-be.

Jake gave her his attorney's number-- she didn't have one yet because she'd filed for the divorce on her own.

Mindy's unfortunate situation made Jake appreciate his own relatively smooth divorce from Rachel. Their's hadn't been nearly as ugly, though hearing about her children surfaced a deep guilty pain he'd been trying to forget.

Mindy gasped, glancing at the smiley-face clock.

"It's almost time to light candles, and you must have a thousand things to do."

"Actually, I'm all set-- stocked my fridge and freezer last week. I'll do my cooking during *Sukkos*. You know you *can*. It isn't prohibited like it is on *Shabbos*."

Mindy perched both hands on her hips.

"Of *course,* I know!"

"I didn't graduate from *yeshiva*, but I do *know* a thing or two."

"Sorry. I didn't mean it that way. It's just– why are you cooking all those meals *now* when you have all that time *during Sukkos* to do it?"

Mindy relaxed her stance.

She wiped her hands and joined him at the table.

"I didn't mean to snap at you like that. Sender always treated me like a moron, as if only *he* could know what the proper thing to do was. I was raised Orthodox-- I know a thing or two. For the record, I like to get my cooking done up front so I can relax during the holiday. For years, I'd spend holidays slaving over the stove while Sender and the boys were at synagogue, serving them when they arrived home famished, then spend the afternoon cleaning up the aftermath. It's about time *I* enjoyed the holidays too."

Mindy sat quietly for a moment, then pushed herself away from the table and stood up. Giving a short nervous laugh, she motioned toward the mountain of food she'd prepared.

"Guess I went a little overboard, being that I'll be eating alone. I was hoping my kids would somehow be back for *Sukkos*."

Jake thought she could use a hug right about now, but didn't dare approach her. He recalled the awkwardness when he offered his hand to her before. If she wasn't comfortable with a handshake, hugging was *certainly* out of the question.

He stood up slowly, trying to think of words to console her. But before he could formulate anything intelligent, she broke the silence.

"Why not join me for the holiday meals-- help me eat all this food? It's the least I can offer you after keeping you all this time going on about my problems. There's a *Sukkah* out back we can use."

He was dumbfounded. This fascinating bundle of energy was certainly more forward than a traditionally

Orthodox woman ought to be.

He liked that.

"Thanks for the invitation– *really*. But I'll take a raincheck."

He watched the disappointment spread across her face.

"But I did enjoy our discussion-- you're an interesting person!"

"Thanks– I *think*. So why not join me for dinner *tonight*, at least?"

Jake tried to think of a painless way out,

"I'm not sure I should."

"Why *not*?"

She gazed into his eyes, scrunching up her forehead, distracting his train of thought.

"It's just that you-- I-- we're so…*different*. That's all."

"Oh. I see."

"No, actually, I don't see!"

"*How* are we different, Jake? We're both extracting ourselves from the Ultra-Orthodox community, we're both single, and we're both looking for a relationship."

"You are, aren't you-- looking for a relationship, that is?"

Jake realized she had him cornered.

"I suppose I am, in the long run."

"So, you need more time before getting involved with someone. I can understand that."

He was relieved at the gracious way out she was granting him.

"Yes. That's *exactly* it."

He thought he was out of the woods.

But Mindy wouldn't let it go.

"Well, we can be *friends*, can't we? There's no harm in joining me for dinner as a *friend*, is there?"

"Mindy, it's not personal. I think you're a nice person– *really,* I do. But I'm not interested in going back to a strict lifestyle."

"What do you mean? You're still Orthodox, aren't you?"

"Well, I suppose I might fall into the very Modern-Orthodox category. But not the way you may think."

"How so?"

"I don't consider myself part of the black-hat community. I certainly don't fall in line with their extremist thinking. I follow some of the basic traditions, but I don't follow the many strict rules Orthodoxy has created for itself. Those traditions and rules seem important to you. I'm practicing my Judaism very differently than you seem to be."

Mindy stood silently, chest heaving, face flushed.

"And what makes you think I'm part of the Ultra-Orthodox community and follow all those rules?"

"Well...the way you were dressed at that party, and your hesitancy to shake my hand when we met. And today, you've got both doors open so we won't technically be alone."

"How can you judge me by the few things you've seen me do?"

Her pitch escalated as she spoke.

"You don't know *much* about me, but you're going to hear *plenty* now!"

She gave him a rapid-fire rundown on her life to-date, then paused to breathe.

"I'm slowly changing, but it's hard to let go. Unlike you, I don't know the *finer* points of Jewish law. I can't determine which rules are basic requirements and which are Ultra-Orthodox add-ons. Even the things I *want* to change I *can't*-- at least not as fast as I'd like to. I have to consider my children too. So, when I'm out in the community, I dress a little frumpy-- but that's not the *real* me. I'm slowly returning to the Modern-Orthodox way I was raised."

Jake waited to make sure she was done.

"Wow!" Mindy exclaimed, as she returned to her seat at the table. "Guess I got a little emotional. Sorry. But that's just how I feel. I'm *so frustrated.* I was hoping that *you*, of all people, could appreciate how difficult this is for me."

Chapter Thirteen

Marsha clicked off the cordless phone, ending the call from Laurie to congratulate her on her new position with the loop-based law firm. Of course, she'd also called to remind Marsha of her undeniable success in being the first of them to bed an Orthodox man.

She tossed the phone onto her bed beside the array of designer outfits she purchased to celebrate her first case on the new job. At least that's how she justified her four-figure shopping binge rather than admit it was really a desperate attempt to console herself over losing Jake.

Marsha had been waiting to hear Laurie declare her victory. It's what she planned and hoped for, for so long.

Revenge was finally at hand.

A simple phone call would take care of everything now.

But her personal loss overshadowed all that for the moment.

She tried luring Jake back.

But when she called him, he claimed to be involved with someone else.

Someone else.

As *if* she didn't know.

It *had* to be that little redhead bitch.

But after this morning's court appearance in the Daley Center, there was no reason to panic. *Now* she had the means to get Jake Cooper back on track.

Marsha spent the rest of the day slipping in and out of her purchases, zipping, unzipping, and prancing before the full-length mirror in the bedroom of her luxury Gold Coast condo– compliments of her new firm. The plush address certainly wouldn't hurt her attempts to win Jake back.

Neither would the clothes.

She knew what had to be done-- the competition had to be eliminated.

She stared at the unopened pill bottle on her night stand and smiled. She stopped taking her medication since her return to Chicago. Today's success *proved* she didn't need it. She'd functioned flawlessly without it. Her head was clear-- her mind sharp.

They wouldn't last long. Not *now*.

Not with the trouble she had in store for Mindy Bloom.

Chapter Fourteen

Jake succumbed to Mindy's persuasive reasoning and joined her for *Sukkos* dinner Tuesday night.

After dinner, Mindy extended the invitation to include the remaining holiday meals. Jake was unable to resist her draw-- *and her cooking.*

He grew more intrigued by the minute.

She was a fascinating meld of the modern world and the fish-bowl life he'd escaped from.

She managed to combine the oil and water mixture into a most delightful cocktail-- one taste, and he *had* to have more.

At the conclusion of *Sukkos* dinner Wednesday night, he asked her out for an evening downtown the following Saturday night. His heartbeat suspended until he translated her flurry of words in response as an acceptance.

Sundown on Saturday was at seven.

Jake picked up Mindy in the Nova at eight-thirty, giving her enough time after *Shabbos* to prepare for their first official date.

Wednesday was the last time he saw her and he looked forward to their evening with great anticipation.

He'd lost all interest in Marsha and found himself completely taken by this fascinating creature named Mindy Bloom.

Jake realized that Marsha was not the woman for him, and in light of that, he didn't understand her anger when he told her it was over.

Mindy was uncharacteristically quiet on the way downtown.

Jake drove south on Lake Shore Drive, trying to make small talk by pointing out buildings of interest. But Mindy didn't respond beyond an occasional nod or grunt.

Where was the vibrant, chatty woman who'd captured his interest this past week?

Thinking she might just be tired, he joined her in silence.

He parked the car and squeezed into the throbbing crowd inside the dimly lit dance club. Mindy's body kept pace with the bone-rattling beat, but her blank expression said she was mentally elsewhere.

Jake took her hand, led her out of the club and sat her down outside.

"So, did you call Michael Wertzberger?"

The question *instantly* broke her silence.

Mindy sighed deeply, looked up at the sky as if

counting the stars, then blurted in rapid-fire fashion, "I-don't-want-to-talk-about-it-so-let's-just-enjoy-the-evening." She didn't even pause to inhale. *"Okay?"*

She tossed Jake a stern look and stood up, arms folded across her chest.

"What's up?" Jake finally asked. "You've been acting strange all evening. Are you okay?"

She slowly lowered herself to sit. "We have a problem," she replied.

"We do?" Jake tried to imagine what crime he'd committed. "What's the problem?"

"You asked me if I called Michael. Well...I *did*."

"And?"

"He set up an emergency hearing for custody."

"That's great-- *isn't it?*"

She tensed her forehead muscles and drew her brows together. *"No.* It is *not* great! Michael set the hearing for Friday morning. I met him there at nine. Sender arrived with *two* attorneys, a man, and a woman. I think the man's name was Rudy Garbacz."

She held out her hand and ticked off her fingers as she recounted the rest of the event. "Rudy requested the judge to order an evaluation. He asked for the case to be referred to mediation. *And,* he wanted an attorney to be appointed to represent the kids."

"What did the judge say?" Jake asked.

"Without letting Michael say *two* words, he granted all their requests-- *just like that*! Like the whole thing had been pre-arranged."

"Didn't Michael ask for visitation for you in the meantime?"

She slammed her fists on her knees so forcefully. "Sender's attorney accused me of *abuse*-- said the kids told Sender they're *terrified* to come near me and pleaded with him not to *make* them visit me."

An ocean of tears welled up in the corner of her big blue eyes.

"The judge refused to grant me *any* visitation until *after* the evaluation."

Jake slowly slipped his hands behind her shoulders, pulled her toward him, and let her head fall on his shoulder.

She let out gulps of sobs. Her ocean of tears broke through her usual dam of strength.

"Mindy, I'm so sorry for you," Jake said while gently massaging her back. "This is awful. Maybe we should call it a night."

Mindy sat upright.

"There's more."

She took a deep breath and slowly blew it out.

"That other attorney-- the *woman*. Rudy requested that *she* be appointed as the children's attorney and guardian. And the judge granted that too."

Jake gave her a puzzled look.

"Her name is Marsha Rein. Isn't that the woman you were dating?"

Chapter Fifteen

Mindy enjoyed Jake's company more with each passing day, but with the children still in Sender's clutches, it was difficult for her to relax and enjoy their budding relationship. The sadistic measures he took to exact his twisted revenge hit her hard. She hadn't seen or spoken to her children since Sender pulled his little stunt.

A week passed uneventfully.

On her way home from work on Thursday, she stopped at Kosher Karry for canned goods and meat, filling her little cart with enough rations to stock her empty fridge and feed herself and her children.

She refused to succumb to despair and hoped that somehow her positive actions would force a miracle, bringing her children home soon.

She battled her way through a herd of Russian-speaking shoppers at Ted's Fruit Market, then hoofed the few blocks home, clutching the plastic handles of her bags stuffed with her shopping spoils.

She began rounding the first landing to complete the climb to her second-floor apartment when she was sideswiped by a dark flash racing past her like the building was about to explode.

One of her plastic bags burst on impact as the black tornado smashed into her, sandwiching the bag between her hip and the wall. The frantic figure careened off the stairwell wall crashing through the door at the bottom of the stairs, barely stopping to open it.

Two of her bags followed the black whirlwind, tumbling down the stairs only to be halted by the door as it slammed shut.

When her heartbeat returned to an inaudible level, she gathered the bags and headed up the stairs.

She dropped the bags outside her apartment door and fished in her coat pockets for the key.

Mrs. Goldstein cracked her door open.

She clutched her threadbare pink nightgown at the neck, as if holding it tightly made it less transparent.

"Is everything alright dear? I heard a frightful noise just as you were coming up the stairs."

The elderly holocaust survivor greeted her the day she moved in and took to her children like a grandmother. When the caring widow learned of Sender's custody ploy, she checked up on Mindy extra-frequently.

"I'm fine Mrs. Goldstein. Someone in a big hurry knocked a few bags out of my hands-- scared me more than hurt me. I'll be okay."

Mindy thought for a moment, contemplating the origin of the black tornado.

"Was anyone visiting you just now Mrs. Goldstein-- did anyone ring your buzzer or knock on your door?"

"No. I wasn't expecting anyone, and you know I never buzz unannounced visitors. Maybe it was one of those awful drunks I've been complaining to the manager about. They come up here during the day and sleep on the landing. I'll call John in the morning-- he'll put a stop to this nonsense. It's getting out of hand."

Mindy unlocked her door and pushed it open.

She reached inside to flick on the lights and dragged the plastic sacks inside.

She didn't notice anything wrong until she tripped on the couch-cushions that now lay on the floor. Their covers had been unzipped and removed from their foam stuffing.

The queen-sized sleeper of the yellow and beige floral couch was open and blanketed with the comics and a Venture ad insert from the unread Sunday Tribune that graced her end table earlier in the morning.

The remaining sections of the paper were shredded, crumpled, and flung about like giant spitballs covering her living room floor.

The antique end-table lamp with the fringed shade that once cast a warm glow upon the cozy room now lay in pieces.

Her photo albums-- former inhabitants of the bottom shelf of her bookcase, now had pages of her life ripped from their spines. The books from the upper shelves were tossed about the floor like chunks of debris chiseled from a prison escape-tunnel.

Mindy stood frozen, waiting for her brain to respond to the message her eyes were sending. A flurry of thoughts raced through her head, causing a temporary mental shutdown.

She slowly waded through the mess, mouth agape, only to find the entire apartment had been trashed.

The bedrooms, the kitchen-- not one square inch had been spared.

She found three file cabinet drawers, sleeping on her bed, buried under a blizzard of tax returns, insurance claims, and dozens of other documents. She only kept them out of fear that trashing them might transgress some obscure felony-- like removing the tag from a mattress. Now seemed like a good time to rethink her record-retention policy.

Slowly, the violation of her apartment-- and her life-- sank in. Her body shook uncontrollably as if Chicago's sub-zero winter had invaded early.

She returned to the living room, slammed the front door shut, and cranked the dead bolt. She fumbled with the security-chain, holding her right hand steady with her left, lining up the metal button with the hole and sliding the chain into its battle-station.

She fished out the cordless phone from the mess in the kitchen, ran to the bathroom and locked herself in.

The sink was filled with the broken remains of her perfume bottles. The intoxicating smell made breathing a chore, but Mindy was more terrified of what might lurk outside the door than suffocating from perfume.

At least she'd die smelling like a lady.

She turned to sit on the toilet-lid, and felt the crunch of broken glass underfoot. She lowered her eyes and saw the silver mirrored perfume-tray her grandmother had given her as a child, now a mangled mesh of twisted metal. The matching sterling brush-set lay amidst the glass-gravel but was unharmed except for minor scratches.

She spent a moment grieving over her childhood treasures and then regulated her labored breathing.

She dialed Jake's number.

She hung up on his answering machine and tried him at work. He'd been staying late recently and was probably still there.

"No, I don't think they took anything."

Mindy spoke with a hushed quivering voice.

"The stereo, my records, and jewelry-- it's all here. Whoever did this was angry, very angry, and *destructive*. This must be Sender's work. You can't imagine what he did here."

"Could that have been Sender who knocked you over on the stairs?" Jake asked.

"I don't think so-- I didn't get a look. Whoever it was, he took me completely by surprise. But I assume it was a man— I saw a black hat, and a flash of beard."

"I know what kind of a person you said Sender is, but why would he go to all that trouble?" Jake asked. "It makes no sense. Not after striking his blow by taking your kids."

"I never *said* he was rational," Mindy retorted. "I can't explain his motive-- unless…"

"Unless *what*?"

"Unless he was *looking* for something."

"When I moved out, I took a bunch of files– just tax returns and medical records, but Sender went *berserk,* screaming that I was stealing his manuscript. I thought he was rambling on about nothing. He's no literary giant by any stretch of the imagination-- he can barely spell. But maybe he did write something and thinks I have it."

"That seems more logical," Jake suggested, "although he could have used the kids for leverage to get it back."

"That would be more his style," Mindy agreed. "But he's capable of *anything*. Maybe he hired some goon to look for it. I don't know."

"But you moved out months ago. Why would he wait until *now* to go after it? Do you think he waited until he was sure your kids wouldn't be around to get caught in the middle of this mess?"

"Oh, I doubt that. He never really gave a *damn* about the kids. Why would he start *now*?"

Venting her anger proved therapeutic-- Mindy's shakes subsided, and her voice steadied.

"Jake, I don't know why or how, but I know in my gut it was him."

She slowly let out a deep, uneven sigh.

"*God,* I hate him."

She opened the bathroom window to ventilate the fragrant room.

"What was that noise?"

"Oh, just me. I opened the bathroom window to get some air."

"You're calling from the *bathroom*?"

"I'm too scared to go out there."

The thought brought on a second wave of the shakes.

"What if-- if it wasn't– Sender? What if-- they come back?"

"Why didn't you say something before? Listen to me. Hang up, take a deep breath, and call 911, *now!*"

Chapter Sixteen

Mindy clicked off the phone and took a deep breath.

Calling the police to have Sender arrested for destroying her home gave her a renewed confidence. With Sender behind bars, Michael Wertzberger could get the kids back in her custody.

She firmly pressed the talk-button. But the cordless device balked, responding with a familiar series of beeps that meant going out *there* to reset the base-unit.

She mustered the courage to leave her bathroom bunker and flung the door open to deflect the phantom attacker on the other side.

Stopping momentarily, she listened for movement, then dashed to the kitchen.

She unplugged the base unit, waited two seconds, then reinserted the plug. When she replaced the base-unit to its spot on the counter, she noticed her flashing answering machine.

She punched the play-button.

The voice she recognized cast her into a mild relapse of the shakes. She couldn't focus on the words-- the sound of his voice was too disturbing.

She played back the message again, this time listening to the amazing words. It took a third and fourth replay until she let herself believe she'd heard correctly.

She listened to the machine spit back the message. His flat nasal voice made her neck-hairs stand at attention.

"I want you to take back the kids. I can't keep up with--"

There was a long period of muffled squeaking like he'd cupped his hand over the mouthpiece.

"It's in their best interest. Come get them tonight. When you get home, come right over. We'll be here– they're all packed and ready to go."

Yes, thank-you God!

Her miracle had arrived.

Why hadn't she thought of this sooner-- he didn't *really* want them.

Sooner or later, he was bound to tire of catering to the needs of three demanding children.

All this time, she'd worried for nothing-- his surrender had been inevitable from the start.

Still, Sender was Sender. Not one to fall prey to yet another ploy, Mindy called for backup.

"What took so long? Did you call the police?"

She recounted the unexpected turn of events for

Jake.

"I've *got* to get the kids back. Calling the police now could ruin *everything*."

"What about what he did to your home Mindy? You can't just forget about it!"

"Right now, *my* only concern is getting my kids. I can always report it later."

"I guess you're right. Let me know how it turns out. I'll stay by the phone."

"Actually, I could use some company. Sender will be less likely to pull another stunt if you're there."

There was a long pause on the line.

"I can't, Mindy. I've got to stay at work and–"

Another brief pause.

"This is between you and Sender. I *can't* get involved in this. I hope you understand."

No. She did not understand.

But she wasn't going to waste precious time arguing with him. There was no telling how long before Sender would change his mind.

Mindy race-walked down Sacramento toward Devon– she was too jittery to drive.

Adrenaline coursed through her veins.

Eventually, her shakes subsided to a mild tremor.

Crossing Devon against the light, she evoked Yiddish and Russian obscenities from angry drivers.

An old oversized Checker cab painted dark green loaded with black hatted bearded men veered just in time to miss her.

She was on a sacred mission. Let them wait.

She desperately needed to hold her three darlings in her arms.

She picked up her pace to a jog, rounded the corner at Mozart and headed south. It was another half-block to the house. Her legs pumped while her mind tried making sense of Sender's violent attack on her apartment, followed by his sudden surrender. Perhaps the break-in was his last attempt at revenge.

The red-bricked Georgian she'd once reluctantly called home came into full view.

She raced up the small front porch and watched the condensation of her breath dissipate as she frantically rang the bell and worked the door knocker.

Both echoed loudly, but there was no response.

Leaning over the iron porch railing, she peered through the dark living room's bay window.

Straining for signs of life in the dark room, she made out the silhouette of the couch, coffee table, and recliner. She caught the reflection of the gilt lettering on the spines of the Hebrew books stacked in the tall oak bookcases lining the walls.

She hoped the silence meant they were all in the back room.

She dashed around to the back yard, mounted the back porch deck, and yanked open the screen-door.

Her nostrils fluttered like fish-gills straining for air.

Her chest heaved as she forcefully slowed her breathing.

The chilled air shocked her lungs as she repeated the bell-ringing/door-knocking cycle at the back door.

Once again, the sounds reverberated off seemingly barren walls.

Cupping her hands around her eyes, she pressed her nose to the window of the darkened back room and hunted for signs of life.

Sarah's doll-house was off to one side.

A glow-in-the-dark kick-ball lay frozen on the carpet in the middle of the room.

A Chinese checker-set resting on the snack-table just under the window had been abandoned mid-game.

Nothing stirred.

Where were they-- where the hell was Sender? Was

this just another twist of the knife?

Was *that* today's game?

She slammed the screen-door and kicked it shut.

She stomped off the deck, shook her tight fists in front of her like a boxer ready for round one and let out an ear-piercing scream that invoked a twist of the neighbor's blinds.

She tried calming herself by sifting through several explanations, none of which were comforting.

She began the journey back to her apartment.

She pulled up the collar of her thick wool overcoat.

Was he at O'Hare or Midway, gloating, all the while ushering the children onto a plane headed for God knows where?

Had he called her from the airport, knowing she'd run to the house full of hope only to plunge back into the depths of despair?

Was this a ruse so that he could squeeze the last ounce of joy from his evil plot?

The nightmare replayed itself in her mind, gaining vivid details with each rerun.

She marched all the way home, as if led by a drill sergeant.

Left, left, left-right-left.

Faster and faster.

The small, feisty redhead turned into a solid freckle-faced muscle-mass, ratcheting one notch tighter with each step. Her body locked into a rigid steel-beam. Her teeth gnashed to the beat of each step.

Enough was enough.

The little bastard better damn well be prepared to play hardball.

This meant all-out *war.*

Stuffing her steel fists into her wool coat pockets, she vowed to do whatever it would take to get her children back.

She marched up Sacramento. The dried leaves blanketing the sidewalk crunched under her angry footsteps.

She nearly kicked a cat darting from behind the shrubs in front of her building.

The wind howled, stirring leaves of every fall-color shade into little whirlwinds.

The nearly naked tree-branches cast ghastly shadows under the eerie glow of the street-lamps.

The few remaining leaves hung precariously from the tree limbs.

A sudden burst of loud voices caused her to stop

abruptly.

She searched the darkness, unable to identify the source of the commotion. For the first time, Mindy realized she was alone in the dark of night.

She dashed the last few yards up her building's walkway.

As she approached the outer door, she heard another outburst. This time she located the source piercing the silent darkness.

Someone was *definitely* on the roof of her building.

* * * * *

Sender wondered if he made a mistake. Had he erred in his judgment of character all this time?

Perhaps the roof was a mistake. But *he* wasn't afraid.

This was a *mind* game – the kind he *always* won. He feared *nothing*.

But the eyes staring him down pierced his very core, exposing his deepest fears.

He took another step back, returning the glare, but his fear rendered his pathetic stare impotent.

He tried to mask the quiver in his voice.

"Let's discuss this downstairs-- *talk* it out."

But the figure before him took another step forward, forcing him closer to the roof's edge.

"You can't do this-- you wouldn't *dare*! You don't scare *me*!"

But the fiery eyes penetrated his thick skin.

His knees knocked uncontrollably.

His body trembled.

How could a person change so drastically in such a short time?

He caught a flash of skin as the steady hands withdrew rapidly from the deep coat pockets, like a dueling gunslinger.

"You didn't even *warn* me. Give me a chance to–"

But the hands were too quick.

They torpedoed toward him, making a direct hit to his chest. The power surprised him.

The tightly clenched fists of steel met his torso full-force, sending him stumbling backward, off the edge.

Grasping wildly at the tree-limbs jutting over the roof, he managed to grab them.

His body swung in the wind and he held back a blood-curdling scream.

But his greasy palms wouldn't hold the grip.

He dropped like a rock straight to the ground.

The hard, cold earth beneath the leaf-covered grass broke his fall.

His foot smacked into the rigid ground.

His leg crumpled.

His torso folded like a lounge-chair.

His kneecap popped.

The intense impact forced his shin bone to splinter and punctured its fleshy housing.

The top half of the human folding-chair collapsed, forcing Sender's head to lunge forward, memorializing his mug with a bloody face-print on the sidewalk.

His black hat cartwheeled and came to rest underneath a black Dodge Ram pickup parked across the street.

A trail of wet blood seeped from his bearded jaw.

Sender's raw flesh and blood melded over the leaf-covered grass and cement like a modern-art experiment gone awry.

Chapter Seventeen

Jake circled his Nova around several blocks, looking for a parking space. He wondered how things were turning out for Mindy.

There were rumors at work that another downsizing was in the works. He stayed late to make a good showing, and that meant scrounging for a parking space in the evening.

After locating a spot on Lunt just big enough to squeeze his Nova into, he decided to walk over to Mindy's after quickly checking his mail and messages at home. He hoped she wouldn't be too upset with him for not going with her to Sender's.

He pulled the collar of his leather jacket up around his neck, and hustled home.

He pressed play on his answering machine and flipped through the mail as the device furiously rewound for several minutes. There was nothing exciting in the mail, another late notice from Visa, a New Year's donation request from the Rabbinical College, and a statement from the IRS for his past due tax balance.

The whirring machine clicked as it reached the beginning of the tape and switched into play mode.

There was a message from his parents informing him his uncle from Israel would be visiting them soon. *That* message was followed by Pinky's voice yelling something about the lottery.

Jake's heart raced.

"Jake-- Pinky. *Call* me! We did it-- we *fucking* did it! We won *big*! Call me-- no, *beep* me as soon as you get in. We've got some *celebrating* to do!"

The time stamp announced the message had been left shortly after four. Jake's first reaction was anger at Pinky for not calling him at work.

A tingling sensation of excitement ran through his body-- could it be *true*?

He lifted the phone's handset with his cold hand, almost afraid to call Pinky.

As his ability to think rationally slowly returned, Jake recalled Pinky's uncanny talent for exaggeration.

Winning big could mean a few hundred bucks.

He dialed Pinky's beeper and punched in his home number.

"Maybe I can finally pay these bills and get rid of them all," he thought. "It's nice to dream about, but let's see what *winning big* really means."

Then he remembered Mindy and called her number

quickly, knowing it would take a few minutes for Pinky to get the beep and return his call. He decided not to mention the lottery until he had details.

But it was a non-issue.

There was no answer at Mindy's.

She was probably still out getting the kids. But it had been almost two hours since she'd called him. He wondered what could be taking so long, though he expected Sender would drag things out once she got there.

The ringing startled him. Jake slowly reached for the phone and lifted the cold plastic receiver to his ear. It was Pinky.

"We gotta *talk,* bud!"

"I know, I know. I just got home and heard your message. What happened-- how much-- when did you find out?"

Jake's questions flew out of control.

"You aren't fooling with me now, are you, Pinky?"

"Jake, the one thing I *never* joke about is my gambling. We won big-- *real* big. That's for sure. But right now, that's the *least* of your worries, buddy."

He knew it couldn't be *all* good news.

"*Worries?* What gives?"

"There's something else."

"What? Are we *rich* or not?"

"I haven't totaled it exactly-- we won on several tickets, and we do have to split it up with the investors-- but that's *not* what I'm getting at Jake."

"Well, I get my percentage, right? How much did we win?"

"Forget about the *damn* money for a second, and *listen* to me! Money isn't going to be a problem anymore. But Mindy's in *deep* shit. You've gotta get over there and get her out."

"Out? Over where? What are you talking about? She called me at work. Is she okay-- where *is* she?"

"Geez, slow down. She tried calling you at work again, but you must have left already. She beeped me about a half hour ago from Belmont and Western asking me to call her attorney, Michael Wertzberger."

"What the hell's at Belmont and Western? What's she doing all the way over there?"

"You really did live in the dark-ages, Jake. That's Area Three Police Headquarters. Mindy's been arrested."

"*Arrested*? For *what*?"

It suddenly occurred to Jake that if Sender thought Mindy took his manuscript and he couldn't find it in her apartment, he might have filed theft charges. Maybe that call about returning the kids was just a setup for an arrest.

"Did Sender accuse her of stealing his *manuscript*?"

There was silence on the line, then, "*Sender* isn't pressing charges. *Sender* isn't *ever* going to bother her again. I think she really flipped out. She's been arrested for Sender's *murder*."

The blood drained from Jake's head.

His knees wobbled.

He collapsed onto the couch.

He sat there with the receiver to his ear, unable to speak.

"Jake-- you okay?"

"Yeah," he grunted, barely audible.

"Mindy needs you now more than ever, Jake. She hasn't got anyone else to lean on."

Considering Pinky's often crass behavior, Jake was amazed at how sensitive and good-hearted he could be when push came to shove.

"Look, I'll pick you up in five minutes and run you down there. Just be ready and wait for me downstairs."

Pinky was a true friend.

Chapter Eighteen

Pinky tugged on Jake's jacket sleeve.

"Jake, this is it, the second floor."

He pointed to a staircase buried in the side of the wall of Area Three Police Headquarters.

Climbing the staircase, they arrived at a large industrial green steel door in dire need of a paint job. Pinky opened it, and Jake followed him into a dark, tiled hallway. A familiar stench emanated from a tiny bathroom to their left. Directly ahead was a door marked DETECTIVES - PERSONAL CRIMES.

Pushing through that door, they entered a large, open, sparsely populated area. Fluorescent lighting filtered through aged plastic dropped ceiling panels casting a yellowish glow over the room. Several lights flashed rapidly, threatening to join their burned-out brothers hanging over some of the darker areas of the large room. The center of the room was divided into cubicles, formed by tattered pea green partitions lined with memos and calendars held up by staples and push-pins.

An ancient PC, dot matrix printer, an electric typewriter, and two old black rotary phones rested on a large folding table at the back of the room. The cinder block walls were lined with an assortment of bulletins and crime statistics. Opaque glass doors hinted at several offices off the sides of the room.

"I can't believe you talked me into coming here Pinky. What good can we do?"

Pinky stared at Jake as if he'd announced he was from Mars.

"I mean, why are we getting mixed up in this? We should let her lawyer handle everything."

"What's with you? Don't you care about her? You can't just *leave* her here now. Whether she did this or not, she's gonna need you *now* more than ever. At least wait around long enough to see what this detective says. Maybe you can visit her."

Jake suddenly felt ashamed.

Pinky was being more of a man about this than he was. She was *his* girlfriend, not Pinky's.

"I suppose I should stick with her through thick and thin."

Then it hit him-- *the guilt.* He wanted to avoid getting involved because he felt guilty.

Guilty for letting her down when she'd asked him to go with her to Sender's. If he'd had the guts to go with her, she wouldn't be in this trouble now.

Jake made a silent pledge to set things right. He just hoped it wasn't too late.

A tall, muscular man with thinning red hair, a clean-shaven baby face, and a cleft chin approached and introduced himself as Detective Joe Roberts. The sleeves of his white shirt were unevenly rolled up, and a blue ballpoint pen flopped around loosely in his shirt pocket.

"What can I do for you?"

"My girlfriend, Mindy Bloom– she's been arrested. I'd like to see her."

Roberts sat down and leaned back in his chair, rubbing his chin, making the cleft grow wider and smaller as he did.

"Well, you can see her, but not until after we're done processing her. I might be able to arrange a few minutes for you before she goes."

"*Goes?*"

"To lock-up."

"You don't think she really murdered him, do you?"

Roberts leaned his large frame toward Jake.

"What I think is the evidence points to her as the prime suspect-- unless there's something *you* want to tell me that we don't already know."

"I don't even know what *happened*!"

"Seems they had an argument on the roof of her building, and she pushed her ex off the edge. The M.E.'s still working on his report, but there's no question the fall killed him, and it happened *sometime* this evening."

"Did you say on the *roof* of *her* building?"

"Yup."

Roberts lifted the edge of a yellow legal pad reading Mindy's address aloud.

"That's where she lives, isn't it?"

"Yes. But I don't understand what *he* was doing on the roof of *her* building. She was going to meet him at *his* place to get her kids back."

Roberts slipped the pen from his pocket, bit off the cap, held it clenched in his teeth, and started scribbling on the yellow pad.

"Spell your name for me." The blue plastic cap bobbed up and down as he spoke.

Jake complied with his request, wondering what he was getting into. But Mindy needed him, and he was now *determined* not to shy away this time, *even* if it meant getting involved with the police.

"Neighbors say she and her ex had a custody dispute. What do you know about *that*?"

"I know she *hated* Sender for what he was doing to

her and the kids, but *not* enough to *kill* him. He left a message on her machine tonight saying he wanted to give her the kids and invited her to come get them from his place."

"*Did* she go there?"

"I don't know. Didn't she tell *you*?"

Jake was too embarrassed to mention the fact that he'd chickened out of going with her.

Roberts ignored the question.

"So, if she went there and found out he was jerking her around, wouldn't she have been pretty upset?"

Suddenly it dawned on Jake that Roberts was interrogating him to get more evidence to pin this on Mindy.

He began to wonder if Roberts knew much of anything at all about what happened.

Jake made a mental note not to mention the manuscript theft or the break-in. Mindy didn't need *more* problems in that department right now.

It was time to take back control of this interview.

"I still don't understand why Sender would have been up on *her* roof. What were they *doing* up there? It makes no sense. Maybe he just *fell* off?"

"The *evidence* says otherwise."

"*What* evidence?"

"Witnesses *heard* her threaten to kill him. She had *more* than enough motive. She had *access* to the roof. *And,* there was *physical* evidence on the body to indicate that *she* pushed him."

"*Physical evidence?*"

"Yep. Two strands of hair caught in the links of the D.B.'s Twist-O-Flex watch band. Lab's doing them up tomorrow. But the color and type are consistent with Mindy's. The positions of the strands were also consistent with the victim reaching to grab at his attacker as he lost his balance."

Jake still couldn't imagine Mindy *purposely* killing him.

"Those hair strands only prove that he grabbed to hold onto her before he fell. It doesn't prove she *pushed* him."

"No, not by *itself,*" Roberts admitted. "But together with their turbulent history and her earlier threat, it takes on a *whole* different context. Plus, there's a witness who heard arguing on the roof. This was no *accident. And,* if he were a *voluntary* jumper, there was no note and no known motive for suicide."

Jake still couldn't believe Mindy had actually done

this, though he didn't have any other explanation for what happened.

"What did *Mindy* say happened?"

"She hasn't said much at all-- very uncooperative."

Great.

Jake assumed she already told them everything. It hadn't occurred to him that the police knew less than he did. Now he'd just provided them with *who knows what* extra ammunition.

"She refused to talk without her attorney present, and he completely shut her down after he arrived."

"Michael's here? Can I talk to him?"

"Wertzberger? Sure, I don't see a problem with *that.* He should be up here in a few minutes."

Jake waited with Pinky for Michael's arrival.

Fifteen minutes later, a short, stocky man in his fifties, sporting a full head of salt and pepper hair with a full manicured beard to match, walked into the squad room, loosening his tie, and undoing the button of his five-hundred-dollar suit.

Jake had so many questions for Michael he didn't know where to begin.

"How *is* she?"

Michael squashed the bridge of his bifocals with his

thumb, sliding them back to the top of his nose.

"Mindy's fine for the time being."

He flashed a reassuring yellow smoke-stained smile.

"I've been chatting with the state's attorney about getting her out on bond as quickly as possible. I'm trying to avoid having her sent down to 26th and California."

"Where are the *kids*, Jake? She's really *worried* about them."

Jake hadn't thought about the kids.

"I'm not sure where they are, but I'd guess they're with Sender's mom if they weren't with him or Mindy."

"What the *hell* happened, Michael?"

Michael glanced around the room.

"Let's go outside. I'm dying for a smoke."

He turned and led Jake and Pinky through the large door they had entered over an hour ago.

Jake held his question until they followed him outside to the parking lot.

"So, what happened, *really?*"

Michael lit up as he related how Mindy said she had gone to meet Sender at his house but found the place deserted.

"On the way back to her apartment, she heard

voices from the roof as she approached her building. She turned to look up and saw Sender flying over the edge. He swung from a branch for a few seconds, then dropped."

He took a long drag on his cancer stick, then continued.

"When she heard what sounded like a window smashing across the street behind her, she ran upstairs and called 911. The police did a preliminary investigation and felt they had enough evidence to make an arrest. *Mindy* is their prime suspect."

"I knew she couldn't have done this!" Jake said. He was relieved that his refusal to go with her had *not* resulted in her losing control. Still, if he'd accompanied her, she'd have another witness.

"Did anyone see what happened that could vouch for her story?"

"Unfortunately, no," Michael said. "At least no one admitted seeing it to the police. But people are often afraid to get involved. Hopefully, we can get her out of this mess. Finding a corroborating witness is our best shot right now. But she's going to need a private investigator."

"Don't you do that kind of thing?"

"Sorry. I don't *do* investigations. Besides, I'll be plenty busy with her bond hearing. I'm hoping we can get her out quickly. She won't hold up well in lock-up. I haven't discussed it with Mindy yet, but do you know if she has access to any sizable funds for bail? State's attorney's talking half a million. She'd have to post ten percent."

"So, we're talking, what, *fifty thousand*? I don't think she has anywhere *near* that. Sender had everything tied up, and I'm not sure even *that* amounted to much."

Jake eyed Pinky looking for some sort of signal.

He didn't want to mention the lottery money without his approval. But Pinky's blank look said he didn't have a clue what Jake was after.

Michael tossed his half-smoked vice on the ground and did the toe-twist. "You boys should go home." He exposed his wristwatch from beneath his coat sleeve. "There's nothing more you can do until morning."

Jake looked back towards the building. "Detective Roberts said he'd try to arrange for me to see Mindy. I'm gonna wait to see her."

Michael flashed a calming smile as he put a hand on Jake's shoulder. "They won't let you see her *now*. Roberts probably just said that to make you feel comfortable, hoping you'd *talk* to him. You didn't *tell* him anything, *did* you?"

Jake's eyes dropped to the ground focusing on

Michael's ground-out stub. "Well, I-- he asked me-- yeah, I did." He kicked the butt across the parking lot. "I spoke to him. I didn't know I wasn't *supposed* to."

"In these situations, the less the police know, the better," Michael said. "They're focused on making an arrest that'll stick. The truth isn't always a concern, and evidence often has a way of pointing in the wrong direction."

"I'm so sorry. I feel like an *idiot*!" Jake admitted.

"Listen, go home kiddo, and don't worry. You're an amateur-- *Roberts* does this for a living. You'll learn. Besides, by the time he's done interviewing neighbors and friends, he'll probably find out everything you told him anyway. It's just easier if we keep one step ahead of them. It's *all* a game."

Michael had a talent for finding comforting words, but Jake still felt like a jerk. He finally mustered the courage to get involved. But instead of helping, he'd screwed it up.

That made him even *more* determined to make it right, *somehow*.

They waved Michael's ancient diesel Mercedes off as he pulled out of the lot.

Jake turned to face Pinky.

"What about our lottery money?"

"What about it?"

"We could use some of that for Mindy's bail."

"*Whoa*! Hold on now. I haven't even cashed in the tickets yet."

"But Pinky, you were right. I've been a jerk, and Mindy *does* need me now more than *ever*. I'm going to do whatever it takes to help her now, and I'm not taking *no* for an answer. I'm not asking you to give the money away. Just park it for a while so she can get out of here."

Pinky reluctantly agreed, and Jake felt like he was finally on track to set things right.

His fear had caused too much pain-- too much needless suffering once before.

He couldn't let it happen again.

He was ready to take whatever necessary action, and he knew exactly where to start.

Chapter Nineteen

Jake pointed to the roof of Mindy's building.

"He probably came off the roof right about there."

White chalk was smudged across the lawn and part of the sidewalk where Sender's body landed.

The top of his head was outlined on the bloodstained cement sidewalk.

Jake turned and stepped into the street.

"Let's see about that breaking glass Mindy heard."

Pinky followed him across the street.

Looking up and down, Jake could clearly see to the end of the street in both directions.

No sign of glass was evident.

At his suggestion, he and Pinky walked all the way up and down the block. Pinky checked the windows on the front and sides of each building while Jake checked the windows of the parked cars.

After coming up empty, they repeated the exercise on Mindy's side of the street, thinking she may have thought the noise came from across the street but may not have. That too turned up nothing.

"Maybe whatever was here has been cleaned up

already," Pinky suggested.

Jake thought about that while staring at the parking space directly across from the roof of Mindy's building.

Jake pointed to an empty parking spot. "You may be on to something. What if a car *was* parked there but left *after* the incident? Maybe someone smashed the window of a car that was here, and *that's* what Mindy heard. The glass might have only gone inside the car, not onto the street. Break-ins are common around here. The window of my Nova's been smashed twice. Of course, that would be a big coincidence to happen at the *exact* same time Sender came flying off the roof. I wonder if anyone called it in for insurance claim purposes. Roberts should be able to tell us that– if he'll tell us *anything*. Let's go inside Mindy's apartment and see what else we can learn."

Pinky stared at the crime-scene tape draped over Mindy's apartment door.

"You wanna break into a crime scene, you're on your *own*, Jake."

"How else are we gonna investigate unless we check it out? You're the one who said Mindy needs my help. So now I'm *gonna* help. Are you with me or not?"

Jake used the spare key Mindy gave him to open the door. Pinky reluctantly followed him under the tape and into the apartment.

Everything was turned upside down and strewn about. The two newly self-appointed sleuths tiptoed through the mess, trying not to move or touch anything.

They made their way down the long narrow hall, toward the kitchen.

The living room, bedrooms, and even the kitchen looked like a tornado had ripped through.

Everything was yanked out of the closets, cupboards, and cabinets and strewn about.

As they made their way back toward the front of the apartment, Jake pushed open the bathroom door.

"That's where she called me from."

Tissues, toilet paper, and bags of cotton balls had been removed from the cabinet underneath the sink. Shiny slivers of glass peeked from beneath the mess, and what was left of the lovely antique hair brush tray he knew Mindy loved was smashed on the floor.

"The cops must really think she did it if they looked this hard for evidence," Pinky said.

"You're forgetting something, aren't you?"

Pinky gave him a bewildered look, begging for an explanation.

"Someone broke in here just before the whole roof

thing happened. Mindy called me, remember? We have no idea what the place looked like right before or after Sender was pushed. Only the police know that now."

"What difference does that make, Jake?"

"Something might have indicated that Mindy and Sender were fighting here before going up on the roof. Now we'll never know for sure."

"Are you thinking Mindy could have actually *done* this?"

"Let's just see if we can figure anything out by looking on the roof."

They carefully stepped back toward the front door, over the books, papers, and furniture obstacle course, and closed the door, leaving everything just the way they'd found it.

A familiar frail voice whispered from behind the neighbor's slightly cracked open door.

"Jake? Is that *you*?"

"Mrs. Goldstein? Yes, it's *me*."

"What's going on? Are they all gone now?"

"Is *who* all gone?"

She motioned the two of them closer to the door.

"Come in. I don't want to talk in the hallway."

After letting them in and carefully checking the hall

for invisible eavesdroppers, she locked the door. She slowly made her way around the apartment, closing every shade.

"Mrs. Goldstein, what's going on? Who are you hiding from?"

"From *them*."

"*Them*?"

"Yes. *Them*-- the *police*."

"*Why* are you hiding from the police?"

"I don't want to get caught up with them. In Poland, we could *never* trust the police."

Jake knew exactly what she meant.

"Don't worry. They're gone. But if you know anything, please tell us. The police arrested Mindy-- they think *she* killed Sender. They believe she pushed him off the roof, and they're trying to charge her with his murder."

"Oh my, that poor, lovely girl. She *couldn't* have done this."

"I don't think so either, but unless we can prove she didn't, the police are trying to make a case against her."

She shook a finger in the air.

"You see. You can't trust the *police*. Innocent people, innocent women, and children, they took us all."

"Yes, I know. But that was a long time ago, in

Poland. Things are different in America. We have a good legal system. We just need to make use of it. And right now, Mindy needs all our help."

Putting his own doubts about Mindy's guilt or innocence aside, He seized the opportunity to glean whatever information Mrs. Goldstein might have to share. He decided to play into her flashback. "She's an innocent woman. Don't let them take *another* innocent woman. Tell us what you know, *please*!"

"Well, I didn't actually *see* much," Mrs. Goldstein confessed. "But I did *hear* something. I fell asleep on the couch waiting for my bread to toast in the oven to have with my tea, which I do every evening. The smoke alarm woke me to find my toast had burned. I went to the kitchen, shut off the oven, opened the oven door, and opened the kitchen window. Normally I'd never think of opening it on a night like this. It's too cold in this apartment-- the landlord keeps it so cold you could *freeze* to death sometimes. Then there was a noise from outside. I looked out the window, but no one was there. At least I couldn't *see* anyone. But then I heard voices, and it sounded like it was coming from the *roof*."

"What exactly did you hear?"

"Arguing. It started as a loud conversation, but then

it got even louder and I heard one man's voice yelling."

"Do you know if any of the voices were Mindy's?"

"No. I couldn't hear them clearly at first. I was startled by the noise. But after I realized what was going on, I heard one voice– a *man, definitely* a man– yelling."

"Did you hear what he said?"

"Yes, I'll *never* forget those words. Very loud and clear as a bell. He yelled 'But you didn't *warn* me!'"

"*Then* what did you hear?"

"*Then*? Then I heard *nothing*. I shut my window fast and minded my own business. I don't need more trouble."

"I appreciate your help, Mrs. Goldstein."

"I tell you this, but only for *your* ears. I don't want to talk to any police. But *you* boys, I can trust, *no*? *You'll* watch out for us, *yes*? Especially for Mindy. Such a dear girl. You *must* help her."

Jake glanced at Pinky nodding his head.

"Yes, Mrs. Goldstein, we'll do whatever we can."

Ms. Goldstein saw them out to the hallway and closed her apartment door behind them.

Jake heard the deadbolt click and the security chain slide into position.

The two newly appointed guardians climbed to the top floor. Jake mounted a short ladder built into the wall

151

that led to the roof-access hatch in the ceiling.

He thought it was odd that there was no lock on the hatch. He gently peeled back the crime-scene tape, pushed the hatch open, and climbed up into the crisp, dark night air.

Pinky followed close behind.

Suddenly, Jake grabbed Pinky's arm.

"What's the matter buddy? Feeling a little woozy?"

"I don't do heights well."

Slowly, he loosened his grip on Pinky's arm and turned around.

"I'll be okay, as long as I don't go anywhere near the edge."

"Some detective *you'd* make!"

"Cut the razzing. We've *got* to help Mindy. If she didn't do this, we need to prove it and get her cleared. And even if she *did* push him, we've got to prove that she had a good reason. Maybe Sender *provoked* her, or maybe it was self-defense. Maybe *he* was trying to throw *her* off. She wouldn't just push him for no reason."

Jake spread his arms out to balance himself while slowly raising his eyes that had been fixated on the roof's floor until he could see out beyond the roof's edge. He let out a nervous laugh.

"It figures, you know?"

"What figures?"

"My luck."

"I *finally* meet a great woman, and she ends up in jail for murder."

Pinky roamed freely around the roof without concern. He sat on the short wall surrounding the roof with his back to the front lawn. Jake slowly shuffled his feet, working his way closer to Pinky but staying well away from the edge.

As he gained more confidence and took note of his surroundings, he noticed the tarred roof was covered with an array of litter.

Several small, familiar candy wrappers and an empty cigarette pack had been blown into one corner of the roof.

Jake pointed to a glass Coke bottle lying near a pile of nut shells near Pinky's feet. "That must be an antique by now. Guess no one cleans up here."

Pinky slid off the ledge and bent down to examine the bottle. He picked it up. "Maybe we should keep it. Could be worth something, don't you *think*?"

"What *I* think is that you just left *your* fingerprints at the crime scene. If they haven't finished fingerprinting up here yet, you're going to have to explain that."

"All the more reason to make sure it's not here for them to find," Pinky said as he slipped the bottle into his jacket pocket.

As Jake followed Pinky back down the ladder, he stopped to pull something sticky off his shoe. "I must have stepped on some gum or something. Hold on a minute."

Jake tugged at several fibers, squashed into the gum under his shoe, and pulled. The gum stretched and draped over the ladder steps. "This gum is fresh."

Pinky held one finger up in the air. "That means whoever was up there with Sender probably left it. Maybe we can identify them with it."

"I doubt it," Jake said. "First of all, I stepped all over it and ruined whatever fingerprints or teeth marks it might have revealed. Second, it may have been left by the police or someone else snooping around, like us, *way before* or *after* Sender's fall."

As Jake pulled at the last few fibers caught in the sticky substance, he caught a hint of a familiar scent. He sniffed the fibers for further analysis.

"Now what Sherlock, you gonna snort that?"

"No Pinky, *wait*. This smells familiar."

Jake shoved the hairy glob under Pinky's nose.

Pinky turned away, but Jake persisted. "Smell it! It doesn't *just* smell like gum. I mostly smell the gum, but there's a hint of another scent. I can't quite make out what it is, but I *know* I've smelled that before."

"Well, it could be anything. Can we get outta here now, Jake?"

"Sure. But there's one more place I want to check out before we call it a night."

Chapter Twenty

Marsha called Laurie's number repeatedly, but there was no answer.

Laurie was supposed to meet her after work at the Dunkin' Donuts on Devon, just down the block from Glatt World, where Laurie worked.

But she didn't show.

Marsha walked to Glatt World to see if Laurie might be working late.

She found the owner working the register, and when she inquired about Laurie's whereabouts, she was attacked with a flurry of complaints.

"She doesn't *even* call-- just decides not to show up-- my wife's mad I'm not home for *dinner*-- my oldest boy isn't speaking to me because I promised to take him to *basketball practice*. If you see that good-for-nothing girl, tell her she doesn't have a job here anymore!"

Marsha drove to Laurie's apartment and gleaned from the building's super that Ms. Smilow stopped by earlier that day to pay her past due rent. She was carrying baggage but left no word about where she was going.

This was *so* unlike her.

But later that night, after learning of the evening's other events, Marsha began putting it all together.

No wonder she'd been so secretive about whom she'd snagged.

Although things had gotten a little out of hand, all-in-all everything was falling into place nicely.

But now, there was another matter Marsha needed to tend to. Sleeping with Laurie wasn't the only thing Sender had been guilty of.

Chapter Twenty-One

Pinky and Jake approached a red-brick Georgian.

"I think that's the one," Pinky said. "The address isn't marked, but Sender's address should be next."

Jake stared at him with a look of astonishment.

"I see your reasoning improves with lack of sleep."

"Very funny. So, mister wise guy– just how are you figuring to get inside? You already got me to break through police tape with you, but I draw the line at actual breaking and entering."

"I have no intention of doing any such thing. Let's just see what we can view from the windows. Maybe we'll get lucky."

"What is it we're looking for here, Sherlock? More signs of a struggle?"

"No. It's unlikely anyone would start a fight here and then go all the way over to Mindy's and climb up to the roof just to continue the argument. What I'm looking for is signs that someone came searching for that manuscript-- the one Mindy thought Sender, or *someone*, was after. He accused her of taking it, but she didn't have it. Maybe someone else came looking for it at Sender's house and when they didn't find it *they* went looking to see if Mindy had it. If his place is also ransacked that might tell us something. And if we get lucky and find an open door or window, we can get in without *breaking* in and see if the manuscript is still here."

They walked up to the front door. The crime scene tape had fallen halfway off the door. Pinky grabbed the loose end and wagged it at Jake. "Looks like we're not the first one's poking around. So, even if the manuscript's not here now, someone else might have found it and already taken it. For all we know, the police took it for evidence."

"Wow! Now you're really *thinking*, Pinky. That's good. But I don't think the police know about the manuscript. And even if they came across it, I doubt they'd know there was anything to it."

Pinky raised his finger in the air. "Unless *something* in that manuscript reveals a motive for someone to kill Sender."

"Pinky, you're an absolute *genius* after hours. I can't wait to hear what you come up with at the crack of dawn."

They pressed their noses to the front window, but the dark interior made it difficult to see anything. As they made their way toward the back, Pinky caught movement through one of the side windows.

"Jake, I swear I saw something moving inside."

"Ah, sleep deprivation finally takes its rightful toll."

Jake nudged Pinky's elbow with his and flashed a smile.

"Maybe he has a cat-- or a dog. Besides, who would be walking around the house in the pitch dark?"

They rounded the corner to the back of the house. There was no crime scene tape on the back door, which seemed odd. Jake lifted himself onto the cement step to peek through the back door's little window. As he leaned forward, the door gave way, and he nearly spilled onto the floor inside.

"Jake? What are you doing here?"

"Marsha? What the hell–"

She cut Jake off mid-sentence, "*I'm* here looking for the children. I've been appointed as their attorney and legal guardian. Now that Sender's dead and their mother's in jail, they're *my* responsibility. But what's *your* excuse, mister snoopy? I see you brought your sidekick. How charming."

A thousand questions raced through Jake's mind. "Why were you looking for the children *here*, and why in a *dark* house?"

"I don't answer to *you*, Jake Cooper. But *you're*

going to have some answering to do to the police when they find out you've come snooping around here."

Marsha pushed her way past Pinky and marched off.

The two of them stood there in silence for a moment.

"You were right Jake-- I can't believe it," Pinky said.

"What are you talking about? Has your intelligence power worn off already?"

"Not all at." Pinky pointed to the open door. "We did get lucky."

They now had full access to Sender's home without breaking in.

They tiptoed around the two-story home, carefully checking for anything that looked like a manuscript. Aside from Sender's inability to keep a clean and tidy house, the place showed no signs of having been ransacked. After a disappointing search in the dark, they made their way back to the rear door. As they passed through the den at the back of the house, Pinky commented on the nice computer system sitting on the desk.

That got Jake thinking.

He fumbled around in the dark for the diskette

drive's eject button until he heard a sweet popping sound.

Jake waved the diskette that popped out at his command.

"*Now* we got lucky."

Chapter Twenty-Two

He took a long drag on his cigarette, savored the menthol, then let out a slow stream of smoke, carefully resting the half-smoked tobacco stick on the ashtray's groove.

The smoker gazed over his left shoulder, studying the figure sitting next to him. He watched as his study partner adjusted his reading glasses, wet his fingers, and smoothed his eyebrows. He waited as the man gingerly ran his fingers through his well-groomed beard and examined his image in a small hand mirror, checking each hair's alignment.

He grabbed a small, yellow, sunflower-seed bag from the desk beside him and with one quick, well-practiced motion, the smoker shook several seeds into his cupped palm and popped them into his mouth. Leaning back in his oversized leather chair, he grew impatient with his neighbor, who continued his grooming ritual. Tipping back the wooden lectern before him, he leaned it against his broad chest. He opened the oversized Talmud resting atop the lectern and rubbed his thick rough-skinned hand up and down the dog-eared, coffee-stained page.

"My friend, will you ever stop *obsessing* with

yourself? We still have much work to do."

The groomer abruptly stopped his ritual and flashed an appalled look at the smoker.

"God-forbid. I would *never* engage in self-indulgence. With all due respect to *The Rav*, a scholar is required to maintain an impeccable appearance. Surely, *The Rav* doesn't discourage this."

The Rav rolled his eyes.

"Ah - yes. Well, come now, let the Creator grant us better luck tonight than we merited last night. Tonight, my friend, we shall succeed."

"*Amen!*"

"Okay then– let's see, I believe we left off on page 49, in the middle of the page, by the two dots."

The groomer carefully returned his little mirror to its leather case and slipped it into the inside pocket of his black wool suit jacket. Half-opening the large Talmud in his lap, so as not to crack the binding, he slowly flipped to the correct page and located the two dots.

"Are you ready to begin, my friend? I believe it's *your* turn to say."

The groomer began reciting the text.

"Rav Pappa says–"

He was immediately interrupted by a soft tapping

on the door.

"Yes?" *The Rav* bellowed.

As the door cracked open, the curls of his wife's wig peeked around the door.

"Fishel is here. He says he has the book you wanted. He's waiting for you in the living room."

The Rav turned to look at the groomer.

"Perhaps you can read ahead a bit while I take care of our friend."

The Rav leaned forward and righted his lectern.

As *The Rav* approached the living room, he watched Fishel, who had sunk into the overstuffed living room chair, struggle to extract his rotund little figure from the chair's depths to stand in respect as *The Rav* approached.

As he stood, he pulled up his baggy, black slacks by the twisted piece of worn leather barely recognizable as his belt.

He straightened his disfigured, dusty, black Fedora with both hands, then wiped the spittle from the corner of his mouth with his right suit-jacket sleeve which was worn to a black mirror-like shine.

"What is it, my friend? Did you get the book? I expected you *much* sooner."

Fishel hung his head.

"I beg *The Rav*'s forgiveness. I lost my watch."

"Speak *up* my friend, and speak clearly!"

"Sorry."

"So? Do you have it or not?"

Fishel responded with a look of bewilderment.

"The *book*, my friend. Didn't you bring it?"

"Oh – yes, yes! I have it right here."

He turned back to the chair to fetch the book, only to find it empty.

"I brought it with me. It must be here *somewhere*."

The Rav watched impatiently as Fishel frantically scanned the room looking for the book.

The Rav lifted a small, worm-eaten brown leather-bound book from the table in the entrance hall.

"Is this it?"

"*Yes*! That's it!"

Fishel grabbed for the book excitedly.

The Rav swung the book out of Fishel's reach.

"Careful! We don't want to destroy it– we want to *study* it. Thank you for your assistance. You've done well, my friend."

Fishel nodded in appreciation and turned to leave.

The Rav made his way back to the study.

Despite his age, *The Rav*'s memory was sharp as ever, and he still had the stamina to study late into the night.

He wondered who would carry on his important work after he no longer could-- work that no other rabbi seemed able, or *willing*, to do.

The groomer waiting for him in the study was a smooth talker and made a good impression. But there was no substance beneath his polish.

Certainly, Fishel wasn't a consideration.

He'd saved those two from the cursed path they'd fallen into. But neither were acceptable candidates.

He slipped his thumb underneath his suspender strap, running it upward to reposition it.

He re-entered the study only to find the groomer immersed in himself again.

"*Enough*, already! We must get on with our work."

The Rav carefully cracked open the book that Fishel had brought. "This is gold, my friend, *pure gold*. We shall use it to the best of our ability and take from it what we can." He removed the Lord Elgin watch from his wrist and wound it several times. "We have the whole night before us. Let us begin, my friend. It's your turn to say– by the two dots, please!"

Chapter Twenty-Three

Jake picked Mindy up from Michael's office in the Loop.

"I'm really worried about how this will affect my kids."

Jake thought she ought to be more concerned about her own fate now that she'd been formally charged with Sender's murder.

"Are you *sure* they're with Mrs. Stein? Last night, Marsha said she was *looking* for them at Sender's house to take custody."

"Marsha is their appointed attorney, but Michael says she doesn't have the right to take custody of them. And, yes– they're *definitely* with Sender's mom. I spoke to them myself from Michael's office. They've been with her since yesterday after school. They weren't even *with* Sender when he called me. It makes no sense why she'd have to go *looking* for them. She *knows* they're with Sender's mother. But I really don't want to think about that now. I just want to be with them. It's been so long. I'm really *worried* about them, Jake."

Michael used Jake and Pinky's winning lottery stub

as collateral to get Mindy out on bail. Jake convinced Pinky they could wait another few weeks to be rich.

Although Pinky agreed and even tagged along to pick up Mindy, he now sat in the back seat and appeared to be upset with Jake for twisting his arm and delaying their good financial fortune.

Jake was also disappointed about delaying his long-awaited take-this-job-and-shove-it announcement at work. But he'd waited this long already, and knew that Mindy needed this more than he did right now. Besides, it was time for him to stand up and do something that *really* mattered.

He felt good about helping and getting involved.

Of course, the whole thing *was* sort of his fault. If he'd gone with Mindy as she requested, this might have never happened.

"The kids will be fine."

"How can you say that, Jake? *How* can they be fine? As bad as Sender was, he *was* their father. Now their father is dead, and their mother is accused of killing him. So how *exactly* do you think my children will be *fine*?"

Jake knew better than to utter another word. When Mindy got this way, *nothing* would be the right thing to say.

He adjusted himself in the car seat and focused on weaving through the Dan Ryan traffic. They were going to Mrs. Stein's home to get the children. The funeral was scheduled for one-thirty that afternoon, and Mindy wanted to see them before that.

Traffic was heavy, and they crept along in silence until Pinky's coughing frenzy caught Jake off-guard.

It was too late by the time he cracked his window open.

After a long period of silence, Jake tried changing the subject.

"Mindy, do you know *anyone* who'd want to kill Sender?"

"I don't know that he *was* killed, Jake. Maybe he jumped. Or maybe he just fell. Why is everyone *so* convinced that someone pushed him off that roof?"

"You don't think *I* pushed him, *do you*?"

After a pause that was just a nanosecond too long, Jake said, "Of course not. Mindy. We have to deal with the reality of the situation. The police really believe he was pushed. Besides, if he jumped, where's the suicide note, and what would be his motive? And, why would he call you to come over and get the kids? Why not just do it?"

"How should I know? Maybe he couldn't handle the

kids anymore and felt guilty about not being a good father, so he jumped."

"Okay. Let's run with that for a moment. Why jump off *your* roof? Why not his own?"

"I don't know."

"And why would he commit suicide at *all*? From what you've told me, Sender had no conscience to speak of, so why would he suddenly feel guilt-ridden?"

"Look Jake, I'm sorry for being so difficult about this, but please hear me out. You're right-- it makes no sense that Sender would kill himself. But you have to admit it is *possible*. Maybe he jumped off *my* roof as his last gesture of revenge, to make me look guilty for a crime that wasn't even committed. His last *hurrah*."

"Okay. I'll accept that as a *possibility*. But we really need to think of every possible scenario and check it out. The best way to prove you're innocent is to find out what *really* happened and then *prove* it. Even Michael said you'll need a viable explanation for what happened other than what the police think."

"Yes, but Michael also said I should hire a private investigator to find out who really did it. He just doesn't understand?"

"Understand *what*? I think he's right on the

money."

"Really? How many Jewish Orthodox private investigators do you know, Jake?"

Jake didn't have to think long about that one.

"None."

"My point *exactly*. And how many people in the community do you think will *talk* to an outsider?"

"I see your point."

"There is another possibility, Mindy."

She looked at him with hope in her eyes for the first time that day.

"Pinky and I did a little investigating of our own last night. I had to do *something*. They wouldn't let me see you. I couldn't just go home to sleep like everything was okay."

"What did you guys do?"

"Nothing dangerous or anything like that. We went back to your apartment to see what we could find out on our own. Come to think of it, Mrs. Goldstein was reluctant—*adamant,* in fact-- about not speaking to or getting involved with the police."

"See-- *nobody's* gonna help me. They're either afraid to get involved or refuse to air the community's dirty laundry in public. They just won't do it."

"You're not letting me finish."

"Sorry. Go on."

"Mrs. Goldstein *did* feel comfortable enough to open up to *me*. Maybe *I* can investigate for you."

"You? I-- I don't know. What do *you* know about investigations? Do you know what you're doing?"

"Well, I think so. At work I investigate computer system problems and interview people to piece together what caused failures, so we can document it and correct the errors. Plus, all those years studying Talmud in the *yeshiva,* I learned how to conduct research and use logic to draw conclusions. Besides, what could possibly be *worse* than the situation you're in now? What have you got to *lose?*"

"I suppose you're right. But where would you *start?*"

"I think the first thing is to make a list of possibilities of what happened and why. Then research each approach and see where it leads us."

"It *sounds* logical. But how do we make a list like that?"

"Well, we've got your suicide theory as one possibility for the *how,* and the *why* could be guilt for not being able to handle the kids and the shame of having to return them to you. Not the most feasible line of reasoning, knowing Sender, but it *is* a possibility. Is there anything else in his past that might have haunted him and driven him to suicide?"

"Not that I know of. Sender never spoke about his childhood. But now that you mention it, there was something strange. Once, when we were with my parents for the *Pesach* Seder, my mom asked Sender what his father, Herman Stein, had been like. Sender said his father died a long time ago from a heart attack but he didn't want to speak evil about him, so he'd rather say nothing."

"That *is* strange."

"I've always wondered about that. In fact, I've never even *seen* a picture of his dad-- not even in his *mother's* home. She's got dozens of family pictures spread out around the house, but not a single one is of Herman. I've always thought that was odd, though she is an *odd* woman, to begin with. She *speaks* of Herman as if he were a saint when his name comes up, but she never says anything *specific*. I never pressed the issue. Sender has no siblings, but I'll bet you could get his mother to open up if *you* tried, Jake. Sometimes she does if you get her just right. Most of the time, she won't say anything bad about anyone. But if you can get her rambling *just* the right way, she might open up to you."

"To me?"

"Yes, Mr. Investigator, to *you*."

"Okay, okay."

Jake felt himself getting deeper and deeper into something he never thought he'd be able to handle. He could never be rid of the pain haunting him from his past failure, but at least he was doing the right thing now.

As he nudged the Nova forward, he noticed Mindy holding a family photograph. He'd never seen that particular picture before.

He pointed to a black-hatted man standing behind the children opposite Mindy in the picture.

"Is that Sender?"

"Yes. I hate carrying this around, but it's the best shot I have of my kids and myself all together."

Pinky sprang forward from the back seat.

"Hey! I *know* that face! He was at the *airport*, with Laurie. I'm *sure* that was him."

"I knew he was seeing *someone*-- we were still together when it started. What did you say her name is?"

"Laurie. Laurie Smilow."

"I've heard about her. I think she is civilly divorced, but her husband won't give her a *Get*."

That got Jake thinking.

"Hmm…I remember Marsha Rein saying they're friends. Maybe she has something to do with this. Maybe Sender found out Laurie was still married, realized he'd committed adultery, and was too embarrassed to face the community. Even *Sender* might have trouble dealing with the guilt and shame *this* community can load up on people."

Mindy smirked.

"Isn't *that* ironic? When I left Sender, his mother insisted it must be because *I* was seeing another man and had fallen in love. She *begged* me to take him back– even offered me money to do it!"

Jake tried to think of more possibilities as he maneuvered the Nova off the expressway at Kimball and headed North toward Mrs. Stein's house to pick up the children.

He turned toward Mindy and pointed a finger at his chin.

"Was Sender involved in any business dealings with anyone?"

"He *definitely* was, but I don't know any details. Sender was secretive about those things. Frankly, I felt better off *not* knowing. I suppose I should have taken more interest."

Pinky once again emerged from the rear seat.

"Maybe someone was blackmailing him. Maybe they threatened to tell everyone about his adultery."

Jake conspicuously checked his watch. "Wow! So, you're capable of intelligent thoughts even during *daylight* hours."

"Funny– you're not the *only* one with an investigative mind."

"No, but think about your theory. Why would anyone blackmail him and then kill him? That defeats the whole purpose. I was thinking he might have been involved with the wrong people and did something to get them mad enough to get rid of him."

"I could see *that*," Mindy added. "Sender did things that could drive *anyone* to murder. I was angry enough to do it myself!"

Jake's raised eyebrows met Pinky's in the mirror.

"Of course, I *didn't*. But I was *angry* enough to do it."

Jake gently rested his right hand on her shoulder.

"Mindy, we know you couldn't have done this. But you'd better watch what you say. Was there anything specific Sender was working on *recently*?"

"He was. I don't know much, but shortly before I

moved out, he met frequently with someone at the *Beis Hamedrash* on California. One time I dropped off his lunch, which he'd forgotten, but I didn't see who he was with. I couldn't even get past the front door-- you know how it is for a woman there. God-forbid I should see the men studying."

Jake nodded. Any woman entering the all-male domain of the *Beis Hamedrash* would be met by a hundred pairs of eyes staring at her until she retreated from their *territory. He* used to be one of those pairs of eyes. "Did you ever see the manuscript Sender accused you of stealing when you moved out?"

"No, I never saw anything that looked like a manuscript."

"Maybe it didn't *look* like a manuscript."

"What do you mean?"

"Maybe he'd been working on a manuscript on his computer, not on paper. Maybe he thought you stole a diskette that had a manuscript on it."

Despite the fact that the diskette Jake retrieved from Sender's computer turned out to be blank, he still felt this was a strong possibility.

"I never thought of that. But from the way he was fussing about the files and papers I took and put in my car, it sounded like a paper manuscript he was referring to."

Jake stroked his beardless chin. "Is it possible Sender made the whole thing up? Maybe there *was* no manuscript at all."

"I'm certain he was telling the truth about this. He got very emotional about it. Sender wasn't *that* good of an actor."

Pinky tapped Jake's shoulder. "Maybe he misplaced it-- took it somewhere else and forgot– at his mother's place, maybe?"

Mindy turned to face Pinky. "I doubt it-- but I guess that's a possibility."

Jake took Foster to Central Park and skillfully guided the Nova down the narrow two-way street.

"What's really puzzling about this manuscript, is that in all the years we were married, I've never known Sender to be much of a *writer*. He needed help drafting the simplest letters. What kind of *manuscript* could he possibly have written?"

As Jake braked at a four-way stop, Pinky grabbed the front seat and pulled himself forward. "Maybe he didn't write it."

Mindy and Jake both turned to face the back-seat detective.

"I mean, maybe he stole it from someone else who took it back and then wanted revenge and killed him."

Mindy shook her head.

"No, I doubt that. Sender was a slime-ball, but an honest slime-ball in a strange way. He wouldn't steal anything outright. He'd peek and snoop where he had no business, eavesdrop when he shouldn't, and maybe stretch the truth a little too far. But he always stayed within certain limits. I don't think he *stole* it. I think it was *his* manuscript. *Especially* since he went on and on about how much work he'd put into it."

But Pinky wasn't giving up that quickly. "But like you said, Sender was no writer. What could he have possibly written?"

Jake thought about the *Beis Hamedrash*, then realized there was another possibility.

"Maybe it wasn't something he wrote from scratch. Maybe he *compiled* something from other books but not actually authored, like from the old *seforim* at the *Beis Hamedrash*."

"I doubt that too. First of all, he was never seriously involved in his studies, despite hanging around the *Beis Hamedrash*. I found out he was a big goof-off at *yeshiva*. But an even *bigger* reason I don't think that's what he

180

wrote is simple. There's no money to be made publishing those kinds of books. Sender wouldn't have been interested. His deals were strictly potential big money-makers."

Jake swung the Nova into a space in front of a dark green Checker cab parked in front of Mrs. Stein's flat on Ridgeway. He tried to connect the dots between Sender's inability to produce literary works, his semi-underhanded value system, and his greed for cash. "You said he eavesdropped and peeked where he shouldn't. Maybe he compiled a lot of dirt he found out about the wrong people. Maybe *they* took the manuscript and did away with the person who could expose them."

"Now *that* sounds like Sender," Mindy said.

Chapter Twenty-Four

"I sent Danny and Sarah to school," Mindy explained as she and Jake sat around her kitchen table Monday morning. "I spoke with Dr. Bulinsky– the child psychologist Sender and I used before we told the kids we were separating. He thought they'd be better off returning to their normal routine. Adam is sitting the entire seven days of *Shiva* with his grandmother. His *Bar Mitzvah* is a few days off, so he's technically not required to do the whole seven days, but he wanted to, and Dr. Bulinsky said it would be good for him. He'll have to catch up on a lot of schoolwork. His teachers were *so* abrupt with me on the phone when I asked about that. They probably think I really *did* push Sender off the roof."

"Jake? *Jake*! Did you hear a word I said?"

But Jake had only been half-listening while carefully examining the two tiny black leather boxes in his hands.

"Oh, sorry, Mindy. These *tefillin* are in pretty good shape, considering how old they are, based on the wear and tear I see on the leather straps."

Adam would be binding these little boxes to his arm

and head for morning prayers using the attached leather straps. His *Bar Mitzvah* would officially mark the date he was required to observe the *Torah*'s commandments, including the wearing of *tefillin*. The handcrafted black leather boxes housed special *Torah* passages. Jewish males over the age of thirteen are required to wear them during weekday morning prayers. Mrs. Stein gave them to Adam on his twelfth birthday. They belonged to his *Zeyde*, Herman Stein. Mindy asked Jake to look at them to see if he thought they were still in the proper condition to be used.

"Adam should have no problem using them." Jake assured her. "As long as he's left-handed."

"Oh? Adam's *right*-handed."

"*Okay*. Well then, he'll still be able to use them, but we'll have to get them changed."

"Changed?"

"Yes. See this knot," Jake said, pointing to a leather knot wedged into a notch carved into the side of one of the *tefillin* boxes. "There are two boxes to each *tefillin* set. One goes on the head."

He placed one of the boxes on his head to demonstrate.

"The leather strap strung through it goes around the

top of the head, securing it in place like this," Jake explained, continuing the demonstration.

"But the other one gets strapped to the arm. Right-handed men place it on their left arm. Lefties strap it to their right arm."

Jake loosely strapped the other box to his right arm.

"See how when it's on my right arm, the leather knot on the side faces inward, toward the heart? Sender's dad must have been left-handed."

Jake pulled the tefillin box off and slipped it on his left arm.

"*See*? When I strap it to my left arm, the knot faces *away* from the body. It needs to be reconfigured so it faces Adam's heart when he has it fastened to his left arm."

"Can't you just untie it and put it on the other side?"

"It's not that simple. The knot has to rest inside a notch on the side, so it touches the main portion of the box where the scrolls are."

Jake pulled on the leather knot, sliding it away from the box and exposing a wide notch carved into the leather.

"This notch allows the knot to be pulled right up against the box, so it's always touching. Even if I knew the correct way to re-tie the knot, which I don't, I'd have to carve a notch into the other side of the box."

"I'm sure I have a tool you could use to do that," Mindy said.

"Trust me. You're better off paying a professional *sofer* to do that rather than take a chance with my limited skills. If I carve just a little too much, I could permanently ruin the *tefillin*. These are very expensive to replace."

"I had no idea. It's a good thing I had you check them."

"I'll take them over to the *sofer* on Devon, Rabbi Stam," he offered. "He can probably handle this for you."

"I really appreciate everything you're doing."

"I just want to help where I can. How are the kids responding to you?"

"Danny and Sarah seem confused. They haven't said anything. I feel a distance between us that wasn't there before. Adam won't even speak to me. He refused to come home-- he's sleeping at *Bubbie* Stein's for now. The whole thing is a nightmare."

"The little ones seemed happy to see you on Friday before the funeral. And I didn't notice any distance between you and them yesterday at the *shiva* house."

"It was nice having them back in my arms again. But it's not the way I would've chosen to get them back."

"What're you gonna do about Adam?"

"That's going to be a long, hard road. I don't know what he's thinking. He refuses to see Dr. Bulinsky. But I've got to keep trying. He might believe I killed his father. Or he may be angry at me because he believes the crap Sender probably fed him about me not being religious and trying to lead them away from Judaism. He's such a sweet boy. Being the oldest shouldn't mean he has to live such a hard life."

"I was the oldest in my family," Jake said. "The oldest child usually bears the brunt of family conflict, *especially* in a divorce."

"I suppose so. He's older and understands more of what's going on."

"That reminds me, what was going on yesterday when Mrs. Stein rambled about Sender not being her oldest? What did you say to set her off? You said she gets nutty sometimes, but she really flipped out."

"It was the strangest thing," Mindy replied. "Sender has no siblings that I know of. But when I referred to Sender as her oldest, she insisted he was not."

"Maybe she had a miscarriage before having Sender. That would mean Sender wasn't technically her first-born. Maybe that triggered an emotional sore spot that was too much for her to bear on top of Sender's death. My uncle is coming from Israel to visit my parents. He might know if she'd had a miscarriage. He lived in Chicago for many years before moving to Israel."

Upon returning to his apartment, Jake was greeted by a call from Pinky.

"I just got back from my vending-machine route," Pinky explained. "The owner of one of my stores told me that back in Cleveland, Marsha was a well-known attorney specializing in child custody cases. She'd been involved in several high-profile cases."

"She's *real* trouble, Jake," Pinky warned.

Chapter Twenty-Five

Jake's boss greeted him at work on Tuesday with the third-degree about the mountain of requests piled up in his in-basket.

Since he and Pinky agreed to use their winning lottery ticket as Mindy's bail, he had to postpone his early retirement and face that mountain for a few more weeks, at least.

But Jake found it challenging to focus with all the thoughts running through his head. Mindy, the murder, or suicide– or *whatever* it was. And now, wondering what Marsha had up her sleeve for Mindy.

His desk phone's sudden electronic beckoning interrupted his thoughts.

"Jake Cooper."

"Is this *Yankel* Cooper?" a man's voice asked.

"Speaking," Jake replied cautiously, responding to the Jewish name he was formerly known by.

"This is Rabbi Gavriel Diamond. I just wanted to see how things were going with you and if there was any way I could be of assistance."

The name rang a bell, but Jake couldn't recall why.

"Thank you. Things are just fine with me. I don't

think there's anything you could help me with."

"How did you get my work number?"

"Of course. Please excuse my rudeness. Rabbi Skumansky suggested you might be interested in meeting someone. There is a very special woman I'd like to introduce you to."

Bingo. Now Jake remembered him.

Rabbi Diamond the Shadchan-- one of several matchmakers competing for Chicago's eligible singles.

The only *help* Rabbi Diamond had called to offer was the opportunity to extract a sizable matchmaking fee for himself.

Jake wondered if, somehow, he'd learned of his lottery winnings.

He hadn't spoken with Rabbi Skumansky since Pinky, and he had purchased their Lulav and Esrog at his backyard sale.

Jake knew *he* hadn't told anyone. Pinky never did reveal the names of his secret investors– perhaps one of them knew Rabbi Skumansky.

"Rabbi Diamond, I'm afraid I'm already dating someone right now."

"Oh," he said disappointedly, followed by a long pause. "You are referring to Mindy Bloom I presume?"

The man had already invaded his privacy by calling him at work-- a number Jake rarely gave out.

Now, he was prying into his personal life.

That didn't sit well with Jake. In fact, it *really* pissed him off.

Before responding, Jake composed himself and calmly replied, "Yes. I *am* dating Mindy Bloom, and things are progressing just *fine*."

"You aren't *engaged* to her, are you?"

"No," Jake said impatiently.

"Well then, I'm not going to suggest you *date* another woman– just *meet* her. There's no harm in that since you aren't engaged. Is there?"

"Look– I'm not interested. Thank you, but I need to get back to work now."

But Rabbi Diamond ignored the hint. "I'm glad things are going well between you and Miss Bloom. You know…I *can* be helpful there too."

Now he had Jake's interest. "Oh? How so?"

"Well, things don't always go so smoothly. Sometimes you need someone to mediate misunderstandings or problems that arise. *Especially* after you've been dating for a while."

Seeing an opportunity to garner support from within

the community, Jake decided to entertain the gesture. "Now that you mention it, there *is* a problem you might be able to help me with."

Jake recounted the story of Sender's demise and explained how false accusations were leveled against Mindy.

"She's having a tough time right now, especially with her children's teachers giving her the cold shoulder. Perhaps you could speak with them."

"What *exactly* is it you would like me to do?"

Jake decided to play on the man's well-known ego.

"Well, you're influential. You could speak with the children's teachers and the principal. Get them to cooperate with Mindy for the children's sake."

"Of course, I *can*, but it's really not up to me."

"What do you mean? Who *is* it up to?"

"I suppose I could discuss it with *The Rav*. I'll see what I can do."

Click.

Jake dumbfoundedly dropped the headset into its cradle. The Rabbi's sudden behavior shift was bizarre-- and what did he mean it was up to *The Rav*?

Chapter Twenty-Six

Jake arrived home from work on Wednesday, thoroughly exhausted. His pending resignation was all the more motivation to resolve Mindy's situation quickly.

He relaxed over a quiet dinner alone, then took a call from his parents and learned that his Uncle Harvey had arrived from Israel.

After updating his parents on the Mindy situation, he spoke with Uncle Harvey.

Uncle Harvey received his S'micha in Detroit but then moved to Chicago, where he lived for many years and was quite involved with the Jewish community before moving to Israel.

"Uncle Harvey, do you remember the Stein family?" Jake asked.

He said he recalled several Stein families but finally pinpointed the right one when Jake mentioned the name *Herman* Stein.

Jake explained Mindy's situation and related how Mrs. Stein insisted Sender wasn't the oldest child.

"Mindy said Sender didn't have any siblings. Herman Stein died many years ago so we couldn't ask him about it. But I was thinking maybe Mrs. Stein had a miscarriage before Sender was born. Do you know anything about that?"

"Jake!" Uncle Harvey corrected. "Herman Stein didn't just *die*. He slit his own throat with his *chalif*."

Jake shuddered, picturing the long, straight, surgically-sharp knife used by a *shochet* to slaughter animals.

"With a *chalif*?" Jake repeated, trying to absorb the shocking revelation.

"Yes. Didn't you know that he worked in the slaughterhouses as a *shochet*? There was a big hubbub in the community at the time. I'm not sure, but I think he was one of two slaughterers who killed themselves that same way. One of them did it in front of a mirror-- I'm not sure which was which. I didn't know the Steins personally, but I knew of the family. As for a miscarriage-- I'm not sure I'd recall even if I'd known at the time. My memory's not what it used to be. But Debby Hoffmeyer would probably remember-- Dr. Debby Hoffmeyer. I used to eat *Shabbos* meals with her and her husband before I married your Aunt Miriam. She lives out in Highland Park now. Her husband's a wealthy big shot in the community-- supports all sorts of organizations, always getting awards and honors at dinners. They're both retired now, but he was in real estate construction, and she used to have a private practice-- she's a psychiatrist. Between the two, they probably know more about the personal lives of Jewish Chicagoans than anyone else."

"Do you think she'd remember you if I mentioned your name?"

"*Absolutely*," he said. "You *know*…you might try Joseph Skumansky too. He boarded at the Stein's for a while. I think he remained close with the family."

After hanging up, Jake dialed Dr. Hoffmeyer's number, left a message with her husband, then phoned Rabbi Skumansky.

His answering machine picked up.

Jake left a message inquiring about a miscarriage before Sender's birth and asked what he knew about Herman's death. Before hanging up, he blurted, "I'm also trying to locate his manuscript. Perhaps you know who has it?"

Jake waited up watching TV until ten o'clock without any callbacks. Then he hit the sack.

The phone rang just after twelve-thirty. Startled, Jake jumped out of bed, eager for any response to his messages.

"Jake? It's Mindy."

"Oh."

"You don't seem too happy to hear from me."

"It's not that-- I was hoping you were someone else." Jake recounted his conversation with his uncle and the two messages he'd left.

"I had no *idea* Herman committed *suicide*," Mindy said. "But a lot of things *do* make more sense now. Herman's suicide must have been extremely embarrassing to the family. Do you think Sender could have had a suicide tendency because his father killed himself?"

"That thought crossed my mind too-- like father, like son," Jake confessed.

"That's actually the reason I called. I can't sleep. I've been tossing and turning for hours, trying to figure out what *really* happened to Sender. The kids are all asleep, except Adam-- he finally came home tonight. He's still up playing Nintendo and..."

Mindy droned on, but Jake was too deep in thought to hear a word.

"Jake Cooper! Are you *listening*?"

"Mindy, what did you mean when you said a lot of things make *sense* if Herman killed himself? What things?"

"Well, I already told you about the lack of a single picture of Herman in Mrs. Stein's apartment. I always thought that was strange. She has so many pictures-- even a picture of herself as a young girl on the nightstand beside her bed. But there's not a single photo of Herman."

"That *is* weird unless she loved Herman so much it's too painful for her to see him. What else?"

"I also thought it was odd they never visited his grave. Most of the Orthodox crowd does, you know-- at least once a year. Mrs. Stein *never* went. I'd know because she'd always call Sender or myself to drive her places-- she doesn't drive. She's afraid of the bus and won't spring for a taxi. In fact, Sender never mentioned going there either."

"But Jake," Mindy continued, "if Sender *did* commit suicide like Herman, why would he jump off *my* building? There are certainly taller buildings he could have used."

"Maybe it was his last way of getting back at you, like you said, framing you for his murder when he committed suicide."

"I suppose that is possible," Mindy conceded.

"But there are problems with that theory, too," Jake said.

"What problems?"

"Well, you heard glass smashing after Sender jumped. It's too coincidental that someone unrelated to the incident just *happened* to break some glass right after Sender jumped."

"How does that connect to Sender jumping?"

"Because Mrs. Goldstein told us that she heard more than one voice on the roof. Unless Sender had two personalities and was talking to himself, that points to at least one other person being present when he flew off the roof. If Sender was jumping, wouldn't he prefer to do that in *private*? Why would he want someone *watching* him?"

"Jake, maybe we should concentrate on finding out who was there with him. That person could clear my name."

"Maybe," Jake agreed. "*Unless*, that's who *pushed* Sender off the roof."

Chapter Twenty-Seven

Jake's conversation with Mindy had his mind racing. Trying to sleep would have been hopeless. He decided to pay Detective Roberts a visit. He'd still be on shift.

Jake threw on a pair of jeans, sneakers, and a Bull's sweatshirt and dragged the Nova down to the Western and Belmont station.

"Get your friend to open up, and maybe we'll talk," Roberts barked. "Until then, I'm not discussing anything with you."

But Jake wasn't letting him off that easily.

"Mindy's decided not to talk-- there's nothing I can do about that. But I have information you might be able to use."

"I'll give you five-- then I've got *work* to do. Talk fast."

"The *building*, detective. Why did he jump off *that* building."

"He didn't jump-- he was pushed. Remember?" Roberts turned away in disgust.

"Okay, so maybe he was pushed. But why from the roof of *Mindy's* building?"

"Do I have to spell this out for you again, son? She argued with him over the kids at her apartment, they ended up on the roof and she shoved him off the edge."

"But Sender left her a message on her machine, inviting her to come to his place to get the kids. She walked to his house but he wasn't there. The whole thing makes no sense."

"*Now* we're getting somewhere," Roberts said, sitting at his desk scribbling furiously on a notepad.

"If he *did* call her, telephone records can verify that. But the physical evidence on the body points to Mindy. She had motive, means and opportunity. That spells G-U-I-L-T-Y in my book. Remember, her hair was caught between the links in his watchband."

"That doesn't mean she *pushed* him," Jake insisted. "That hair could have gotten there any number of ways. Mindy lived in the same house with Sender. That hair could have been caught in his watchband in his own house."

"*Possible*, but not likely."

"Or, Sender could have been pushed by someone who wanted to frame Mindy. Maybe they planted her hair there on purpose."

Jake thought more about that for a moment, then added, "That could be what they were after during the break-in."

"Hold on now," Roberts dropped his pen, pushed his chair back away from his desk and braced his hands on his knees. *"What* break-in?"

For the first time he questioned the logic of Mindy's silence.

"Mindy found her apartment ransacked when she got home, *before* she went to Sender's." Jake decided to go for broke.

"She thought it might have been Sender looking for a manuscript he'd accused her of taking."

Roberts shook his head. "We attributed the mess in her apartment to a confrontation between Mindy and Sender, before they went up on the roof."

"Wait here a minute."

Roberts walked over to a half-open office door, briefly poked his head inside, then returned, grabbing his pen and pad of paper, and a file from the rusted metal cabinet behind his desk.

"Come with me."

Jake followed Roberts into a conference room off to the side of the squad room.

"This is new information we didn't have before. Your girlfriend should have spoken up when she was questioned. If this checks out it could–. Let's just get down the details so I can check it out. Then we'll see."

Jake recounted the details he remembered about the break-in.

"There's more," Jake added. "Mindy says she heard glass breaking-- like someone smashing a window, just after she watched Sender hit the ground. Did you check for any broken windows in the area?"

"We thoroughly checked the entire area, all up and down the block-- standard procedure. There's nothing in the report about a broken window or glass."

Jake thought for a moment, stroking his once-bearded chin. "Maybe a car *moved* between the time of the incident and your inspection of the area. *Maybe* something or someone smashed the car window from the outside, causing all the glass to land *inside* the car. That would explain why you didn't find any broken car windows or glass in the street. In fact, maybe the *real* murderer *escaped* in that car."

They were both silent for a moment, then Jake added, "Detective, were all the parking spaces across from Mindy's building occupied?"

Roberts flipped through the report in the file and began reading, "...said officer searched the perimeter directly adjacent to...went to the end of the block in both directions…" After perusing the report for a few more seconds, Roberts looked up and announced, "There's nothing in here about an empty space. But it is possible a car left, and another took its spot before we arrived."

Now taking a different tone with Jake, Roberts thanked him for coming in and escorted him out of the squad room.

Jake was just about to head down the stairs when he remembered he hadn't discussed the main reason he'd come there in the first place.

He turned back toward Roberts and said, "I still don't feel suicide should be entirely ruled out, detective."

Jake recounted what his uncle told him about Herman Stein's suicide, then asked, "Wouldn't there be a record of that in your files?"

Chapter Twenty-Eight

The little red flashing light pierced the darkness of the musty study like a lighthouse beacon on a foggy night.

It was several hours past midnight as Rabbi Joseph Skumansky stepped into the tiny book-filled room and flipped on the light switch. The single-bulb fluorescent ceiling fixture flickered as it woke up, finally flooding the room with pure white light.

His wife, the *Rebbetzin*, as he called her, was fast asleep in the bedroom.

He entered the study, slid into his chair, and shook a handful of sunflower seeds from the little yellow package on his desk into his hand, then popped several into his mouth.

He swept aside the mound of papers covering the answering machine, then switched the dial to rewind, then to play.

"Rabbi Skumansky? Hi. This is Jake-- *Yankel* Cooper. I'm wondering if you remember Sender Stein's father, *Herman*. I'm trying to verify whether or not his father committed suicide."

The rabbi shot up straight in the chair and replayed the message that instantly resurfaced memories he thought had been carefully buried and forgotten.

"Would you please call me when you have a moment?" Jake's message continued. "I'd really appreciate it. Oh– and do you know anything about the manuscript Sender was working on?"

Those last words caused the rabbi to gasp and inhale a sunflower seed shell. He coughed uncontrollably until he expelled the shell, sending it flying across the room. He heard a little ping as it hit the glass door on the weather-beaten, overloaded barrister bookcase across from his desk.

His loud cough woke the *Rebbetzin,* who now poked her babushka-clad head into the room. She squinted through the thick bifocals that were slid halfway down her nose.

"Is everything alright?"

"I'm fine. Go back to sleep, *Rebbetzin.* There's nothing wrong. I was just listening to my messages."

The Rebbetzin retreated, but Rabbi Skumansky remained frozen in his seat. How could Yankel Cooper *possibly* know about that manuscript?

It was so long ago.

He'd been so careful.

Herman was dead and buried, what else really

mattered now?

Why did Yankel Cooper *insist* on dredging up all this history now?

He sat there, taking deep breaths to dissipate the anger, almost coming to a boiling. As he did, anger gave way to more pleasant memories. It had been a wonderful yet painfully difficult time of his life that he'd put completely behind him, or so he thought– until *now*.

But there was no way he'd ever *really* be able to forget his beautiful Malka. He longed to see her– to tell her so many things.

But he'd been forced by the twisted evil that fate delivered to only watch her from afar, as if through a one-way mirror.

What about all this could *possibly* interest Yankel Cooper? He picked up the phone and dialed, ignoring the late hour.

"If Yankel Cooper wants to know about these things, he'll have to learn about them on my terms," he decided.

Several rings yielded no response. The rabbi was about to hang up when a groggy voice mustered a "Hello?"

"Perhaps I've caught you at a bad time *Reb Yankel*, but now is the only time I have to answer your questions about Herman Stein."

"No. Okay. That's fine," Jake said.

"You ask questions about memories I prefer to forget, my friend. So, you will listen carefully because I will not repeat myself. Herman Stein was a sick man-- a *very* sick man. No one in the community believed it was so, but he was a sick, *abusive* man who did terrible, disgusting things in the privacy of his own home."

Rabbi Skumansky cleared the lump that had caught in his throat. "There was a young girl-- an innocent, beautiful, young thing. It was disgusting-- shocking, what he did to her. You asked if he committed suicide. What does it matter? That question only leads to more shame for a family who has suffered more than enough already. Herman Stein is dead and buried. He will never harm anyone again. So, leave things *be*, my friend. Leave it alone. All is well. Do not concern yourself with ancient history."

"Sorry," Jake said. "I had no idea. It's just that when I heard Sender's father committed suicide, I thought Sender might have felt it was an acceptable way out of whatever it was that troubled him. His wife, Mindy, has been charged with murder. The police think *she pushed* Sender off her roof-- surely, you've heard. I think it's possible that no one

pushed him-- that he jumped on his own. I was just trying
to gather more information. I meant no harm."

"You understand, this brings back very ugly
memories. I suppose Herman couldn't bear the shame.
When people found out what he was doing in the privacy of
his home-- going into her bedroom every night, doing those
things to a poor innocent young girl-- it must've been an
unimaginable sense of embarrassment for him. But Sender
Stein was not like his father. My understanding is that
Sender was a respected member of the Orthodox
community. A man who was trying to do right by his
children-- not like their mother, I might add. Why do you
insist on involving yourself with a woman like that, *Reb
Yankel*? She is not for you. You are a wise and learned
man. A woman like that is not for a *Talmud Chacham* like
yourself."

An uncomfortable moment of silence passed.

"What about the manuscript?" Jake asked.

Jake's relentless questioning caused the rabbi's
hand to squeeze the yellow bag he was holding, sending
sunflower seeds scattering across the wooden floor.

His right hand gripped the now near-empty bag
while his left trembled, knocking the receiver against his
ear like a woodpecker.

The rabbi tried to steady himself and calm down.

How could Yankel Cooper even *know* about that manuscript?

His heart pounded furiously as he replied, "I'm not sure I know what you're talking about."

"The manuscript that Sender was working on before he died," Jake explained. "It seemed to be important to him."

"Whatever Sender Stein wrote would certainly not be of any value to anyone living. Bring it to me-- I'll see it gets back to someone who will appreciate his work."

"Oh– I'm sorry if I misled you. I don't have it. I was asking about it because it's *missing*."

"*Reb Yankel*, I don't have time for games at this hour. Bring that manuscript to me *first thing* in the morning!"

Chapter Twenty-Nine

Jake met Pinky at Blind Faith for dinner on Thursday. He recounted his meeting with Roberts the night before as he watched Pinky wolf down a huge helping of shepherd's pie, a tall glass of carrot juice, and a large date bar.

"If someone was up there with Sender, why don't we just ask *them* what they know?"

"Gee, why didn't I think of that?" Jake mocked, pointing at his forehead. "All we have to do is– *find out who it was!*"

"Laurie Smilow," Pinky said smugly, then slurped the last drop of juice from his orange-stained glass.

Once again, Pinky's flash of genius caught Jake off guard. "That must have been a very potent batch of carrot juice," he said.

"My god, Pinky! Laurie is the married woman you said Sender was seeing. If that were proven, she would be worthy of the death penalty under Jewish law."

"Was Sender blackmailing *her*?"

Chapter Thirty

Jake received a call from Dr. Hoffmeyer's assistant early Friday morning before work. She was responding to the message he had left for her. She could meet him at her home at ten in the morning.

Jake called in sick and picked up Mindy.

They drove up to Dr. Hoffmeyer's Highland Park address together in his Nova. Wishing to avoid the embarrassment of being spotted exiting his old beater in the upscale neighborhood, he sheepishly parked behind an oak at the end of the street large enough to hide behind.

They approached the white stucco mansion and trekked up the circular walkway approaching the estate.

Jake noted the oversized foliage surrounding the home and a fenced tennis court off to the right rear of the massive edifice. His uncle had said that Dr. Hoffmeyer's husband was some type of real estate construction tycoon.

A bell ring resulted in the large, double oak doors swinging open simultaneously, revealing a heavy-set black woman in her late forties clad in a gray uniform adorned with a heavily starched white apron.

"Can I help you?"

"We're here to see Dr. Hoffmeyer," Jake replied.

"Whom shall I say is calling?"

"Jake Cooper."

"One moment."

The doors gently closed.

Jake glanced at Mindy and shrugged his shoulders.

Their surroundings seemed completely sheltered from the recent nasty events that had infiltrated their West Rogers Park neighborhood.

As much as logic dictated that suicide was still possible, Jake didn't believe Sender jumped voluntarily.

But after his strange conversation with Rabbi Skumansky, his curiosity about Herman's death grew. He sensed a connection between the father-and-son deaths, though he didn't know why.

Their silent wait ended abruptly when the maid swung the doors open again, announcing, "Dr. Hoffmeyer will see you now. *Please*, come in."

They followed her into a large marble foyer surrounded by massive Greek columns supporting a huge domed skylight. The black, white, and gray marble floor gleamed, causing sun rays to bounce off the highly polished, slippery surface. The foyer ceiling rose a full three stories to the back of the foyer, a winding staircase leading to second and third-floor landings. To their right was an antique wooden bench/coat-rack combination that seemed out of context with the decor. Off to the far right was a large paneled parlor room. To the left, a gleaming white door concealed what Jake guessed to be the kitchen.

The maid pointed toward a wooden bench. "Have a seat. The Doctor will be with you momentarily."

They sat for what Jake felt seemed like a good half-hour, staring at each other in bewilderment, taking in the ostentatious glory of the structure's interior.

He'd never been in a home like this, and from Mindy's expressions, neither had she. She seemed intently focused on an oil painting hanging near the front door. The gold-leaf wooden frame housed an old rabbi studying an open page of the Talmud. Mindy stood and approached the painting, examining the engraved brass plate affixed to the wall just beneath the work.

She pointed to the bronze engraved plate. "*The Rav*," she said, looking over her shoulder at Jake.

Jake shrugged and gave her palms up.

"That's why I couldn't remember the name of the rabbi Sender insisted on using for our Jewish divorce. He didn't give me a name. He just called him *The Rav*."

Jake wanted to tell her that the term *Rav* was a common term used by followers and disciples of a beloved rabbi.

But before he could utter a word, a wide, short, sixty-something woman wearing an orange and blue Muumuu and pink furry slippers adorned with cat heads bearing pink bows as whiskers came flouncing down the winding staircase.

Her tightly curled, flaming red hair seemed too youthful for her body. She had a large round face and bouncy black eyes.

As she approached, Jake detected gray hairs peeking out from beneath the tight curls.

The reek of perfume sent his nose into spasmodic twitches. The closer she got, the harder it became for him to breathe.

"Dr. Hoffmeyer?"

"Hello Jake," she said in a high-pitched, singsong voice. "And this must be the lovely Mindy. Come with me, children. We have *lots* to discuss."

She did an abrupt about-face on the marble floor, causing her pink slippers to graciously rotate like a ballet dancer who'd practiced the movement a thousand times.

They followed her up the stairs to the second floor as she floated from step to step, and watched her Muumuu sway rhythmically as she climbed.

They followed her into a room at the end of a long hallway. The back wall was mirrored from ceiling to floor.

A fireplace graced another wall below an ornate mantle above, which hung a poster-sized photo of a cat snuggling up to a pair of pink slippers matching their hostess's.

"Sit, children," she sang, offering them the pink-striped velvet love seat next to an overstuffed white armchair occupied by a curled-up ball of fur.

"Run along, Pitzel," she commanded, scooting the cat out before plopping into the seat herself.

"So, you want to know about Herman Stein's death, do you? Why such a peculiar interest in ancient history, child?" She asked in her sing-song tone.

Jake explained how his interest related to Sender's death. "If we prove it was suicide Mindy will be off the hook."

"Yes, yes, I know *all* about that *unfortunate* incident. But you are wandering off in the wrong direction, Jake Cooper. You are not *focusing* on the problem at hand."

"What do you mean?" Mindy broke in.

"Your boyfriend here is the only person who can get you out of this mess. But he isn't acting like a real *friend*, now *is* he?" She gave Jake a nasty *bad boy* look.

Jake's head bounced from Mindy to the Doctor, then back to Mindy. "What do you mean by *that*?"

"Ah, there it is. Your masculinity *is* alive dear boy. *Use it*! Stand up and *fight* these people like a man!"

Jake stared at her, not uttering a word, in complete shock.

"These people?"

The Doctor entered a trance-like state. She began rocking, bouncing her open-palmed hands up and down alternately on the overstuffed arms of her chair as if conducting a silent symphony.

She stopped abruptly, leaning forward, her voice taking on a melodramatically serious tone. "Listen closely and carefully to what I'm going to tell you. I can help you, but there are limits to what I will do."

Jake glanced at Mindy, as the Doctor leaned in closer, switching to yet a third voice– this one barely above a whisper.

"I've been involved with the *Get* Committee for many, many years, long before you were brought into this world, child. It's one of several underground organizations led by *The Rav,* who is also Chief Judge of his very own *Beis Din*. He takes a particular interest in saving children from abusive situations. This type of thing is not only harmful to the children, but it is shameful to the community. He feels, *as do I,* that we must be careful not to give the outside world any further reasons to hate us. You may think this type of thing doesn't happen in our religious community. But it happens more than you can imagine. While his *cause* is praiseworthy, *The Rav* has demonstrated time and again that he has the common sense of a dumb ox when dealing with these matters. Our committee has saved many children from terrible situations, to be sure. But the methods employed to achieve these results have shown he has grown into a power-hungry monster who feels aloof. He disregards his expert advisors, such as myself, and trusts accounts from complainants without verifying them. Too many times, he takes matters into his own hands, making terrible blunders-- resulting in an awful mess of people's lives.

"Unfortunately, my husband has fallen under his influence and gives him substantial financial backing. So, you see, just having this conversation with you is *risky* for me, *personally.* But this I *can* tell you," she continued, turning to face Mindy, "I've *never* seen *The Rav* destroy a family like he has yours, dear girl."

She stared at Mindy silently, her own eyes became smaller and more intense. "You will not be prosecuted for

Sender's murder. Of that, you have my word. But that should not be your primary concern now. Your *children* are the ones you should be concerned about."

"I *am*! *Of course* I am. I've been giving them all the love and attention I can-- even to the point of putting the rest of my life on hold."

"You don't understand, child. Your children are in *danger*. Things have been discussed with the *Get* committee-- things concerning you and your *children*. You have left the strict ways of those people and have placed your children in jeopardy."

"I take exception to that! I follow all the basics– I keep kosher, and I keep *Shabbos*!"

"I can *vouch* for that," Jake chimed in. "Those were false rumors that Sender spread."

"Ah, but you did *change*, child. You changed how you dress in public when the children are not with you. You took a job in a non-Jewish environment, in the *goyishe* world. You've been seen walking the street talking with strange men," she said, turning toward Jake. "I realize this is normal behavior for the secular world, but *they* don't think like that. To *them,* you're a heathen, leading your children away from *their* version of Judaism. As a professional, I must tell you that these changes *do* affect your children. The differences they see between your actions and the way the rest of the community behaves confuses them. I'm not saying you *shouldn't* do these things. Just be aware of the impact it has on them now. But also, be aware of what is in store."

"What can this *Rav* do about it," Jake said smartly. "He can't just meddle in someone else's family like that."

"You are mistaken. He's *not* alone. I told you, there are organizations-- and he is at the helm. He has aides that carry out his every whim. For years he has preyed on the guilt of Orthodox wannabes, cultivating strong financial and political connections with enough clout to accomplish the impossible. Surely a Talmudic Scholar like yourself understands the ramifications of that, don't you?"

They sat silently for a full minute, then the doctor added, "Your primary concern must be keeping Mindy and the children protected from more trauma than they've already endured."

She waved a finger at Jake. "Take *action,* young man, and take it *soon.* You are the only one who can help Mindy. You *alone* can stop this train wreck. Do it!"

He begged for more details, including the mysterious *Rav*'s identity. But Dr. Hoffmeyer responded only by repeating how only he had the knowledge to stop them. For the life of him, Jake couldn't figure out what she meant.

Perhaps that's what scared him most.

Chapter Thirty-One

Jake met Mindy and her children for Saturday morning services at the Young Israel *synagogue* on Touhy, then joined them for a traditional *Shabbos* lunch. It was an unseasonably warm, sunny day so they took the kids to play at the petting zoo in Indian Boundary Park, just a few blocks from her apartment.

The echo of Dr. Hoffmeyer's warning that more trauma was lurking just around the corner for the children and Mindy made Jake feel helpless.

She hadn't been specific about what was about to happen or when. The only thing she did reveal was that someone referred to as *The Rav* was going to do something terrible to them.

He wasn't sure what to make of her warning. She told them that Mindy would be cleared of murder charges. But that had yet to materialize and seemed unlikely at this point.

Was there really any credibility to anything she said? Dr. Hoffmeyer had really snowballed him. She hadn't even disclosed a damned thing about Herman's death-- his reason for calling her in the first place.

And what did she mean that he was the only one

that could stop it? What qualified him as their only savior? He had no idea what miraculous skill he supposedly possessed that would enable him to ward off the evil lurking around the corner.

Mindy and Jake sat on a wooden park bench while keeping an eye on the children.

"Rabbi Skumansky claims Herman abused some girl in his own home and killed himself out of embarrassment when people found out," Jake contemplated.

"That explains why there were no pictures of Herman in the Stein house and why no one visited his grave," Mindy added. "But what could that have to do with *Sender's* death?"

"It's possible Sender learned from Herman that suicide was an easy way out. But everything we know seems to tell us that he *didn't* jump– he was *pushed*. But my gut tells me there's some connection between the two deaths."

Mindy leaned back and stared up at the blue sky.

"I agree. I can't see the Sender I knew committing suicide. But getting involved in something that would cause someone to push him-- *that* I could see."

After congratulating themselves on ruling out the

suicide theory, they realized they'd raised several new unanswered questions.

Who pushed Sender?

Was it an accident or done on purpose?

If it was an accident, what exactly happened?

"Mrs. Goldstein told me she heard yelling," Jake said. "Not just yelling. She definitely said it sounded like an *argument*. And she said one man was yelling about not having been warned."

"Was the man yelling Sender, or his *attacker*?" Mindy asked.

"She wasn't sure who it was. *Maybe* Sender was angry he hadn't been warned about something, and he pushed someone who simply shoved him back. Or, perhaps someone *else* was angry at Sender for not warning *them* about something, so they *pushed* him off the roof."

"What if Mrs. Goldstein was wrong about both voices being male?" Mindy suggested. "What if his attacker was a *woman*?"

Jake recalled Pinky's suggestion that it may have been Sender's girlfriend, Laurie Smilow. But as Mindy posed that question, his thoughts turned once again to the one question he was afraid to ask yet had no real reason to let go of.

Did he really know it *wasn't* Mindy that pushed Sender?

He hated himself for even thinking it, yet other than her own word, he had no logical reason to rule her out. If she *did* do it, it certainly would have been understandable. That would mean *Sender* was the one yelling about not being warned. But what would he expect Mindy to warn him about?

And it didn't answer the question of why Sender was on *Mindy's* roof in the first place.

By late afternoon they were mentally exhausted, and the children were amply tired from running around the park all afternoon.

They returned to Mindy's apartment for a light dinner.

Nightfall arrived, and Mindy began preparations for the *Havdalah* ceremony, marking Shabbos's conclusion. She removed a large candle, a silver goblet, and a jar of cloves from one of the kitchen cabinets.

Holding up a corked bottle of wine in one hand and a half-empty jar of grape juice in the other, she asked, "Grape juice or wine?"

"Grape juice," Jake replied. "I don't want any alcohol before driving. I was thinking you could get a sitter, and we could go out tonight-- take our minds off things. See a movie, perhaps?"

"I'd rather just spend a quiet evening together."

"How about I rent a video while you finish up here? When the children are asleep, we can feast on a bowl of popcorn and watch a flick."

"*Deal*!"

After *Havdalah,* Jake hiked back to his place and took the Nova on a five-minute ride to the Blockbuster on Western.

The after-*Shabbos* crowd had already converged on the premises. He caught several *yarmulkes* peeking over the ocean of video racks filling the showroom floor.

Jake scanned the *New Releases* section looking for something that fit Mindy's request for a romantic comedy-- not his personal first choice, but he probably wouldn't be concentrating on the film much anyway.

Mindy seemed to be ignoring Dr. Hoffmeyer's foreboding of danger-- or at least she hid it well.

He was grateful either way.

If he was to be their guardian, he didn't need the added pressure of a panic-stricken client.

Jake scanned the *G* shelf. He crouched to view the bottom row, then shifted his eyes to the bottom of the *H*'s, working his way up. When he stood up, an unwelcome yet familiar voice greeted him.

"*Well*, look who's on a video hunt. What's the matter? No date tonight, *hotshot*?"

"Marsha? What brings you to this neck of the woods?"

"Maybe I was looking for you."

"*Funny*. I *swear* we broke up."

"*No*, Jake. *You* broke up. *I* wasn't a willing party to that– or have you forgotten?"

Her ice-cold stare instantly froze the hairs on the back of his neck.

"Not to worry, Mr. *Talmudic* Scholar-- no harm done. I'm still all yours if you want me. Why don't *we* spend the evening together?"

"Marsha, I really meant what I said last time. I *don't* want to continue a relationship with you. Besides, I'm seeing-- I just don't think it's a good idea."

"*Who* are you seeing?"

Her intense eyes narrowed.

"I'm involved with *someone*."

"Oh, come now. At *least* be man enough to tell me. You're still with that redhead, *aren't you*?"

A burst of tears quickly replaced her ice-cold stare,

like a two-sided head from a flick in the Horror section.

Unfortunately, her obviously tactical move worked.

Jake pulled her aside, wiped away her crocodile tears, and wondered what the *hell* he was doing. He just couldn't resist the lure of this beckoning, gorgeous woman.

"Marsha, you know the last thing I want is to *hurt* you. But I'm really involved with Mindy. We've been seeing each other regularly for a while now."

The mask rotated, and he was once again facing the ice woman.

"*Idiot*! I already knew that. Do you think I'm *stupid*? But you don't *belong* with her, Jake. You're not one of *them* anymore. You know you *need* someone like me. How can you have anything to do with those people? I hate them-- and I'll hate you too if you have anything to do with them. Besides, Mindy's *quite* the little murderer now, isn't she? How can you date her? Aren't you afraid *you'll* be next?"

Marsha rambled on, shuffling her feet, and repeatedly clenching her fists. Her eyes froze once again.

He'd never seen her this way before.

He let her continue until she ran out of steam, said his goodbyes, then waded through the small crowd that gathered to eavesdrop while pretending to video hunt.

He quickly made his selection, checked out, and left the store. He regretted the day he'd met Marsha and wondered if he'd ever be free of her.

The way she acted sent a chill up his spine.

Chapter Thirty-Two

A short, rotund man made his way toward Jake's three-story brick apartment building. Fishel Fogal pulled up his baggy black wool slacks by the twisted leather strap that had once been his belt while checking the building's address against the one *The Rav* had given him as that of Reb Yankel Cooper.

Scratching his head through his mangled Fedora, he concentrated on the four oversized numbers on the door, comparing them one by one to those on the slip of paper in his hand. After reviewing the numbers several times, he decided they matched.

Tripping over his weather-beaten wing tips' untied laces, he stumbled toward the front door, then stopped short.

The back door would be more discreet.

Slithering along the building's outer wall, Fishel pressed his rotund yet muscular body as flat against the brick as possible, squeezing behind the rows of shoulder-height bushes hugging the building's perimeter.

He didn't see the old woman on the sidewalk with the shopping cart, mouth agape,

watching a mangled Fedora float across the top of the

bushes.

Smug with his sleuth-like accomplishment Fishel mounted the wooden back staircase, kicking aside the yellow Tonka dump-truck parked on the first step. The sound of grating metal sent the cat nestled on the basement apartment's windowsill scampering to safety. The inept sleuth stomped up to the second-floor landing and fished out a long, flat-head screwdriver from the depths of his worn-to-a-shine black wool suit jacket. He was no amateur-- he'd come prepared, he assured himself, popping the lock with ease.

It was lucky that *The Rav* chose *him* to get the manuscript. Otherwise, he might never have learned that Mindy had a boyfriend. Then again, *The Rav* always chose him for the *dirty* jobs.

He realized he was being used and felt he had more than paid his debt for *The Rav*'s silence. The whole thing was so long ago.

He was young and foolish.

It hadn't been his fault, really.

Gavriel had dumped him into it, yet Gavriel always ended up with the *clean* work. Gavriel was *The Rav*'s mole holding a respectable position with the Illinois Rabbinical Board. He handled the matchmaking, brought in new clients for *The Rav*'s Beis Din, and researched *Talmudic* laws for cases when needed.

When *The Rav* dished out praise, it was always *Gavriel, Gavriel, Gavriel.*

Fishel was certain that when *The Rav* retired, he'd name Gavriel as his successor-- the *ultimate* insult.

But he wasn't about to wait around for that– *no sir*!

That's why it was doubly important to clear up the pending trouble and get out now while he still could. He dreaded what he thought Gavriel might do with him after *The Rav* was gone.

Gavriel never said anything outright– just hinted here and there. But he sensed Gavriel was patiently waiting all these years only to pounce the minute the opportunity presented itself.

The thought made even the dirt on *his* skin crawl.

Fishel should have been surprised to learn that Reb Yankel Cooper was seeing Mindy.

She wasn't worthy of a man of Reb Yankel's stature. But after what he'd observed and experienced over the years, *nothing* surprised him anymore.

After searching Mindy's apartment and Sender's house and still coming up empty, Fishel concluded he'd find what he was looking for at Reb Yankel's apartment.

The Rav may have sent him on this mission to get the manuscript Herman wrote, but Fishel's *personal* agenda was to retrieve that manila envelope and *Sender's* manuscript.

That would constitute his ticket to freedom.

Sender had only begun collecting money from it. Once Fishel found it, he could collect more and then disappear to live the life he deserved.

To *hell* with *Herman's* manuscript.

It wasn't really *his* fault he'd left it behind the first time. *The Rav* had given him far too many tasks to carry out. He should have asked Gavriel to look after that detail. He shouldn't have been expected to do it all.

Fortunately, no one had discovered anything, despite the oversight. So, what difference did it make after all these years? If he happened to find it, fine. If not, let *The Rav*, or better yet, let *Gavriel* find it.

Fishel Fogal will no longer be their personal gopher.

Fishel rummaged his way through the apartment in spurts.

He rifled through a few drawers in the kitchen near the back door, then went to the bedroom and pulled the closet apart.

He ricocheted to the front door, searched the coat closet, then bounced to the linen closet.

Racing through the small bedroom apartment, he toppled lamps, smashed nick knacks, and dumped everything on the floor as he frantically continued his futile search.

He was tired of this routine.

This was his third time in a month. It *had* to be here somewhere.

Who else could possibly have it?

After exhausting every searchable area, he considered the possibility that Reb Yankel Cooper may not be the man everyone thought he was.

Look who he'd involved himself with.

Perhaps he'd found it and decided to take advantage of the opportunity himself. Perhaps he was out collecting the money right now. *That* would explain Sender's manuscript. But what could he hope to do with the manila envelope?

Its contents were worthless to anyone but him- and the authorities.

Unless Reb Yankel intended to blackmail him, as Sender attempted.

Fishel's stubby fingers clenched into steel fists as he

contemplated that possibility. There was no way that he was going to let anyone steal his venture's booty. Not after all the work he'd done-- sneaking and snooping, hiding in dark, dank places gathering material.

It had been the most difficult plan he'd ever executed. But it would all be worth it. He'd worked it for almost a year, mustering every ounce of his imagination and effort.

Ultimately, he'd almost fallen victim to the same scheme– the attempted perpetrator being his own partner.

Fishel recalled that late Friday evening at the Maplewood *Shteeble*– the little make-shift *synagogue* housed in the basement of a two-story apartment building.

He was running late.

Tiptoeing down the creaking staircase, Fishel selected a tattered prayer book from the metal shelving.

Scanning the faces across the room, he spotted mostly regulars and a few newcomers. His man was at the back.

Sender Stein sat along the back wall schmoozing in a hushed tone, catching angry glances from the *Shteeble*'s *shusher*.

To his left stood a tall, thin man in his fifties. A salt and pepper five O'clock shadow peeked out from under his dusty black Fedora. A black scarf hung loosely from his neck between the thin open lapels of his tired gray herringbone overcoat. Peering through tiny reading glasses at the prayer book in his open palms, he tipped his ear toward his neighbor's lips, catching Sender's whispered gossip.

Fishel slid into the open spot to Sender's right.

"Good *Shabbos,* Reb Sender," Fishel whispered, nudging Sender's elbow.

Sender turned and nodded, "Reb Fishel," then returned to his *schmooze*-in-progress.

Fishel leaned in toward Sender's ear, whispering, "The envelope. You can give it back to me now."

Sender turned abruptly. "What envelope?" he replied, barely containing a smirk.

"Reb Sender, *surely* you remember. I asked you to take special care of it. They're done searching. Now I need it back. I *must* have it."

Sender let the smirk out. "Really. And why is *that*?"

"Reb Sender, please. Don't play with me. You know they accused me of tax fraud. I could go to prison." Fishel's alarmed voice escalated above the whisper he'd intended, drawing scornful glances from the congregants.

The *shusher* simply glared and shook his head in

disgust.

"I *need* that envelope. I asked you to hold it for me. You'll give it to me after *Shabbos*, no?"

"Perhaps I can *look* for it after *Shabbos*," Sender said.

"And you'll have a check for me then too?"

"Not yet. This is a delicate operation. You must have patience."

"But *you* got paid already, *no*? So why shouldn't I? *I* did most of the work." Fishel beat his chest. "Without *me*, you have *nothing!*"

"Correction. Without you, I *had* nothing. *Now* I hold everything. *You'll* get paid when I'm *ready* to pay. Perhaps we should work out an arrangement. You know, it may take a while for me to *locate* that envelope. In fact, Mindy ransacked the house when she left. So, I may not even *have* it anymore."

"Reb Sender, please. Don't tease me. I *must* have that envelope– I *must!* And it wouldn't be fair for you to take my share of the manuscript profits. I worked hard and took many risks for that information. I can't just give it all up now. *Please*, I *must* have that envelope!"

But Sender simply laughed at his desperation.

That was over a month ago.

Sender was no longer a problem, but neither the envelope nor the manuscript had turned up. He checked everywhere-- Sender's home, Mindy's apartment.

Nothing.

That's when Fishel concluded that Mindy must have given it to Reb Yankel. But it wasn't here either.

Sender had tried cutting him out of the deal. Did Reb Yankel have the same thing in
mind?

No. He would not let that happen. Not after all this.

He waited for Reb Yankel's return home, making himself comfortable on the front room couch.

* * * * *

Monday after work, the hair on the back of Jake's neck was still frozen at the thought of Saturday night's chilling encounter with Marsha.

He took the Edens to Touhy and headed home. Traffic was backed up past the Jewish Community Center, so he ducked down a side street to Estes, cut across California, and pulled in behind an old green Checker cab near the alley.

Marsha's little act not only gave him the creeps, but

it also rekindled his deep-rooted connection with the right-wing Orthodox community.

Each time she denounced *those* people, he took it as a personal attack. Despite his grievances with the community's reaction to his divorce, his new mode of dress, and the unorthodox measures of some of its members, a part of him still identified with those people deep down inside.

Those people were *his* people, whether he liked it or not.

He took the back stairs to his second-floor unit, stopping at the open back door.

Thinking the super finally came to fix the bathtub, Jake crossed the threshold, stepped into the kitchen, and immediately balked.

The super wouldn't toss his kitchen drawers upside down.

"These break-ins are reaching epidemic proportions," he thought. "First Mindy, now *me*?"

From the extent of the mess, he assumed it was a crew.

He reached for the phone to report the break-in, then decided to assess the damage before calling.

Disaster had struck the bedroom too. He recalled Mindy's apartment after her break-in.

These guys had their routine down pat.

As he rounded the corner toward the living room, he smacked full force into a short, fat brick wall whose round head was adorned by a squashed Fedora accessorizing his rumpled suit. The sparsely bearded, seemingly older man was surprisingly strong and withstood the direct hit he'd taken when they'd crashed.

Jake took note of the man's long, oily *payos* pasted across his forehead. He took him for an overzealous *meshulach,* trying to extract a donation. This one apparently had taken his open door as an invitation to let himself in.

The perfect end to a perfect disaster!

"*Give-it-to-me-now!*" the man growled from behind clenched teeth.

Thinking the guy wasn't playing with a full deck, Jake asked, "What are you doing in my apartment?"

Jake felt violated by the intruder, not to mention the apparent break-in that left the door open for this guy to waltz in. "I don't care *who* you're collecting for! You can't just barge into my apartment and *demand* a donation."

But the man just stood there, staring at Jake with a

stupid grin. "Maybe this guy doesn't speak English," Jake thought.

He decided the best way to get rid of him was to write him a check and see him off. The international language of money always worked magic with these guys.

"Who are you collecting for?" Jake asked. "Who should I make the check out to?"

"*The Rav* sent me," he mumbled, clenching his hands into fists. "Cooperate, or you will suffer the consequences. No one keeps *The Rav* waiting."

The Rav.

Jake was almost afraid to ask as he blurted out, "*The Rav*? Who *is The Rav*?"

But the little man's lips curled into a delightful smirk, letting Jake know he detected the panic spreading across Jake's face like a billboard.

"*Vantz*!" the man spit the word flying from his mouth. "You don't know who you're dealing with, *do you*?"

Jake wasn't sure what *Vantz* meant, but he could tell it *wasn't* a compliment.

The foul-mouthed intruder wiped the spittle from the side of his mouth.

Jake stared beyond the gray puffs of beard into his

raw pockmarked face. There was something strangely familiar about this man.

Jake mustered every ounce of courage he had and stared down into the monster's sunken

eyes.

"Look, I don't know who the hell you are, but if you don't leave right now, I'm going to have you arrested. In fact, I might anyway. How dare you come in here and trash my apartment. And I don't give a damn about your *Rav*."

As the words rolled off his tongue, he realized *why* the man seemed familiar. He'd never met him, but he'd seen this ugly mug before.

Jake tried stepping behind him to push him out of his apartment, but the grimy little man was too fast.

He grabbed at Jake's legs, sending him flying backward.

His head smacked against the corner of the wall, then bounced twice off the green carpeting.

He was dazed but conscious.

"Who the hell is this goon?" He wondered.

Jake shook his head vigorously, trying to clear his vision, then dropped it back onto the comforting thickness of the carpet.

He suddenly recalled *where* he'd seen that mug

before.

"Give me the manuscripts and the envelope now, *vantz*! Don't make *The Rav* wait. Rabbi Skumansky is a great and powerful man. Don't be a fool. Now, tell me where you put them?"

"*Rabbi Skumansky– Joseph* Skumansky?" Jake surmised, recalling the man who sat beside him, studying in the *yeshiva*.

"The *esrog* guy?" Jake asked aloud. "*That's The Rav*? Surely, you're joking. A *great and powerful man*? That's not the Joseph Skumansky I know."

Jake perceived him as a kind and pious man. But he never thought of Joseph Skumansky as great and powerful– until *now*, he decided, recalling Dr. Hoffmeyers' warning about *The Rav*. The little black ox stood over Jake, arms folded, managing a semi-intimidating stance.

"*Nu*? Give it *now*!"

As Jake's vision cleared, a sense of relief set in.

If this was the impending evil Dr. Hoffmeyer foretold, it wouldn't be a problem. Jake now realized *why* she said he was the only one that could help Mindy.

They weren't the best buddies, but Jake did maintain a certain rapport with the man.

He recalled his last conversation with Skumansky

about Herman. He'd become quite upset when Jake mentioned the manuscript-- downright nervous and demanding.

"Now it makes *sense*," Jake thought. "He thought *I* had it and *demanded* I give it to him. He must have sent this goon. Was he planning to steal it? This pit bull seems willing to *beat* it out of me. What could be so *damned* important about that manuscript?"

"As I told Rabbi Skumansky earlier," Jake responded aloud, "I don't have Sender's manuscript-- it's missing. That's why I asked *him* about it in the first place."

"You asked Rabbi Skumansky about *Sender's* manuscript? He sent me to get the *Eicha* commentary that *Herman* Stein wrote."

Jake's clarity dissipated. He stared up from the floor at the man in genuine bewilderment, "*Eicha commentary?*"

"*Yes*! Herman's manuscript," he explained, shaking his head in disappointment. "You haven't forgotten *Eicha*– the book of Lamentations, have you, Reb Yankel?"

"Herman wrote a manuscript too?"

"*Vantz*! Herman wrote an English commentary on *Eicha*." As he barked his response, he squashed Jake's still throbbing head with his shoe, placing his full weight on his forehead.

Jake winced in pain, drawing his knees up to his chest, and repeatedly whacked the bully's tree-stump legs.

But the man didn't even budge.

"Personally, I don't care about the *Eicha commentary*. They can come get it themselves. But I *must* have *Sender's* manuscript and the manila envelope. Now tell me where they are or–"

"Hello? Mr. Cooper?"

Someone was in the kitchen.

"Mr. Cooper, are you here?"

Thank God for clogged drains and Frank the Super.

"I'm in the front room!"

Rabbi Skumansky's goon bolted to the front door.

He had it unlocked and was halfway down the stairs by the time Jake saw Frank's head poke into the front room.

The intruder was long gone.

Chapter Thirty-Three

Jake joined Pinky for dinner at Blind Faith later that evening, recounting his visit from *The Rav*'s human Pit-Bull.

"So, you think it was Fogal?"

"I'm sure it was. That's the mug from the Sun Times photo you shoved in my face– the one in the article about him cheating on his taxes."

"Not just *cheating*-- fraud." Pinky clarified. Licking his finger and striking an imaginary notch in the air he added, "Rabbi Fogal strikes again. A real upstanding Orthodox fellow, don't you think?"

"You *know* what I think, Pinky. I just wish you wouldn't hold it against the entire community. He's one bad apple in a healthy orchard. I can't wait to get the charges against Mindy dropped, get the lottery cash, and put all this far behind us."

"*Amen!*"

"I think I should give Rabbi Diamond a call," Jake said. "He called me about fixing me up with a woman-- said Skumansky had referred him. Maybe he can fill me in on the Joseph Skumansky I *thought* I knew."

"Are you nuts?" Pinky warned. "I wouldn't talk to

Gavriel Diamond if my life depended on it. He and Fogal *both work* for Skumansky, and Gavriel's a real snake-- you can't trust him, Jake."

"You *know* him?"

Pinky tilted his head backward and released a deep sigh. "I never mentioned it before because it didn't have anything to do with you or Mindy. These guys are dangerous, Jake-- half-cocked religious lunatics who know no limits."

Pinky slurped the last drop of carrot juice from the glass tumbler in his hand and parked it near the table's edge. Spreading both hands wide, palms down, on the wooden table, he let out a long deep sigh.

"Two years ago, when I was going through my divorce, my wife, Shaindel, refused to let me see my kids-- just like Sender did. We hadn't finalized our civil divorce, and fortunately, I hadn't given her a *Get* either. That gave me leverage because I knew she wanted to remarry right away. Without the *Get,* she'd be stuck. Then one day, I heard she announced her engagement to some guy from L.A., and that our *friend* Rabbi Diamond was the matchmaker. Shaindel began harassing me for a *Get,* calling me all hours of the night at home, beeping me on the road-- it became a real nuisance. She refused to let me see the kids-- just kept insisting I meet her at Rabbi Skumansky's to give her the *Get*. I told her I would, but only after she signed a visitation agreement. Skumansky officiated at several bigamist marriages, where one or both parties had a *Get* but no civil divorce. The community treats him like a hero, taking great personal risks to help Orthodox men and women held hostage by uncooperative, estranged spouses. So, I figured she planned to marry this L.A. guy once I gave her the *Get*. But there was no way I'd do that without getting to see my kids. Next, I start getting calls from a Rabbi, Gavriel Diamond, *suggesting* I give her the *Get*. She means no harm-- *blah, blah, blah*. I agreed but insisted she sign a visitation agreement first. Diamond followed me around-- approached me at the *Shteeble* while I was shopping on Devon, *everywhere*– always peddling the same pitch. The guy was getting on my nerves, but I stood my ground. I wasn't giving up my trump card. Without it, I knew I'd *never* see my kids."

Jake was troubled by Pinky's revelation. His heart certainly went out to him. But he also took offense that Pinky had kept this from him. He'd thought they'd grown close-- he knew Pinky had been through a divorce but hadn't the slightest idea he even had any kids, let alone the torture he'd been put through. Jake could see the pain in

Pinky's eyes as he recounted the events.

Pinky took another deep sigh and wiped a budding tear from the corner of his eye. "My lawyer petitioned for a visitation schedule, but we couldn't get a hearing date set. The case had been assigned to Judge Rabinowitz, an Orthodox Jew with ties to *your* friend, Rabbi Joseph Skumansky. Shaindel's lawyer managed to keep putting off the visitation hearing. I held strong and refused to give her the *Get* until she signed a visitation agreement. She never did. Next thing I know, my picture's posted on flyers in every *synagogue* and Jewish establishment in West Rogers Park. I even noticed them slipped under the windshield wipers of cars parked outside Mi Tsu Yun, that Chinese kosher place on Touhy."

"Just your *picture?* On a flyer?"

"No Jake. They put me in *cherem*-- the bastards excommunicated me. I couldn't get into the *Shteeble*. People shunned me on the street. The Jewish establishments where most of my vending machines were placed demanded I remove them. My life and livelihood were in the crapper, and I hadn't seen my kids in months."

"What did you do?"

"Actually, their little stunt turned out to be a blessing for my vending business. It forced me to establish

247

new, more lucrative routes outside the community. But that took a while. I had a few bucks stashed away, so I managed to get by. I was determined not to cave into their crap."

Pinky slouched back in his chair, taking deep breaths, causing his muscular chest to heave. He raised his arms and cupped his hands over his head as if holding down a toupee in a blustery winter storm.

"But all that was *nothing* compared to what they did *next*."

Pinky leaned forward again, lowering his voice to a whisper. "I'll never forget that day. It was a Thursday, late afternoon. It had been pouring like hell. I had one more stop to finish my route, the Howard-Western Coffee Stop. I backed the van close to the rear door, so I wouldn't get soaked carrying boxes inside. I had just swung the back doors of my van open when a powerful shove from behind sent me flying into the van. My attacker climbed in behind me and slammed the doors shut. Someone was already sitting in the driver's seat-- I'd left the doors unlocked with the motor running. The guy smashed my head. My nose broke when I hit the floor. Blood filled my nostrils. I struggled to breathe. My teeth felt like they'd rattled loose, one by one. The bastard cuffed me and pinned my head, face down, on the floor, mopping my face in a pool of my own blood. The van took off with a jolt. I later learned the muscle man's name-- Rabbi Fishel Fogal, our *friend* from the Sun Times. Pretty strong for an *old* guy. Gavriel Diamond was behind the wheel. Fogal duct-taped my mouth shut. They drove me around like that for about a half hour. Neither of them uttered a word."

As Pinky continued, Jake watched him absently grab his left wrist with his right hand and flex his huge biceps, then alternate, holding his other wrist, flexing his other steel arm. As he continued the story, his whisper ratcheted up a notch with each cycle of this ritual.

"I don't know where they took me, but Diamond slammed on the brakes suddenly, sending my head into the metal seat leg I'd been chained to. Diamond spoke first, softly, kindly-- as if he were my *mother* coaxing me to take my medicine in a spoon of applesauce. He said I was being foolish, that I'd left them no other choice. He said *The Rav* had ruled, so I wasn't going home until I authorized them to deliver a *Get* to Shaindel on my behalf. Fogal ripped the tape from my mouth. I can still feel the sting on my throbbing face," Pinky said, rubbing his upper lip. "I spat a glob of blood as Diamond gave me another lecture. He just smiled, spewing some gibberish about my Jewish soul being trapped in its corrupted earthly vessel-- my body. He said they'd have to beat the evil out until my Jewish soul was free to cooperate. Fogal fished a pen from his jacket pocket. A hand reached out, extending a sheet of legal paper, which Fogal grabbed. I hadn't noticed the third man until then. Diamond told me to authorize them to write the *Get* on my behalf by signing the legal document. I shook my head in refusal. The third man, a pug-nosed thug with a mean crew cut and a face that looked like a brick wall flattened it, zapped me with a stun gun. I can still feel the burn coursing through my body when I think about it. He pinned me down while Fogal shaved off my hair and eyebrows. I spat in their faces, kicked, screamed-- anything I could muster to fight back. The pug-nosed guy reached into his leather jacket and whipped out a steel-blue pistol. He pressed the cold metal barrel against my temple and cocked the gun." Pinky demonstrated as he spoke.

"Diamond smiled again and repeated his good-soul/evil-body hogwash. He calmly demanded that I authorize the *Get*. I refused. The pug-nose guy whacked my head with the pistol's butt. I heard my skull crack. I remember hot blood dripping from my head, and then I must have passed out. But they were kind enough to revive me with smelling salts, only to repeat the stun gun, pistol-whip, and gibberish routine over and over. I couldn't take it forever Jake.

Eventually, I nodded in agreement to have Fogal write and deliver the *Get* and signed their damn document."

When Pinky finished, Jake gathered his jaw off the floor. "*Pinky*, you should have told me-- I had no *idea*. That's *awful*. I can't believe--."

Pinky smashed the table with his fist, sending the glass perched precariously near its edge to its death on the tiled floor. "Don't even say it, Jake!"

The entire restaurant froze, all eyes upon them.

"Sorry," he said, kicking the broken shards under their table with his foot. His color peaked at crimson-red, leaving his cheeks with a ruddy tinge.

A tumbler-paramedic clad in a white apron rushed to the scene, sweeping the shards onto his flat metal stretcher.

Pinky ran his hand through his thick blonde curls.

"That's *exactly* what everyone said-- *I can't believe it-- it can't be true*," he mocked. "I'm *sick* of hearing those words. Why the hell can't anyone believe it? It's true Jake— every word, damn it! No one can *believe* that Rabbi Joseph Skumansky, their hero-- *your* buddy, the *esrog* dealer-- and his henchmen can be so cruel. They all took Shaindel at her word about how I was making my kids non-religious, feeding them non-kosher food-- the exact same shtick

Sender pulled. I should've guessed who was behind his shenanigans. I just didn't put it all together," he said, smacking one hand's fist into the other's open palm. "I *know* it because they told me in the van, but I couldn't actually prove to the police that Skumansky was the one who'd put them up to beat me-- *until* today. Diamond only referred to *The Rav* as the one who made the ruling. Now *you* tell me *The Rav* is definitely how Fogal referred to *Skumansky*. The day after they beat me, Skumansky officiated at her bigamist wedding, and she disappeared with the kids. I haven't seen them since. Legally she's still married to me-- we never finished the civil divorce. I'd love to nail Skumansky for the bigamy and the beating, but I can't prove he had anything to do with it. I'll never get anyone to testify against him."

"Didn't the police do *anything*?"

"I filed a report, and they pulled in Diamond, Fogal, and the third guy, whose name I later learned is Harold Winke-- he lives in Skokie."

"So why aren't they behind bars now?"

"Skumansky sent one of his money men to me-- Marvin Fox. I still hadn't recovered from the business I'd lost at that time. Fox offered me cash if I dropped the charges. He said the whole thing was a big misunderstanding, that they'd apologize to me-- offered to let me put my machines in all his restaurants. He owns the Shalomski chain. That's a *big* account, and my business was hurting-- *badly*. If I prosecuted them, what would I have had to show for it? Nothing but more grief from the community. I didn't pursue the complaint, and the police dropped it. I took Fox's offer hoping to get back on my feet financially and hire a private investigator to find my kids."

"Wonderful," Jake said facetiously. "Now they're cocky enough to think they can get away with whatever they want-- all they have to do is flash a few bucks and pull a few political strings."

"Jake, they're probably right. Do you have any idea how many judges and cops Skumansky has access to via his supporters? Especially Fox. He's *really* connected. A lot of Chicago's *Jewish* machine is under his influence. Besides, I couldn't think of everyone else after that. I *had* to look out for myself at the time. No one else was."

* * * * *

Despite Pinky's advice, after dinner, Jake went home and flipped through the white pages, locating the number for Rabbi Gavriel Diamond on Albion.

He punched the numbered buttons and counted

three rings before the familiar voice answered.

"I met someone today and was wondering if you knew anything about him," Jake said. "His name is Fishel Fogal."

"Yes, I know who he is."

"He paid me an unexpected and most *unfriendly* visit today. Actually, he broke into my apartment, trashed the place, and threatened me. He claims Rabbi Skumansky sent him to get Sender's manuscript, a manila envelope, and a commentary he claimed Herman Stein wrote. I was hoping you could shed some light on that."

"Reb Yankel, I can assure you personally that *The Rav* would never have any part of what you described. Rabbi Skumansky detests violence and would surely have discouraged Rabbi Fogal's behavior had he known what he was up to. I wouldn't trust anything that *low-life* said."

This was odd.

"*Low-life*? Why do you call Rabbi Fogal a low-life?"

"Well, I really shouldn't tell you this, but that unfortunate man doesn't quite have all his marbles. He hasn't been well ever since his dismissal from the *yeshiva*. He was a student there many years ago."

Dismissed...Hasn't been well...

"Did he have a nervous breakdown?"

"No. More of a *moral* breakdown than a nervous one."

"Meaning? He ate non-kosher food-- he drove a car on *Shabbos*-- what does that *mean*, Rabbi Diamond? What *exactly* did he do?"

"Fishel Fogal was asked to leave the college after he was caught with another boy in a broom closet. Both of them were *disrobed.*" He paused for a moment, then continued. "You really can't believe anything that low-life says. He's harmless though-- talks tough, but he wouldn't really harm you."

This was absurd.

Diamond spilling all this gossip about another Rabbi-- at the toss of a hat? What did Fishel Fogal's homosexual tendencies have to do with his honesty? An outcast in Orthodox circles, maybe, but not an automatic liar.

Then Jake recalled Pinky's nickname for Rabbi Diamond-- *the snake.*

"Reb Yankel," he added, "what do you want with this trouble? It's all because you are with that woman, Mindy. She's not for a scholar like you. I tried telling you, but you're a stubborn man. Come to your senses, Reb

Yankel, before it is too late."

Chapter Thirty-Four

Jake used the bump on his head that lingered from his encounter with Fishel Fogal as an excuse to call in sick on Tuesday. After plopping the bedroom phone back into its cradle, he tried to get back to sleep with little success.

Until now, he hadn't given much credibility to Dr. Hoffmeyer's doomsday warning-- she seemed more flaky than factual.

But after hearing about Pinky's run-in with Skumansky's goons, he had no doubt every word she'd said about *The Rav* was true, and that she too was referring to Rabbi Skumansky.

"What the *hell* have I gotten myself into?" he thought.

He *wanted* to be brave this time. But this was *beyond* his abilities-- or so he wanted to believe.

Jake was determined to help where he could with her murder rap, but Mindy would simply have to find another way to deal with Rabbi Skumansky.

He couldn't be held responsible.

Stun guns, pistol-whipping-- they held a gun to Pinky's *head,* for God's sake. Jake wanted to help, but there *had* to be a limit.

He pulled the sheets over his head, hoping to dream the whole thing away, and finally dozed off. But when he woke, the nightmare continued to haunt him.

He shaved, showered, strapped on his *tefillin,* and mumbled through morning prayers. He sat on the couch nibbling whole-wheat toast between sips of chamomile tea while immersing himself in the *seforim* he slipped from the bookcase. He quickly located the passages he was looking for and confirmed that memory had served him well. Skumansky had no right to take *any* action against Pinky.

Only a real, qualified *Beis Din* had the right to even make such rulings. But even a qualified *Beis Din* is not permitted to carry out violent punishments-- they violate local civil laws.

The physical coercion Skumansky and his goons exerted on Pinky was entirely out of the question. Even Skumansky's ruling to coerce Pinky into authorizing a *Get* was inaccurate.

It seemed like Skumansky was heading up some sort of Jewish religious Mafia-- running off half-cocked, like Pinky said, using a little knowledge to implement dangerously inaccurate rulings.

Jake wondered who'd given Skumansky his *S'micha*-- his rabbinical ordination?

Pinky said Skumansky officiated at bigamist ceremonies before. He seemed certain that Skumansky had officiated at Shaindel's wedding.

A quick call to Michael Wertzberger confirmed his suspicion that bigamy is indeed a felony in the state of Illinois.

He opened one of his large *Talmud* volumes.

He definitely recalled Jewish law prohibiting violations of civil laws.

Flipping through the pages, he scanned the familiar text he'd once labored over until he found it.

The passage clearly stated that the law of the land is the law, except where local law requires a direct *violation* of Jewish law.

If the state of Illinois *required* a Jew to light a fire on *Shabbos*, he'd be required to violate Illinois state law rather than the Jewish law forbidding that.

Short of that, however, it was uncontested-- there was to be no violation of the local laws.

There is no *Talmudic* law prohibiting Pinky's ex from remaining married to Pinky. Skumansky should have waited to marry off Shaindel until after Pinky's civil divorce was complete. He had *no basis* for violating the local bigamy laws.

Then there was the issue of Skumansky and Company coercing Pinky to authorize a *Get*. Jake cracked open the *Talmud* volume dealing with divorce law. Once again, memory served him well.

They had no grounds to excommunicate Pinky, let alone coerce him with physical force. Pinky never *refused* to give her a *Get*. He simply wanted assurances he'd see his children. A coerced *Get* isn't even valid. Technically, Shaindel was still Pinky's wife, even according to Jewish law. That meant she was now a married woman living in sin with another man-- a crime punishable by death under Jewish law.

Skumansky's rulings were absolutely wild-- *dangerously* off the wall.

It was beyond him how anyone could have granted Skumansky *S'micha*. In Jake's eyes, he now seemed nothing more than a Mafia boss running his own version of Judaism.

Thugs.

Physical violence.

Guns.

This was a war Jake had no way of combating. He couldn't possibly get involved in something this huge. Besides, he had a far more serious matter to resolve-- Mindy's murder rap. He couldn't afford the diversion into Skumansky's pranks right now.

Yet something just wouldn't let him shelve it.

He went into the kitchen for a chamomile refill. Sipping the hot soothing liquid at the kitchen table calmed his nerves. He rolled his shoulders, slowly relaxing the muscles he'd unwittingly tangled into knots.

He contemplated other avenues of attack-- less risky means than direct confrontation. What he needed was someone with more clout than he had. Someone who'd be willing to stick their neck out. Someone with the *authority* to do something about it.

He thought of Detective Roberts but didn't think he'd be too keen on helping Mindy right now. Besides, the police wouldn't care, and the courts probably wouldn't do much. Pinky seemed to think Skumansky had connections with the courts anyway.

No, it would *have* to be someone else. Some other legally empowered entity like...a *Beis Din*!

Why hadn't he thought of this before?

Surely Skumansky and his clowns could be summoned to the Illinois Rabbinical Board's *Beis Din*.

In all his years studying *Talmud* at the *yeshiva*, Jake

never expected to be able to actually *use* much of what he'd learned in a practical way.

Years of dedicated study that were dormant memories of *Talmudic* texts suddenly emerged.

He felt a rush of excitement course through his veins.

He chug-a-lugged the rest of his tea, threw on his leather jacket, and dashed out to the Nova. He raced up McCormick to Skokie, swung left on Dempster, and pulled into the tiny building's lot.

After being told Rabbi Miklin was in a meeting, Jake announced that he'd wait. He took a seat on the chrome and orange couch next to the receptionist's desk. Several copies of Kosher Times Magazine and the Jewish Press were strewn on the end table next to him. He thought about picking them up to pass the time, but he was too charged up to focus on reading anything. He was sure the receptionist could hear his heart racing inside his jacket.

An elderly man wearing a black suit entered the building. He stood in the doorway for a moment, straightening his short beard hair while peering into a hand-held mirror.

After slipping the mirror into his pocket, he leaned over the receptionist's desk, whispering and pointing in

Jake's direction. As he passed Jake, he nodded a curt Hello and took off toward the open doors of the courtroom at the far end of the hall.

"Who was that?" Jake inquired of the receptionist.

"Rabbi Gavriel Diamond, the court clerk," she responded without looking up from her typewriter.

"That guy really gets around," Jake thought. "Matchmaking was evidently not providing his desired level of income if he had to *clerk* for the *Beis Din*."

Jake thought it strange that he was so friendly on the phone, then cut him off. And now he all but gave him an icy cold shoulder.

Eventually, a tall, stately figure wearing a long black coat strode straight as an arrow down the hallway toward Jake. His shoes tapped louder with each step as he got closer. As the smiling figure approached, Jake noted the Rabbi's long, trimmed white beard, and polished appearance.

"Mr. Cooper?"

As Jake rose from the plastic couch, it took a deep, life-saving gasp as if he'd nearly suffocated it to death.

He exchanged greetings with Rabbi Miklin and followed him into his cozy office. The rabbi picked up several *seforim* and returned them to their rightful places on the bookshelf, making room for Jake to sit.

Jake recounted all that had occurred with Mindy since Sender's death and related Pinky's new revelation about his being beaten until he authorized a *Get*.

"What gets me," Jake explained, "is who would have granted *S'micha* to such a man to bestow the title of Rabbi on him?"

"Mr. Cooper, I am bound by the laws forbidding evil gossip. What possible good could result from discussing this?"

"With all due respect Rabbi," he replied, "the laws restricting gossip are not applicable when there is a direct need to know the information for a legitimate reason."

He recounted how Dr. Hoffmeyer had specifically identified *The Rav*, whom he was now certain was Rabbi Skumansky, as the man plotting to keep Mindy's children away from her.

The Rabbi sat quietly, humming to himself while stroking the white fur on his chin. Then he abruptly arose from his chair and carefully shut the door.

"What I tell you in here today must remain in strict confidence. I can't even trust the people in these offices. I've known for some time now that there is a connection between someone in our office and Rabbi Skumansky.

Many of the more controversial cases that come to us suddenly disappear. Then I hear that Rabbi Skumansky is handling the cases only a few days later. He runs his own little *Beis Din* from his apartment. I have a cousin living in the same apartment building. He's retired and keeps himself entertained by keeping me informed of who comes and goes from Skumansky's apartment. The first few times, I thought it was just a coincidence. But this pattern has repeated itself too many times to be coincidental. As a matter of fact, Sender Stein was here discussing *his* situation with me. He wanted me to issue a ruling granting him custody of his children. After discussing the case with him, I determined we could not intervene on an official basis because the case was already pending in civil court. Shortly thereafter, I received a detailed report from my cousin that Sender visited Rabbi Skumansky."

"You think Skumansky's been stealing cases away from you? Why would he do that? Doesn't he have his own followers to draw his business from?"

"Of course, he does. But there's more than dollars and cents going on here. There's the issue of lost honor. There is a certain perceived prestige that comes with the position I've been entrusted with here. At the time I applied for this position, Rabbi Skumansky also applied. I didn't know until later, but he actually had been tendered an offer to take the position. During the time he took to respond to the board's offer, someone had reason to question his *S'micha*. Precisely during this time, my application was received. The board withdrew their offer and tendered it to me instead. I felt bad about the way things turned out. Shortly after moving into this office, I received several disturbing telephone calls from Rabbi Skumansky accusing me of stealing his offer. He was *extremely* angry. Eventually, I learned what happened, but decided it had been destined for me to serve this post rather than Rabbi Skumansky, and I went about my business. So, you see, Mr. Cooper, I would be foolish not to conclude that Rabbi Skumansky is resorting to stealing my cases as a feeble attempt to usurp the authority of this *Beis Din* to exact political retribution."

Suddenly Jake realized *why* Rabbi Diamond hadn't bothered to introduce himself. *He* was the likely mole.

"Specifically, in answer to your question about his *S'micha*," Rabbi Miklin concluded, "I'm afraid I know little more than you do."

Jake appreciated the Rabbi's candor and repaid him with a tip of his own. "For what it's worth, Rabbi, your mole is probably your clerk, Rabbi Gavriel Diamond."

"*Gavriel*? Why would you say that?"

"He's Rabbi Skumansky's right-hand man. He was one of the three men who assisted in Pinky's beating."

"H'mm. Interesting. I had no idea. All these years...I guess you just never know."

All this was intriguing, but Jake hadn't accomplished what he'd come for.

"Rabbi, surely there's something you can do to prevent Skumansky from interfering with Mindy and her children."

"What is it you would like me to *do*?"

"For starters, you could summon Rabbi Skumansky to your *Beis Din* and make a ruling barring him from meddling with this family."

"Mr. Cooper, surely you understand the political ramifications that would entail for me. Unfortunately, Rabbi Skumansky has support from many influential community members. To do what you ask would be political suicide for me. I wish I could help. My heart really goes out to Mindy and her children, but-- I'm *sure* you understand."

But Jake didn't understand it at all.

Chapter Thirty-Five

On the way back from Miklin's office, Jake rehashed his conversation with Gavriel, *the snake*, Diamond. He obviously wasn't going to get straight answers from *him*. What could he really trust about *anything* the snake said? And why had he so easily gossiped about Fogal's homosexual tendencies?

Jake supposed he threw him that bone in an effort to gain his confidence. But who knew if that was even true?

Inching his way back to Rogers Park down McCormick, he glanced at his watch.

Five-thirty. That explained the crawling traffic. But it also meant he'd wasted an entire day obsessing over Skumansky instead of focusing on proving Mindy innocent. He located a spot for the Nova and made a bee-line for his apartment, determined to salvage the few hours left of the day.

The morning after the murder, after he searched Sender's house with Pinky and found that diskette, he tried to view whatever might be on it. But the damn thing was blank. It had been his only lead.

Then he thought of something.

He nuked a frozen burger, squashed it and a slice of

tomato between two slices of a whole wheat bun, and munched on it, hunched over his computer.

Eureka!

A *hidden* file on the disk.

But his excitement vanished when he discovered it was password protected.

He spent the better part of an hour trying to crack the password until he concluded his efforts were futile.

Feeling the need to accomplish *something*, he called Pinky and arranged to meet at Sender's house. Perhaps they'd find Sender's password hidden in the house somewhere. At work, he'd often locate passwords of vacationing employees somewhere in their cubicles, either in a drawer or under their telephone or calculator.

The odds were decent that Sender stashed his password somewhere.

Pinky was waiting at the corner when Jake turned down Sender's block. Their luck held out as they found the back door unlocked, as they'd left it the morning after the murder.

Jake checked the obvious spots on Sender's computer desk, then led Pinky through the other rooms.

"Maybe Sender's manuscript had something in it Skumansky doesn't want to be made public," Pinky suggested after Jake had explained how he'd wasted most of the day.

"Gavriel Diamond works at the Illinois Rabbinical Board's office," Jake said. "He clerks for Rabbi Miklin."

"*So?*" Pinky screwed up his face into a twisted mass.

"Rabbi Miklin's *certain* Skumansky's stealing cases from him. Shortly after Miklin refused to help Sender, he showed up at Skumansky's. He might have realized Skumansky was stealing cases, figured out how he was doing it, and wrote about it in his manuscript."

"Even if he did, how would Skumansky or Gavriel know about it, Mr. Smarty Pants," Pinky mocked.

"Maybe Sender *blackmailed* Gavriel Diamond."

"*Yeah*– and Diamond pushed Sender off a roof just to save his pathetic little clerking job," Pinky said sarcastically.

He didn't understand the sudden attitude from Pinky. "Hey, you of all people should be able to consider the possibility-- look what they did to *you*!"

We continued our search in silence after that but turned up nothing.

"Maybe you should talk to Marvin Fox," Pinky suggested. "He didn't seem too happy with Skumansky when he offered me that deal. He might talk to you."

"I still can't believe you *took* that deal, Pinky. But then again, I'm not judging your situation. I suppose you felt it was the only thing you could do."

"Look, maybe it *was,* and maybe it *wasn't.* All I know is that it was better than coming out of that mess without my kids *and* being broke."

As Jake took one last look around Sender's computer desk in the den, there was a noise at the front door. He realized they'd left the hallway light on. Before they could find a hiding place, Detective Roberts stormed into the den. Mindy trailed behind him.

"What the hell are you two doing in here! Did you not see the tape across the door," he demanded, pointing toward the front door. "This is still a restricted area!"

"Sorry-- I thought it was just left behind," Jake lied. "I didn't think you'd still be interested in anything here."

"Well, we most certainly *are*! The charges are going to be dropped against Mindy here, but we're still considering this a homicide investigation. Seems that the hair pulled from the victim's wristwatch was dyed a slightly different shade of red than Mindy's hair color at the time of the murder."

"I just had my hair colored at the salon," Mindy

explained. "The hairs caught in Sender's wristwatch were dyed with a shade I only use when I do my own hair. I don't see how some of my hair with *that* shade ended up in Sender's wristband. The Detective now thinks someone planted those hairs and tried to frame me. We were coming here to see if a brush from my apartment made its way here somehow. Sarah may have taken it with her the last time Sender picked the kids up."

"Maybe *that's* what they were after," Jake suggested. "Whoever broke into your apartment did a real job on your hairbrush set, didn't they? Maybe *that's* what they were really *focused* on. The rest of the mess may have just been a ruse to make it look like a robbery or vandalism."

Jake could see tears welling up in the corner of Mindy's eye as she asked, "Who would want to do that to *me*, Jake? Who could be so *cruel*?"

"Of course! Why hadn't I thought of this before!" Jake thought. "I only knew one person, other than Sender, who had a *personal* vendetta with *Mindy*."

Because he was at the center of that mess, Jake left his thoughts unspoken for the moment.

"You still haven't answered my question, gentlemen," Roberts bellowed. "What are you two doing here? Tell me why I shouldn't pull you both in right now!"

Jake explained to the Detective that they were searching for Sender's manuscript, leaving out the details of the diskette and Fogal's demands for the mysterious book. "Sender's manuscript might have been a motive for his murder if he'd written something and blackmailed someone with it."

"An interesting theory," Roberts responded. "Any thoughts on what he may have uncovered about whom?"

Jake felt Pinky's thumb jabbing his rib cage, tapping out his own version of Morse code to share their brilliant theory about Diamond with the Detective.

As tempting as that was, now was not the time.

He returned the attack with an elbow jab to Pinky's gut-- his own, more concise, version of the code.

"Well," Jake said sheepishly, dramatically twisting his toe into the carpet pile, "not really."

He wasn't letting on any more than he had to for the moment.

The charges were being dropped against Mindy. That's all he cared about now. Putting additional information in Roberts' hands might end up giving him the ammunition he needed to twist the facts around and come up with another theory to pin this on Mindy.

"Even if your speculation is correct," Roberts pointed out, "it still doesn't answer the very question *you* asked *me*-- why push him off *Mindy's* building? It still points to someone framing Mindy and we haven't got a single lead on that angle just yet. This crime scene is still important. You two had best keep your asses out of here. Next time I might not be so understanding."

Roberts motioned them toward the door and saw them out.

"By the way," he said, "expect a call from Detective Morton Wolfe. He's retired now, but he worked the Herman Stein death investigation-- you were asking about it the other day. Seems he's got a few unanswered questions of his own about that case."

Chapter Thirty-Six

Jake arrived home after midnight but dialed Marsha's number anyway. He'd certainly been naive. Not so much about the dirty laundry hidden within the community as he was about how far a crazy woman might go to get what she wanted.

But if she wanted the chance to take away Mindy's children in some sort of jealousy vendetta, she had the perfect opportunity to do so. Marsha was the only person he knew angry enough with Mindy to try and frame her like this. When Mindy innocently asked who'd be so cruel to her, he flashed back to Marsha's cutting, angry remarks and the contemptuous fire burning in her eyes. It happened both times. Once when Mindy had approached him with her phone number at the singles event and again when her name came up during their video store encounter.

There was also the night he broke up with Marsha and told her he was seeing Mindy. At first, she directed her fury toward him. But as he turned away to leave, he heard her grumble,

"I'll show that red-headed bitch."

After several rings, Jake realized he had no idea what he was going to say and was thankful when Marsha's voicemail picked up. He asked her to call him and said it was urgent.

Then he hit the sack only to enjoy a repeat of the restless sleep he'd been having since Mindy's arrest. He thought about Pinky's children and how he'd been so cruelly separated from them.

He knew all too well the pain of missing a child. He couldn't let that happen to Mindy.

On Wednesday Jake dialed Marsha's work number several times throughout the day, each time receiving a tacky excuse from her secretary.

She was definitely avoiding him, and that fueled his suspicions.

After dinner that night, he drove the Nova down Lake Shore Drive to the Gold Coast. If Marsha was avoiding him, he'd have to step up his efforts to see her. It took nearly an hour to find a parking spot. He was lucky enough to spot a woman jogging as she turned down Banks and then slowed to a walk.

He followed her in the Nova, slowing in step with her. When she climbed into a red Porsche and pulled away, he slipped the Nova into the tight spot, wondering if his jalopy was worthy of the holy Porsche ground.

He walked back to Astor and waltzed up the tight

circular drive gracing Marsha's building. He peered inside, past the double glass doors at the doorman or Concierge as he was sure they called them in Gold Coast country. He bravely climbed the steps announcing himself as a guest calling on Ms. Marsha Rein. After a hush-hush chat with his mission-control desk phone, he informed Jake that Ms. Rein was "unavailable" and promptly ushered him out the door.

It was eight-thirty when he crawled back into the Nova and reluctantly yielded his prized Gold-Coast real estate to an overeager Beemer.

Too keyed up to go home, he headed to the Shalomski's near his apartment. It wasn't their kosher polish delicacies that lured him there. It was Pinky's suggestion to reach out to Marvin Fox, the owner. Nothing else had panned out today-- so he gave that a shot.

The manager at Shalomski's informed Jake that Mr. Fox would most likely be at their Albany Park location near Lawrence and Kedzie. Jake didn't think much of a Jewish community still existed in the Lawrence area-- it was mostly Korean now, but he didn't presume to second-guess Marvin Fox's business acumen.

The blaring blue and white neon sign was impossible to miss amidst the darkened street. Business in

Albany Park had pretty much shut down for the night. Shalomski's Kosher Polish Cuisine was one of the few establishments with a hint of life.

Jake crossed the Polish border, stepping inside the uniquely decorated eatery. "We're closing up, mister," a mop-in-hand teen announced.

"I'm not here to eat," Jake assured him. "I came to see Mr. Fox."

"Oh. He's in the back, but he'll be out soon. Should I tell him you're here?"

"That's okay. I'll just wait."

Jake sunk into a vinyl booth at a corner table, watching the teen flip overstuffed padded wooden chairs onto butcher-block tables that filled the middle of the room, then proceeded to mop up the bricked floor.

A commotion at the front door caused the teen to look up suddenly.

The Devon wheelchair beggar rammed his vehicle into the half-open door repeatedly, trying to get his wheels to clear the threshold.

Evidently, Lawrence Avenue was also part of his territory.

Jake started toward the door to help the beggar, then stopped short, recalling his miraculous self-healing capabilities. He watched him lean halfway out of the chair, pull the device over the threshold and wheel himself inside, leaving dirt tracks across the freshly mopped floor.

The teen propped his mop under his chin, shook his head, and pointed toward the counter. "Over there," he said. "The two paper bags next to the empty bins."

The beggar wheeled himself a few feet, then halfway to the counter, he leaped out of the chair and sprinted to the bags. He meticulously inspected each of the empty bins next to the bags, verifying he hadn't been deprived of a single leftover scrap.

With his attention focused on the miraculous abilities of the beggar, Jake didn't notice the appearance of a short fifty-ish man emerging from the back door.

The beggar held up the bags and mumbled in a thick Russian accent. "May you, your children, and a thousand generations beyond be blessed for your charity, Mr. Fox," he said.

Marvin Fox saluted the wheelchair-bound faker and flashed him a smile.

The beggar returned to the wheelchair, rummaged through the bags, popped bits of food into his mouth like rock candy, then repeated his door-ramming routine on the way out.

"We're closing up now," Fox said, turning to me. "My man here needs to mop around your table."

Jake stood up. "Sorry I didn't come to eat."

"Oh? You *should* have– don't know what a treat you're missing. A hundred years of secret polish recipes for your delight," he said, holding up a menu.

"Have you been to any of my joints? Fourteen in the Chicagoland area and counting," he boasted.

"Actually," Jake muttered, "I was just hoping to speak with you for a minute."

"I was just about to leave." He fumbled with his shirt pocket, fished out a card and handed it to Jake. "Give my secretary a call, and we can set up an appointment."

"It's about Rabbi Skumansky," Jake blurted, mustering the sternest look he could. "I really only need a few moments of your time, but it *is* urgent."

He motioned to the mopping teen. "That's enough for tonight. I'll finish up."

The teen flashed a surprised look, tossed his apron behind the counter, grabbed a Bulls cap off the hook, and left.

Jake briefly explained all that had happened and gave a more detailed description when he got to the part about Fogal's visit to his apartment.

"Among other things, he kept asking for a manuscript that Sender–"

Marvin's face exploded.

"If you gave that *goddamn* thing to him, I'll–. Where is it now? Do you still have it?"

This manuscript sure made a lot of people jumpy.

"What's so important about Sender's manuscript?" Jake asked.

"*Important*? I wouldn't say it's *important*. It's *not* important. But Sender had a pretty wild imagination-- liked to make up stories. That slimeball thought he could threaten people that he would publish them. Came to *me* asking me for financial backing."

"Some things just shouldn't be hung out for the world to see."

"Like what?"

"*Things*."

"Things Sender made up about people in the community?"

"*Fantasies*-- that boy had a wild imagination."

"Would these *fantasies* include Rabbi Skumansky?"

Marvin looked at Jake quizzically. "Skumansky wanted Sender's book? I thought you said Fogal was after it."

Jake thought carefully for a moment, trying to recall Fogal's exact words. Marvin was correct. When Skumansky had called him, he'd never said it was *Sender's* manuscript. He just referred to *a* manuscript. Jake was referring to Sender's manuscript, but Skumansky must have thought it was Herman's *Eicha* commentary. He must have sent Fogal searching for that. But Fogal asked specifically for *Sender's* manuscript *and* an envelope. He didn't seem all that interested in the *Eicha* commentary Herman wrote.

"Come to think of it, you're right," Jake admitted. "So why would Fogal want Sender's manuscript? Did the fantasies include *him*?"

"I only wish," Marvin replied. "Him, even *I* could write a book about. Bestseller, no doubt. Those two were really something else."

"Fogal and Skumansky?"

"*Skumansky*? No. Fogal and *Sender Stein*."

Marvin took a deep breath, then flipped a chair off one of the tables and sat down. "You never *did* answer my question. Did you give anything to Fogal?"

"I don't have, nor did I *ever* have Sender's manuscript, Herman's commentary, nor any envelope."

Jake flipped a chair and joined Marvin at the table.

"Even if I did, I don't understand Fogal's loyalty to

Skumansky. Breaking into my apartment and attacking me was risky. I could have him arrested. How did he know I don't have a gun or something? I could have killed him for all he knew."

"If Skumansky asked him to, he'd probably rob the First National Bank."

"Why's he *so* loyal to Skumansky?"

"*Loyal*? I wouldn't call it *loyalty*-- more like fear. The guy's frightened to death of Skumansky."

"Why?"

"Don't really know. It's just when I see those two together that's how I read it."

"What about Rabbi Diamond? Is he also afraid of Skumansky?"

"Gavriel Diamond? Now there's a *whole* different piece of work. If he'd spent half as much time studying *Talmud* as he did primp himself, he might actually have become something. No. I don't get the sense that Gavriel's *afraid* of him-- more like he's a Rabbi Skumansky wanna-be. Kisses up to him, does white-collar stuff for him-- more like an *aide* than a goon-gopher. *That's* Fogal's job."

These three amigos were sounding stranger by the minute.

"How'd these three hook up?" Jake asked.

"They've been...*acquaintances*," he said, choosing the word carefully. "Ever since their *yeshiva* days. Skumansky was the dorm supervisor when those two attended the *yeshiva* out in Deerfield. That was before the fire when the dorm was housed in an old farmhouse. Eventually, Skumansky left and worked as a traveling *meshulach*, raising funds for the *yeshiva*. Got pretty good at it too. The man knows how to play people-- a real *schmoozer*. Shoulda been an insurance salesman. He stayed single well into his late twenties until people began talking-- you know how it is. Eventually, he married and settled down in Chicago. But he needed a new source of income. He approached a couple of other businessmen and me about financing his *Beis Din*. Told us he was gonna help poor unfortunate women-- those with husbands who beat them, left them penniless with a house full of kids, or whose ex's wouldn't give them a *Get*-- stuff the Illinois Rabbinical Board wouldn't touch."

"*You* financed Skumansky?"

"I still give him a few bucks now and then. He's a hard man to refuse. But he's got a slew of followers chipping in now. He's actually done *some* good things-- I've seen that first hand."

"Yeah, I've heard some of the *good* he did. I had a

long talk with Pinky Greenberg. Is that what you call *good?*"

"Look, the guy gets a little overzealous once in a while. Everyone makes mistakes. Besides, he patched things up with Pinky."

"With a little help from *you*, I hear."

"Hey, I do what I can," Marvin said, touching his fingertips to his chest, then spreading his hands outwardly. "Everyone came out happy."

Happy– right.

How happy could Pinky be never seeing his own children-- not even knowing where they were? Jake wanted to tear Marvin Fox a new one, right then and there. But that confrontation would lead nowhere and he wanted to leave the door open with Fox, who seemed to be talking freely.

"That book of Sender's turns up you let me know now." Fox said as Jake bid him goodnight and stepped out into the chilly night air.

Jake made his way back to the Nova, wondering if Fox knew more than he let on.

Marvin's reaction to Sender's manuscript was so intense. Now even he wanted to get his hands on it. But Jake still had no idea if that had anything to do with Sender's murder. Just how many people Sender had threatened with that manuscript? Had he gone beyond this community, writing about others? Marsha Rein, perhaps? Maybe she killed Sender and then figured out how to get back at Mindy at the same time.

Jake arrived home and was immediately beckoned by the flashing light on his answering machine. He prayed it was a message from Marsha. She couldn't avoid him forever.

Chapter Thirty-Seven

Thursday, Jake met Mindy downtown for a lunch date. They picked up tuna bagels at a café on Michigan Avenue, then sat on a bench in the tiny park near the old Water Tower and devoured them.

Mindy pursed her lips. "How's my lipstick?"

"You could use a touch-up."

Mindy unclasped her purse, paused for a second, then extracted something a lot bigger than lipstick.

She waved a half-folded legal pad at Jake.

"I almost forgot about this. I found it today in a large manila envelope, stuck in the bottom of this purse. I must've taken it the day I moved out from Sender. Maybe you can figure out what it is. It's not Sender's writing."

Jake examined the cryptic writing, finally assessing it as a ledger of some sort. "This right-hand column has different grades of *esrogim* written in Hebrew," he explained. "The left column looks like prices." He flipped through the ledger, noting that the Jewish year was scribbled on the top of each page and incremented every few pages, ending with the current year.

"Rabbi Skumansky sells *esrogim*," he said. "Pinky and I bought ours from him this past

Sukkos."

Mindy ran her fingers through her red hair. "Why would *Sender* have Rabbi Skumansky's ledger?"

"I didn't say this was *Skumansky's* ledger. But it sort of fits with what I found out last night." He updated Mindy on his chat with Marvin Fox.

"So why was Sender's *uncle* interested in it?"

"Sender's *who*?"

"Marvin Fox. Didn't he tell you he was Sender's *uncle*?"

"No. He didn't."

"Maybe he just assumed you knew."

"Well, I didn't. It is *odd* that he didn't mention it. Anyway, Sender's *Uncle* Marvin said Sender made up stories about people and wanted to publish them. He claims Sender approached him for financial backing."

"It's not dirty laundry unless it's true," Mindy pointed out. "So, what kind of dirty laundry could an *esrog* ledger contain?"

"When Fogal burst into my place he was after three things." Jake ticked them off on his fingers. "Sender's manuscript, a manila envelope, and Herman's *Eicha* commentary, which he said Rabbi Skumansky had sent him for. But it sounded like he *really* came to get the first two for himself."

"You think *this* was in the envelope he was after?"

"Sounds like a match to me. Skumansky must make a nice buck on his annual sale. Maybe Sender somehow got this ledger and was going to prove that Skumansky wasn't claiming the income on his tax return."

"But didn't you say Fogal came for the envelope for *himself*-- not for Skumansky?"

"Yes. You're absolutely right, Mindy. I see what you're saying. If Skumansky had noticed the missing ledger and he was cheating on his taxes, *he* would have sent Fogal to look for it. If Fogal was looking for it on his *own accord,* then there's something else we're missing here."

"Now I remember!" Mindy's excitement scared off the flock of pigeons congregating around our lunch crumbs. "I was trying to remember *exactly* where I pulled this envelope from. I couldn't figure out why I would have taken it. Now I remember taking it on my way out the door, the very last time I went back to get any important papers I thought I might need. I saw this envelope sticking out from underneath the *Talmud* that Sender carried to his study sessions. It looked like the envelope we keep our tax returns in, so I took it."

Jake thought about Fogal's run-in with the IRS.

"You said you never knew who Sender was studying with, didn't you?"

"That's right. I never *did* find out."

"Don't you wonder how Sender would have gotten his hands on this? Marvin Fox said something odd that now makes some sense. He said those *two* were really something-- I thought he meant Fogal and Skumansky. I even commented on it but he said he meant Fogal and *Sender*. I didn't give it much thought at the time. But maybe Sender's mystery study partner was *Fogal*. *He* might have had access to Skumansky's files."

"You mean he and Sender were partners in gathering dirt, and Fogal stole the ledger from Skumansky so Sender could write about Skumansky?"

"You're close, but I think you're missing one *twist* to the whole thing. I'll bet the handwriting on these ledger sheets is Fogal's. Fogal seemed *very* nervous about the envelope. More so than the manuscripts. I'll bet he was skimming merchandise from Skumansky's shipments and selling the stolen *esrogim* on the side. Skumansky wouldn't notice a few here and there. The way they put them out for sale, anyone could lift an *esrog* or two. He wouldn't care. The markup is so high he probably makes a nice profit just selling half the shipment. There's always stuff left over that can't be returned-- can't even mark it down. Who'd need it after the holidays? This is probably *Fogal's* ledger, accounting for the *esrogim* he sold out from under Skumansky's nose without claiming the income on *his* tax returns. Marvin Fox said he sensed that Fogal feared Skumansky. Skumansky has some dirt of his own on Fogal that he's been keeping secret. But if he found out Fogal was *stealing* from him, he might just blow the whistle."

"Jake Cooper!" Mindy sprang to her feet, sending her purse chasing a pigeon who'd cautiously returned. She slammed her hands onto her hips. "How could you say such things? These are *rabbis*!"

"Maybe. But they're still *human*. And the title doesn't *guarantee* their moral character. I had trouble believing anything like this could be true myself, until Pinky told me what happened to *him*."

He filled Mindy in on Pinky's encounter with the rabbinic clan. Mindy slowly sat down, listening intently, as he provided the details of Pinky's abduction.

When he was done, they both sat in silence and watched the pigeons inch their way back into the park, slowly making their way toward their lunch crumbs.

"What I *still* don't get," Jake finally said, "is why Marvin Fox seemed *so* desperate to find Sender's manuscript?"

"Maybe he's just worried about protecting his reputation," Mindy suggested. "Sender obviously knew about Fogal's *esrog* scheme. If Marvin supports Skumansky and it gets out that Skumansky's trusted assistant was involved in a scandal, that would reflect poorly on Marvin."

"He got pretty hot under the collar-- let himself go there for a second. He definitely sounded angry and *desperate*. I think he had something *more* at stake. He was pretty upset at the thought I'd given that manuscript to Fogal. As if that would be the *worst* hands it could be in now."

"If Fogal works for Rabbi Skumansky and he had access to his financial files," Mindy hypothesized, "he'd *also* have access to his case files-- peoples' private business."

Jake could see she was with him on this now.

She continued, her wild hand gestures scaring away the pigeons once again, "Which *means* he could have supplied Sender with a boat-load of dirt on *all sorts* of people. Maybe they got something on *Marvin*. Marvin said Sender asked him to *finance* the book. Was the financing to publish it or to keep it secret?"

"Blackmail his own uncle?"

"That was Sender."

"*Boy*, you really picked a winner there, didn't you."

"Okay. You don't have to rub it in."

"Sorry."

"But we still don't know who killed Sender and *why* they want to frame me," Mindy declared.

Until he had something more concrete than a hunch, there was no sense getting Mindy riled up about Marsha. Jake still hadn't been able to reach her.

"I must have *something* to do with that manuscript," Mindy said. "Everyone seems so hot on the trail for it. But whoever did kill him wouldn't have done it before they got hold of it."

"Unless," Jake pondered, "Fogal got the idea to cut Sender out of the deal." He wanted to give Mindy something to grasp onto without mentioning Marsha. "He does seem to move in on other people's money-making schemes-- like stealing and selling Skumansky's *esrogim*. Maybe he got into a fight with Sender, killed him to keep the blackmail money for himself, and framed *you* to throw suspicion off himself."

"Then why doesn't he *have* the manuscript?"

"Good point," Jake admitted.

He was going to have to do better than that.

"Maybe it was the other way around. Maybe *Sender* used *Fogal* to get the information, and when he was through, *Sender* got greedy. Maybe *he* tried killing *Fogal* and tried to frame you. They had a scuffle on your roof, but maybe Sender went over instead. He probably figured he could overpower an older guy like Fogal. But Fogal's a lot stronger than he looks. He pinned *me* down."

"I still don't think Sender would have crossed that far over the line. Still, he was awfully greedy. But even supposing you're right, Jake, how would *Sender's* plan have framed *me*? What would have been *my* motive for killing *Fogal*?"

She had him there.

Jake abandoned the notion of providing her with anything solid. Instead, he added one more question for her to ponder. "While we're on the topic of things that don't fit, you're forgetting one more-- Herman's *Eicha* commentary. Why would Rabbi Skumansky want that bad enough to send Fogal after it?"

Mindy thought momentarily as three pigeons waddled toward the crumbs at her feet. "I haven't the foggiest idea," she replied.

Later that evening, they met at Mindy's apartment.

She returned a call from Michael Wertzberger and put him on speakerphone so they could both listen.

"I've got good news and bad news," he said. "Good news is the States Attorney officially dropped the murder charge. Based on Detective Robert's input, they agree there's not enough evidence to prosecute you"

"That's great!" She paused, then added, "What's the bad news?"

"We've got to be at the Daley Center for a court hearing Monday morning."

"Why? I thought you said we're done."

"New petition– filed by Marsha Rein. She's still your children's court-appointed attorney."

"Petition for what?"

"I'm afraid it's serious. She petitioned the court to remove the children from you because it's not in their best interest to live with the woman who murdered their father."

"But you said the charges were dropped," Mindy insisted.

"Dropped because there wasn't enough evidence to prosecute you in criminal court," Michael explained. "Domestic Relations is another story. There, the rules are completely different. All you have to do is convince a judge that the children are *probably* in jeopardy. You don't have to actually prove it."

"*My God*! When does it all *end*?"

"I wish I could say soon kiddo, but I'd be lying. Anyone's guess is as good as mine. There's no telling. Get some rest and enjoy the rest of the week with the kids. Don't mention anything to them-- no point in upsetting them. Unless I can make this go away on Monday, the court will probably request a psychiatrist to evaluate the kids and render an opinion for the judge to consider. But for now, let them just be kids. Focus on one step at a time, Mindy. It's the only way to get through this. How are you doing otherwise?"

"Fine. I'll be okay."

"Good girl. Just show up Monday at the Daley Center. 10 AM, 8th floor, room 802. Dress modestly but don't overdo it. *Don't* come early, and *don't* come looking for me. Just wait for me in the courtroom. I'll be in the judge's chambers meeting with the children's attorney, Marsha Rein."

Chapter Thirty-Eight

Monday arrived too quickly. Jake still hadn't pinned down Marsha, nor had he learned anything new about Sender's death or Skumansky's little trio.

On the bright side, he would have an opportunity to corner Marsha after the hearing. Mindy hadn't stopped wringing her hands since Jake had picked her up in the morning.

On the ride down Lake Shore Drive toward the Loop, she'd alternated between long periods of silence and bursts of long-winded stories about her kids. Hearing her recount those memories caused Jake's old wounds to resurface, but he hid his pain for Mindy's sake.

Marsha no doubt had reveled in the filing of this petition. It was an easy shot at Mindy. Jake deeply appreciated Mindy's refrain from blaming him for this attack, though it didn't do much to lighten the guilt that weighed heavily on him.

The only part of this morning's battle he was confidently blameless for was the part neither Mindy nor he had verbalized. They both knew Rabbi Joseph Skumansky was somehow behind this court business. Dr. Hoffmeyer may be strange, but she was right about everything so far.

Mindy had been cleared of Sender's murder. Now, her prediction that *The Rav* would interfere with Mindy's children was materializing. Dr. Hoffmeyer was either a prophetess or privy to the manipulations of the wizard behind the curtain. Since he doubted her psychic ability, he was sure that someone with a lot of clout was pulling the string.

The odd part was it also meant Marsha was involved with Rabbi Skumansky. She was the *last* person Jake figured would hook up with Skumansky. Though she'd never said as much, it was obvious from their conversations she was raised strictly Orthodox and now resented it in the worst way. Why she would even *talk* to Rabbi Skumansky was beyond him.

Mindy and Jake arrived downtown shortly before nine-thirty. Following Michael's specific instructions, they killed a half hour over coffee in Marshall Field's, then at a few minutes to ten, they made their way to the Daley Center. After clearing security on the ground floor, they rode a crowded elevator to the 8th floor.

The case was set before Judge Morris Handelman. Michael said he was a decent judge, although that wasn't saying much in the Domestic Relations Division of Cook County Circuit Court.

"Thank heavens they hadn't assigned it to Judge Frederick Jay Barris," Jake thought. During Jake's own divorce proceedings, Michael had educated him about Barris. He'd been reassigned to the Domestic Relations Division-- tossed into the dregs of the system as political retribution. Since his reassignment, he'd been doing everything possible to get removed from his post, making the most absurd, off-the-wall-rulings he could manufacture.

They approached the smoked-glass double doors of the courtroom. Jake tugged on the door, half-noticing a hand-written sign on the glass. He read the note and said to Mindy, "Handelman's out. That note says all cases have been reassigned."

When they swung the doors open, a tall, thin, mustached bailiff in his late fifties barked, "Stein?"

Mindy nodded.

He spun on his heels, "Come with me."

They followed him into the hallway behind the back wall of the courtroom. He grunted and pointed toward the end of the hall where Michael and Marsha were chatting. As they approached, Marsha touched Michael's shoulder and left via yet another door.

"I've been trying to learn as much as I can from Marsha," Michael explained, "but she's one clever cookie--

not letting on to a thing, other than what's written in the petition."

He placed a hand on Mindy's shoulder. "I tried to make this go away, kid, but I'm afraid it's going forward. Also, there's more bad news. We've been reassigned," Michael said.

"Sometimes these things happen. Handelman's out indefinitely on sick leave. All his cases are being sent to Judge Barris," he said, giving Jake a knowing nod.

"Nothing permanent can come out of today's ruling," Michael explained, "Marsha filed this as an *Emergency* Motion. By the time we get a full hearing, I'll try to get the case reassigned. Don't worry about it. Just keep in mind, whatever happens, today is only temporary."

They followed Michael through a maze of hallways and entered Barris's courtroom from the back. Squeezing into a corner of the standing-room-only courtroom, they waited for Mindy's case to be called. Another hearing was already in progress.

A dark blue vein throbbed across Judge Barris's temple as he yelled, "*Both of you*, go out in the hallway with your attorneys and flip a coin. Winner gets the Honda. Loser rents a car until the plates are reinstated on the wagon. *That's* my ruling."

"Who's the next and last victim before lunch?" he bellowed, motioning to the clerk.

"Stein," The clerk replied.

Marsha and Michael approached the bench. Jake couldn't make out what they were saying. Marsha motioned to the back row. He turned to see the tall, familiar man standing just inside the double glass doors at the back of the room, stroking his long white beard while swaying as if he were praying. Marsha motioned Rabbi Joseph Skumansky over to the bench.

As Rabbi Skumansky made his way through the crowd, Judge Barris smashed his gavel with such force that Jake thought it had surely broken.

"I'm *not* in the mood to hear *sermons* from *rabbis* today! Motion denied. Next case!"

Stunned by Mindy's good fortune, they silently followed Michael out into the hallway like sheep. Michael waited for Marsha and Skumansky to make their way past them before speaking.

"We got lucky, kids. But that's one hell of an angry *bitch*-- pardon my French," he said, referring to Marsha. "She brought in a rabbi– Rabbi Skumansky, to testify that you're an unfit mother and that he *personally* heard you threaten to kill Sender."

"Rabbi Skumansky doesn't even *know* me!" Mindy retorted furiously, twisting one hand with the other. "I've never even *met* the man. What does *he* know about my mothering? And how could he *lie* like that?"

"Seems Marsha had something lined up, and it backfired on her," Michael said. "No way they'd even think they could have pulled this off without connections. But sometimes you get lucky. Today was your day, kid. But I'm sure we haven't heard the last from Marsha Rein."

"Did you find out who's behind all this?" Jake asked.

"She won't reveal a thing-- claims she's doing it on her own in the kids' best interests. She *is* their legal Guardian Ad Litem. She has the legal right to do this if she wants to."

But Jake sensed Michael had another theory he wasn't sharing. "You don't think *she* really wanted this done, *do you*?"

"Well, if I had to bet on it, I'd put my money on the Rabbi there. Remember when I was talking with Marsha in the hallway before you arrived? Each time I proposed something in an attempt to negotiate our way out of this mess, Marsha wouldn't respond until she went to the ladies' room and returned. Either she's got an awfully weak bladder, or she was conferring with someone out in the hallway. I didn't put it all together until the Rabbi showed up inside the courtroom. My guess is *he's* the one calling the shots."

This was too much. Jake couldn't keep his thoughts silent any longer. "I wonder if you haven't got it backward," he said. "I think Marsha *is* the one calling the shots, and *she* arranged for Rabbi Skumansky's testimony to help her. Marsha may have left you on purpose to make you think it wasn't her own doing. But I'm afraid she's got it in for Mindy, and it's all *my* fault."

Jake waited for Mindy's reaction. But all he got were her tear-filled puppy-dog eyes pleading for clarification. She was going to make him drag this out.

He supposed he deserved it.

Jake confessed to his bungled breakup with Marsha and how he'd sort of blamed it on Mindy.

"You had no way of knowing she was a crazy woman, Jake," Mindy said. "It's not your fault."

"*Now* I know," Michael mumbled.

"Know *what*?" Jake asked.

"When you two followed the bailiff into the hallway, I sensed something strange about Marsha. For a split second, she seemed to become another person. I'm not sure if it was the way she was standing, the look in her eye, or her voice. Maybe it was a combination of things. But she transformed from what appeared in every way to be a professional attorney doing her job with finesse into what I can only describe as a mad hunter looking for a kill."

"*Now* I know *why* she had that hatred in her eyes."

"Michael," Jake asked, finally coming out with his entire secret, "do you think Marsha had anything to do with Sender's death?"

"I don't know, but you might consider another possibility."

"What's that?"

"I'm not trying to be sacrilegious or anything. But if a rabbi's willing to give false testimony, which if I recall correctly is a violation of one of the big ten, isn't it possible he could just as easily be involved in violating another of those big ten?"

"Thou shalt not kill," Jake mumbled, pondering the thought.

"It makes no sense," Jake concluded aloud. "If Skumansky wanted to get the kids away from Mindy based on the crap only Sender could have told him, he wouldn't want Sender dead. He'd need him alive. Sender was the best way to get the children away from Mindy. They could have made a good case for custody. Now it's a much tougher sell."

"But Sender didn't *want* the kids," Mindy reminded him. "Remember, he called me to give them back."

"I still don't see what motive *Skumansky* could have to kill Sender. But that does bring up a good point. Why *did* Sender call you to return the kids? I can't believe he had a change of heart. Not a cold, calculating guy like that. And besides, his mother did most of the caring for the kids."

"Maybe it wasn't Sender's choice," Mindy rebutted.

"What do you mean?"

"Well, what if he was fixed up with a woman who didn't want three kids around."

"I never thought of that. It's an interesting theory. If Skumansky does a lot of divorce work, it's a natural offshoot to do matchmaking. With all those divorce cases he'd have all the contacts needed for a successful matchmaking business. And that could be far more lucrative than running his *Beis Din*. People in that community pay handsomely for a good match," Jake explained for Michael's benefit. "A couple grand at least-- a lot more for matching up damaged goods with baggage. Some families pay a small fortune to get the shame of divorce off everyone's tongue quickly."

"*Exactly*," Mindy went on. "Maybe Skumansky set up a match for Sender. He'd want to get paid for the match, but he wouldn't have been able to endorse Sender's giving the kids back to me if he believed I was such a terrible mother."

"So, he bumps off Sender? He'd collect no fee and risk murder charges," Michael joined in. "That clearly doesn't work."

"What if Sender tried *cheating* Rabbi Skumansky out of the matchmaking fee?" Jake suggested.

Michael asked, "How could he do that?"

"Suppose he told Skumansky the match was off because of the kids. Then, after waiting a bit, he tried giving the kids back and marrying the woman on his own."

"Skumansky would have been *pissed*," Michael agreed. "But even *I* can't see him committing murder over a matchmaking fee."

Jake saw Rabbi Skumansky walk away from Marsha from the corner of his eye. He headed for the elevator bank while she made a dash for the ladies' room.

"C'mon," Michael said, breaking the three-way trance. "If I don't get outta here and take a smoke, I'm gonna bust."

"I'll meet you guys downstairs," Jake said. "There's

someone I've got to speak with before she gets away."

Chapter Thirty-Nine

Jake waited outside the women's washroom, leaning against the wall.

She can't stay in there forever. This time, *I* have her cornered.

It really bothered him that Rabbi Skumansky would testify against Mindy. Mindy was right-- the man didn't even *know* her. But then he recalled their visit to Dr. Hoffmeyer. The picture in her foyer had reminded Mindy that Sender had said he wanted to use *The Rav* to officiate their *Get*.

It all made sense now that they knew Rabbi Skumansky is *The Rav*. The lies Rabbi Skumansky wanted to testify about must have come from Sender. He must have believed what Sender told him about Mindy leading their children away from Orthodoxy.

According to Marvin Fox, this definitely qualified as a case Rabbi Skumansky would pursue-- stuff the Illinois Rabbinical Board wouldn't touch.

Jake didn't realize how menacing he looked, perched just outside the restroom until he noticed the angry glances from the women stepping out of it. He strode down to the end of the hall to a less conspicuous stakeout location, where he still had a clear view of the door.

Marsha is certainly taking her time. It was almost fifteen minutes since she'd gone in there. She had to surface eventually.

The moment she did, he'd make his move. There were a lot of questions he wanted answers to, starting with her whereabouts at the time of Sender's murder.

He waltzed back toward the restroom, stopping at the water cooler. He sipped the cool, refreshing liquid, monitoring the door from the corner of his eye when a hand gripped his shoulder. After snorting water and nearly choking from the surprise attack, he turned to face Rabbi Skumansky.

"Reb Yankel, my friend," he said, flashing his tobacco-stained teeth in a smile. "It's good to see you again." He stroked his long white beard, fishing out half a sunflower seed shell from deep within. "I just wish it were under different circumstances-- I'm sure you understand. It really is a shame to see how you have fallen so far. *Surely* you know better than to be involved with a woman like Mindy Stein."

"She goes by Mindy *Bloom* now," Jake retorted, buying time to formulate his response. "And there's nothing wrong with her, regardless of what you may have heard from Sender to the contrary."

"Really, Reb Yankel? Whom do you think you are fooling, my friend?" He stroked his beard several times, then said, "I didn't approach you now to interrogate you about Mindy Stein or Bloom, whatever the case may be. But I did want to see if you'd turned up Herman Stein's manuscript."

Though the intruder he sent to Jake's apartment was still fresh in his mind, he decided to take a diplomatic approach. "As I told your *representative*, Fishel Fogal, I do not have, nor do I know, where the manuscript is. Even if I did, why would *you* want it? What's so important about Herman's commentary on *Eicha*?"

"Surely, Reb Yankel, you have not lost all appreciation for scholarly works. Herman Stein wrote a brilliant commentary that deserves to be published."

As sincere as the Rabbi sounded, Jake didn't buy it. "What's so important about *that* commentary? There are plenty of others available today."

"It's very sad indeed, Reb Yankel, or is it *Jake* now?" the Rabbi said as he repeatedly stroked his beard, looking upward as he spoke. "It pains me to see how far you've strayed. You don't seem to appreciate the works of a true Orthodox Scholar. Of *course,* there are other commentaries. Some were authored by non-Jews, and others by Conservative Jews. Herman's was the only one written by an Orthodox Jew. He consulted prominent *Orthodox* scholars on the slightest details, ensuring nothing deviated from Orthodox interpretations. You raised my hopes of finding it when you asked about it. It was a gem. Now, apparently, it remains lost."

Rabbi Skumansky distracted Jake long enough to miss Marsha's exit from the restroom, but he managed to catch a glimpse of her rounding the corner toward the elevators. He couldn't help but wonder if the move had been deliberate. He missed the elevator Marsha stepped into but caught the next one seconds later.

* * * * *

Marsha was relieved things turned out this well. She fulfilled her obligation to Rabbi Skumansky without wasting too many otherwise billable hours. Plus, she enjoyed watching Jake and Mindy sweat it out today. Mindy got the scare of her life, and Jake now surely understood that Marsha Rein was not a woman to mess with.

When she saw Jake emerge from the courtroom, she knew he would seek her out. But she wanted to be in control of when and where they next spoke. So, she ducked into the ladies' room and waited. She was curious to hear what Jake had to say. But she dodged him to make him wait until *she* decided otherwise.

"Just what that worm deserves," she thought.

She had fallen for him badly like she had for Mark all those years ago.

She met Mark at the firm where she worked in Cleveland. He occupied the office next to hers. At first, they just flirted and enjoyed an occasional working lunch. But Mark came to be much more than a colleague for Marsha. It was the first time the emptiness inside her was filled.

Mark treated her like a queen, and his kindness melted her heart in a way that no other man ever had.

She fell for him– *hard*.

Flirting blossomed into love, culminating in Mark's proposal six months later. She was madly in love with him and shared that with only two people-- her therapist and her best friend, Laurie Smilow.

Laurie still lived in Chicago, but they faithfully maintained their childhood friendship remotely. Marsha spoke with her at least once a week.

Laurie promised to spend the week before the

wedding with Marsha in Cleveland.

Marsha anticipated it being the most fun they'd enjoyed together in years.

The day before their wedding, Marsha decided to surprise Mark. He insisted they not see each other the week before the wedding. But she couldn't wait. She took a day off from work, bought a new dress, and had her hair and nails manicured. She planned an entire surprise evening down to the last detail.

She was going to give him the night of his life.

She let herself into his condo, unpacked the groceries she'd picked up, and prepared her lover's feast. Everything was going as planned, and the big moment finally arrived.

She heard him unlock the door. She killed the lights.

She uncorked the champagne in the dark, knowing Mark could hear it, then flicked on the
lights.

Then it happened– *he wasn't alone.*

He was embraced in a kiss, with *Laurie.*

Marsha felt the familiar ugly darkness rear its head deep inside her. How *could* they?

The champagne bottle sailed across the room,

barely missing Mark's head.

Marsha didn't utter a sound.

She left them standing there, still embraced. It was the last time she saw Mark. But it wasn't the last she wanted to see of Laurie.

In the flick of a light switch, Laurie had ripped her heart out *twice*. The only love of her empty, dark life, *and* her lifelong best friend, were both gone in an instant.

It took years of therapy to heal those scars. The medication helped her through it, but she hadn't loved any man since that– *until Jake*.

For years Marsha pondered the perfect way to deal with Laurie.

Then, she got wind that Laurie got engaged to a wealthy Orthodox man in Chicago.

Bingo.

The elaborate scheme she concocted would be well worth the effort. Everything went according to Marsha's plan.

She moved back to Chicago.

She convinced Laurie that she'd forgiven her-- that their friendship was more important than any man. Laurie bought it and opened up about the rich, handsome man she'd married.

She didn't care for his Orthodox ways or their right-wing wedding, which Rabbi Joseph Skumansky officiated. But she ignored all that to revel in the lavish lifestyle she rapidly became accustomed to-- a beautiful custom-built home filled with nothing but the finest furnishings that *she* hand-picked, a closetful of designer clothes, shoes, and fur coats. And, of course, the *unlimited* credit cards, a limousine, and a driver to whisk her to Magnificent Mile shopping sprees.

Her life was perfect, and Marsha knew *exactly* how to take it all away.

Everything began to unravel just as she was ready to put her scheme into play.

Laurie caught her new husband cheating and saw an even bigger opportunity. Her lawyer expected her to walk away with hush-hush settlement money well into the seven-figure range. Her cheating husband would never want his infidelity leaked to the Orthodox community's gossip mill.

But that backfired. Thinking *he* would turn the tables on *her*, he withheld her *Get*, until she signed off on a more reasonable settlement.

But he didn't know Laurie as well as he should have. She didn't give a rat's ass about a religious divorce.

She wanted the *cash*.

315

Meanwhile, Marsha improvised an alternate revenge scheme.

Marsha challenged Laurie to a familiar competition as a ruse to take her mind off her divorce woes. When they were between steadies, the two of them would see who could string a guy along without giving it up and run up the biggest tab before getting cut off.

Marsha emphasized how this would demonstrate to Laurie's ex-to-be just how little she cared about obtaining her *Get*. But, *this* time, she suggested the contest involve the opposite of the usual goal. This time they'd target an Orthodox man from the community.

Men who would have to be craftily lured across the line.

This time, the goal was to be the *first* to get an Orthodox guy into bed.

Not only would that help Laurie demonstrate she didn't need a *Get* to sleep around, but she'd be doing it with an *Orthodox* man to boot!

Marsha couldn't have devised a better trap. It was the perfect and ultimate revenge.

Laurie didn't know the ultra-Orthodox community as intimately as Marsha did.

Best of all, no one would ever point the finger back

at her. Marsha would have nothing to do with it.

Everything was progressing according to plan until Marsha met Jake. He was so much like Mark, handsome, intelligent, and kind. Yet, there was something special about him. Something that told her if she could be his, it would be forever. She wanted that more than anything.

Just when she was sure he was attached to her, along came that little red-headed bitch, *Mindy*. Once again, her man was snatched away.

She wanted them to suffer– *both of them*.

Seeing the two of them sweat out today's events had been satisfying.

After speaking with Mindy's attorney, Marsha ducked into the restroom until she figured Jake would leave.

She knew he wanted to speak with her.

When she finally emerged from the restroom, she realized she had misjudged Jake's tenacity. Rabbi Skumansky's convenient distraction was just what she needed.

She did plan on talking to Jake, but it was going to be on her own terms.

She followed the crowd exiting the elevators on the ground floor and ducked around the corner to wait.

She knew he'd be down soon.

*****

"Hey there, big boy," a sultry voice beckoned as Jake strode toward the courthouse exit. "Looking for me?"

Jake was pissed but didn't want to come across as desperate.

Mustering every ounce of charm, he replied, "Look, Marsha, I'm sorry if I hurt you when we broke up. I suppose I should have handled that better. And for that, I apologize. But using Mindy just to get revenge against me– *really*?"

"Don't flatter yourself, Jake," Marsha said. "I have no feelings for you-- there's no need for me to seek revenge. I'm simply helping out a *friend*."

"A *friend*? What *friend*?"

"The Rabbi."

"*Skumansky*? What have you got to do with him? I thought you wanted nothing to do with that community."

"Hey-- when a guy like that does a favor for me, I return the favor. Business is business, right-wing Orthodox or not."

"Rabbi Skumansky, did *you* a favor?"

"He got me this job," she replied, examining her perfectly manicured ruby-red fingernails. "He's got connections. I owe him. And besides– it would be foolish *not* to leave the door open for future opportunities. But it has nothing to do with *you*, Jake. I didn't tell you to get messed up with that woman. You *had* your chance. Now it's *too* late. I certainly don't need *you* anymore."

But Jake caught the fire in Marsha's eyes that said otherwise.

"Is that so? Just like that. You seemed pretty hot and bothered the last time I saw you."

"All a ploy, my dear. Part of the game. Nothing more."

He gave her a puzzled look. *"Game?* What the hell are you talking about?"

"Laurie Smilow and I had a little competition going-- who could be the first to bed an Orthodox guy." Marsha gnawed on a fingernail. "When I first met you, I thought I had won– you were ripe for the picking. But Laurie beat me to the punch."

"So, it *was* her and Sender Stein!" Jake concluded aloud, slamming one fist into the palm of the other.

Marsha pulled a cracked fingernail from her teeth. *"You* knew about them?"

"I heard things. Mindy had her suspicions." He was glad the conversation had taken a shift on its own toward the topic of Sender.

"The way I figure it," Marsha said, "Sender couldn't take the heat. Someone must've found out. He took the easy way out. Too bad."

"Funny," Jake said, "Sender Stein wasn't the type to care about what other people think."

"Jake, I'm surprised at you. You know the kind of pressure that community puts on a person. Some learn to shrug it off. Others literally die of embarrassment. Besides, the apple doesn't fall far from the tree."

"Oh? What do *you* know about *that*?"

"Ha, ha! Never mind. Now I've really got to run along."

Chapter Forty

Jake spent Friday trying to locate Laurie Smilow, based on Pinky's not-too-shabby hunch that she'd been the one on the roof with Sender. Even if she wasn't the pusher, she might know who was.

Directory assistance provided a Lincoln Park address.

A trip to her apartment led to a conversation with her landlord who informed Jake that she packed her bags and left with no forwarding address.

When Jake inquired exactly when that was, he learned she left the night of Sender's murder.

He left a message for Detective Roberts with this new revelation.

Jake shaved and showered, preparing to attend Friday night services.

But his plans were curtailed by a call from retired Detective Morton Wolfe– the call Roberts had told him to expect.

Jake returned the call and was promptly invited to the retired detective's Albany Park flat to discuss the Herman Stein death investigation.

It was already dark out– past sundown. *Shabbos* had

begun, which meant driving was a no-no. But Jake felt compelled to break the rules to take advantage of this opportunity.

"Second floor," a tired, deep, raspy voice called out from above. Jake climbed two flights up the creaky staircase, carpeted with what once was a pretty floral pattern. He noted the dingy walls desperately in need of fresh paint as he grasped the sticky varnished banisters to pull himself up the steep steps.

Waiting on the second landing was a gray-haired man appearing to be in his seventies, wearing a dark green cardigan over a sweat-stained undershirt. A pair of oversized loud polyester plaid pants, supported by wide, black suspenders, completed the outfit. Detective Wolfe's feet were squashed into badly worn leather slippers. Reading glasses hung from the chain strung around his neck.

The old man welcomed him eagerly, as if Jake was his first visitor in years.

"I'm so glad you came. Can I get you something? I'm afraid since my wife passed I haven't really mastered my hosting skills. But I can rustle up a mean pot of tea. My coffee's not bad either. Care for anything?"

Without waiting for Jake's reply, the detective

disappeared into the kitchen. Jake followed him, taking in the time-warped apartment that shouted modern fifties.

The musty smell drove Jake's nose into a tizzy. He dared not touch a thing for fear it would disintegrate into a giant dust-ball.

Morton, or Mort as he insisted Jake call him, busied himself with a banged-up metal teapot on the gas range. He carefully metered out two cups of water into the ancient device, then fiddled to get the gas pilot lit. After striking his way through half a matchbox, a gas fireball erupted, nearly singeing Mort's cardigan.

Jake wasn't in the mood for a hot beverage but politely said, "I'll have some *herbal* tea if you've got it."

Mort steadied the rickety pot over the flame, pointed to the cracked cushion of a kitchen chair Jake once saw in a museum once, then said, "Make yourself at home while I get the file."

He disappeared through the tiny kitchen's back door into a screened-in porch. The sight unleashed childhood memories of Jake's great-aunt's flat, not two blocks from here.

He heard Mort wrestle with a squeaky metal file cabinet drawer.

Mort returned, short of breath, and tossed an

oversized manila envelope onto the table as he sat himself across from Jake.

"I'm afraid I'm not quite in the shape I used to be. Ever since Miriam passed, I haven't been myself. Can't seem to shake it. We'd been together for thirty-three years–almost to the day. High-school sweethearts, we were. Bet you think I look a lot older than sixty-three, huh?"

Jake responded with a noncommittal gesture and pointed toward the rattling pot on the stove. "I think it's boiling now."

Mort extinguished the flame and prepared two glasses of piping hot herbal tea.

Examining the box Mort had extracted from the back of his tiny pantry, Jake wondered if the tea was older than he was.

"Now," Mort said, slowly blowing out a deep breath. "Let's talk."

He squeezed off the metal clasp gripping the manila envelope labeled *STEIN, HERMAN* in thick, black magic marker.

He slipped out an overstuffed file folder.

"It's been a lot of years, but I just can't get some of these cases out of my head. Besides, without Miriam around, it gives me something to do with my golden years.

These files I took with me when I retired keep me going. This Stein case has been officially listed and solved as a suicide. But that has always troubled me. The Medical Examiner said he ruled it a suicide after Herman's brother-in-law tried leveraging his political clout to pressure him into a natural causes ruling. But that backfired. Joe DeLaney was the M.E. back then. And *nobody* told old Joe what to do. That pressure only made him dig in *harder* to rule it a suicide."

"What made him so *sure* it *was* suicide?" Jake asked.

"Let me show you the picture that tells it all."

Fumbling through the file, he pulled out a set of large black and white glossy photos.

"It's lucky I even got these. The original file was mysteriously lost. But I managed to locate the negatives. I had these reprints made after Miriam passed on, and I also have my personal copy of the incident report."

Mort flipped through the half-dozen photos, then passed one to Jake.

"Here. This one gives you the overall idea."

Jake felt soured herbal tea back up into his mouth and jerked his head away, trying not to spit tea onto the table. He slowly regained his composure and took hold of the photo.

"You look a little green there, Jake. You alright?"

"I'll be fine. I never-- it's my first-- I just wasn't ready for it."

It was a photo of a small room with a closed door to the rear. To the right was a twin-size bed supporting an obese, fully clothed man on his back. His huge round face was clearly visible, but his beard, neck, and chest were saturated with blood, as were the sheets beneath him.

Grasped in his right hand was the handle of a long knife. Across from the bed was a desk.

"This was Herman's study," Mort explained. "According to his wife, he napped at three in the afternoon every day. Check out the desk."

Jake scanned the desk-top. There was a leather desk-pad complete with matching accessories. The wooden swivel desk chair had been pulled back away from the desk. A leather-covered pencil-cup held the usual assortment of writing implements and a pair of scissors.

There was a sloppy stack of papers off to the side.

A leather-covered ink blotter, a wood ruler, a pack of cigarettes, and a heavy brass lighter populated the rest of the desktop. On the wall, behind the desk, was a mirror through which Jake could make out the reflection of dozens of books crammed into a tiny bookcase in the corner of the room opposite the back door. The bookcase was out of camera range, but its reflection was visible in the mirror.

"Looks like a typical desk," Jake said. "What in particular were you referring to?"

Mort's face came alive as he explained, "The *note*– look at the *note*," he said excitedly, pointing to the desk pad's leather edge, under which a small strip of paper had been tucked as if someone had purposely placed it there to prevent it from blowing away.

Jake could see there was something hand-written on it, in script. "What does it say?"

"Hold on– see for yourself," Mort said as his eyes beamed.

Years vanished from his forlorn face as the detective's passion for the unsolved case pumped new life through his weary veins. Mort fished a yellowed piece of paper out from the file. The handwriting was messy, but Jake could make out the crudely formed words:

I have become the laughing stock of all peoples.

"At first, we didn't know what this meant. But it makes sense if there was something Herman became overly embarrassed about and couldn't face the community. The *frustrating* part was that no one would talk—all those people living in a fish-bowl like that. *Somebody* had to know *something*. But they wouldn't breathe a *word* to me. I understand being in a community and not liking to talk to outsiders. But I'm Jewish too– am I not part of the community too? I'm no Orthodox right-winger, to be sure, but they made me feel like a goddamn Nazi."

"Old Joe latched onto that note and the fact that Herman was found with the knife in a position consistent with having slit his own throat while lying in bed. There were no fingerprints on the knife other than Herman's."

"So, what *is* it that makes you suspect it was anything *but* suicide, Mort?"

"It isn't any one thing specifically. Maybe more of a gut feeling than anything else. But take the note, for instance. It's *strange*, don't you think?"

"Well, like you said, maybe he did something he was terribly embarrassed about. Now that I think about it, Rabbi Skumansky claims Herman molested a young girl. That might be why the community clammed up. A scandal like that in the Orthodox community-- and we're talking how many years ago? Yeah, I could see that happening. So, he wrote that he was too embarrassed to go on. *Where's* the problem?"

"You've got a lot to learn if you want to be a real

detective, young man. It's not what he wrote or why he wrote it. It's the *way* he wrote it."

"Look carefully at that piece of paper."

Jake carefully examined the slip of yellowed paper. It was a thin strip of paper. It appeared to have been cut from a larger sheet of blank paper.

"Don't you think it's *strange*," Mort impatiently asked, "that he used such a *tiny* strip of paper to write the last statement of his life? Now me, I'd wanna write it on a big gigantic poster, so it would be sure to be seen. I mean, isn't that the whole point of a note-- to announce to the world, or at least to your loved ones, *why* you felt compelled to take your own life?"

"And yet, Herman chooses to use a little tiny strip of paper? I didn't buy it then, and I still don't buy it now."

"Maybe he was just habitually cheap," Jake suggested, recalling his wealthy great-aunt's obsession with recycling pop cans for a nickel a pound and stockpiling hundreds of dry-cleaning safety pins. "I've seen people save every last scrap of everything. Or, maybe he was torn, half of him not wanting the note to be found."

"Look at the stack of papers on the desk," Mort insisted. "There were plenty of unused blank sheets sitting *right* there. If he knew he was about to die, he wouldn't

329

hesitate to use one of those."

Mort shook his head, "No. It just doesn't add up for me. Plus– there's *more*. The words, Jake– who says *I have become the laughing stock of all peoples*? It just doesn't sound like something a person would naturally write to convey their embarrassment as the reason they were about to take their own life."

Mort continued, "I kept searching for a way to make sense of it all. Eventually, I went back to re-interview the widow, *Elaine* Stein. This time she mentioned that Herman wrote some kind of Hebrew book he wanted to publish. He wrote the entire thing by hand. She showed me the manuscript and *bingo*! One of the pages had a piece missing– looked like it was cut out, and this little note matched perfectly. Unfortunately, I can't show it to you now. The case had already been closed, so I couldn't confiscate it as evidence, and she refused to part with it. She got all sentimental-like. She probably still has it for all I know."

"I doubt she has it," Jake said. "Rabbi Skumansky thought I somehow had it. Said he was looking to make sure it got published. I doubt I was the first person he asked. He *must* have checked with Sender's mom before asking *me*."

"So, there's no mystery about the *source* of the tiny paper note," Jake added. "But it is *odd* to leave a suicide note that way. Unless–. Unless there was foul play!"

"*Precisely!*" Mort's eyes lit up like the fourth of July. "Now you're getting the hang of it, Jake."

Seeing he was on a roll, he continued. "Herman's manuscript was a commentary on the Book of *Eicha*. He would have used the original Hebrew text for reference, but those words– *that* phrase, is an exact *English* translation of one of its Hebrew passages."

"If someone wanted it to look like a *genuine* suicide note and knew about the manuscript, it would be a near-perfect solution. It sort of says the right thing, and it *is* in Herman's own handwriting."

"So…," Jake said, drifting into deep thought. After a short pause, he began counting the ideas aloud on his fingers as they crystallized. "*First*, the killer had to know Herman was writing a commentary on the Book of *Eicha*. *Second*, they had to be intimately familiar with the contents of the Book of *Eicha*. *Third*, they'd have to know that Herman wrote it *by hand*. *Fourth*, they must have had access to it. And *fifth*, they must have had access to Herman's study at the *time* he was napping."

"Jake– I'm *impressed*! You'll make a *fine* detective,

young man!"

Jake thought Mort was going to pinch the life out of his cheek right then and there, as he asked Mort, "Didn't you go back to Joe, the Medical Examiner, with that information?"

"I did, but the case had already been closed. As far as he was concerned, it wasn't enough on its own to contradict his suicide ruling. Once old Joe locked onto that suicide ruling, I don't think he would have changed his mind if I had a murder confession on the table."

They sat quietly for a moment as Jake finished his herbal tea, despite his reservations about its expiration date. He picked up the photo of Herman's death, still out on the table, then asked Mort for the rest of the set. As he flipped through them, he realized they were all just different angles of the same room. Nothing new.

Then Jake noticed something in one photo.

"What's *that*, down there, Mort? Looks like shoes covered with something." Jake squinted and took a closer look. "The shoes are covered with a *yarmulke*."

"That was another odd thing," Mort explained. "According to the widow Stein, Herman always lay down for a nap precisely at three every afternoon. He had a very set routine. First, he removed his shoes and placed them neatly on the floor, then slipped off his yarmulke and placed it over them. Then, he laid down for his nap. Once he was out, she said he snored loudly until he woke at four."

"That day, she remembers seeing him go through his routine, and then sometime later, hold on–," Mort said as he flipped through the incident report, "Here it is. She heard him start snoring at around ten after three. So, he was definitely alive until then. Old Joe put the time of death between ten after three and four. If he always rose at four and he was definitely alive and asleep at three ten, doesn't it seem strange for him to take his nap and *then* wake up to *kill* himself?"

"What's more," Jake added, "is this all points to someone killing Herman during his nap time, meaning it also had to be someone that knew Herman's napping schedule!"

Chapter Forty-One

Shabbos morning was Adam's *Bar Mitzvah*. There was a nice turnout and Mindy busied herself greeting and chatting with guests at the small reception following the service. Afterwards, Jake joined Mindy and her children for the lavish luncheon Mrs. Stein insisted on hosting, in the gymnasium of the Bernard Horwich Jewish Community Center.

The non-stop stream of people flowing in seemed as if the entire Orthodox community had been invited. Mindy wanted Adam's affair to be small and intimate– family only. But Mrs. Stein insisted on a big public affair. They compromised by keeping the service and reception small, but hosting this big luncheon afterward.

The luncheon was an open house style, all on Mrs. Stein's tab. The feast consisted of a huge buffet and an open bar. The buffet tables ran from one end of the regulation sized gym to the other, surrounded by banquet tables and chairs. A bar had been set up near the doors leading to the hallway. One wall was lined with sweet tables draped with white tablecloths to protect the delicacies from being devoured by any early-birds.

Marvin Fox was off to one side of the room in a

heated discussion with a short, hunchbacked elderly man, bearing a long white beard, and a dusty black hat.

The buffet line was packed and people inched forward circling around the tables. But the line at the bar was almost non-existent.

Jake made a bee-line for the bar and ordered a Ginger Ale. He nursed his soft-drink while circling the buffet to preview what might be left for him once the vultures dissipated.

There were enormous bowls of hot *cholent*, an endless train of silver platters overflowing with roast chicken, stuffed Cornish hens, *kishka*, farfel, a choice of chicken noodle or mushroom-barley soup served in thick mugs, roast beef, rice pilaf, and scalloped potatoes swimming in an ocean of oozing margarine.

Tuxedo-clad waiters circulated rapidly proffering trays of faux pigs in a blanket, potato puffs, and stuffed mushroom caps. This only served to drive the crowd wild as they swarmed to grab wildly at the trays. Some had to make split-second decisions between their choice spots in the buffet line or risking it all for a grab at the mobile delicacies.

When Jake spotted a wheelchair spinning around the room, he knew the guest list had been exhaustingly complete.

The familiar faux-invalid sped past him, tipping a hello with his crumpled black hat on his way to the bar. He scowled at the bartender waving him off like he was chasing away a thousand bats. He grabbed a bottle of Smirnoff, slipped a little flask out of his pocket, and carefully poured himself a drink. He skillfully maneuvered his vehicle over to the buffet tables and grasped at the sparse remains of a roast chicken platter. He then roped Mindy's nine-year-old son, Daniel, into filling a brown paper bag he handed the boy with anything he could get his hands on. When Daniel faithfully returned with the bag full, he produced another and asked Daniel to repeat the procedure at the covered sweet table.

Jake heard Daniel admonish the grimy man, "Bubbie said no deserts until *after* the meal!" The young boy then escaped, joining a brood of children chasing each other like chickens.

Jake watched as the bearded, half-gloved, middle-aged man studied the crowd, largely seated at the round tables filling the room, intimately involved with their own feasts and conversations.

He slowly rolled his wheelchair up to the covered sweet tables, and quickly popped out of the chair, slid his hands underneath the tablecloth, and proceeded to fill the bag himself.

Jake wondered which of the children would get blamed for that.

Mindy interrupted Jake's musings with a jab to his ribs, "That's someone we should speak to, Jake," she whispered in his ear. "He worked with Sender's father in the slaughterhouse. I think his name is Sidney. I can't get away now, but *you* can."

Jake wanted to refuse, but she gave him her best puppy-dog eyes and it was all over before he knew what hit him.

"You'd better do it now. The speeches will start soon."

Jake introduced himself to Sidney, "Mindy tells me you knew Adam's grandfather. There's something I'd like to ask you. Would you mind sharing a few minutes with me, perhaps somewhere a little quieter?"

Sidney agreed and followed Jake across the hall and into the empty arts and crafts room. Jake squatted on a kiddie-chair after offering Sydney the only adult-sized chair in the room. He improvised and embellished, explaining that things were getting serious with Mindy and he wanted to learn more about her family's background.

He asked Sydney what he might know about Herman's influence on Sender.

Sidney obliged. "Oh, I doubt Herman had much influence on Sender. He died when Sender was an infant."

Jake shifted the topic momentarily, talking about the lavish affair Mrs. Stein was hosting for the entire community. "I guess Herman put away a few dollars before he went," Jake supposed.

That struck a chord.

"You know, I really never really forgave Herman, even after *all* these years," Sydney said.

"Never forgave him? For *what*?"

"Well, it's not that I'm complaining, you understand. I make a decent living, I provide for my wife and children, and support two sons-in-laws studying for *S'micha*," he proudly added. "Herman and I started our jobs as a *Shochet* the same day, at Henderson's slaughterhouse, on the Southside. The FDA shut them down over thirty years ago. But until then, that slaughterhouse was booming. The Henderson family fortune was built on that business. Herman and I did okay. We made a nice living, but not enough to ever make us wealthy. Herman and I would share opportunities that came along now and then to make a little extra money. Substituting for a sick or vacationing

338

Shochet on our days off, taking odd jobs as a *Mashgiach*, supervising the food prep at a wedding or Bar Mitzvah.

"One day Herman tells me he's leaving the job. Just like *that*. Said he acquired a Shalomski restaurant franchise. Now, I *know* how much Herman made. He had a wife and kids. He wasn't a big spender and neither was Mrs. Stein, but there's no *way* he could have saved up the fifty-thousand-dollar down payment. I know how much it was because afterward *I* inquired about a franchise for myself. I thought if Herman could do it, so could I. Sure, he had family connections. But I know his brother-in-law well enough to know he wouldn't just waive a fifty-thousand-dollar fee for anyone, *especially* not Herman. He didn't care much for Herman. So, I knew he must have come up with the money *somehow*. I was angry at him for leaving me behind the way he did. You'd think he'd at least offer his long time chum a position with his new big-shot enterprise. After that, he wouldn't say two words to me. But that's okay by me. Look where it got him. Six feet under is where it got him. No sir, I'm glad l kept my little career. Now, thank God, I can enjoy my family."

Jake played dumb and asked, "you said he had family connections. What did you mean by that?"

"His brother-in-law, of course. Marvin. Surely you

know Marvin. Marvin Fox-- Mr. Shalomski himself. But he wouldn't have given Herman the time of day, let alone a restaurant franchise worth fifty-thousand for nothing. Marvin hated Herman. Couldn't stand the man. Was angry at his sister just for being married to him."

Chapter Forty-Two

Jake returned to the buffet luncheon surprised to find Rabbi Skumansky addressing the crowd. The man certainly had balls. Jake was so absorbed in his disgust that he only half-heard the Rabbi drone on about the wonderful Stein family and his blessings for Adam's future.

After attempting to help take Mindy's children from her, he couldn't fathom how Skumansky could show his face at Adam's Bar Mitzvah, let alone *speak*.

Mindy seemed to be taking it all in stride. She leaned over to Jake's ear. "How'd it go with Sidney? Did you learn anything?"

"Yes, but nothing really conclusive," Jake replied. "There was something about what he said that just didn't sit right with me. But for the life of me, I can't put my finger on it."

After Mindy bid the last well-wisher good-bye, Jake escorted her and the kids home. The younger two children ran ahead, raced to the end of each block, then waited at the corners until they all crossed together. Adam lagged behind, dragging his feet.

They reached Albion and were just about to turn off California, when a voice called out from across the street.

"*Jake*! Good *Shabbos*!"

Jake spun on his heels to see Rabbi Miklin crossing the street, waving a hand. They exchanged greetings and chatted. Mindy gave Adam the key and he led the younger children to their apartment while Jake and Mindy spoke with the Rabbi.

"How's your little *problem* at the office?" Jake asked, wondering if Rabbi Miklin had plugged the leak after he'd tipped him off that Rabbi Diamond was involved with Skumansky and was most-likely the mole he was looking for.

"Oh, yes. I meant to call you. We did indeed confirm the leak was our court clerk, Rabbi Gavriel Diamond, as you suggested. We checked the files and found he'd even been present at *your Get*, Mindy. He probably overheard the accusations Sender made about you when he first approached me and passed that along to Rabbi Skumansky. I wouldn't be surprised if Sender went to see Rabbi Skumansky, repeated his story, and possibly received some guidance from him. That's more than likely why Rabbi Skumansky feels compelled to pursue his mission of separating your children from you. How *are* things on that front?"

Mindy and Jake told of Skumansky's attempt to

testify with the help of Marsha Rein, and his failure in that regard.

"Rabbi, if you have a moment, I'd like to discuss something with you...," Jake said, then glanced at Mindy as he added, "privately. Mindy, do you mind?"

"Not at all. Will you join us afterward, Jake?"

"Sure thing. I won't be long."

That night Jake caught his first good night of sleep in a long time. He finally had a plan of action.

Chapter Forty-Three

Early Sunday morning, Jake wolfed down a batch of scrambled egg whites and a tall glass of O.J., then set out on phase one of his mission.

Rabbi Gavriel Diamond was an early riser. Seven o'clock Sunday morning, and he'd already returned from an early morning service. He was finishing breakfast when Jake arrived. The Rabbi graciously invited him into the kitchen corner of his tiny studio apartment.

Guiding him to a seat at the table, he offered Jake a bite to eat.

Jake declined. He didn't want to take a chance in upsetting the delicate balance of acid and scrambled eggs in his stomach. He needed to keep his nerve and maintain an even-keeled attitude for this phase of the plan.

"I'd really rather get right to the point of my visit," Jake said.

"Ah, yes. And what *is it* I can do for you this morning?" Gavriel inquired, flashing a small mirror before his face, plucking a few microscopic crumbs from his white beard and mustache.

"After our brief meeting at the Illinois Rabbinical Board's offices, I inquired and learned that you are employed there as a legal secretary."

"Legal *clerk*," he corrected, glancing abruptly away from the mirror. "But do go on." He resumed his grooming routine.

"You're also under the employ of Rabbi Skumansky's *Beis Din*."

Rapid eye movements.

A return to the beard and mustache ritual.

"*Go on.*"

"Mindy and Sender Stein had their *Get* officiated at the Illinois Rabbinical Board's *Beis Din*, despite Sender's insistence on using Rabbi Skumansky."

Acting on Rabbi Miklin's hunch, Jake moved in for his first line of attack.

"Shortly afterward, Sender was advised by Rabbi Skumansky to withhold the children from Mindy."

"What *is* your point, Reb Yankel? Oh, excuse me-- *Jake*."

"My point is, you've been stealing cases from Rabbi Miklin's court and directing them to Rabbi Skumansky."

The hand with the mirror dropped to his side.

"*Stealing*? I invite you into my home and you have the audacity to accuse me of *stealing*? Where are you getting this nonsense? There's no law against a man seeking out help wherever he can. Rabbi Miklin refused to help Sender, so he went elsewhere. You're leaping to foolish conclusions. Perhaps your absence from the *yeshiva* study-hall has finally taken its toll on you. I expected better from *you*, Reb Yankel. We *all* did. Did you really come up here at this early hour to disturb me with this ridiculous nonsense?"

Despite his smooth-talking deflection, Jake pressed on. "That's not all. I know about the *other* cases."

More rapid eye movements.

"I have no idea what you mean."

Back to the mirror.

"I know you've been systematically helping Rabbi Skumansky build his caseload by *redirecting* cases from Rabbi Miklin. You've undermined the trust placed in you. I have enough evidence to take to Rabbi Miklin."

Rabbi Miklin assured Jake they hadn't taken any action yet, or even discussed the matter with Gavriel. Jake wanted to catch Diamond before he learned they already knew.

The mirror hand dropped again.

"Whatever you *think* you've discovered doesn't bother me. Feel free to discuss these matters with Rabbi Miklin if you like. I keep no secrets. I've done nothing wrong. Rabbi Miklin already turned down the cases I referred to Rabbi Skumansky. I most certainly do not *steal* cases away from anyone. I'm quite shocked you'd even *think* that of me."

"Damn," Jake thought. "He *is* slick."

He'd diffused Jake's threat so naturally and didn't seem the least bit concerned. But Jake was too pumped to stop now.

"I *also* know you participated in beating up Pinky Greenberg and kidnapping his children. I think the police would be *very* interested in the evidence I have."

Jake wanted to be sure this punch would land, so he delivered the next line just as he'd rehearsed it the night before. "I also know you match individuals who've only received their *Get*, but no civil divorce, then arrange their bigamist weddings under Rabbi Skumansky's auspices. I may not hang around the *yeshiva* anymore, but I haven't forgotten a thing. Apparently, *you* have. Bigamy is against the law, Rabbi. It's even against Jewish law. You should know better."

The mirror dropped to the floor, shattering against the worn, yellowed tiles. Gavriel leaned over the edge of his seat, slowly bent down, and lovingly picked up the larger pieces in silence. He returned to an upright posture with the remains cradled in his hand. His now intense eyes focused directly on Jake's.

"What is it that you want from *me*? Make your point and get out. I still have errands to run this morning."

Bingo! Jake succeeded in shaking him. But the battle had only begun. Jake's hands balled up into tight fists. His pulsing shirt-buttons gave away his rapid breathing and racing heart. It was time for the grand finale.

"My point is, if you don't convince Rabbi Skumansky to back off-- stop trying to get Mindy's children away from her-- I'll report these crimes to the police, then go *straight* to the press."

He watched Gavriel's hand tighten. A trickle of blood ran down the side of his palm. He nursed the mirror-shard wound with a napkin while struggling to regulate his breathing.

"I don't expect this from *you*, Reb Yankel. You may have once been the pride and joy of the *yeshiva*, but what has become of you *now*, *Jake* Cooper? Why do you turn so angrily against Judaism?"

Jake was infuriated by his rhetoric. "I'm not turning against Judaism, I'm standing *up* for Jewish values-- for what's right and good. You can't break civil laws simply to accomplish whatever you *personally* think is right. The

Talmud clearly prohibits violating civil law. The laws of the land we live in are to be complied with, *absolutely*. As Jews, particularly as religious Orthodox Jews, we're supposed to be model citizens as an example for others to emulate. Yet you undermine all that, breaking laws as you please."

"You are making a *foolish* mistake, Jake Cooper. God's word is our utmost concern. No matter what the laws of any state, we cannot violate *His* command."

"What's that got to do with having a gun held to Pinky's head and kidnapping his children? What *holy command* were you fulfilling that justified violating Pinky and his kids that way?"

"If you must know, Pinky Greenberg was leading his children astray from Judaism. He wasn't acting like an *Orthodox* Jew. He went places an Orthodox Jew shouldn't go, dressed in inappropriate clothing, wore no black hat, and prayed at *questionable synagogues*. He was teaching this to his children by example! The law of the land cannot stand in the way of protecting Jewish children!"

Jake was not only angry at his absurd comments-- he was ashamed. Ashamed to have ever been associated with the likes of Diamond and his corrupt mentality. "And how did you *determine* that Pinky was teaching his children anything but–"

"This is futile," Jake thought. There is no arguing with a man who openly states that Pinky shouldn't see his children just because he didn't wear a black hat, or act the way he *thought* an Orthodox Jew ought to. As if Gavriel Diamond has a monopoly on the definition of an Orthodox Jew-- as if Orthodoxy has a monopoly on the definition of a *Jew*!

There was no arguing with this insanity. There was only one thing left to say.

"Look. It's very simple. I'll report you for kidnapping and each and every case of bigamy you and Rabbi Skumansky participated in. I have it all documented. Everything is recorded in detail. Dates, names, locations, sworn statements-- I have it *all*."

He bought Jake's bluff.

Gavriel lost it, his calm demeanor now that of a mad dog.

"Have you lost your *mind*? You're going to report *The Rav* and myself to the *police*! Think what you're saying. Surely you haven't forgotten the punishment for a *moser*. To turn another Jew over to non-Jewish authorities is *forbidden*! A Jew cannot turn in another Jew-- you *know* this! If you did such a thing-- and God-forbid you should--

you'd give our *Beis Din* no choice but to excommunicate you. You know what that *means*? Do you have any idea how serious that is? Think about what you're *doing* here!"

Jake replied calmly, "Frankly, I don't care about being excommunicated by Rabbi Skumansky's *Beis Din*. He may have followers that will comply, but the people I now associate with won't give a *damn* about *his* excommunication order."

Jake could see a vein in Gavriel's neck begin to throb. He shook his bloody fist in the air. "If you do this, we can sentence you to *death*! You're talking about something *extremely* serious!"

This wasn't a threat Jake took lightly. He *knew* what they were capable of.

Mustering his last ounce of bravery, he cocked one eye, put on his best pit-bull face, and leaned over the kitchen table, staring directly into Gavriel's eyes. "I'll hold off for a *very* short while. But you *will* help me with Rabbi Skumansky-- he's *got* to *stop* going after Mindy's children."

Jake stood up abruptly, sending his chair flying backward, smashing it into the fridge, then added, "And if there's any more talk of excommunication or physical violence, you *will* be arrested. Everything is documented. If anything happens to me, others have instructions to take this information directly to Detective Roberts of the Chicago Police Department."

Jake let himself out in an outwardly calm fashion. But the moment he exited the building, his entire body began trembling uncontrollably.

There was no turning back now.

Chapter Forty-Four

Pinky finally cashed in their lottery ticket and set himself and Jake up with an investment advisor who assured them they'd both be comfortable well into their old age. Jake wasted no time in quitting his job, leaving his schedule wide open for phase two.

The lunch hour was in full swing when Jake entered Shalomski's. The sounds of clanking utensils, wait-staff barking orders to the kitchen, and a dish crashing against the bricked floor, followed by a mocking Mazel Tov, filled the air.

Instead of shedding light on Herman's death, Sidney left Jake more puzzled than ever, and Jake had a hunch Marvin Fox could put the pieces together.

Making his way past the bathrooms, he located a door marked Private. He knocked briefly, cracked open the door and took the seat Marvin waved him into while wrapping up a call with a supplier.

Jake got right to the point.

Marvin's smile vanished as if the eleventh plague had arrived. "What do you mean, *how*?"

"I mean how could Herman afford the franchise fee? I hear it was pretty steep. You didn't just give him a franchise free and clear, did you? You didn't exactly get along with him."

Marvin rubbed his chin and examined his watch. "He was my sister's husband. Why *shouldn't* I help out my own sister?"

"So, you just *gave* him a franchise? Just like *that*?" Jake asked, snapping his fingers.

"Let's just say Herman was smart enough to figure out how to *get* one."

"And how was *that*?"

Marvin's eyes roamed the ceiling searching the water-stained tiles for the answer. "He *leveraged* his way into the business."

"You mean he took out a loan?"

"Look," Marvin snapped, sliding his reading glasses to the tip of his nose, tilting his head forward and staring down, "why are you poking around about Herman Stein? He's long dead and gone. And now, so is Sender. Leave it alone."

His face reddened as he adjusted his black velvet *yarmulke*.

"Mindy's no longer being charged with anything, so why do you persist sticking your nose where it doesn't belong? Let me give you some advice, young man. Don't look for trouble. Enough comes your way in life without looking for it."

If there was trouble behind the questions Jake was asking, he knew there were answers too. Jake knew he was on the right track, but he had no idea where it led. It was time to grab the bull by both horns and hang on for dear life. "Which bank did Herman borrow from?"

Marvin stared Jake straight in the eye, over the edge of his glasses.

Jake stared right back, holding back a blink. Finally, the bull subsided.

"If I tell you more, you've gotta promise two things-- hear me out completely, and don't run your mouth off about this. Can you promise those two things?"

Jake nodded. "You have my solemn word," he said, holding up one hand.

Marvin took a long, deep, drag on the cigarette that had been smoldering in the ashtray on his paper-laden desk, beside a half-empty pack of Winston's. He slowly let out a stream of smoke trailing right up Jake's nose. Jake felt his lunch backing up into his throat, but swallowed hard and tried to relax.

Marvin stood abruptly, opened the partly closed office door, checked the tiny hallway, then shut the door.

Sinking back into his leather chair he leaned forward, parked his elbows square on the desk and laced his hands together.

"Herman originally worked as a *Shochet*. He did that for many years, before Shalomski's was even conceived. On one of his days off, Herman filled in for a vacationing *Shochet* at another slaughterhouse that happened to be *my* meat supplier at the time– they've since closed. You probably don't know this, but at the time they had an excellent reputation. Every faction of the right-wing community accepted their meat as *glatt* kosher– the ultimate level of kosher– without question. You know how it is, everyone's gotta be stricter than the other. It's ridiculous, of course. You wouldn't *believe* the politics-- or maybe you would. The base of my business is from the black-hat Orthodox community. Just about everyone eats by me.

"The following week, Herman comes into my office and slams the door shut like he owns the place. I remember like it was yesterday. Had this big grin on his face. Made himself comfortable in *my* chair-- this very one," Marvin said, stabbing the arm of his chair with his finger. "Puts his feet up on the desk and tells me I'm gonna *give* him a franchise. I laughed, of course. He got angry-- had a wild temper, that animal did. I said, 'I'll *sell* you one, if you've got the cash. But I'm not *giving* you anything.' Herman said he had something *better* than cash. He insisted that if I didn't give him a franchise he'd tell everyone the *glatt* kosher meat I was serving wasn't genuine. Now, of course, I was serving *glatt*, as advertised. But what most people don't know is that there are two kinds of *glatt*. One is considered the purest *glatt,* without question– the kind where no lesions are found. The other has lesions but is still considered *glatt* as long as they can be removed without leaving a hole. The slaughterhouse *I* bought from was selling the latter."

Jake knew exactly what Marvin was referring to. The practice of accepting an animal as *glatt* kosher even though it had lesions that could be removed was introduced about a century ago, meeting with heavy resistance at first but eventually widely accepted.

Jake thought about that for a moment, then asked, "Why did Herman think you'd care if he made it known you were using that type of *glatt*? Everyone uses it now. Most people aren't even aware there's a difference."

"Jake, you've obviously forgotten your black-hat *yeshiva* days. Back then the *bulk* of my business was black-hatters. The slightest hint of a scandal, legitimate or not--

357

who would be the first to set foot in my place and eat after that? Who'd risk facing the gossip and finger-pointing? The *yenta*-gram machine lets everyone know everybody else's business. Anyone walks in my place after that– the whole community's gonna know before they finish ordering! If Herman spread that around, no one would have dared come to eat by me. *These* days I'm not so vulnerable. I get a mostly Modern-Orthodox crowd that doesn't care about that nonsense. But back then, I'd have been out of business overnight."

After a moment he added, "That doesn't mean this information needs to get around. I expect you to keep this to yourself. Anyone wants to know which *type* of *glatt* I serve, let them ask me. Over thirty years– not a single inquiry," he added, shaking an upright finger.

Jake had no intention of blabbing this minor detail around town. That didn't bother him. But something else *did*. "So, you gave Herman a free franchise in exchange for keeping his mouth shut?"

"It's not a crime, *is it*?"

He took a moment to let Marvin's story sink in. Something didn't add up. "So, you're telling me, Herman blackmailed you into giving him a free franchise, and then after he got it and made all kinds of money, he goes and *kills* himself? That makes no sense."

Marvin folded his arms and leaned forward heavily on the desk. "Look, I gave you the answer to what you were after. Why do you insist on digging up more old dirt? Let it rest, Jake."

But Jake ignored the request. Thoughts raced through his head faster than he could verbalize them. Suddenly he realized that the answer might be sitting right before him.

"No, really. I can't understand Herman killing himself *then*. I met Morton Wolfe, the detective who investigated Herman's death. He *never* bought the suicide ruling."

Without considering the consequences, Jake continued his thinking aloud, "Now, that would make sense if someone *killed* him and made it *look* like suicide. Maybe someone Herman was...*blackmailing*?"

Marvin shook a fist as he barked, "Look here. Making wild accusations will get you nowhere fast. Just who the *hell* do you think you *are*?"

Despite the barking, Jake saw fear in Marvin's eyes. Running on pure adrenaline, he decided to play this to the hilt. Jake leaned back, crossed his legs, and laced his hands above his head. He stared at the ceiling tiles Marvin extracted his information from earlier.

"Seems to *me,* an innocent man wouldn't get so jumpy about this. I'm sure Detective Wolfe would be very interested to learn about Herman's blackmail scheme. Might give him a new lead, don't you *think?*"

Marvin buried his head in his arms.

Slowly sitting upright, he rubbed his face with both hands, as if washing up in the morning. "*Vey is mir. Vey, Vey, Vey.*" He let out several deep sighs. "Alright, look. If I tell you more, it's only for your ears-- *understood?* There's no reason to spread this around. You'll see what I mean when I tell you. Innocent people can get hurt. It's very sensitive. Far more sensitive than the *glatt* issue."

"Sorry," Jake said. "No promises this time. I'll have to decide after I hear it."

Chapter Forty-Five

After a long pause Marvin began his tale. His voice now sounded like that of a defeated warrior. "There was trouble in the family. My sister wanted everything to look okay to the outside world. She kept her secret for a long time. But sooner or later it was *bound* to come out."

"One day, after closing up, I took some leftovers to my sister. It was something I often did, despite my distaste for Herman. It saved my sister the trouble of cooking and the food would have gone to waste anyhow. I serve everything made fresh every day-- no leftovers. That's one of my secrets to success. I also give leftovers to a few street people who come by around closing time. Anyhow, that day, I parked in the alley behind her apartment. I carried the box up the back staircase and knocked on her back door. No one answered. I pressed the buzzer and then I heard...," Marvin took a deep breath, let it out slowly with his eyes closed and finished, "...a scream. Then another. I didn't have a key but I tried the door. It was unlocked. The screams were coming from Malke's room."

"Who's Malke?"

"You don't-- Mindy didn't--. Well, of course-- even *Sender* probably didn't know. We never mentioned it. *I* never told him. *Elaine* may not have either. Malke is Sender's older sister."

Suddenly, something clicked in Jake's mind. "That's it!" he realized. "That's what Sydney said that didn't sit right. He said that Herman had a wife and kids-- *plural*! Now it made sense."

Marvin continued, "I went in through the back room. I could see my sister through the hallway, nursing Sender in a rocking chair in the living room. The screams came from behind the closed door of Malke's bedroom. I rushed toward my sister and asked what was going on. I'll never forget the look on her tortured face. She just sat there, cuddling Sender with one arm, holding out an open, pleading palm, her mouth opened wide, but words just wouldn't come. The doctors said she was *physically* fine, but she was never the same after that. If only I'd never--." Marvin lowered his face into his cupped hands, breathed deeply into them. "The screams didn't stop. I burst into Malke's room. Herman was-- it was-- *horrible*. I wish more than anything that I could erase that from my mind. To tell you the truth I did nearly kill him *right* then and there-- at least I *wanted* to. That *monster*! What he did to that beautiful, innocent child-- she'll never fully recover from that kind of damage."

Jake's adrenaline rush was a faint memory now. He was embarrassed, *ashamed* even, that he'd intruded into this private family matter in his quest. But there was no turning back. He thought about this unknown sister, tried to picture what she might look like. Then he remembered the picture Mindy had spoken of. The one she'd thought was that of Mrs. Stein as a young girl, parked on Mrs. Stein's night stand. Perhaps it was a photo of Malke, who probably looked a lot like her mother.

After a short period, Jake broke the silence. "How come no one ever said anything? Mindy doesn't even know Malke *exists*. Why all the secrecy?"

"Elaine *begged* me not to say anything, for Malke's sake, and her own. The shame it would have brought on them. She was afraid, and rightly so. If it got out, Malke would never find a match. Elaine convinced herself that Herman meant no harm– it was just his way of expressing his love for his daughter. My stomach still turns just talking about it. *Vey is mir.* I thought these feelings had long been buried with Herman."

Jake was feeling less impressed with himself.

Marvin continued, "Elaine insisted Herman would stop now that I knew about it. She promised he'd get help– *pleaded* with me not to say anything. What good would

363

come from everyone knowing, she begged? Perhaps it was a mistake, but I kept my mouth shut."

Despite Jake's sensitivity to his pain, his curiosity just wouldn't stop, "So what happened to Herman?"

Marvin indulged him.

"After that incident, I kept quiet about it, though I didn't think anything had really changed. Part of me didn't want to know. I didn't *ask*, Elaine didn't *tell*. She still won't. I'll never know for sure. My sister is so messed up in her head now that sometimes, I'm not sure *she* even knows what happened.

"Herman got his franchise up and running smoothly. But his greed knew no bounds. It was a Thursday-- a humid, stormy, summer day. I'd stopped by after running errands on Devon to visit with Elaine. She'd progressively slipped further into her own little world and I found myself spending more time with her than I could really afford. But she's my *sister*. Who else did she have? Once the restaurant was up and running, Herman spent most of his time at home, letting his staff run the joint. Whenever I visited, he secluded himself in his study in the back room. Elaine claimed Herman was working on some kind of book. I had to walk through his study on my way out the back door– I usually parked in the back. He usually stuck his nose in a book without so much as a grunt in my direction. That was fine with me. I had no desire to speak with the man, nor see his ugly mug. We rarely encountered each other. When we did, we either exchanged mumbled greetings for Elaine's sake, or flashed angry glances at each other.

"But on *this* day, Herman stopped me and began chatting, at first in a friendly tone. It took me by surprise. He explained that he'd been writing this manuscript. Then his tone changed. He *demanded* I finance the publication of his *Eicha* commentary. The man fancied himself a scholar. The sheer *gall* of that *schmuck*! A molesting monster like that wanting *me* to finance a *religious* work to make him look like a scholar? It was more than I could bear. I refused him outright, taking a whack at the manuscript he was holding and sent it flying. Herman went ballistic, swore he'd tell everyone that *his* was the only Shalomski's franchise serving legitimate *glatt*, even though I tried pressuring him to use the cheaper *glatt* that we serve in all the locations."

"So, you *killed* him?"

Marvin hung his head low. "Not exactly."

Jake waited for more.

"I *do* feel responsible, in a way. But to be perfectly

honest, I haven't the slightest regret. The man got what he deserved. I lied and told him that I had already switched to serving the better *glatt*, and that I put the word out that he was a child molester. His face turned colors so fast, I thought he was gonna have a heart attack. Without saying a word, he shoved me out the back door and slammed the door. Somehow, I knew that was the last of Herman's outrageous demands. But I didn't expect to get that result the way I did."

"So, you're saying Herman killed himself after you told him you already spread it around that he molested his daughter?"

"I suppose the embarrassment was more than even Herman-the-monster could bear to live with. After his death, word *did* get out that he abused Malke. But *I* never told a soul. Elaine had a complete nervous breakdown after that. I thought it best for Malke to disappear from the community and start fresh somewhere else. I sent her off to live with our other sister, Hannah, in Cleveland. Hannah told everyone she was a distant cousin who'd been orphaned. She gave Malke another name. I managed to keep a lid on things here, and the rumors eventually died down after I repeatedly denied them. It was Malke's only chance to grow up without that stigma following her around for the rest of her life."

Marvin slouched back in his chair, rubbing his forehead with his thumb and forefinger repeatedly. He opened a drawer from an old oak dresser to his left, pulled out two shot glasses and a bottle of Krupnik.

"Care for some? It's good stuff-- the *best*." Marvin twirled the bottle in front of me as he read the label, "*Vodka, honey, water, vanilla, nutmeg, cinnamon, cloves, and lemon peel*. Some people like it hot, but I like mine room temperature."

Jake politely declined.

Marvin poured himself a full glass. *"Now* you understand why I ask you to keep this quiet, don't you? Malke *still* hasn't married. Spreading any of this around would gain nothing. It would only hurt Malke. It would all be for nothing, nothing at all. It wouldn't help you or Mindy in any way. I *beg* of you, Jake, *please*."

Jake had no intention of unnecessarily repeating this, but obviously Marvin was very concerned and Jake tried to take advantage of that.

"Maybe we can help each other," he said. "You remember when I asked you about Skumansky and Fogal?"

Marvin downed a shot of Krupnik, winced, then responded, "Yes."

"And you know Rabbi Gavriel Diamond, *don't you?*"

"Sure, I know who he is. What of it?"

Jake explained how Rabbi Skumansky attempted to testify and get Mindy's kids away from her.

Marvin didn't seem the least bit surprised.

Marvin had stepped in after Pinky had been beaten, so Jake knew he was connected with this bunch. He thought he might enlist Marvin's help, now that he had him over a barrel.

"I can't help you there," Marvin responded. "You're going down a dead-end street, Jake."

"How can you be so sure without even *trying*?"

"Those characters have a three-way *arrangement—*." Marvin winced off another shot of Krupnik. "I think we've opened enough wounds for one day, Mr. Cooper. Have you no compassion?"

He knew Marvin was right. But his unquenchable thirst for the truth blinded him to the man's pain. "What am I becoming?" Jake wondered. He didn't know if he liked this new side of himself.

He thanked Marvin for his candor and apologized for the buried pains he'd resurfaced. He shook his hand, went to the door, then abruptly swung back around.

"Just one more question, Marvin." Jake just couldn't help himself. "Besides the gossipers, who actually *knew* that Herman abused Malke?"

"Other than Elaine and myself, absolutely no one, except Malke herself, and my sister Hannah, of course. We kept it *very* tight-lipped. That was key to Malke's fresh start. If word had spread, it would have followed her to the ends of the earth."

Jake thanked Marvin and left.

As he coaxed his sputtering Nova home, he mulled over their conversation.

Marvin's explanation certainly rationalized Herman committing suicide. But the inconsistencies remained to be explained. Could Marvin have killed Herman and simply explained it away as suicide? If he did, he was one hell of an actor.

Marvin's comment about the three-way arrangement between Skumansky, Diamond and Fogal made him wonder what dirt was being swept under *their* carpets?

Even more puzzling was Rabbi Skumansky's confident statements about Herman doing something terrible to a young girl. That didn't sound like repeated gossip. It sounded like he was *certain*. Like a man speaking with conviction.

But if Marvin Fox was so sure about their tight-lipped code of silence, how could Rabbi Skumansky *know*?

Chapter Forty-Six

Absentmindedly cracking a sunflower-seed between his teeth, Rabbi Skumansky's tongue guided the tiny seed to one side of his mouth and the empty, salty shell to the other.

After extracting the salty flavor, his fingers slid reflexively across his lips, snatching the shell as his tongue expelled it and deposited it in the ashtray on his desk.

Leaning back into his leather chair, he wondered about Reb Yankel Cooper-- *Jake* Cooper.

What could transform such a quiet, naive boy into the fierce menace he'd become? Was it perhaps his desire to protect his girlfriend, Mindy?

He knew all too well how a woman could lure a man. Still, there was no choice now.

Jake Cooper *had* to be dealt with.

He had no idea what was in store for him. The situation demanded appropriate and swift action, within the framework of Jewish law. Jake threatened to go to the authorities about serious matters. Matters that were left to the community to deal with, in its own way-- matters that *had* been dealt with appropriately, regardless of their compliance with secular laws.

If Jake carried out his threat, the answer would be simple.

But the Almighty's work had to be done, and he was the only one willing to do it. Nothing would stand in his way. Not even Jake Cooper.

Rabbi Skumansky leaned back farther in his padded, leather chair and stretched his legs beneath his tired, oak desk. He dragged one hand across his forehead, down his right cheek, and then pulled it through his beard. He repeated the process several times, as though pulling deep thoughts out of his head.

The Jake Cooper matter was a difficult one.

Turning another Jew over to secular authorities violated Jewish Law– *that* was clear. But Jake hadn't turned anyone over, *yet*. He'd only *threatened* to.

As he continued his thought-provoking ritual, he flipped through the open *Talmud* on his desk with his free hand. There was no way to *prevent* Jake from informing the police, the law only prescribed the punishment for having done so. The Rabbi ended the last draw on his beard with a wiry hair trapped beneath his fingernail– a victim of his thought process. He twirled it, examining the precious follicle. He lovingly buried it in the fold of a *Talmud* page, resting his treasure amongst the ancient rabbinical discourses running through the pages.

Turning the page to seal his follicle's tomb, Rabbi Skumansky relaxed his sternly wrinkled face.

This was particularly frustrating. Until Jake *acted* upon his threat, it seemed that nothing could be done.

Chapter Forty-Seven

Jake was the tenth man to arrive, including Adam. Since he was now thirteen, he could be counted as one of the ten men required to constitute a *minyan*– a quorum. *This* minyan gathered to hear Adam complete his review of an entire volume of the *Talmud* as he recited the last paragraph aloud before the crowd. Adam's grandmother hosted the event.

After the ceremony, Mrs. Stein asked Jake to join her in the dining room because she wanted to ask him something. He threw Mindy a puzzling look which she returned with a shrug of her shoulders.

He pulled himself out of the overstuffed wingtip chair he'd settled into and sauntered into the living room. Though he had no clue what she wanted to ask him, he figured this might be an opportunity to ask her a few questions of his own.

They sat at the dining room table and Jake eagerly waited to hear what Mrs. Stein wanted to ask him. But she just rambled on about the weather, repeating the same thing over and over.

Jake broke the cycle by asking, "Mrs. Stein, what was Adam's *Zaydie* like?"

"Would you like some *cholent*? There's plenty left over from the *Bar Mitzvah*."

Jake politely refused and repeated the question. "I'm really curious what Herman was like."

She responded by saying how much she missed Sender. "He was such a good boy, and a wonderful father. Who will be their father now?"

Jake said something comforting, then steered her toward Herman once again, only to be offered the *cholent* again.

"Mrs. Stein!" he finally said, firmly. "I really need to *know* something about Herman."

She sat up, stiff as a board, scrunching up her nose and eyes as if squinting to see him through the thick eyeglasses, now rising above her eyebrows.

"*Why*, Jake? Why do you have to ask about *Herman*?"

"I need to know if the information I have about him is true. What was he like?"

She shifted uneasily in her chair and tugged on her dish-water blonde wig. "Herman was--. Herman never--," she stuttered, unable to get the words out.

Then came the flood, "He was a good husband. He always provided for us-- we *never* went hungry. And he was always there for us. Herman was a good *husband*."

She sounded as though she were rattling off a memorized shopping list. "What about Sender's sister?"

Her body froze.

She let out a long, deep sigh, then asked, "Who told you about Malke?"

Jake thought about telling her, then decided to let her draw her own conclusions. "That's not important. But I *must* know the truth now, Mrs. Stein."

"Jake, maybe you're hungry. I'll get you a bowl of *cholent*. I kept it warm in case anyone was hungry after the *siyum*. Come in the kitchen."

"*No!*" Jake took a deep breath realizing he'd raised his voice a little too high. "Look, I know it's hard to talk about, but I *need* to know the truth– this is *very* important. We still don't know exactly what happened to Sender. You don't want him remembered as a suicidal coward, do you? And *now*, someone is trying to take the kids from Mindy. Several odd things have happened that need resolving so I can understand what's going on, clear Sender's name and help Mindy keep the kids with her."

Jake waited a moment to see if he had her full

attention.

When he was certain he did, he explained, "The detective who handled Herman's death investigation believes that Herman may not have committed suicide. He and I believe Herman was likely *murdered*. Who would have wanted to harm Herman, Mrs. Stein?"

"No. *Herman*--. No one did *anything* to him."

"What about your daughter? The one you don't talk about-- *Malke*? I hear that Herman was abusing her. Is that true?"

Shaking her head vigorously, she firmly said, "*No*! Of *course* not! He *loved* Malke. Herman would never abuse anyone. Everything he did was out of *love*."

"What about the nights he visited her in her bedroom-- and the *screams*?"

"*No*! Never *abusive*!" Her head oscillated once again. "He had a different way of expressing his love toward her. *That's* all. But no one understood that. *Malke* didn't understand that. But I *know* it was because he loved her so much."

Her head slumped as she confessed, "It was really all my fault."

"How so?"

"Jake, let me fix you a bowl of *cholent*."

Eating was the last thing Jake wanted to do right now, but he hoped allowing her to feed him might get her to *really* open up.

He followed her into the kitchen and took a seat at the table while Mrs. Stein dished out several huge scoops of *cholent* into a gold-speckled melamine bowl and set it down before him. After downing several spoonfuls, he tried again as she sat down across from him.

"Why do you feel it was *your* fault, about Malke and Herman?"

She stared distantly at the dish-towel in her hand.

Jake patiently waited for her reply.

"I was always so busy cleaning, shopping-- *cooking*. Maybe I didn't give Herman the attention he needed, so he drew himself closer to Malke."

Jake was startled by her profound, yet twisted, logic. "Mrs. Stein. You have *nothing* to feel guilty about. Herman was a sick man. You did *not* cause him to do that."

She looked up at Jake, wide-eyed, pushing her eyebrows above her glasses. "Do you really think so, Jake?"

"*Yes*, I do."

"Because *really*, I tried everything I could think of to make things better. I cooked his favorite meals *every* night. His meals were always hot and ready for him when he came home. Sometimes he worked far away and slept at the slaughterhouse during the week. But I always made a nice *Shabbos* meal for him. I invited his friends for meals. We had *lots* of guests. Herman liked that. I stayed up late with him while he read his paper. I tried *everything*, Jake. Really, I did."

"I'm *sure* you did," he responded in a comforting tone.

"When he didn't stop, I thought maybe if another person lived with us, he would *have* to stop. So, I took in a boarder-- a *meshulach* who used to stop by. He traveled collecting money for charity. Herman always invited him in for a drink and gave him a few dollars. He said it was a *Mitzvah* to invite guests into our home. At first, he only stayed with us while he was in Chicago making his rounds. When he was *here*, things were quiet. But most of the time he traveled. Nothing changed. Eventually he decided to settle down, here in Chicago and became our full-time boarder."

Her eyes grew distant and her stiff body suddenly relaxed. Her head tilted to one side. "He was a gentle, loving, man. I thought Herman would be pleased, but he wasn't. When he pressed me asking *why* I wanted a boarder, I said it was to help with the money. Herman threw a *fit*. He was *so* hurt. He was insulted that I challenged his ability to provide for us. Shortly afterward, he somehow got into the restaurant business. He did well. But I kept our boarder on, just the same. His presence helped the situation with Malke, even though it didn't completely stop. Herman still went into her room when our boarder was away."

"Such a *nice* man," she added.

Jake wasn't sure which man she was referring to– the boarder, or Herman, but he let it go.

"What happened to Malke?"

"After Herman-- *died*, we sent her to live with my sister. I was in no condition to take care of her. I had a--. I was *ill* after Herman died. It was best for Malke to get away from all this."

Her hands trembled as she collected Jake's half-empty bowl to top it off with a *cholent* refill. He knew where he'd be spending the rest of the evening if he downed any more of the volcanic mixture, but eating her *cholent* to get her to open up seemed to be working.

He wondered what she originally called him into the dining room to ask him, but first there was one more thing he wanted to know. "I understand Herman wrote a commentary on the Book of *Eicha*. Did he ever get it published?"

The pain that had filled her face dissipated. "*Yes. His manuscript.* That's what I wanted to ask you about, Jake. It was Herman's pride and joy. He desperately wanted to be recognized as a scholar. We couldn't afford for him to continue studying after we got married like many of his friends did. Some became respected rabbis and teachers. Herman wanted to show them all that he could work and *still* be a scholar. He worked on that manuscript for *three years*. He nearly had it finished and was trying to get backers to publish it when--. He never lived to see that. That was a shame. He was working on it the *day* he died."

"I was the one that found him in the study, you know. That day started out no differently than any other. He was meticulous about his routine. He went to morning services, came home for breakfast, then worked on his manuscript, in the study. He continued working on it after lunch, then laid down for his usual nap, on the day bed in his study."

"I had no idea he would--."

Jake tried taking her mind off the pain her face revealed. "Do you know where his manuscript is *now*?"

"*Yes!*" She said, suddenly perking up. "*That's* what

I wanted to ask you about. I came across it this afternoon when I was preparing for Adam's party. I hoped Sender would have been interested in his father's work. But when he was *Bar Mitzvah,* I asked him about it. He wasn't even interested enough to read it. I suppose it was foolish of me to think he would. He never knew Herman. Sender was an infant when Herman--. I wanted Sender to know his father was a scholar, that he authored a religious work. But Sender wasn't interested. He had other interests. You know how thirteen-year-old boys can be. The Cubs were his interest-- baseball, and his friends. That's all he had on his mind. *And gossip.* Sender *loved* to gossip. You'd think he was a girl, the way he was about that. But shortly before he died, Sender took a sudden interest in Herman's manuscript. He had questions, *so many* questions. I was delighted he finally wanted to know more about his father. I wanted him to know the *good* things about Herman. The week before Sender's…*accident*, he asked me to take it back. He refused to tell me why, just *insisted* I take it from him. After that, he never asked a single question about Herman."

She got up from the table and went into the dining room. Jake followed. She opened the top drawer of the mahogany buffet and retrieved a six-inch stack of musty, yellowed, papers. Several dehydrated rubber bands were fused to the outer sheets. One large, fresh band held the stack together.

Jake cradled the treasured work in his hands, examining the Hebrew lettering scribbled on the front page. The writing was in *Yiddish*.

He gently placed the handwritten work on the dining room table and gingerly removed the fresh rubber band.

Herman lost his life as he was finishing this manuscript. Sender lost *his* just after returning it to his mother. And apparently, Sender had produced his *own* manuscript to boot.

There *had* to be a connection.

Perhaps, Sender gleaned something from Herman's work that led to the odd repeat of history.

But *what*?

"Before everyone arrived tonight, I asked Adam if *he* wanted it," Mrs. Stein continued. "He seemed to have no interest. *Now*, I'm not sure *anyone* wants it. But I was thinking that being a *Talmudic* scholar, you might appreciate Herman's accomplishment. He was *so proud* of this. I've always felt bad he never got to see it published. Do you think it has potential to get published now?"

"I doubt it," Jake replied, flipping through the pages, looking for a particular passage. Some of the pages had notes scribbled in the margins. Personal notes. *Call at four-thirty. KEY-7690 - Mr. Krupp. Four cases of wine...* Each page was meticulously numbered.

"There are several good *Eicha* commentaries on the market now," Jake explained. "I don't see the need for another one."

"*Oh*. I see," her voice trailed off disappointedly.

Sensing her dismay, Jake added, "But I can certainly ask around-- see what I can find out."

Where was it?

Realizing he'd passed it, he began with the top page once again, carefully separating each page so as not to miss one. Sure enough, it was on the second of two pages stuck together by the dried rubber bands.

It was plain as day. A missing section-- smoothly cut with a razor, or scissors. No rips, no jagged edges.

Just as Mort said.

Jake was excited to get his hands on this manuscript, but not for its publication potential. "Where *was* this when Herman died?" Jake asked. "Do you remember *exactly* where it was?"

"It was awful," she replied. "He was *napping*, that's

all-- just his *regular* nap. I didn't hear a thing, except his snoring. But then, it got real quiet. But that's how it always went with the snoring until he woke up. It was on a Thursday. I was already preparing the *cholent* for Shabbos. Herman liked it best when it was slow-cooked for *two* days, so I used to put it up Thursday afternoon, bring it to a boil, then leave it in the oven on a low flame until *Shabbos* afternoon. I had just put it in the oven when I poked my head into the open door of his study to check on him. It was too early for him to wake up but I *didn't* hear his snoring. The first thing I noticed was the manuscript on the floor. Herman would *never* put holy words on the floor. It was *so* odd. At first, I thought it must have slipped off his desk somehow– maybe by the *wind*. But the windows were shut tight, and Herman *always* kept that back door locked. Many times, I had to drag groceries around to the front when I forgot my back door key if he was napping. Herman was a little *crazy* about keeping that door locked. I was trying to think *how* it could end up on the floor. When I bent down to pick it up, that's when I saw he was--."

After giving her a moment to let that painful memory pass, Jake asked, "Mrs. Stein, did you ever figure out *why* Sender suddenly returned this to you?"

"No. He never said-- no explanation. But he *did*

seem frightened about *something* at the time. It seemed *so* important to him to not have this in his possession." Her face transformed into a horrified look of panic. She got all teary eyed and slumped in her chair. Her lower lip began quivering. "Dear God. You don't think-- this didn't have anything to do with--. Oh, my poor, poor, boy. What have I done? How could I be so *foolish*? There must be something about this manuscript that caused Herman to take his own life. I was afraid that might be what Sender had done as well. Now it might all be *my* fault."

"You didn't do anything wrong Mrs. Stein. Herman probably didn't kill himself. And Sender's death was not likely a suicide either."

"I think they were *both murdered*."

She looked up, abruptly. "*What*? Who would want to hurt *them*?" Her eyes roamed about their socket's as if searching for suspects.

Then, her face went rigid.

Jake replied, "I wish I knew, *believe* me, Mrs. Stein. But I *do* know that whoever killed Herman *must* have known his napping schedule, and that he was working on a *handwritten* commentary on *Eicha*. Detective Wolfe assured me there *was* no forced entry. You said the door was locked when you found Herman. So, the murderer also must have had a *key* to access Herman's study from the back door, and then locked it when they left."

Jake sat in deep thought for a moment, stroking the five-o'clock shadow that had once been a full beard. "Who knew about Herman's precise napping schedule?"

"Well, let's *see*. Besides myself, my brother Marvin knew. Oh, and of course our boarder knew. Some of Herman's staff may have also figured it out. They called here so many times throughout the day asking for him. I would always tell them if he was busy working in his study, or if he was napping. Oh *my*! It *was* my fault, *wasn't it*? I told too many people about his schedule. It was *all my fault*."

"Mrs. Stein, whoever did this would have found a way no matter *what* you did. You can't blame yourself."

"It's just that I feel, *somehow–*." her voice trailed off into an indiscernible whisper.

Suddenly a wild idea occurred to Jake, though he couldn't imagine Mort would have overlooked asking about it.

"Mrs. Stein– Did your boarder have a *key* to the back door?"

Her face relaxed. "Herman would be furious with me, but yes. I gave him keys to the front *and* back doors. It was easier for him to get up from the back if he was lucky enough to find an open parking space back there, late at night."

"Was *he* home when Herman died?"

"No, he was out working that week. I think he was filling in as a substitute *mashgiach* at a cheese factory in Wisconsin, supervising a run of kosher cheese."

"Who *else* had a key to the back door?"

"Well, *me* of course. And Malke had a key, *and* of course my brother– *Marvin* had one. I gave him one, just in case, you know– in case we got locked out, or were away and needed him to get in for a water leak or something. I remember the day I gave it to him. It was the same day we moved in-- before Malke was born. Marvin came by with a bottle of wine and some leftovers from his restaurant. I wanted him to have a key. He resisted a first, but I made him take one. Like I said, in case I got locked out. But also, because Herman worked so far away. Most of the week he would sleep near the slaughterhouse-- I was all alone. But all that changed after Herman got the restaurant. *Then* he was home with me *every* night."

"Great," Jake thought. "Home *every* night, going into *Malke's* room. No wonder he couldn't stay away the whole week. That's probably why he was so desperate to get a business that would keep him in town."

"What about Malke? Who *else* knew about Malke? I mean, after you sent her away. Who knew where she *went*? Who else knew about Herman going into her room?"

"We never told anyone. *Never!*"

"Until now," Jake concluded.

Chapter Forty-Eight

Jake waited in the car, outside Target, while Mindy dashed in to pick up the snapshots from Adam's *Bar Mitzvah*. Taking pictures on *Shabbos* is prohibited, so she re-created the event by having everyone dress up before *Shabbos* and meet at the gym so she could take the snapshots.

Jake flipped the radio to WNUA, the *smooth-jazz* station. Popping the side-lever of his seat he reclined all the way back and closed his eyes. He thought about trading in the old Nova for something flashy, now that money was not a concern. But he'd grown attached to the old relic and couldn't let it go just yet. For now, he just imagined the threadbare seats were fine Corinthian leather. He conjured up memories of that new leather smell...

...*Tap. Tap, tap, tap.*

Smooth Jazz...

TAP-TAP-TAP!

Jake sprang up.

Mindy had returned. He'd locked her out and dozed off.

He heard her muffled voice from beyond the window. "Wake up *sleepy*." He reached over and opened the passenger door's lock. Mindy slid into the bucket seat beside him.

"Are they nice?" he asked, pointing to the packet of photos in her hand.

"I haven't seen them yet. I figured we'd look at them together, Jake."

Mindy flipped through the pictures handing Jake the extras. "Keep these separate," she said. "I had three sets made-- one extra for Mrs. Stein and one extra for my parents."

Jake took the pictures two at a time, scanned them briefly, then placed them in separate piles on the dashboard. He wasn't all that interested, but they seemed important to Mindy.

"Something's weird about these pictures, Jake. They look odd, but I'm not sure why."

Jake examined the shots a little closer.

"Wait a minute– *here!*" he declared, pointing to a picture of Mindy, Adam, Sarah, Danny, and Mrs. Stein posing for a shot in front of a *Mazal Tov* banner written in Hebrew. "Look at *this* one."

"What about it? I don't see what's wrong."

"Look at the banner, at the Hebrew *lettering*."

"It's *backward!*" she said, laughing.

"Yes, the negatives were processed *backwards*," Jake concurred.

"You're right! I'll go back and see if they'll re-do them," Mindy said as she opened the door to leave.

"Now if they were processed backwards," Jake thought, "the layout of *everything* was backward."

He knew *something* was odd about those other pictures– the ones Mort had shown him of that horrible, bloody mess. He closed his eyes and conjured up images of those photos, letting his eyes wander across Herman's desk, and examined the reflections in the desk mirror.

The books!

The Hebrew lettering on the books were NOT backwards, as they should be as reflections in the mirror.

That means *everything* in that photo, and possibly the *entire* set of crime-scene photos, were *backwards*!

Everything that was on the *left* was really on the *right*.

The books in the bookcase were actually stacked in reverse of the order they appear in the photos.

Mindy rapped on the window, startling Jake once again.

"They said *no problem*," Mindy related as she got

back into the car.

"Mindy, remember what I told you about Herman's picture-- the one *Mort* showed me?"

"Sort of. Lots of blood and gore. Why?"

"The Hebrew lettering on the books in the mirror. The lettering *wasn't* backwards!"

"So?" Mindy said, giving Jake a puzzling look. "Police film developers pay more attention to detail than Target. *So, what?*"

"No– I don't think they *did*. The lettering was *not* backwards. But it *should* have been. The lettering should have appeared backwards in the mirror. But I was able to read the Hebrew words normally-- *right-to-left*. That means *that* negative was *also* developed backward. Mort said he had those shots remade from the negatives on file because the originals went missing. So, when they made the new shots, they had nothing to compare them to and no one caught the mistake."

"Okay. How does *that* change anything?"

"It means that everything else in the picture was in reverse *too*."

Stroking his absent beard Jake began swaying rhythmically, back and forth and speaking in the sing-song rhythm he used when thinking through a complex section of the *Talmud*.

"In the photo, the knife was in Herman's right hand. If he killed *himself,* he'd have used the hand he was most comfortable using-- *don't you think?*"

"I suppose so."

"Well, remember when we took Herman's *tefillin* to get them changed for Adam because he's right-handed, and Herman was left-handed."

"But you said the knife *was* in Herman's left hand."

"*Exactly*! In the photo it *seems* like it's in his left hand. But if everything was reversed, that means Herman was holding the knife in his *right* hand. Why would he use his *right* hand to kill himself? Herman was definitely murdered!" Jake announced. "Mort suspected it wasn't suicide but didn't have enough evidence to convince anyone, including the Medical Examiner. *This* might be enough to re-open the case."

Jake wondered again about who might have killed Herman. Marvin Fox had a strong motive to get rid of Herman. He knew Herman was abusing Malke. Herman blackmailed him into handing him the keys to a Shalomski's franchise and was hitting him up for more money to publish his manuscript.

"I'm going to pay *Uncle* Marvin another visit," Jake

said. "I think he's got some more explaining to do."

"I wish you'd leave that to the police. Why not just tell Mort-- let *him* handle it."

"I can't explain it. I just feel like this is something I *have* to do myself." Jake wasn't letting fear hold him back.

Never again.

"I don't think Fox is dangerous," he assured her. "I'll turn everything over to Mort when I confirm what I suspect is going on. I *promise.*"

Chapter Forty-Nine

Mindy left work at four-thirty on Thursday and headed to the boys' school to pick up the kids. Sarah would be waiting with the secretary at the boy's building. The girl's school let out at four-fifteen. Mindy arranged for her to be brought to the boy's school so she could pick them all up together. Sarah would sit in a corner of the school office doing her homework, reading, or just watching the goings on.

"Hi Rachel," Mindy called out, waving to the twenty-something secretary seated behind the metal desk, wearing a long, brown braided wig. "Where's Sarah?"

Rachel gave Mindy a startled look, then said, "She's not here. She never showed up. I assumed she was sick or something. I thought you just forgot to tell me."

The blood drained from Mindy's face. "She's not sick– I put her on the school bus myself, this morning."

"Oh." Rachel paused, then stood and came around the desk toward Mindy. "I'm sure she's okay. Maybe she's still at the girls' building. Let me call over there."

Rachel went into an inner office and placed the call. She muttered something Mindy couldn't hear into the phone. Cupping her hand over the mouthpiece she yelled back to Mindy,

"Mrs. Bluestein is checking out front and in the hallways. I asked her to check the washroom too. I'm holding."

Mindy fought horrid thoughts threatening to race through her mind. But it was a losing battle. Was Sarah wandering the city streets, lost? Had she been attacked in the bathroom? Has someone taken her?

Her panic spiraled.

She sat down, taking long, deep breaths.

Checking her watch, she saw it was just five minutes until the boys' classes let out. Trying to think rationally, she decided she would wait for them, drive straight to the girl's school, and look for Sarah herself.

They could all look for Sarah together.

A comforting thought passed through her mind. Perhaps Sarah had been taken to Mrs. Stein's house for some reason.

She picked up the phone on Rachel's desk and dialed Mrs. Stein's number.

One ring.

No answer.

Two rings.

Still, no answer.

As the line rang a third time Rachel returned. "She isn't there– they can't find her," she said apologetically. "Maybe she got a ride with someone else and they're still on the way somewhere, maybe dropping off other girls. Mindy, you know they make sure they account for every girl before closing up. I'm sure you'll get a call soon, or she'll turn up at home."

Five rings.

Still, no answer.

The school bell drowned out the sixth ring.

Mindy dropped the phone back into its cradle. Good. The boys would be out in a moment.

She'd take them straight over to the girl's school.

Mindy stepped out of the tiny office, into the sea of young boys surging into the hallways from the classrooms lining the walls, each one maneuvering to reach the safety of his own locker. The hall was full of hundreds of little men, wearing black *yarmulkes*, dark clothing, and sneakers. Some of the older boys wore black fedoras. Eventually, the boys began making their way to the front door, backpacks and overcoats in tow.

Mindy couldn't see down the entire hall, and she knew what a panic it would cause if a woman mingled into the all-male crowd.

Adam was usually the first of her boys to emerge. She'd often send him back to get Danny who preferred making his exodus slowly, strategically waiting out the crowd in the comfort of his empty classroom.

Once Mindy spotted Adam, her heartbeat began settling. She sent him immediately to get Danny. He dumped his backpack against the wall and disappeared into the deep, black, sea once again.

Slowly, the hallway cleared. All that remained was the occasional stray homework sheet or candy wrapper. Mr. Hix, the janitor stood at the end of the corridor armed with a broom, shaking his head right on key.

Mindy spotted Adam popping in and out of the last few classrooms at the far end of the hall.

"I can't find him," he shouted.

Mindy felt the gold, apple broach affixed to her sweater rise and fall in a pulsating motion. Leaving Adam inside to continue looking for Danny, she dashed out to the parking lot in time to catch Danny's teacher, Rabbi Moskowitz, getting into his car.

The young lanky rabbi's red-bearded face whitened. "Thank *God* you're okay!"

"What are you talking about-- of course I'm okay!"

"Where's Danny?"

"He went with his aunt," the young rabbi explained. "She knocked on my classroom door about fifteen or twenty minutes ago asking for Danny. She said you'd been in a terrible accident and she came to rush Danny to the hospital to be with you. I thought the *worst*– you can imagine. I suppose there was some kind of mix up. *Obviously,* you're okay."

Mindy's knees buckled under the weight of Rabbi Moskowitz's revelation. She grabbed his open car door to steady herself.

"*Are* you okay?"

Mindy looked pleadingly past the Rabbi's gold-rimmed spectacles, into his eyes, and said, "Rabbi– Danny doesn't *have* an aunt."

She rushed back inside the building, grabbed Adam, then raced to the girl's building, weaving through traffic.

She arrived just as Sarah's principal was locking the front door.

Mindy quickly learned that the bogus aunt had also visited Sarah's classroom with the same story just minutes before her class ended.

Her teacher left a note in the office that wasn't discovered until a few minutes ago. Mindy also learned the bogus aunt's name.

Malke Stein.

Chapter Fifty

Jake squeezed the Nova into an empty spot in front of Mindy's building, just shy of six-thirty in the evening. He was lucky to find a space. It wouldn't be long now before the snow arrived along with rickety kitchen chairs, laundry baskets, even an occasional milk crate, reserving prized parking spots.

Earlier that day, he had cranked the engine of his frost-covered Nova, and the old beast slowly came to life. When he flicked on the windshield blower and cranked up the heat, he heard a strange flapping noise, like that of the imaginary motorcycle noise made by kids fastening baseball cards to their spokes with clothespins.

A quick fishing expedition into the depths of the dashboard vent, landed a dandy catch. One of the photos he stacked on the dashboard when he and Mindy were looking over the *Bar Mitzvah* pictures, had slipped into the vent.

It was an interesting shot of Mindy and the kids.

Mindy had a worried look on her face.

Adam seemed angry, annoyed, or perhaps a little of both.

Daniel had rabbit ear fingers popped up behind Sarah's head, who had one finger up her nose.

He was sure Mindy would be looking for the third copy of this shot and decided to drop it off tonight.

The fourth time Jake pressed Mindy's buzzer, the vestibule door's glass pane rattled in response. The door gave way as he pushed it, and he began his climb. As he rounded the landing, he was greeted by Mrs. Goldstein's head, poking out of her slightly ajar door.

She watched Jake knock on Mindy's door several times with no response before motioning him inside her apartment.

"I don't think Mindy's home yet. I can usually hear the children's racket as they climb the stairs. When I heard her buzzer, I looked out front and saw your car. I figured it was you."

Sinking deeply into her living room sofa, Jake recounted the reason for his visit tonight, showing her the photo. "Do you mind if I wait here until she gets in?"

"Of course not. Actually, I'm glad we have this time. I've got something to tell you, Jake. Something *very* important."

"I wasn't sure *how* to tell you. I guess there's no good way."

Not wanting to miss a word of the old woman's frail voice, Jake struggled to pull himself upright and forward

403

out of the depths of her couch.

"What is it?"

"The day before yesterday, I was coming back from the fruit store, pulling my cart of bags when I bumped into Mr. Shapiro. He's the handyman for many of the buildings on our block. We talked about the Stein's and I mentioned how terrible it was what happened to the children's father, right *here* in front of our *own* building. Mr. Shapiro was *shocked* to hear this. He'd been visiting his son, Jonathan, in Jerusalem, for his oldest grandson's *Bar Mitzvah*. He'd left for an El Al flight, the day it happened. He just returned to Chicago the day I chatted with him."

"Mrs. Goldstein, is there a *point* to all this?" Jake didn't understand his own impatience. He had nowhere to go anyway.

"Of *course,* there is– let me *finish*."

Clutching her housecoat, she slowly lowered herself into the worn upholstered armchair across from him. "Mr. Shapiro had *no idea*. This news came as a particular shock because he was *here* that *very* night, replacing a broken window in the back of the building across the street. He said he's *always* careful to dispose of the broken glass far away from these buildings. There are *too* many children playing around here. He puts the broken glass in the back of his pickup. It was parked right across the street, around the time Mindy *says* she saw Sender fall."

That got Jake's attention.

"What do you mean by, *says* she saw? Don't you *believe* her?" He didn't mean to get defensive and his question got no direct response.

"I've watched Mr. Shapiro work. He *is* very careful. He said he put two large pieces of glass in the back of the truck, then went back to get the rest. When he came back with the remaining glass, he saw something fly off the roof of our building toward him. It landed in the back of his truck, and *smashed* the glass. He said it sounded like Kristallnacht all over again."

"No one ever figured out what the breaking glass sound was," Jake thought to himself. "The police didn't find any broken windows because Mr. Shapiro fixed it and they didn't find any broken glass because he hauled it away."

"So *that* was the breaking glass Mindy heard," Jake said aloud.

That earned him a cold stare and the shake of her head. The elderly widow silently lifted herself from the chair and disappeared into the kitchen. A moment later she returned, lugging a brick.

She held the dark block above Jake's lap. "*This* is what landed in the back of Mr. Shapiro's truck," she announced, releasing her grip.

Springing into action to defend his family jewels, Jake quickly cupped his hands into a net, catching the deadly object.

He escaped with light scrapes to his palms.

He examined the rather odd brick. The words Purington Paver were embossed across the top.

"An old *paving* brick," she announced. "When I moved here after the war, all the streets were paved with them. But I haven't seen one of these in years. So *where* did this come from? *I* want to know. Mr. Shapiro doesn't care, but *I do.*"

"This is an odd brick for someone to have," Jake commented half-mindedly, bewildered by the amazing revelation. "Mr. Shapiro saw *this*, but he didn't see Sender *fall*? That's hard to believe."

"Oh, so now you're a Mr. *big-shot*, like the police. You won't believe an *honest* man like Mr. Shapiro now? Well let me tell *you* something, mister fancy pants. When Mr. Shapiro *says* something, it's *always* the truth-- the *absolute truth*. He couldn't tell a lie if his *life* depended on it. *I* ought to know-- it once *did*. Sender Stein either came off that roof *after* Mr. Shapiro left, or maybe while he was in the back getting the rest of the glass. He *couldn't* have seen him fall if he was in the back, and by the time he returned to his truck, all the parked cars would have blocked his view of Sender laying on the ground."

"Mr. Shapiro saw nothing but *this* brick flying off that roof!" She again insisted.

"Did he see *who* threw the brick?" Jake asked.

Mrs. Goldstein carefully lowered herself back into the armchair before answering.

"*Yes*, he did."

"That's *great*! Whoever threw it probably killed Sender, or at least *knows* who did. Who *was* it?"

"*That's* what I wanted to tell you. When Mr. Shapiro looked up to see who was on the roof he saw–"

The sound of a stampede, racing up the stairs distracted her attention.

"*Oh*," she said, holding a quivering hand to her mouth. "They're *home*, though not quite as noisy as usual."

"*Mrs. Goldstein*! *Who* did Mr. Shapiro see on the roof?" Jake pleaded.

Lowering her voice to a whisper she said, "Mr. Shapiro told me that he shined his flashlight up and saw *Mindy*, look down over the edge of the roof, and then back away into the dark. He didn't understand what she was doing, but didn't have time to ask. He had to get ready for his flight."

The blood drained from Jake's head.

Shock set in, then disbelief.

"*Mindy?*"

"How *could* she–? *Why* would she throw--. But she said--." His heartbeat accelerated.

His thoughts spun out of control.

He waited with Mrs. Goldstein until the hallway stampede subsided. She said Mr. Shapiro *insisted* on going to the police with the information. "That man is too straight for his own good sometimes. I convinced him to wait until I could discuss this with you, Jake. I *promised* him you'd look into this quietly first."

"There was no hurry in the matter and getting the police involved again so soon after Mindy had been reunited with her children, even if she *had* done the unthinkable, would be devastating to the children."

Jake mulled over his next move carefully.

He needed to confront Mindy and find out what really happened. Perhaps, there was *some* explanation, other than the obvious.

Jake contemplated how to approach the subject with

Mindy. He realized he was doomed. If she *didn't* do anything wrong, she'd never forgive him for the accusation. And if she *did* do it--. *That* was somewhere he wouldn't let himself go just yet.

Evidently, he had deeper feelings for Mindy than he wanted to believe.

*****

Before knocking on Mindy's door, he hustled back to the car and tossed the paving brick into the trunk of his Nova.

Mindy was hysterical when she finally opened the door. A flood of tears ran down her cheeks.

She grabbed Jake with both arms in a tight bear hug, holding on for dear life and cried through her sobbing, "They're *gone* Jake. She *did* it. She took Danny and Sarah, just like she *said* she would."

Jake couldn't understand a word of it.

He tried calming her.

"Mindy, everything will be okay. Just tell me *slowly*, what *exactly* happened?"

After holding her in the doorway for a moment, he walked her inside. Adam was at the dining room table, blankly staring at the wall.

"Danny and Sarah are *gone*, Jake. A woman *claiming* to be their aunt rushed into their classrooms saying I'd been in an accident and the children had to get to the hospital right away. No one questioned her. She was *dressed* like them so they *trusted* her! Dr. Hoffmeyer was right. This *must* be what she warned us Rabbi Skumansky would do. And the woman who took them said she was their aunt– *Malke Stein*. They don't even *have* an aunt. The teachers didn't *think*– they just *trusted* her!"

Jake decided this was *not* the time to ask her about the brick. That would have to wait. Right now, finding her kids was the priority.

Part of him wanted to back away from this whole mess. But when he pulled the photo he found in his car, out of his pocket to give to her, all he could think about was those two wonderful, innocent, beautiful little children.

"I *can't* let them down. I did that *once*," he thought. *"Never* again."

He calmed Mindy down as much as possible under the circumstances, then dialed Detective Roberts. Midway through dialing, he realized that with this brick complication in the mix it might be better not to deal directly with Roberts right now.

He called Mort, instead.

"I'll see what I can do, of course," Mort said. "I'll put in a few calls. This is *awful*. How's Mindy?"

He took the cordless phone into the kitchen, out of earshot, motioning to Mindy and Adam, who were now both seated on the front room couch, to stay put.

They obliged.

"She'll be okay once we locate the kids Mort."

Checking over his shoulder to make sure he was out of earshot, he whispered, "I haven't told Mindy or anyone yet Mort, but the kids really *do* have an aunt Malke Stein. They've never met her and no one here knows about her. She's been sort of underground since she was a young girl. I'll tell you the rest later, I'm at Mindy's right *now*. She doesn't know. I can't really talk."

"Of course, of course. Just thinking out loud here. Why didn't she take the *oldest* son?"

"He might have blown the whole thing, Mort. He's thirteen, so maybe she figured he knew he didn't have an aunt."

"Jake, if this was the work of Skumansky, and he's the half-cocked zealot you described, he might still have another scheme for nabbing Adam. You'd better keep a close eye on him till we get this all resolved."

Just as Jake clicked off the cordless and placed it on the kitchen counter, it vibrated with a loud ring. Jake grabbed the phone and poked his head back out to check the living room where Mindy was still shaking on the couch.

"This could be about the kids," he shouted. "Should I get it?"

He waited through two more rings for her answer, then went into the living room, grabbed the extension next to the couch and handed it to Mindy, and listened in on the extension he was holding.

"*Hello?*"

"Hello Mindy," a woman's voice said. "I'm *so* sorry to hear about your children, dear. Is Jake Cooper there by any chance? I've been trying to reach him. Please tell him Dr. Hoffmeyer wants to talk to him."

"*Hello!*" Jake interrupted, not even bothering to pretend he hadn't been listening in. Mindy hung up.

"*Jake Cooper*! Why didn't you call me right away? You *know* I can help. Now be a good boy and listen closely."

Mindy watched me, with bated breath.

"You're on the right track Jake. You know I can't name names, but I know *you'll* figure it out. Just stay with

412

these people. It's the most *awful* thing he's done yet. Everyone's always afraid to stand up to him. But he's the biggest *chicken* when it's *his* neck directly on the line. You've got to file charges against *him* personally. He'll back down. *You'll* see. Those *poor* children. They must be frightened to *death*."

"Look, Dr. Hoffmeyer. I know you're *trying* to help. But I can't play these games anymore. We both know we're talking about Rabbi Skumansky. Can't *you* talk to him? You must have *some* influence with him. Your husband is one of his backers. Can't *he* say anything to him?"

The last thing Jake wanted right now was to deal directly with the police. Even if Mindy *had* some other explanation for lying about being on the roof and throwing the brick, the police could use Mr. Shapiro's statement to make a case against her anyway.

"Look, Jake. I'm sticking my neck out as it *is*. If my husband finds out I've been collaborating with you he'll be *furious*. For personal reasons, I'm *just not willing* to risk that– for *anyone*. Besides, you don't *need* me. Use that *Talmudic* brain of yours. You *have* all the information you need to figure this out for yourself. Just *put* the pieces together. But you'll have to *hurry*, Jake. I can tell you this much– the children *are* still in Chicago. *You-know-who* is connected with a woman– an Orthodox woman, who is part of an organization that rescues exploited children from bad home situations. For the most part, they do a much needed and good service. Some homes, even *religious* homes, are dangerous places for young children. Not even the police can help them because neither the spouse, nor the children will talk about it to outsiders. Even if I wasn't concerned about my husband, I couldn't jeopardize that operation just for you and Mindy. Too many children are saved from *truly* horrible situations. You don't need to know any more about them."

"Can you at least tell me if the kids are *okay*?"

Mindy stood up, clutching her fists to her chin, her eyes full of hope.

"The children are *fine*. *Trust* me. I *know* the woman. But she listens to *him* and takes him at his word. Most often they act on a mother's request. But they have acted upon his word alone before. This is not the first time. However, as a safety measure, they have a mandatory three day cooling off period to prevent rash decisions made in the heat of the moment. If the request is not revoked within three days, the children are transferred to another part of the organization. Neither party knows the exact identity of the other, for security reasons. Once the kids are transferred, they are never contacted again. As I said, the organization is a *good* one, and they follow *strict* protocols."

Her voice dropped to a faint whisper, "Oh *pooh*, the front door just opened. You'd better get going before it's too late. Once they're gone there's no way to get them back. Don't waste any more time. Use your head!"

Click.

Chapter Fifty-One

Jake recounted most of Dr. Hoffmeyer's words to Mindy, except the part about the three-day deadline. There was no point adding that to her anxiety.

He left to brainstorm with Pinky over a late dinner at Blind Faith.

Jake guided the Nova past Touhy to Ridge. He wondered if the children wouldn't be better off away from all this, particularly if Mindy was indeed the one who murdered Sender. There was no denying Mr. Shapiro's account. What other reason could there be for Mindy lying? At the very least, the way she said she heard the sound of breaking glass, was a clear attempt to conceal that she was on the roof and threw a brick.

Jake thought about where Mr. Shapiro's truck would have been parked. If he left, there should have been an empty space, yet the police report hadn't noted it. Shapiro had left after most people were already home from work. He decided Roberts was probably right. Someone else must have pulled into that spot after Shapiro left, but before the cops arrived.

Pinky already had a seat waiting when Jake arrived. Eager to discuss the recent events with Pinky, Jake placed his standard order– a large carrot juice and a tempeh burger. Pinky however, took his usual leisurely time perusing the menu and interrogating the waitress about the specials. He was serious about his food and Jake needed his mind at its best, so he indulged the ritual.

Jake recounted everything for Pinky, this time including the three-day deadline. "I need help trying to think this through, Pinky, I can't handle it all on my own."

"Yes, you *can*. You've become *quite* the private eye. Look how much you've already uncovered."

Jake shook his head in disagreement. Then buried his head in his hands. "God. What am I gonna do?"

"Don't worry buddy. I'm *here* for you. Run those thoughts by me."

"Okay, here goes. Dr. Hoffmeyer claims I already *know* everything I need to figure this out– that I just need to put the pieces together. *Damn* that woman. She's put me in a real *spot*."

"As much as I hate to say it," Pinky said, "it seems you already *know* who killed Sender. *And* you know who took the kids and why. All that's left is to get them back. But, do you really think it's best for them to live with their father's *killer*?"

"Look," Jake responded defensively, "in the first

place, I'm not willing to fully concede Mindy did it. At least not until I have a chance to ask her about it. So, let's shelve that one for now. *Besides*, saying the kids will be better off is a cop-out– they'll never see their friends or family again. They have a brother, a grandmother, *and* a great uncle here. That will be traumatizing for them. And to Mindy– it would be like they're dead to her. *You* of all people, should understand *that*. And I *definitely* know what it's like to really lose a child, *believe me*. I don't wish that on her, even if she *did* kill Sender. Our focus *has* to be getting the kids back, and we need a way to pressure Skumansky into giving them back. He's not going to do anything just because we ask him to. Dr. Hoffmeyer says he's a big chicken when attacked *directly*. She suggested I file charges against him *personally* with the police. But *I* think we can just pressure him with something."

"How are we going to manage that, Sherlock?"

"By getting some *real good* dirt on him. Something he personally fears, more than Mindy getting her kids back."

"We'll *never* find anything on him like that," Pinky said hopelessly.

"I disagree. And I think we start with figuring out *why* all these people jump at Skumansky's command?

Malke Stein came out of hiding to kidnap those kids, and risked jail time. Fogal could have gotten himself killed breaking into my place the way he did. And Gavriel Diamond feeds Skumansky cases from his employer, jeopardizing his own job. What compels them to risk so much?"

"Maybe they truly believe in Skumansky and are just fanatically loyal followers?"

"I don't think it's *loyalty*."

"What then?"

"I think Skumansky's got some really good dirt on each of them. People in this community stick their head in the sand and ignore everything, pretending it doesn't exist. They put on a good face for the public– *Heaven forbid,* the world should know we're not perfect. That kind of pressure breeds the opportunity to control people if you know their secrets."

"Assuming you're right, what could Skumansky *have* on them? Malke Stein, I just heard about now. But I asked around and no one seems to know anything inappropriate about Fogal or Diamond."

"Maybe it's something from their past," Jake pondered. "I *do* know Skumansky was their dorm supervisor when they were students in the *yeshiva*. Marvin

Fox told me that. I think he described them as being *acquaintances*. An *odd* way to describe it, don't you think? I bet he knows more than he told me."

"Maybe you should take another run at him," Pinky suggested. "Maybe you just haven't asked the *right* questions."

Jake agreed and left Pinky to wait for their orders while he went to the pay phone at the rear of the restaurant to call Marvin.

This time he got lucky-- he asked the *right* questions.

Jake returned to their table just as their food was delivered. Pinky grabbed his asparagus and slid them down his throat like a worm.

"Fox was more talkative this time," Jake reported. "Turns out that when Rabbi Skumansky was the dormitory supervisor, he caught them *doing* something. Something that should have resulted in them getting expelled."

Jake recounted his knowledge of similar experiences when he was at the Rabbinical college. Occasionally, a student was expelled– sometimes they were caught with a banned publication, a radio, or a dirty magazine. He recalled one student who got caught watching television in the A/V closet.

"No, Jake," Pinky said. "I don't buy it. Those don't seem like reasons for them to take the risks they have. It has to be something even *more* embarrassing. Something that would ruin their lives if it were divulged."

Jake considered that for a bit.

Dormitory Supervisor. Dirt.

Ruin their lives.

Jake recalled Gavriel Diamond, telling him that *Fogal* was dismissed from the *yeshiva*– that he was caught with another student-- a male student, in a closet and both of them were disrobed at the time.

"H'mm…," Jake thought out loud. "*That* could be it. *Yes*! It all *fits* now." He announced, slamming one hand's fist into his other hand's open palm.

"What? *What*! Spill it, *c'mon*!"

"Okay. think about this. If Skumansky kept the reason for Fogal's dismissal a secret to hold over his head, how the *hell* would Gavriel Diamond know about it, *unless*…"

"*Oh*!" Pinky smirked. "Unless *he* was the other naked boy in the closet!"

"*Wow*. Those must be some really *potent* asparagus. *You got it*!"

"Ya– I can *see that*. Hell ya– now *that* would be

worth a lifetime of loyalty in exchange for silence. It *fits*."

"Like a *glove*."

"*Huh?*"

"It fits like a glove. That's what Mort told me. You know you've put the pieces together correctly when everything fits perfectly, *like a glove*."

"And what's more," Jake added, "Gavriel Diamond is an odd guy. He's never been married that I know of, and he's always primping himself with that little mirror. And when I see him with men and young boys, he gets a little too physical for an Ultra-Orthodox rabbi– caressing their cheek, a lingering touch on the shoulder. In fact, I could see *Diamond* being the one that *lured* Fogal into the closet. Fogal's an aggressive bully, but he's feeble-minded. A little coaxing from Diamond could have put him *right* there."

"*See?*" Pinky cheered on, "You've *already* unlocked another piece of the puzzle. I *told* you you're good at this."

"I guess, it gets easier as I go."

Jake took a long drag on the straw in his glass of carrot juice.

"There's something else I remembered when I spoke with Marvin Fox," Jake said.

"He told me that after leaving his dorm supervisor position, Rabbi Skumansky traveled raising funds for the *yeshiva–* he was a *meshulach*."

"Okay, now I'm completely lost Jake. How's *that* connected to anything?"

"Bear with me. *Mrs. Stein* took in a boarder hoping someone in the home would stop Herman from molesting Malke."

"Guess what she said this boarder did for a living?"

"I give up– *what?*" Pinky responded.

"He was a *meshulach!*"

"Jake, there are tons of *meshulachim*. What makes you think *Skumansky* was the one staying with the Steins?"

"It was just a hunch, but now I'm *sure* it was Skumansky boarding at the Stein's."

"How can you be *sure?*"

"It's like you said. Sometimes you just have to ask the right questions."

"I asked Fox straight-out if Skumansky was the boarder. Fox confirmed it. Skumansky stayed with them overnight, sometimes a few nights, when he was collecting in the Chicago area. When he decided to settle here, he became a full-time boarder, until he got his own place."

"*O-kay*...so what?"

"*So*...suppose Skumansky was there and overheard Herman threaten Marvin about revealing his questionable *glatt* meat supplier unless he financed the publishing of his manuscript. Mrs. Stein said her boarder was in Wisconsin, supervising a run of kosher cheese on the day Herman died. But suppose he wasn't *really* out of town. Or even *better*– suppose he was, but he came *back*! It's only a little over an hour's drive from here. Maybe he returned, came up the back staircase, and overheard their blowout. When Herman was found dead, maybe Skumansky confronted Marvin, accusing him of killing Herman to stop the blackmailing. Further suppose that Marvin convinced him to keep quiet, rationalizing he'd be of no use locked up in prison, but offered to finance an organization that Skumansky could head up. I could easily see Marvin sweet-talking him into that with money, like he did with *you*, when you were going to prosecute Diamond for beating you up."

"Even supposing *all* your assumptions are right, how does that *help*?"

"It helps because applying the right amount of pressure on Skumansky is the right play. But that doesn't mean *we* have to apply the pressure. If I'm correct, the only person in a unique position to do *that* is Marvin Fox."

"Why *would* he?"

"For starters, he *is* the children's great uncle. He *should* do it just for them. But I got the distinct impression

424

on the phone with him just now that he's *not* willing to intercede, *voluntarily*. However, I do think Marvin *is* the one that killed Herman. If I'm right and I tell Marvin I have real evidence, he might be *persuaded* to volunteer."

Pinky shoveled a spoonful of brown rice into his mouth and began coughing loudly.

Jake instinctively pinched his nostrils.

"Hey, give me *some* credit," Pinky demanded. "I just choked on the rice– *okay*? We *are* in a restaurant."

Still coughing, he grabbed Jake's now half-full glass of carrot juice and took a swig. Gesturing to return it to Jake's side of the table.

"Keep it," Jake said.

Pinky proceeded to explain what *triggered* his coughing-attack. "Jake, don't be foolish. Think about it. If Marvin Fox *did* kill Herman, he can do it again. You'd be giving him a pretty strong motive to kill *you!*"

Once again, Jake was stunned at Pinky's amazing flash of brilliance.

"You know, sometimes I think you'd make a pretty good *Talmudic* scholar yourself."

Considering there may be eavesdroppers nearby, Jake continued in a hushed tone. "I hadn't thought of that, but I *have* to get Mindy's kids back– I just *have* to!"

"I'll say one thing," Pinky said, slapping Jake's cheek lightly, "You're certainly not the scholarly wimp I thought you were when I first met you at that singles party."

"Oh, I *am* that wimp, Pinky. But I don't have *time* to be one right now. The clock's ticking. I've *got* to do this."

"Speaking of that, what if Marvin doesn't come through, Jake? Have you thought about that? There might not be enough time for a Plan B."

"I'm a step ahead of you. I'm not waiting for a Plan B– I plan on attacking this from multiple angles at the same time. I'm gonna pay Fishel Fogal a little visit. If I'm right about his skeleton in the *closet,* he'll be vulnerable. He may know where the kids are and tell me straight out. After all, he does all the *dirty work* for Skumansky. He beat *you* up in the van. And he broke into my apartment and attacked *me*. Even if he *doesn't* tell me where they are, he'll run straight to one of his cohorts, Gavriel Diamond or Rabbi Skumansky. And, even if I'm wrong about what Skumansky's got on those two, just *threatening* to spread a rumor like that is bound to shake them up. Once the word's out, it'll be nearly impossible to convince enough people otherwise. Skumansky would be forced to kick them both out. My chat with Fogal will definitely force them to do *something* desperate. *That's* for sure."

Chapter Fifty-Two

On the way to Shalomski's, Jake rehashed his theory until he was sure that confronting Marvin Fox was the right key to unlocking everything.

The key.

Marvin Fox.

The back door.

"Marvin said he knocked, and rang the buzzer," Jake recalled. "He said he got in because the back door was unlocked. But Mrs. Stein said Herman was adamant about keeping that door locked. She also said Marvin had a key."

"Marvin was *lying* about that," Jake concluded. There was nothing Jake hated more than a *liar*.

Nine-thirty at night and Shalomski's was still crowded. A waiter was flipping the OPEN sign to CLOSED, just as he walked in.

"We're closed," the teenage boy announced.

But Jake was so focused on his mission that he didn't register the comment. He motioned the boy aside and stormed toward the back office. He banged on Marvin's office door angrily. His adrenaline was out of control.

Not bothering to wait for a reply, Jake burst in to see Marvin sitting behind his desk with the phone to his ear.

Marvin sprung to his feet, reaching for his glasses.

Cupping his hand over the phone, he whispered angrily, "What the *hell* do you think you're *doing*?"

It took Marvin a moment to realize *who* stormed in.

He took a deep breath, then whispered, "Next time, wait for a reply before barging in."

He peered at Jake through the reading glasses perched on the tip of his nose as he mumbled something into the phone and hung up.

"I'll tell you what would be *nice*, Marvin! You want to talk about *nice*? It would be *nice* if you told me the truth. Stop *jerking* me around."

"What the hell are you *talking* about?" Marvin asked with an angry, puzzled look.

"You had a key."

"A *key*? What? What are you *talking* about?"

"You had it with you," Jake insisted. "You're messing with the wrong guy, Marvin." Jake thought he had the door blocked, but Marvin was faster, and *stronger* than he anticipated.

"I don't need to hear this *nonsense*," he barked, as he shoved Jake aside and burst out the door.

Jake followed him to the front of the restaurant just

outside the kitchen's side door. "Well, you're *damn well* gonna hear it, Marvin!" Jake shouted. "Here and *now*! I want *answers*!"

Every customer in the house had their eyes glued to the pair, soup spoons and forks frozen midway to their mouths.

Jake realized that he had raised his voice louder than he meant to.

"Okay, *look*," Marvin said in a hushed tone as he turned towards Jake. "*Calm down* and we can discuss this back in my office."

The veins in Jake's throat throbbed as he replied, "*No way*! *Here and now*, Marvin."

Jake's body trembled. He knew he was losing it, but couldn't regain control.

Marvin nodded towards the crowd behind him as he quietly insisted, "You want to ruin my *business* or you want to *talk*? I'll talk, but *not* here."

Jake took a deep breath and quietly followed Marvin back to the office.

He closed his eyes trying to regain his composure just as Marvin hand-signaled toward the kitchen.

Marvin opened his office door just as Jake heard approaching footsteps behind him. Marvin slipped into his office and quickly slammed the door shut.

Jake turned to face a tall, obese, middle-aged man in a white blood-stained apron giving him the stink-eye while flashing a meat cleaver.

Jake slowly backed toward the rear exit door. The beast relentlessly followed.

Forcing the door open with his butt, Jake stumbled backward into the alley falling into oil-slicked gravel.

The monster followed.

Towering over him waving the shiny weapon once again, he growled, "No more bothering Mr. Fox. Stay out or I'll put *you* on the menu."

With that, the beast retreated, slamming the back door shut with a force that rattled its rusty hinges.

The stench alone should have motivated Jake to get up off the ground. But as he moved, pains shot through every bone and muscle.

He heard rustling from within the trash bin and assumed a rat or raccoon was scrounging for sustenance, until his eye caught a familiar unoccupied wheelchair parked beside the bin. The restaurant's last seating would be leaving soon, leaving Jake wondering why the faux-invalid bothered with trash when he could get the day's leftovers wrapped to go in less than an hour.

The man slowly peeked out from inside the bin, climbed out and slid back to his wheelchair, as if Jake wouldn't notice him.

Still laying in pain, Jake said, "Hey look, I know you can walk. Everyone does. Can't you give me a hand?"

The man stared at him for a moment, looked around the alley, then slowly rolled the chair toward Jake.

As he approached, he rose to his feet with the ease of a five-year-old and held out a hand. Jake grabbed it and the man easily pulled him upright.

"Thanks," Jake said.

Jake brushed off his clothes, and nodded toward the wheelchair. "Why do you do that anyway?"

But the man just cocked his head, staring strangely, as if he'd just heard a Martian speak.

"You know," Jake repeated, gesturing back and forth to the chair and the man's legs, "why the wheelchair act if you can walk?"

He smiled revealing a gold tooth that reflected the streetlight brightly in the dark alley and replied in a thick Russian accent, "A man's gotta make a living. I *dress for success*. If I didn't dress and act the part, I wouldn't get the attention– *farshteyt*?" He gave Jake a nod and a crooked smile.

Jake returned the smile and replied, "I get it. Thanks for the help."

Jake pressed a few bills into the man's hand who responded by muttering his repertoire of blessings while wheeling himself toward the street.

Jake tried to shake the aches and pains as he made his way back to the Nova. At first, he figured that despite the result, Marvin's reaction was a *good* sign. He'd hit a nerve, meaning *something* was *bound* to pop.

But then he realized all he *really* accomplished was getting tossed out for disturbing the customers. Losing control got him nowhere. He vowed to do better next time—he had one more trick up his sleeve. He was determined that his next visit would result in his opponent raising *their* voice out of control.

Chapter Fifty-Three

There was no answer when Jake pressed the apartment buzzer marked FOGAL. His address had been easy enough to find-- there was only one Fogal, Rabbi F., listed in the white pages.

He waited nearly an hour, sitting in the Nova, planning and rehearsing his lines. He wasn't blowing it this time.

At ten-forty-five, the rumbling of an unmuffled car pierced the quiet street.

A Checkered Cab, painted green, passed by, then backed into an illegal spot at the end of the block. Jake watched Fogal kick the beater's rusted door open. The loud creak reverberated throughout the crisp night air. As Fogal started up his building's walkway, Jake hopped out of the Nova and silently followed him.

Fogal opened the front door.

Jake slipped in behind him.

As Fogal fumbled with his mailbox keys, Jake calmly said, "*Hello*, Reb Fishel."

The short, plump, blob of a man spun on his heels, revealing a crazed look-- the same look that stared down at Jake when Fogal used his neck as a boot scraper.

"Do I *know* you?" Fogal asked.

Obviously, a memory for faces was not his forte'.

"We *met* recently. I was hoping to have a few words with you." Jake sensed his hesitation and impatience. "I feel bad about what happened. I want to explain and apologize, that's all."

That hooked him.

"*Apologize*? Sure, *go ahead*," Fogal said leaning against the wall with his feet crossed, as if waiting for a bus against a lamp-post.

"I'd prefer not discussing it out here. Can we go inside for a minute? Not more than five minutes, *I promise*."

He begrudgingly led Jake to his third-floor apartment. Veering right at the top of the stairs, he opened his apartment door without unlocking it. There was a hand-written note taped to the dirty, dark-stained, wooden door. Jake slowed to read it as he followed him inside.

DO NOT ENTER THIS APARTMENT.

Fogal saw Jake lingering inside the front door, with a bewildered stare. Jake bounced his glance from Fogal to the sign and back.

"I don't like to lock my door. I forget my keys a lot."

The Wise Men of Chelm immediately came to Jake's mind, but he let it go. He followed Fogal into the living room.

Fogal sat on the couch, propping his feet up on a beaten block of wood constituting his coffee table. Jake took a seat in the broken recliner in the corner.

"So, what is this about *Reb*..."

"*Cooper. Jake* Cooper."

Blank stare.

"You don't recognize me?"

Before he could answer, the phone rang. Fogal took the call on the kitchen phone.

He was gone less than a minute before returning to the couch.

"You visited my home recently," Jake explained. "I suppose I wasn't very cordial with you and I just wanted to apologize."

Fogal's feet quickly retracted from the table.

His rotund torso rolled to an upright position, palms down on his knees. Jake had his full attention.

"I also wanted to let you know I'm aware of your little incident at the yeshiva when you were a student there. I know *all* about it, *and* I know who *else* knows."

Fogal's jaw flopped open, hanging there until saliva

drooled from his lip. Using his rumpled suit-jacket sleeve to wipe it, he scrunched his face into an intense stare.

Jake's rehearsal was paying off. Now for the punchline.

Jake's pulse escalated.

He took a deep breath and let it out slowly.

"My girlfriend Mindy Bloom, formerly Mindy Stein, wants her children back." Jake could feel his blood pressure rise. Struggling to maintain his composure he said, "I know you know where they are. And if you don't tell me I'll--. I'm *going to*--."

Where were the words he'd lined up?

Before he knew what was happening, his mouth finished the job for him. "It would be a shame if the community found out about your little incident."

Fogal's face transformed into a purple mass beneath his scraggly beard. His eyes bulged.

"What do you *want* from me?" he growled under his breath.

"You know where Mindy's children are," Jake said. "You're going to tell me where they are and help me get them back, starting *right now*."

"I *remember* you now, you little *vantz*. There's nothing I can do for you, even if I wanted to. *The Rav* has

437

ruled. There *is* no going back."

"The *ruling* was made in error," Jake replied.

Fogal leaned back on the couch and lapsed into a nervous bout of laughter.

"*The Rav* never makes *mistakes*! He's saving the Jewish souls of those children. Their mother was turning them away from Judaism, dressing like a whore, wearing pants, and going around with her hair uncovered. *No mistake– The Rav* is a hero. A Jewish hero. A *leader.*"

As he spoke, he removed the twisted remains of the fedora perched atop his head, revealing the *yarmulke* fastened to his hair with rusty paper-clips.

"Well then, I'm afraid your hero has really done you in," Jake retorted. "Because if you don't help me now, your life will be *ruined*. You'll be *shunned* by the entire community. Your family will *disown* you. You'll be *blacklisted* from every *synagogue* in the community. Even the precious little job your *hero* gave you will *vanish*. He'll be *forced* to distance himself from you."

"*Ha*! *The Rav* already knows all this. It makes no difference to *him*. He's a great man. Something you know nothing about, you *vantz*!"

Jake's hunch was right on the money.

"He doesn't care now," Jake responded, "because

it's still a *secret*. But how long do you think he will tolerate you once your disgraceful incident becomes common knowledge? Especially when he learns that you've been stealing his *esrogim* and selling them from under his nose. There's a certain manila envelope I came across that *The Rav, and the IRS* would find very interesting."

Jake let him mull that over while he abruptly stood and headed to the door before adding, "I'm not gonna argue with you. Either make sure the children are returned to Mindy pronto, or pack your bags and look for a place to hide."

Jake opened the door as Fogal gave chase, nearly tripping over the coffee table.

"*Jake Cooper!*" he thundered, "I'll do everything in my power-- I'll move *heaven and earth* to make sure neither you, nor Mindy, *ever* see those children again! You *filthy vantz!*"

Breathing deeply to keep his temper in check, Jake slowly opened the door. He slipped one hand along the side of the door and located the lock's metal toggle buttons. He pushed one into place, knowing what would happen when the door closed.

He stepped out onto the landing and turned back toward the raging bull following him. "*Goodbye* Rabbi

Fogal," he said, polite as pie, save for his wide grin.

As Jake closed the door, Fogal grabbed it and followed him out to the landing. What he didn't realize was that he'd grabbed it so hard, it bounced off the inside wall of his apartment and then slammed shut.

Jake continued down the stairwell.

Fogal peered at him in silence, too angry to find words.

He leaned over the railing watching Jake leisurely descend to the ground floor. Jake heard Fogal's deep angry breathing through his nostrils.

"How come *now* you wear your *black* pants? Where are your *white* pants, Mr. Modern Dresser! Where are they now, *vantz*?"

Jake looked up to see the wooden railing shake, trapped in Fogal's twitching vice-like grasp, revealing his anger, now coming to a full boil.

Jake smiled and calmly replied, "When I'm with *good* people I wear *white*. When I visit *evil* people, I wear the *black*."

Smugly proceeding to the ground floor, he heard Fogal growling and muttering, presumably hurling indiscernible curses at him.

Jake calmly exited the building as Fogal fought his

doorknob, nearly ripping it off until he finally realized what happened.

Jake had locked him out.

Chapter Fifty-Four

After a fitful night's sleep, Jake rose sensing he could do more. He met Mort at Dunkin' Donuts to get any updates he might have, and to brainstorm on other things that could be done. Mort said Roberts mentioned he was still looking for Laurie Smilow. Roberts had learned that Laurie was in the midst of an ugly divorce. Being that Laurie and Sender were together, he was looking into that angle for a connection.

Jake said he'd heard nothing more about Laurie since trying to locate her. The timing of her disappearance seemed too coincidental *not* to be related to Sender's death. Two cups of coffee later, Jake still had the feeling there was more to do gnawing inside him.

He called Mindy.

The police took her report and instructed her to stay near her phone. She'd been diligently complying ever since.

So far, no news.

After returning home, Jake too sat by the phone, waiting for something to happen. His heart raced when the phone rang a little after Ten O'clock in the morning.

Pinky.

He'd been asking around, seeing what information

he could rustle up. More of the same-- no news.

As the hours dragged on, Jake's feeling intensified. There had to be something *more* he could do. He called Marsha's work and home numbers. Her voice mail greeted him twice. By noon, he was a wreck.

He counted on his plans to pressure Fox and Fogal into doing his dirty work *for* him. But so far, nothing had come of either of his visits.

Time was running out, *fast.*

Twenty-four hours since they'd snatched Mindy's kids and less than forty-eight to go before it would be too late.

Finally, it dawned on him.

"*Of course!*" Jake realized. "There *is* something else I can do. I should confront Rabbi Skumansky directly."

Figuring the exercise would help walk off his frustration, he hit the pavement to head for Rabbi Skumansky's apartment. Skumansky sat behind a large wooden desk in a bedroom converted into an office, at the back of his flat. He casually put on his glasses and looked up as Jake entered the room.

"Reb Yankel. It's good to see you, my friend. What can I do for you? Everything is well with you I presume?"

Jake said nothing.

He slowly shut the study door only to reveal Gavriel Diamond sitting behind it in a folding chair, legs crossed, stuffing a little mirror into his pocket with one hand, while grooming his beard with the fingers of his other.

The steam emanating from the clanking radiator near the window instantly filled the room.

"Please, leave it open," Skumansky requested. "Otherwise, it gets too hot in here."

"Not *nearly* as hot as it's going to get in a minute," Jake thought.

"The matter I'd like to discuss is extremely sensitive. I'd prefer it to stay closed."

"Very well," he said as he turned around, lifted the blinds, and cracked the window open. He motioned Jake to sit in the empty chair across from him.

"It's about Mindy's children," Jake jumped right in. "They've been kidnapped."

Not a flinch.

Skumansky busied himself opening a pack of sunflower seeds, seemingly half-listening. "That's a *terrible* thing, my friend. I'm sure she must be upset. But what can *I* do about it?"

Have to happen.

Bastard.

He was playing the game. Jake played along, trying to goad him, "Surely, you'd be interested in helping *find* the children."

That got no response from the rabbi, though he heard a brief chuckle from the gallery.

"To hell with this cat and mouse crap," Jake decided.

He sat upright, chest out, stomach in, shot a cold stare at Skumansky, and rattled off the lines he practiced on his way over. "Whoever did this crossed a dangerous line. Kidnapping is a *felony.* The police have *already* been notified and when they find out *who did this,* they'll be seeking *serious* jail time."

"Reb Yankel. Your emotions have understandably got the better of you. Calm down and think about this rationally. You were right to come to *me* with this, my friend. Perhaps, I can help you think this through. You realize reporting a fellow Jew to the authorities is a serious matter. The *Talmud* is clear. Surely there are other ways to resolve this matter."

A fellow Jew.

Jake hadn't said anything about the kidnapper being Jewish.

"You *know* who did this– *don't you*? You *assume*

the kidnapper is Jewish, yet I haven't mentioned the slightest detail."

The rabbi continued his seed-cracking ritual. His complacency irked Jake. His voice rose several octaves as he said, "Mindy has *every right* to be with her children. *No one* has the right to interfere with that! Her kids could be in danger. This might be a matter of *life or death*!" He rambled faster with each word.

Jake realized he was losing control again.

The rabbi continued with the seeds, piling the empties into a battered metal ashtray, not even bothering to glance at him.

Jake turned briefly to see that Diamond was back to his mirror ritual. It was more than he could bear. Jumping to his feet, he slammed his fist on the rabbi's desk, sending the ashtray of seeds flying in all directions.

"The police *have* been informed! Charges *will* be filed, I *assure* you!" The strapping, yet elderly man, released the bag of seeds from his oversized hand, sending them plopping onto his desk. With the back of his hand, he sent everything on his desk flying to the floor, papers and all.

He leaned forward, placed both hands squarely on the table. His fiery eyes bore down into Jake's, as he began drumming his fingers, each pounding the battered oak desk with the force of a steel hammer.

Jake shot up to stand, sending his metal folding chair flying backward. He stood there frozen, unable to respond. His foot groped behind him, searching for the chair.

Skumansky adjusted and re-adjusted the black velvet *yarmulke* perched on his head of closely cropped, coarse white hair. He began to rub his skull with it, as if to help him formulate some profound thought.

"You cannot just take matters into your own hands," he announced in a deep, authoritative voice. "The sages teach us what to do, and *how* to do it. You should be delving into the laws of the *Talmud*, searching out the right path– not running to the *police*. How quickly you have forgotten, Jake Cooper. Running wild on an emotional warpath is the *worst* thing you can do. No matter how serious the matter, you cannot run to the police and report another Jew. Regardless of your previous stature in the community, you are *not* the end, all and be all of Jewish law. The *Beis Din* alone has that right."

He paused briefly. "You speak of kidnapping charges and felonies. These are American laws, not *Jewish* laws. First and foremost, Jewish law must be complied

447

with. A colleague of mine, was once forced to approach his pulpit one Shabbos morning, sadly announcing that he had the grave task of placing one of his congregants in an irrevocable *cherem*. He was forced to excommunicate him because he'd reported another member of the community to the IRS. Despite the tears in his eyes, he complied with what the *Talmud* compelled him to do. *Jewish* law *is* the law. You cannot take matters into your own hands, my friend."

He was good.

Damn good.

But instead of scaring Jake, his little guilt-trip speech fueled Jake's fire. While he'd been selling his wares, Jake regained his composure. He righted his chair, seated himself in a relaxed position, hands on his thighs, taking even, slow breaths.

"My dear rabbi, as you well must know, the very same *Talmud* clearly requires us to comply with the laws of the land. As citizens, we are all bound by local and federal laws, not just *Talmudic* law."

Pounding the desk with his fist Skumansky yelled, "*Never*! Jewish law is *never* to be cast aside in favor of the laws of the *goyim*. Turning any Jew over to local authorities is *absolutely* forbidden!"

His escalated tone confirmed that Jake was gaining the advantage. Now *he* was losing control. Jake went in for the kill, "That *only* applies in cases where the authorities have no due process. But this is *America*, Rabbi Skumansky. We *have* a judicial system. We *have* lawyers, hearings, and rules of evidence. The American legal system *overflows* with due process. No rabbi, in this situation, Jewish law is *not* violated by turning in the kidnapper."

The ancient words Jake labored over year after year in *yeshiva* suddenly came alive. His toiling had been worth arriving at this juncture, heavily armed. *Nobody* was snowing over Jake Cooper.

"Was this what Hoffmeyer meant?" he wondered. "Is *this* why she said that I am the only one who can help Mindy?"

Rabbi Skumansky spoke slowly and firmly, "You are being *very* foolish, my friend. Or perhaps, merely *naive*. This is Cook County-- one of the *most* corrupt judicial systems in the *country*. This does not constitute the due process exception to the rule. Make no mistake."

Jake briefly pondered his rebuttal.

Rhetoric.

Quick thinking rhetoric.

Once again, Jake wondered about his credentials--

where did he get his *S'micha*?

"Rabbi, please. I am not a fool. Even if your assertion is correct, the *Talmud* does not advocate punishment for reporting another Jew except in the extreme case of a *repeat* offender who turns people in to satiate his hunger for revenge against the community. This would *not* constitute a *repeat* offense. It would constitute an *isolated*, *justifiable*, incident."

Jake wasn't giving him an inch.

Leaning back in his chair, the rabbi visibly relaxed his tensed muscular frame and said, "Please, Reb Yankel. Let us focus on the solution to this problem. Not *quibble* over semantics. And besides, the *police* won't help you."

"How can you be so sure? What do you *know* about this kidnapping?"

"What *The Rav* knows is not important," Gavriel piped up from behind. "What *is* important is that Mindy turned her back on Judaism, dragging her children down with her. It's the absolute duty of every member of this community to save those children. Let's not mince words. She's *your* girlfriend, so *you* know. You can't deny the way she acts and dresses-- the places she goes. Orthodox women don't *do* such things."

Gavriel stood and approached Jake. He chucked

450

Jake's chin as he advised, "Don't get sucked down with her, Reb Yankel."

Jake escaped unscathed from Skumansky's reproach. But Diamond's words stung.

At one time, Jake shared his attitude. Yet now, hearing it so brazenly stated, he found it shocking.

He was furious.

Focus, Jake. Focus.

"There's nothing wrong with the way Mindy dresses. You just don't like it. You and I both know it. Have you even taken the time to ask her directly about her actions? *No!* You have *not*. In my book, *you two* are the ones judging without due process!"

Nudging his voice back down, he added, "I *will* get Mindy's children back, *with* or *without* your help. And I'll *definitely* be reporting the responsible parties to the authorities, Jewish or not."

Jake turned abruptly, directing his next comment to Rabbi Skumansky. "As for your threat to excommunicate me– *be my guest.* I don't care to associate with a community that condones this behavior."

Rabbi Skumansky sat quietly, seemingly unaffected.

Jake desperately grasped for more ammunition.

He wanted to hit a nerve that would force one or both of them to act. Though he had no idea where to go with it, he said to Skumansky, "By the way, I understand you boarded with the Stein's at the time Herman Stein was killed."

Skumansky responded by leaning back in his chair, popping another handful of sunflower seeds into his mouth.

"The police might reopen Herman's death as a murder investigation. You should expect a call from--."

Skumansky leaned forward abruptly and slammed an iron fist on the desk, sending more shells scattering in every direction.

"Do you have *any idea* what you're doing?" his voice boomed.

"When *police* get involved people-- *good people* can get *hurt*, my friend. Now that you've dragged the police into this matter, this *Beis Din* has no choice! You will suffer the consequences, my friend. Jewish law *will* prevail– make no mistake. *This* court will see to *that*!"

Once again, the cheerleader chimed in from behind, "*The Rav*'s *Beis Din* does not let these things go on unchecked!"

"You will soon see the power of this *Beis Din*."

Chapter Fifty-Five

Fishel Fogal paced back and forth in the rear of *The Rav*'s apartment building, waiting in the blustery cold Friday afternoon, per Gavriel Diamond's instructions.

Gavriel assured him a more prominent position in the organization once he took over. That moment was now close at hand. But Fishel wasn't sure he wanted any part of it. Not that he could afford to forfeit his only source of income-- *especially* with the IRS still breathing down his neck for back-taxes. But Jake Cooper's threat panicked him-- he was coming after him for the *unthinkable* things he performed for that very same *Beis Din*.

If Jake exposed him, years of stooping to perform those menial tasks will have been for nothing. After Jake's visit, he had to break back into his own apartment to call Gavriel to say he wanted out-- and demanded those children be returned to Mindy!

But Gavriel calmed him by guaranteeing their incident would remain secret, though he wouldn't say how. He promised more details if Fishel waited to meet him outside *The Rav*'s apartment.

But, where was he?

*****

Gavriel needed Fishel's help if he was to continue the operation successfully. There was no one else who could, or *would* do the things Fishel did on behalf of their *Beis Din*.

Gavriel was delayed by Jake's interruption. Now hustling down the wooden back staircase, he hoped Fishel would still be waiting. Though he had bigger fish to fry, the twist Jake introduced into the *Beis Din*'s latest venture, just might solve all his problems.

Leaning over the railing as he rounded the first landing, Gavriel searched the backyard for signs of Fishel, but he was nowhere to be seen.

He thought about the file lacking his name. *No way.* This was *not* going to happen. But he needed a *plan.* Fortunately, today's turn of events provided just what he needed.

If *The Rav* were arrested as a *kidnapper-*, or *worse–that* would be perfect. With *The Rav* unable to remain in his position, Gavriel could just step in and take over.

Eliminating Jake Cooper could easily be pinned on *The Rav* as well.

Gavriel was certain *The Rav* would invoke the rarely exercised power of the *Beis Din* if things escalated, and he had the perfect plan to make that happen.

But the timing would have to be just right.

Rounding the back stair's ground-floor landing, he was relieved to finally spot the lovable rotund figure, bouncing around the backyard like a soccer ball.

"This is *it*, Gavriel! I won't *take it* anymore," Fogal yelled. "*You* created this problem and *I'm* the one that's *paid* for it *all these years*. Make it go away or I'll-- I'll--."

"Calm down, my dear Fishel," Diamond said soothingly, placing his hand on the shorter man's shoulder. "I didn't *force* you to do anything, *did I*? Besides, I'm *way* ahead of you. I think we can finally put all that behind us, once and for all."

He reached to caress Fishel's cheek, but Fishel's arm smacked his hand away.

"Don't touch me, you *vantz*! I was weak. I made a mistake. I shouldn't have to pay for it the rest of my *life*. I'm tired of this. All these years I've done– and for *what*? For his *silence*? Now Jake's going to expose me anyway. I *know* what needs to be done and if you don't help me get those kids back to Mindy Stein, *I'll* turn you in myself! You *know* where they are. *Start talking*!"

"No, my dear friend. You needn't resort to such extremes. I have a *better* plan-- one that solves *more* than just *this* problem. Leave the thinking to me," he coaxed, pointing at his forehead.

"*I'll* take care of you. I always *have*."

Chapter Fifty-Six

After leaving Skumansky's, Jake's body shook like an autumn leaf, desperately clinging to life in the cold, howling wind. He headed on foot to meet Mort again at the Dunkin' Donuts on Devon.

"You look *terrible*," Mort exclaimed as he approached Jake's stool. "What *happened*? You know something I don't?"

"Not exactly," Jake explained. He let out a deep breath then downed the last drop of sediment from his hot chocolate. "Any news from Roberts about the kids?"

"Afraid not."

"Isn't there *anything* you can do, Mort?"

"Jake, usually these things end up with the kids running off on their own, or at a friend's house."

"But Mort, we *know* they were taken out of school under false pretenses." Jake spilled what he knew about Malke Stein-- the abuse, her being sent away for a fresh start. "She lied to get the kids. Isn't that *enough*?"

"For you and me, *maybe*. But the department isn't considering this a high priority. I've tried pleading your case, Jake, believe me. I wondered why they were dragging their feet. But now that you mention this Malke Stein thing, it makes sense. Isn't it possible they're with her– with *family*? She *is* the children's real aunt. Have you considered that possibility? There may not even be any *dangerous* foul play here. You yourself questioned Hoffmeyer's reliability. She's the only one feeding you this line about Skumansky *kidnapping* the kids. Can you really believe her? Be patient, Jake. Patience and discipline are the cornerstones of a good detective."

"But Mort, you can't just look at this as an isolated incident. I was just at Skumansky's. There's no doubt in my mind he's behind the kidnapping. I *know* it!"

"Did he actually say he did it?"

"Well, no but–."

"Did you gather any solid evidence by talking to him?"

"No," Jake admitted.

"Then, in the department's eyes, you don't *know* squat."

"But you have to put it all in context," Jake insisted. "Sender convinced Skumansky that Mindy was an evil mother. I know Skumansky helped Sender keep the kids away from her then. Diamond didn't deny it when I confronted him. Even after Sender's death, Skumansky was there to testify after having Marsha Rein petition the court to take the children away. The man just hasn't *stopped*."

"Suppose you're right," Mort continued the thought. "Why *now*, Jake? They've been trying to get the kids away from Mindy since before Sender died. If they were willing to *kidnap* them, why didn't they just have Sender take off with them, like Pinky's ex-wife did?"

Jake thought about that, then suggested, "Maybe Sender didn't feel like going into hiding."

"Good point. Good point." Mort downed the rest of his coffee, plopped it down on his saucer and motioned the waitress to hit him again. "So why not nab the kids right after Sender died? Why wait until now? And why bother hiring Marsha to file a petition-- why shoot a *pistol* when you've got a *cannon*?"

Jake thought about that and responded, "Because, why chance something illegal when they could do it legit? According to Pinky, Marvin Fox has political ties. He could have lined up a judge to take away Mindy's kids *legally*."

Mort wrapped his hands around the fresh mug of hot java, staring down into it, searching for the answer hidden in the hot liquid. Mort raised two fingers. "Two thoughts." He redisplayed the count, starting at one. "I now understand how *and why* I was ordered to shut Herman's death investigation down so quickly. When I questioned

Marvin Fox about his brother-in-law's death, he insisted we couldn't do an autopsy-- said it was against his religion. But I was adamant about following the regs– wouldn't give him an inch. He probably called in a favor before I'd even left the scene. Those things can happen fast."

"Second," he continued, releasing another finger, "if they've got connections, why didn't filing that petition pan out?"

"We got lucky, Mort. There was a scheduling problem. The judge originally assigned, called in sick. It got reassigned to a judge with no patience for Rabbi Skumansky's antics." Motioning skyward Jake added, "*Somebody* was looking out for Mindy."

"Interesting-- *very* interesting, indeed Jake. You've got a good, solid, hypothesis. Now follow up and see where it leads. Can't convict on a *hunch* you know."

"What about the kids, Mort? Do you think you could convince Roberts to at least check out Skumansky?"

"I hate to say it, but I wouldn't expect too much. Fox probably put the kibosh on that already– that explains Robert's reluctance to move on this. I'll see what I can do. Meanwhile, regardless of what *we* think, tell Mindy not to worry. Tell her the kids'll probably turn up soon."

"*Now*, young man, what did you mean before,

nothing's new, *exactly*?"

"He really was a good detective," Jake thought. He didn't miss a trick. Jake recounted his confrontation with Skumansky.

"*Unbelievable*," Mort said, shaking his head. "These people call themselves *religious*? How can they do this to their *own* people?"

"Is that the file?" Jake asked, pointing to a familiar large envelope, parked halfway inside the outer pocket of Mort's coat.

He slapped the envelope onto the counter. "Like I said before– when I retired, I went to get the original file. I was told it had been lost, but I managed to get the negatives from the lab. I finally had the reprints made, after Miriam passed on-- figured it'd take my mind off things. I didn't make much of them until *you* noticed they'd been made *backwards*."

Mort slurped his coffee.

Jake rescued the file from the coffee dripping from the bottom of Mort's mug. "Mind if I take another look?"

"Be my guest. Been looking at it every which way since you told me it was backwards. Not like me to miss something like that. My granddad used to drag me to High Holiday services. Guess I shoulda paid more attention--

might've learned to at least recognize the Hebrew alphabet. Never know what you'll need to know to solve a case. I shoulda caught that." He ran his fingers through his hair, shaking his head. With the wave of a hand he said, "*Aaach!* I'm getting too old to be any good at this. Who'm I kiddin'? Go ahead. *You* look at 'em. Maybe you'll catch something *else* I missed."

Mort emptied his second cup of coffee, then covered the cup when the waitress headed his way.

"You ever thought about it, Jake?"

"About what?"

"Bein' a detective-- police work? You'd be *good* at it. Got an eye for detail, know how to talk to people. Most of all, you got *guts*, kid."

"Is he talking about me?" Jake wondered. "*Guts?* Where were my guts on the lake? I didn't even have the guts to jump in the water! I had *no* guts *that* day."

"Hey son," Mort said, snapping his fingers in Jake's face. "You drop into a trance? Should I call a shrink?"

"Sorry," Jake replied.

Jake felt he'd come a long way in the past few months. He certainly accomplished more than he ever thought possible. But *police* work? He'd never even entertained the idea.

Jake opened the file, examining the black and white shots, again picturing everything in reverse. There was no mistaking it. The reflection of the Hebrew lettering wasn't reversed. That meant despite being a lefty, Herman was holding the knife in his right hand, *not* his left, like the backward photo suggested. The little slip of paper beneath the desk blotter, the cup holding pens, pencils, and those scissors-- all were actually on the opposite side of the desk.

Scissors.

"Mort," Jake said, pointing to the faux suicide note that had been cut from the manuscript, "we established the murderer knew about Herman's manuscript, this excerpt in particular. They not only knew that was in it– they knew the *exact page* to cut it out from. That means the murderer must have *read* Herman's manuscript. Fox said Herman wanted him to finance its publication. He *says* he wasn't interested, but maybe he *was*."

Jake related how Fox lied about not having a key to the Steins' back door. "If he lied about *that* he could be lying about *other* things. Maybe he *didn't* turn Herman down, flat out," Jake hypothesized. "Maybe he *took* the manuscript to *read* it, then decided it couldn't make any money. He could have snipped out this section, used his key to access the apartment when he knew Herman would be napping-- he *probably* even knew where Herman kept his slaughtering knife– his *chalif*."

Mort's face lit up. "That's *good* Jake-- *very* good! His motive would have been the blackmailing. He was so damn adamant about me wrapping up that case quickly, and without an autopsy. Having political ties, he may have known the M.E.'s reputation and exploited it, knowing if he insisted it wasn't suicide, the M.E. would do the opposite. It's beginning to fit like that proverbial *glove*, Jake. You may be *on* to something here. Motive, means *and* opportunity. You've just identified our number one– and *only*, solid suspect. More than I've accomplished in all these years. It's embarrassing."

Jake thought about the other suspect he discovered– Sender's murderer. It would have been cruel to drop that one on Mort too just now, so he kept that to himself. Besides, he wasn't ready to discuss it, even with Mort, until he confronted Mindy and decided for himself. But there were a few other things it was time to share with Mort.

When Jake had finished, Mort said, "*Wow*! Talk about *motive*! This Fox guy was *double-loaded* with motives. You think he killed Herman because Herman abused his niece-- the Malke Stein you mentioned before?"

"I think it at least fueled his fire. Add that to

Herman's threat to go public with the *glatt* kosher meat situation at Shalomski's, and you've got one *hell* of an angry man."

"So, you think Fox executed this fake-suicide murder by himself, and nobody ever knew?"

"Oh, I think *someone* knew."

"Well, you're just *full* of surprises tonight, aren't you?" Mort flopped his hands over backwards toward Jake. "Okay. Who knew, *Mr. Detective*?"

"Did you know that Rabbi Skumansky was a *meshulach*? He went door-to-door raising money for the *yeshiva*. Traveled around the states for a while."

"So, what?"

"*He* was the one boarding at the Stein's home when Herman was murdered." Jake recounted the theory he shared with Pinky, about Skumansky overhearing Herman blackmail Fox and then blackmailing Fox himself into financing his organization, hoping to shut him up.

"Maybe Skumansky actually *saw* Fox kill Herman," Jake speculated. "Maybe he saw him cut the note from the manuscript and *everything*. Skumansky seemed all bent out of shape when he thought *I* had Herman's manuscript. Maybe he knew that would lead me to Fox. He'd lose a big supporter-- take a big financial hit. What else could *possibly* be so important about Herman's manuscript? It has no real commercial or scholarly value."

"Jake, didn't you say Fox also asked you for Herman's manuscript? Maybe Skumansky told Fox you had it."

"Actually, no. Fox never asked me for *Herman's* manuscript, only Skumansky asked me for that. But Fox *did* ask me for *Sender's* manuscript. He practically went berserk when he thought I had it. Maybe Sender discovered what Fox had done, drafted a little telltale manuscript, then threatened his rich uncle with it."

"Gotch'ya," Mort said, shooting an imaginary target with a finger-gun. "And, maybe Fox, who'd already killed once, killed again to get rid of Sender."

Jake hadn't thought it that far through, but having him concentrate on Fox as the prime suspect in Sender's murder would keep him off Mindy as a suspect-- at least for the time being.

"You're right, Mort! I hadn't thought of that, but come to think of it, Mrs. Stein still has Herman's manuscript. She showed it to me, hoping I might be interested in it. She said Sender asked for it, then gave it back to her in a panic, shortly before he was killed."

"See Mort," Jake said, patting his back, "you

466

haven't lost your touch."

It was time to pay Marvin Fox another visit.

Chapter Fifty-Seven

Jake made it home just before sundown and rustled up a *Shabbos* dinner from the meager rations in his fridge-- two slices of pita-bread, leftover vegetable soup and a week-old bottle of Manischewitz wine. He flipped a white cloth over the dining room table, laid out his spread, and rushed through his Friday night prayers before downing his feast.

The white pages listed only one Marvin Fox on the 6300 block of Central Park-- Peterson Park-- the upscale, right-wing, Orthodox hood.

It was a half-hour's hike away. The weather turned slick.

Gusts of freezing rain smacked Jake's face as he hustled south on McCormick until it became Kimball.

He marched on as the pitch-dark rush hour wound down.

Making his way over to Central Park, he located the Georgian bearing the listed address. It seemed disappointingly narrow-- not what he expected for the wealthy entrepreneur's abode. But as the door opened in response to his knock, it revealed a grand, high-ceilinged entrance and rooms extending beyond his view.

A large Hispanic woman, clad in a starched, gray and white uniform, greeted him silently. She uttered something Jake couldn't decipher and waited expectantly.

"I need to speak with Mr. Fox."

"Martina, who is it?" Marvin inquired as he popped his head through the doorway behind

her.

The instant Jake locked eyes with him, he said, "It's okay Martina. Go back to the kitchen-- I got it."

Examining Jake through the reading glasses balanced on the tip of his nose, Marvin folded his arms tightly around his maroon smoking jacket and silk tie and snapped, "We're in the middle of our *Shabbos* dinner, for God sake! What do you want *now*?"

"Good *Shabbos*," Jake said politely, offering the customary greeting that Marvin had failed to proffer. "Sorry for interrupting your dinner, but I just couldn't stop thinking about the way I behaved at the restaurant. I want to apologize."

Marvin's stance relaxed.

He slipped the glasses off his nose, letting them dangle from their gold chain against his chest.

"I walked all the way from Roger's Park. It's nasty out here. Can I come in for just a minute?"

He gestured Jake inside.

Wiping his feet on the inside doormat Jake said, "I was an emotional basket-case and got way out of line. I meant no harm. I hope you understand that and can forgive me. I'd really like to just *talk* with you for a minute."

Jake gave up trying to dry his soaked shoes and abandoned them beside the door. He draped his wet jacket onto the coat tree and followed Marvin inside.

As they passed the formal dining room, Marvin leaned into its doorway, announcing, "I'll be back in a minute, dear. Start dessert without me. I'll be back for dessert."

He led Jake through a maze of rooms that extended far deeper than a standard Georgian's lot size.

He led Jake downstairs to a full-fledged underground floor.

Walking past a home-theater, Jake noted the viewing pit, wet bar, and popcorn cart.

Peeking through the open door of a utility room, he caught a glimpse of metal shelving loaded with restaurant supplies, and neon Shalomski signs. He also noticed a huge pile of familiar looking bricks-- *antique paving bricks*.

Marvin opened a door on the far back wall, revealing a miniature *synagogue*. The room was lined with intricately carved mahogany bookcases, stuffed with Jewish books, and a velvet-curtained Ark, positioned at the front. Fluorescent lighting bounced off beige Berber carpeting. The room was filled with conference tables surrounded by padded folding chairs.

They sat across from each other at one of the tables. "So, let's *talk*," Marvin said.

Struggling to keep his cool, Jake delivered his spiel. "I just figured, being you're family to Mindy I– I just don't want to cause a rift. I don't know what happened. I just kept thinking about the kids– a *real* sore spot for me *personally*, not just about Mindy' kids. I'm sorry I went off the deep end. I'm trying to get a handle on *who* took them and *where* they are. I'm fairly certain that Rabbi Skumansky's behind this."

"You could be right. He *has* been known to do some wild things."

"If you *know* that, why do you support him? Unless, maybe, you *have* to."

No response.

"I also want to ask, why you lied to me about not having a key the day you found Herman with Malke."

Silence.

"You're not gonna let this go, *are* you?"

"Not until Mindy gets her kids back. I need to know the truth about everything even remotely connected to this. I have a feeling it's all connected somehow. Herman's death being no exception. I want those kids back home, *safely*. That's all I'm really after right now."

"Damn it!" Marvin's fist slammed the table. "Don't you think I want the same thing? They're *my* great nephew and niece for God's sake!"

Jake let him stew for a moment.

"I can't just--. I couldn't possibly--. *Damn it!*" His second fist landed beside the first. "Look. It's like I told you in the first place. I went there like I said, except, *yes*, I had a *key*." Marvin's eyes fixated on his hands as he spoke. "I thought you'd get the wrong idea so I said I didn't. But everything else I told you was one hundred percent straight. That bastard molested his own daughter. When he tried blackmailing me into funding his manuscript to help him gain a reputation as a scholar, I blew a cork. We were in his study, in the back room. I threatened to expose him and stormed out the back door. On my way out, I heard something on the landing but didn't see anyone. But as I opened my car door, he approached me with a proposition."

"*Who* approached you?"

"Skumansky. Claimed he was tired of schlepping

around collecting door to door– tired of being treated like a second-class citizen." Marvin looked up. "You know how they're treated. Most people tolerate them, but no one really likes them. They board with people who really don't want them around. My sister was a rare exception to that rule. Skumansky *insisted* he was destined for greater things. That he should be a great rabbi, not a *meshulach*. He said it would be most unfortunate if people knew where I got my meat for Shalomski's. He must've overheard Herman threaten me with that crap about the lower-grade *glatt* meat I used. He suggested that with a thumbs-up from the right rabbinical authority, people wouldn't question it. He proposed that I set him up as the head of his own *Beis Din*, so *he* could endorse Shalomski's. Of course, I knew his endorsement wouldn't mean squat. Nobody recognized him as an authority at that time. But he had me over a barrel."

"So, you've supported him all this time for *that*? Wouldn't it have been better, and cheaper to serve the higher-grade *glatt*?"

"No, no," he stammered, putting up a hand. "Let me finish. I told Skumansky off. Hell, I called him a– I believe my exact words were *hypocritical, bloodsucking, scumbag*."

Marvin hesitated for a moment, giving Jake the

once over. "I have a feeling I can trust you, Jake. I presume you've kept quiet about Malke. You'll have to keep this to yourself as well."

Jake nodded.

"When Skumansky boarded with Herman and my sister, I noticed he'd spend time in the apartment with her alone-- a big *no-no*, even for a *meshulach*. Certainly not appropriate for a great rabbi. Then, the day I'd caught Herman with Malke, my sister confessed she'd been having an affair with Skumansky. She blamed herself for Herman turning to Malke for something she should have provided."

"So, you countered *his* threat with a better one?"

"The *best*. I told Skumansky if he didn't keep his trap shut about the meat, I'd let the world know he'd slept with a married woman-- a sin worthy of the death penalty under Jewish law-- you know that. He'd *never* serve as a rabbi, anywhere. I told him to go to hell with his *proposal*."

He paused, then added, "Course I'd never hurt my sister that way, but he couldn't know that for sure."

"So why do you support--."

"My, you're an eager beaver. *Let me finish*. I know you mean well Jake, but a little patience goes a long way." He took a deep breath, then said, "After Herman was found with his throat slit, I got another visit from Skumansky-- in the cemetery, while we were burying Herman. Being a suicide, there was no funeral per se. But here he comes, playing the close friend of the family card, all weepy-eyed for my sister's benefit. He's a shrewd, cold, and calculating man Jake. He took me aside and said if I didn't fund him, he'd tell the police he heard *me* threaten to *kill* Herman. He knew I had a key *and* a reason to kill him. He said he'd tell them I planted the suicide note and staged the whole thing. I panicked. The man had me by the *you-know-what.* I repeated my counter-threat to expose his affair if he did that, but *he* claimed-- and rightly so, that no one would believe me. They'd assume I made up the affair to discredit him. He's one shrewd operator. I was trapped, same as if I'd been the one nailed into that coffin. What choice did I have but to pay him, and keep on paying?"

"So, you gave him the seed money to start his little *Beis Din.* I understand that now. But how did he get so much *clout* in the community?"

"Skumansky's no dummy. He desperately wanted to be a big-shot rabbi. It was his life's dream. He had me talk him up to my friends and associates, build up his reputation, and recommend people to him to advise on personal and eventually, community matters. In his second year of operation, he got involved in a high-profile divorce case. He helped the daughter of a prominent, and politically connected community member get sole custody of her six kids. Skumansky realized he had a good thing going and muscled his way into every divorce case he could, the nastier the better, racking up favors like poker chips to be cashed in at the appropriate time."

"He really doesn't need my support anymore. He's made a big name for himself– got an arsenal of supporters. But every once in a while, he drops a subtle hint to keep me in line. Matter of fact, he called me after you asked him about Herman's manuscript. Told me he was doing me a favor, tipping me off about a potential problem. What he really did was drop one of his hints that he could still go to the police with his fairy-tale about me doctoring up Herman's suicide. That's why when you asked me about the manuscript, I thought you were after the one that *Herman* wrote. But then it became clear, you were asking me about Sender's manuscript. Sender and Fogal had a little business going. Fogal was providing dirt on wealthy community members and Sender wrote them down. Then Sender offered those portrayed in it, the opportunity to finance his book's demise, though he phrased it more like he was selling the rights to the highest bidder who could do with it as he saw fit. I still wonder if Skumansky spilled some beans in exchange for a cut. Sender claimed he wrote that *I* killed his father. I'm sorry he suffered such a horrible death, but he wasn't exactly my *favorite* relative. He turned up dead before I even had a chance to think my way around that problem. The police should *really* be looking into the *other* victims of his novel. I would've come forward about it if the charges against Mindy hadn't been dropped. Fortunately, they were, so there's no reason to reveal this circumstantial evidence pointing at me. I *didn't* do it, of course. But it could easily be used to make a case against me."

"I was right about one thing," Jake thought. "Like father, like son. But it was *blackmail* they shared, not *suicide*."

"*Now* you know why I got so angry when you told me Herman's death was being investigated as a murder, and started accusing *me*. That trapped feeling I had in the cemetery, came back to haunt me."

Marvin dropped his head into his hands, ran his fingers through his hair and leaned back in his chair. "You know, it actually feels good to finally tell someone the whole story, lock, stock, and barrel. I never even told my *wife*-- she's better off not knowing. The *whole community's* better off not knowing what monsters lurk amongst us."

Though Jake strongly disagreed on that last count, he let the comment go unchallenged. A voice wailed down the stairs. "Marvin, your tea's getting cold. Are you almost done?"

"I really should be getting back upstairs," Marvin said.

"Just one more thing," Jake pleaded.

"*Shoot.*"

"I noticed the bricks in your utility room-- the paving bricks. What are they for? Where'd you get so *many* of them?"

"Oh, *those*? I have several antique dealers collecting them for me. I'm going to remodel my stores. I want something unique for Shalomski's besides the name. Like a trademark– a distinct look."

Jake knew that Mindy having one of these was no coincidence. That brick *must* be from Marvin's stash. But how would *she* have one?

"Do you ever give any to people in the community?"

"Over the years, I've given some to friends here and there for little backyard projects and the like. As long as it's not used in a manner that will undermine the new Shalomski image. I want to capture the sense of dining at an old Polish street cafe."

"Did you ever give any to Mindy or Sender?"

"Not that I recall. Why do you ask?"

"No reason, really," Jake lied. "They're unusual bricks. I'm sure I've seen them somewhere besides Shalomski's. That's all."

Marvin invited Jake to join his family for dessert and tea. Recalling the dastardly weather awaiting him, he graciously accepted. It was nine-thirty when he finally headed home.

The wet weather had transformed into an icy chill. Skate-walking along the ice-slicked sidewalks, Jake passed a bank thermometer reporting the temperature at twenty-nine. It was nearly ten-- time was running out fast. Despite the new information, he felt no closer to locating the children. Passing block after block of row houses, he wondered if Mindy's kids were inside one of those tidy, cozy little homes. Perhaps, they'd even been told their mother was dead-- killed in the fictitious accident announced at their classroom door. It would devastate them. First their father, now their mother. He hoped Mindy had heard something positive by now, though he didn't really expect it. Either way, given the prohibition of using the phone on *Shabbos*, he'd have to wait till morning. Jake was due there for lunch but figured he'd run over there early.

Marvin seemed genuinely sincere. This time, Jake believed he hadn't held back. Despite his innocence, he was right to be nervous about his dealings with Herman getting leaked to the police. Heavy-duty circumstantial evidence like that could definitely be used against him. The bad news for Jake was that he still didn't know who *really* killed Herman.

Picking up his pace to keep warm, Jake rehashed everything he'd learned, searching for another possibility.

He thought of Fishel Fogal and Gavriel Diamond's sexual secret at the *yeshiva*. Herman might have learned about it-- maybe he overheard Skumansky tell someone while he was boarding with them. That had possibilities. Fogal was a physically powerful man for his age. He must have been a *real* powerhouse in his youth. And he was *definitely* capable of violence. Herman clearly demonstrated *his* blackmailing skills to Marvin. He even came back for seconds, although he failed. Perhaps he tried blackmailing Fogal after Marvin didn't pan out and Fogal killed him instead of paying.

Jake mulled that theory over most of the way home, methodically stepping through the mechanics of how Fogal would have done it. But the theory eventually fell apart.

How would he have read Herman's manuscript?

How would he have accessed Herman's study, undetected by Mrs. Stein without a key?

There were no signs of forced entry. Was it possible Herman woke up in response to a knock at the back door that his wife didn't hear? Maybe he let Fogal in, not expecting violence. But how would Fogal have known about that passage in Herman's manuscript? Did Herman give it to him to read, to consider it for financing publication? Fogal didn't seem wealthy. Why would Herman approach him for that?

Too many things just didn't add up– the *glove* didn't fit.

Jake dismissed Fogal as a viable suspect as he rounded the corner to his building. He concluded that both Mort and he must be overlooking something. Maybe the whole thing was a mistake. Maybe they were too quick to scream murder when there simply was none.

Maybe Herman did himself in, after *all*. So, *what* if Herman was left-handed and the knife was in his right hand? Maybe he cut with his right. He was a *shochet*, and old-world thinking stigmatized lefties. The *Talmud* relates how being a lefty was considered one of several blemishes disqualifying a Levite from performing the full gambit of their ritual duties in the ancient Jerusalem Temple. That could explain why Herman slaughtered himself with his right hand. Sure, the note he left was odd, but not enough to conclude it wasn't suicide.

An odd note from an odd man?

Possibly.

Sender's death however, was another matter.

Snuggling under his quilt, Jake searched for a pocket of warm air to chase the chill from his bones. But there was only one thing that could chase away his biggest chill. He'd put it off long enough.

Chapter Fifty-Eight

Jake overslept Saturday morning and arrived late for lunch at Mindy's. It was time to confront her about Sender's death. Though his bones had thawed from his Friday night trek home from Marvin's, the icy chill deep within, remained.

Would the truth melt it, or become an icicle that would pierce his heart?

After lunch, Adam went to his room, and Mindy and Jake went for a stroll in the park.

They strolled through the park's mini-zoo where children of all ages enjoyed the unexpected park hurrah granted by the day's unusually warm weather.

A boy about Danny's age, raced past them. A young girl dangled over the log fence, squealing, and pointing excitedly to a pygmy goat.

Jake watched tears well up in the corner of Mindy's eye. But she was watching him as well.

"Jake, what's the matter? You're trembling. There's something you're not telling me, isn't there?"

"I'm fine. *Well*, maybe *not* so fine."

He wasn't ready to come out with it yet, but he couldn't deny that something was wrong. "I've been threatened," he explained as they circled the duck pond.

"Rabbi Skumansky threatened to excommunicate me if I go to the police about the kidnapping. But I'm sure it's just a scare tactic to get me to back off. But I'm *not* backing off. I'm close to finding Sarah and Danny. I can *feel it*. Don't worry about a thing, Mindy. They're not being harmed. That much I've learned from Dr. Hoffmeyer. She says the kids are with an Orthodox woman somewhere right here, in the community. I'm sure Skumansky knows where they are. I'm also certain *he's* behind this kidnapping."

"Jake, you know I appreciate everything you've done-- *are* doing. I'm sorry they threatened you. Can't the police *do* something? What does Mort say?"

He wanted to reassure her that the police were helping, but he knew otherwise.

"Mort says this isn't a priority for the police. My guess is someone with powerful connections is pulling strings-- probably Skumansky or one of his groupies. If I'm going to find the kids-- and I am-- I've got to push forward. I'm *so close*. But according to Dr. Hoffmeyer, we've only got twenty-four hours left to find them before they get shipped off to an unknown destination."

"*Darn!*" Jake realized, "I forgot. I haven't told her

about that yet."

The dam, holding her welled up tears at bay, finally burst. Jake reached to wipe the salty-streams from her cheeks but his arm was smacked aside by a suddenly feisty powerhouse.

"*When* did she tell you that?" Mindy asked.

Her shove nearly sent him stumbling onto the bench behind him. The small redhead he'd grown so fond of, packed a punch more powerful than he ever imagined.

"A punch powerful enough to send a man off a roof," he thought.

"What *else* aren't you telling me, Jake? These are *my* children. Don't you think I have a *right* to know," she yelled, thumping her chest. "How *dare* you!"

Mindy collapsed onto the bench, sobbing hysterically. A small crowd gathered, keeping their distance. People gawked from all across the park. Jake returned the invasive stares, particularly from the Orthodox men and women. He studied their faces.

Did *they* know where the kids were? Were they involved?

He sat down beside Mindy.

"Don't worry," he assured her, "I'm *going* to find them."

Chancing another blow, he reached to wipe the tears from her cheeks. She succumbed to his comforting gesture.

"You'll hold them both in your arms very soon."

"Sorry," she said. "I can't help it. They're all I can think about. You said they're not being harmed, physically. But what about *emotionally*, Jake? And what about *me*? What have they been told? Why isn't their mother there for them? What if they told them I didn't want to see them anymore?"

"Mindy, you know they love you. They're old enough to realize something's not right. They know if you could, you'd be there for them."

Painfully aware of the ramifications of not finding them before the rapidly approaching deadline, Jake decided it was time. He had to have all the cards on the table. "There's something else, Mindy."

She stopped, turned toward Jake, and looked up tearfully, into his eyes. "Let's have it– *all of it*. No more secrets, *okay*?"

"*Deal*," he said.

He explained how he learned about the brick thrown off the roof into Mr. Shapiro's truck. "That was probably the breaking glass you said you heard."

No reaction.

"Mindy, if I'm not going to keep secrets, neither can you. *Okay*?"

"What is it, Jake?"

"Here goes," he thought. "Mr. Shapiro saw *you*. It *was* you, wasn't it?"

"Oh God!" she said, burying her head in her hands.

"*Yes*," she said. "It was *me*."

"I hope you don't hate me, Jake. You must think I'm an awful person."

His body went numb.

He felt light-headed.

He gripped the bench with his arm.

The worst was over, but the shocking truth was more than he could handle. He didn't know *what* to think of her. Sure, she was provoked. But she *killed* the father of her own children. How was he *supposed* to feel?

"You *killed* Sender and then *conned* me into helping you get away with it?" he muttered angrily. "What the *hell* am I supposed to *think*!"

Slam! Mindy shoved him again, this time sending him three feet off the bench. Jake's head nearly hit the pavement.

"How *dare you*! How could you even *think* I did such a thing?"

"What the hell are you *talking* about? You just *admitted* it. What else *should* I think?"

"I said I was *there*-- *I* threw that brick. It's not something I'm proud of. But I didn't *kill* him. I was angry-- *damn* angry. He taunted me. Told me he'd return the kids if I came over to the house. I rushed over there only to find the place deserted. Sender was a cruel man. I don't know what possessed me to ever marry him. When I got back home and saw him lying there, dead, I felt cheated-- someone had stolen my only chance for revenge. I *wanted* to kill him, but I could never actually *do* such a thing. As cruel as Sender was, I could *never* do *that*. He was *already* dead. I went up to the roof to try and figure out what happened. That's when I saw that *brick*. It was my last chance. I *needed* to throw that brick at him, Jake. So, I just *did it*. I took my revenge in my own way. But I didn't *kill* him for God's sake! I didn't think it was important for the police, or anyone to know. I'm ashamed of what I did, Jake. I didn't want anyone to know– *especially* not you."

"*Hallelujah!*" Jake thought. "She *didn't* do it."

He knew there had to be a good explanation. Though she originally lied, he was certain she was being truthful now. "I won't tell a soul," he said. "It'll be our secret. I don't blame you. I can only *imagine* how you must have felt."

They returned to Mindy's apartment just before sundown. Adam was still napping and Mindy woke him in time for the *Havdalah* ceremony marking the end of the *Shabbos*.

Jake helped Mindy prepare by setting up the candle and taking out the *besamim* spice box while she customarily over-poured a silver goblet of wine.

"I thought we could sniff *this* instead of the regular besamim," Adam said, holding up a shriveled *esrog* with cloves jammed into it.

"Sure, we can," Jake replied.

"His father used a home-made *besamim* like that one," Mindy whispered in Jake's ear as he took the dried clove-studded *esrog* from Adam.

Jake held it in one hand and raised the goblet with his other.

Adam held the candle as Mindy lit it.

"*Hinei...*" Jake recited over the wine, cloves, and fire, holding the *besamim* to his nose, and reflecting the candle light with his fingernails at the appropriate moments.

Afterward, Jake took one more sniff of the aromatic studded dried fruit.

Breathing deeply, he closed his eyes, letting the scent overtake him. He distinguished the musky scent of the cloves from the tingling citrusy aroma of the lemon-like *esrog*.

Thoughts of *sukkos* past flashed before him– happy thoughts.

He recalled this past holiday, when he'd taken Pinky to shop for an *esrog* at Rabbi Skumansky's backyard sale.

But the smell also surfaced memories of another event. A more *recent* event.

When Adam left the room Jake said, "Mindy– the *esrog* smell. Now I *remember* what smelled *so* familiar when Pinky and I checked out the roof, the night Sender was killed. Those fibers I pulled from my shoe smelled like the horsehair wadding wrapped around an *esrog* to prevent it from bruising. It must have been left on the roof either by Skumansky or Fogal-- more likely *Skumansky*. He's probably got a stockpile of that stuff left over from his yard sale."

Yard.

"*That's it! That's* where I've seen those paving bricks besides Shalomski's. When Pinky and I went to Skumansky's to buy our *esrogim,* we entered the yard from the *side* of the building instead of the alley. The walkway

490

was *paved* with *those bricks*. I'm *sure* of it. Marvin must have given him some to pave his walkway and he brought extras to carry out Sender's death sentence. They used those bricks to carry out a sentence of *death by stoning*. He must have found out Sender was sleeping with Laurie Smilow. She didn't have a *Get--* Sender was committing a sin punishable by death. I'll bet Skumansky carried out the sentence."

"But what about Laurie," Mindy asked. "Isn't she guilty of the death penalty too?"

"Yes. *That's* probably why she took off when Sender was executed."

"Now it makes *sense*," Mindy said. "Didn't Mrs. Goldstein tell you she heard Sender screaming about no warning?"

"You're right! A prerequisite for a finding of the death penalty is for two witnesses to warn the offender of the specific violation prior to the transgression."

"So, Sender was saying he wasn't warned," Mindy added.

"*Right*. But they killed him anyway."

"But why on *my* roof?"

"Well, it could be to meet the height requirement for a stoning death. They throw the sinner off a cliff or high place and if they aren't killed by the fall, they throw stones to finish him off. That's how stoning is carried out. But I think there was *more* to it. All along Skumansky's been trying to separate you from the kids. He bought everything Sender told him about you. When he determined Sender was to die, he decided to use *your* roof and had Fogal break into your apartment to get *your* hair into Sender's watchband, to frame you for it. *Remember–* your mirror was smashed on the floor. He was probably fumbling with your brush to get the hair. It would have been the perfect solution. He could kill two birds with one stone– *eliminate* Sender *and* separate your kids from *you*."

"But that failed when the charges against me were dropped," Mindy said.

"Exactly! *That's* why Skumansky had Marsha file that petition. And when even *that* didn't work, he went to plan C-- *kidnapping*."

"Now it all fits," Jake said. "Like a *glove!*"

Stroking his beardless chin, he added, "Now we just have to figure out how to use this information to get your kids back."

Chapter Fifty-Nine

"You think Rabbi Skumansky *actually* sentenced Sender to death and then *executed* him?" Mort was having a hard time swallowing Jake's theory. Jake ran it by him because he was the only one qualified to help Jake really think this through. Pinky would be good for support, but Jake needed a genuine detective consultation right now.

"I never doubted he'd make a *finding* of death," Jake said. "But I couldn't imagine him carrying out sentencing. In ancient times, when the *Sanhedrin* convened in the Jerusalem Temple, they carried out an execution. Back then, Jewish law *was* the law of the land. But today, it's just a *formality*, an embarrassment. They excommunicate you, but that's as far as it goes. The *Talmud* requires compliance with local laws. Skumansky has no authority to carry out a death sentence."

"But your friend, Pinky-- *he* was physically beaten," Mort insisted.

"That's *precisely* what got me thinking Skumansky might not let the law of the land stand in his way. He ignored the law before. In fact, now I've learned that he violated Jewish law himself while boarding with the Steins. He had an affair with Mrs. Stein, according to Marvin Fox.

And, he incorrectly applied the law several times–
including kidnapping Mindy's kids on Sender's word alone,
coercing Pinky into authorizing a *Get*– conducting *bigamist*
marriage ceremonies. Plus, he accused me of just being a
moser for saying I would turn over the kidnappers to the
police. Clearly, he knows *just enough* to be dangerous, but
has no idea how to properly apply the law."

Jake didn't hear Mort get up, nor did he see him
refill his tea. "Jake, are you there?" Mort waved a hand
before his eyes.

"Yeah, I'm with you. I was just thinking about
Skumansky's sidekicks, Gavriel Diamond and Fishel Fogal.
They carried out Pinky's beating, surely ordered by
Skumansky-- they don't make a *move* without his approval.
Fogal's the one who broke into my place and attacked me.
He's *definitely* capable of physical violence, but--," Jake
massaged the back of his neck, pausing to think before
continuing. There were three pieces still missing from this
giant puzzle.

"Nah. Forget it. That's crazy."

"Jake, *don't stop*. Verbalizing hunches is
important."

"Well, I was *thinking*, there are four methods of
death that can be called for by the Jewish court. Stoning,

burning, beheading, and strangling. Sender was sentenced to stoning, which called for throwing him off a high place-- Mindy's roof, then pelting him with stones-- in this case bricks, if he didn't die from the fall."

"You're back-tracking, Jake. We've already gone over this."

"Stay with me, Mort. I'm getting to the *good* part."

Jake sipped his tea ignoring the scalding his lips received.

"Herman's throat was slit-- pretty close to a beheading sentence, *no*? I'm not sure which type of death incest calls for, but it doesn't matter. Skumansky doesn't seem to get these things right anyhow. Technically, Sender should have been strangled, not stoned. Stoning is for sleeping with a woman *engaged* to another man. But Laurie Smilow was *married* to another man-- she hadn't received her *Get* yet. Sleeping with a *married* woman calls for *strangling*, not stoning."

"You may be right, Jake. Skumansky was *logically* the only other person who could have known Herman was abusing his daughter. He lived there. He might have decided to rule Herman guilty of death. Maybe that was the beginning of his little underground *Beis Din*. It was shortly after that he set up shop, *wasn't it*? But it still seems a little far-fetched from a *motive* standpoint. If Skumansky's religious convictions aren't what they should be, isn't it odd he'd risk civil *murder* charges to carry out religious death sentences? He seems to be selective about his victims. He's probably got ulterior motives. I believe we've got the right man, but we haven't nailed down the motive just yet."

"The *Talmud* says a Jewish court that rules in favor of the death penalty more than once in seventy years is considered an unjustly murderous one," Jake said. "And now, we think Skumansky ruled for death *twice* in half that time."

Now that Mort had time to take it all in, Jake moved on to the next stage.

"All this is great, Mort. It fits like the glove you always talk about. But where do we *go* with it? The kids'll be gone by tomorrow afternoon. I'm *sure* Skumansky knows where they are. But we can't prove *anything*. How do we use our theories to get the kids back?"

"Honestly, there's only one thing to do at this point. Skumansky doesn't know what you can, or can't, prove. So, make him *think* you have proof. You might get a confession or provoke him to do something incriminating. It's our only shot right now."

"I *knew* you'd know what to do next. How do we go

about it?"

"We don't. If you're right– and I think you *are*, Skumansky and company are murderers. They won't hesitate to take either of us out. It's far too dangerous."

"I have to do *something*. I'm willing to take the chance. But I need you to back me up on this."

Mort silently cleared the table and dropped the dishes into the sink. He emptied the kettle, then plopped down beside Jake and said, "I can't believe I'm saying this but, *you're on*! I've got to do *something* with the rest of my life. Might as well start with this. Ever since Miriam passed, I've been hiding from life, not taking any chances. It's time to live again. God, this is *great*! I can feel the juices flowing already!"

Mort grabbed pen and paper, and constructed a step-by-step plan of action for Jake.

Jake watched the master at work.

He wanted to nail Skumansky, but there was a *right* way and a *wrong* way. Mort was steering him *right*, from a police perspective. But he needed *more* and he was too involved to decide for himself.

"There's just one thing I've got to check out before proceeding," Jake explained when Mort finished. "Skumansky may ignore the law, but I refuse to stoop to his level. I want to run this by Rabbi Miklin-- make sure we do this within the framework of Jewish law too."

*****

"Thanks for seeing me on such short notice," Jake said, taking a seat in Rabbi Miklin's office. The elderly Rabbi removed his crisp, black, Hamburg, carefully placing it on the desk.

"Now, how can I be of assistance?"

Jake reviewed his theory and Mort's plan.

"My main concern is getting Mindy's kids back. If I capture a couple of murderers in the process, *great.* Skumansky's dangerous. I suspect his actions are motivated by more than pure religious conviction, despite his stature in the community. But I don't want to violate Jewish law *myself* in the process of flushing him out."

"Don't worry about turning Rabbi Skumansky over to the authorities. We live in a society of due process. He'll get the benefit of the American justice system. What *does* concern me, however, is *your* safety. Mort's plan sounds like a good one, but also a *dangerous* one, Jake. Should you be risking your own life to catch this man, even for the children's sake?"

"Who else is there? Time is running out, *fast.* The

police aren't acting on this. Mort's passing my hypothesis along to a friend at the FBI, but who knows where that will lead, if anywhere, or how fast?" Bolstering his case Jake added a quote from the sages, "If not me, *who*? And if not now, *when*?"

The Rabbi smirked at his reference, nodding in agreement.

"Anyway," Jake said, "if things go according to plan, Mort will make sure nothing happens to me."

Chapter Sixty

Rabbi Skumansky checked his watch. It wouldn't be long now. But the timetable changed when Reb Yankel Cooper-- *Jake* called. He tried putting him off– to meet with him later. But Jake was adamant, saying he was going straight to swear out the complaint he already filed with the police unless he met with him no later than three.

It meant cutting things close-- the children wouldn't be transferred until five. Jake could ruin everything. It was time to deal with him, once and for all.

Immediately upon hanging up after Jake's call, the rabbi dialed the number to secure the assistance he needed to deal with Jake Cooper.

That settled, he called to have the children's time-table escalated.

Chapter Sixty-One

Sunday afternoon– *D-day.*

On his way to Skumansky's, Mort's words ran through Jake's head, over and over.

"We don't," Mort said, when advising Jake how to proceed. "If you're right, and I think that you are, Skumansky and Company are murderers. They won't hesitate to take either of us out. It's far too dangerous. *"*

But it was the only option. He *had* to take the chance.

He couldn't let those kids down.

Not again.

He was barely coping with the pain of losing his own.

He recalled being the happiest man alive that Father's Day. He took Debra for pizza and ice cream. She fell asleep as he drove up to Lake Geneva. He felt drowsy himself, after all the cheese and cream.

She woke as he parked near the lake and was ecstatic.

Boats Daddy! Can we *go*?

He secured Debra's life-vest, carefully tightening the strap. But she squirmed as if the foreign life-saving bulk surrounding her was smothering her.

It hurts daddy. Take it off.

He explained the importance of leaving it on. He *thought* she understood. But how much can a three-year-old really understand? He rowed out onto the lake in the lazy, sweltering June afternoon and located a secluded, shady spot. He leaned back, enjoying the peaceful moment while Debra scanned the water's surface for signs of marine-life.

He dozed off for what he thought was just a moment.

The loud splash and rocking of the tiny row-boat woke him up. But it was too late.

She was gone. Just like that.

He remembered hearing her words in his half-sleep.

Look Daddy, fishies!

He recalled steadying the boat by gripping the sides firmly, praying it wouldn't capsize, then shouting. "Debra! *Debra!*"

But there was no answer.

He mustered an inner strength, overcoming his aquatic-fear enough to lean over the side, and peer into the lake's murky depths.

But there was no sign of her except the miniature vest her little body occupied only seconds earlier, now dangling on the seat.

Shivering despite the ninety-degree heat, he shouted for help. But he'd done too good a job locating a secluded area.

He *knew* what he had to do, but he *froze*.

Jake cursed himself for never learning to swim. His parents had sent him for lessons. His grandfather, a retired, high school swimming coach, had tried his best. But it was no use. Jake couldn't overcome his fear of the water.

Debra's tiny body was eventually recovered just before midnight. Feelings he thought had healed, now surfaced. But a scar like this never completely heals. He just lived with the pain and tried not to think about it.

But now, it was foremost on his mind. It had been since Mindy's kids were taken. He let Debra down, his precious, only child.

He let them all down that day.

The trouble between Rachel and himself began shortly after, all because he was afraid.

There was only one way Jake could live with this pain now.

He could not make the same mistake twice. Two beautiful children would be emotionally scarred for life, *unless* he took a chance.

The time had come for him to see what kind of a man he really was.

"This one's for you, Debra."

The thought renewed his determination to beat Skumansky at his own game. He was *sure* he'd take the bait. Jake just hoped Mort would be there to catch him in the act.

Mort arranged to meet Jake with the police in an unmarked car at three, the time he'd originally arranged to meet with Skumansky.

But a few minutes shy of one-thirty, there was an unexpected call from Gavriel Diamond informing him that the timetable had been moved up. They wanted to meet at two. Jake didn't hesitate to agree because it bought him extra time. The kids' departure was imminent. He tried calling Mort but there was no answer at his place. Pinky was out on his routes today. Mindy didn't answer her line, and her machine didn't pick up either. Jake called Pinky's beeper, but there was no time to wait by the phone for a reply.

Gavriel instructed him to wait outside the garage, in the back of Skumansky's building, saying that they'd meet him there. Jake didn't have time to question why they weren't meeting in the rabbi's study. He made it there with five minutes to spare, carrying a briefcase containing his bag of tricks.

He paced the alley waiting for someone to show. By two thirty, Jake wondered if he'd been duped. He ran down to the corner, dialed Mort's number from a pay phone and left him a message.

He followed the brick-paved path around the side of the building, retracing the steps Pinky and he took earlier that year.

"Reb Yankel. Where are you going?" The voice came from behind.

Jake turned.

Skumansky smiled. "I apologize for the delay. Come, let's talk." Gavriel Diamond and Fishel Fogal lurked behind in Skumansky's tall, husky shadow.

Following them to the side door of the garage, Jake watched Skumansky flip up the tail of his long, black coat and fish out a key ring chained to his belt. Several tumbler clicks later the door popped open.

He followed Skumansky inside, with Diamond and Fogal prodding him from behind.

Just inside the garage's main door, small cartons were piled roof-high, stencil-stamped with the words *Product of Israel-- Esrog Exports Ltd., Tel Aviv, ISRAEL.*

The floor was littered with the same horsehair wadding Jake pulled from his shoe the night Sender was killed.

A large room divider blocked his view of the back of the garage. Skumansky parked himself at one end of a long, folding table, then motioned Diamond and Fogal to flank his right and left sides. He instructed Jake to sit opposite himself, at the far end of the table. It felt to Jake like a movie scene, where a wealthy couple rings for the butler to bring the salt from one end of the table to the other. The distance between them starkly contrasted the rabbi's cramped office they'd met in before.

"Now then, my friends," Skumansky began. "Reb Yankel Cooper-- excuse me, *Jake* Cooper, has made some rash decisions and taken action hastily-- very *serious* action. He has reported to the authorities that Sender Stein was murdered at the hand of this *Beis Din*. We are all aware of the serious nature of his actions and the inevitable consequences."

A broad grin spread over Skumansky's face. He fiddled with a pack of sunflower seeds, tossing the contents onto the table, then surrounding them with one arm, protectively.

"Although these accusations against us are false, the

police have a way of barging ahead without concern for the truth. Lawyers, district attorneys, and prosecutors looking to make names for themselves may latch on to this and press forward. We are aware how innocent people are convicted of crimes-- *serious crimes*, serving prison time, occasionally facing death, when in *fact* they have done nothing."

"Jake Cooper," the Rabbi bellowed, "Do you admit to the things that I have said?"

"Yes. This is all true. But there's more."

They were heading just where he wanted them to, but he needed to make certain they couldn't resist the bait. He plopped the briefcase he'd been carrying onto the table. Dramatically opening one latch, then the other, he opened the lid, drawing out a long, thin, velvet case. He cracked the case open, exposing the razor sharp *chalif* knife.

"*This* was used by *this very Beis Din* to *execute* Herman Stein, nearly thirty years ago."

Jake watched three pairs of eyes bug out at the display laid before them. Slipping a small envelope from the briefcase, he extracted a tiny slip of paper and laid that beside the knife. *"This* is the phony suicide note you left at the scene, and…" Reaching back into the briefcase for a third time, Jake withdrew a stack of rubber-banded, yellowed, papers. He slowly slipped off the bands and carefully flipped to one particular hand-written page where a piece had been cut out. "*This* is the page you cut that fake suicide note from," he announced, reuniting the slip of paper with its long-lost parent, demonstrating the perfect match. "It was in Herman's own handwriting, so you *knew* it would look like a legitimate suicide note."

Skumansky gripped both ends of the table leaning forward. His face twisted into an ice-cold stare that took on a certain familiarity. "You *foolish*, foolish man. And *why* would we do these things?"

Without flinching, Jake returned the rabbi's odd stare. It was the second time he'd seen it, only the first time it wasn't on Skumansky's face.

That look was familiar.

Yes. It was the same stare.

Of course, it was.

How could he have missed that before? It made so much sense now. Mort was right. Religious convictions were Skumansky's *means*, not his *motive*.

"You *killed* Herman Stein because you were sentencing him to death for incest with his daughter, Malke Stein."

Skumansky glanced quickly at his sidekicks, then

said, "I see you've done some research, my friend. Very interesting-- *impressive* even. But you are wrong."

"Of course, I am," Jake replied. "Because Malke Stein is *not* Herman's daughter. There was a *meshulach* boarding with the Steins-- a man who went on to become a respectable rabbi, heading up this very *Beis Din*. Yet, he was a man who did some very *un-respectable* things with Mrs. Stein. Things he would have preferred remain a secret."

Skumansky's face grew redder by the minute.

"This *meshulach* got *friendly* with Mrs. Stein while Herman was away at the slaughterhouse-- friendly *enough* to have a child with her. But Mrs. Stein never told Herman-- he believed Malke was his own. One day, this *meshulach* returned to the Steins' apartment unexpectedly. Coming up the backstairs, this *meshulach* overheard a conversation between Marvin Fox and Herman. A conversation revealing that Herman had been sexually abusing his *own daughter*-- a daughter he could never acknowledge. That *meshulach* was *you*, Rabbi Skumansky!"

Jake turned to Fogal and Diamond, "That's right! Your *holy* Chief Judge here committed adultery with a married woman– worthy of the death penalty himself."

Jake stared into Skumansky's eyes. "You listened as

the conversation erupted into an argument and gathered enough details to coerce Marvin Fox into financing this very *Beis Din*. But Herman discovered your affair with his wife, didn't he? He threatened to expose you. So, you came up with a plan to protect your daughter *and* keep your little secret. You convened this little *Beis Din*, perhaps for its very first case. You declared Herman Stein guilty of the death penalty, then proceeded to carry out the sentence in a way that protected the *Beis Din* members from prosecution. Clever. *Very clever*, I must say."

Diamond and Fogal just sat there, wide-eyed, ears at attention. Clearly, Skumansky's affair was big news to them.

"To the outside world, it appeared like a sad case of suicide. Rabbis Diamond and Fogal here actually believed Herman was abusing *his own* daughter, a crime punishable by death. They assisted you without doubting they were carrying out a justified sentence. They never suspected that Malke was in fact *not* Herman's daughter, but *yours*-- that he was not deserving of the death penalty at all. They never suspected the great Rabbi Joseph Skumansky had an illegitimate daughter named Malke."

Jake stared directly at Fogal and Diamond, "Until *today*, that is. And the police now know too. In fact, there's

also one other person who learned about this before today–
Sender Stein. He threatened to tell the police unless you
paid him off. But you took care of him before he had the
chance, once again using the ruling of the death penalty for
his adultery with Laurie Smilow as a cover, duping these
fine rabbi's here into helping you."

Skumansky began laughing uncontrollably, then
clapped. "A *wonderful* performance, Reb Yankel. A *most*
wonderful imagination, I must say."

But as quickly as he burst into laughter, he stopped.

"*Nonsense! All of it. Absolute* gibberish. We've
known each other too long for them to believe a word of
your fantasy. Isn't that so, my friends? They can tell you I
did *none* of those things."

But Diamond and Fogal remained silent.

Jake swore he caught a smirk flash across
Diamond's lips.

Skumansky pulled an envelope from his jacket's
breast pocket and extracted a folded sheet of paper.
Carefully unfolding it, he placed a pen on top of it and slid
it down the table toward Jake. It stopped just short of the
velvet *chalif* case.

Jake picked it up and read it aloud. "I have done a
foolish thing. I have given the authorities information that

jeopardizes Rabbi Joseph Skumansky and others. I now realize this was wrong. I am ashamed and know that I should never have done this."

"You committed a serious crime by going to the police, my friend. But I know you have a good soul and want to repent. Sign this now, in our presence so we can be assured you have seriously repented. We wouldn't want to invoke the death penalty against *you* if you do it again."

Jake smiled, thinking, "*Ya, Right.* A glorified *suicide note* was what Rabbi Joseph Skumansky had just handed me. All it needs is my signature."

Jake checked his watch-- *two forty-five.* Still a full fifteen minutes before Mort's scheduled arrival. There was no way to stall for that long. But he had to try.

If Skumansky wanted a suicide note by golly, he was going to get a beauty. Jake faked some tears and sniffled, letting his tears drip onto the paper. He signed it in big, bold, script and slid it back across the table.

He noticed Fogal whisper something to Diamond, but Diamond shooed him away.

Skumansky took the document, examined it, and handed it to Diamond who inspected it, then handed it to Fogal. "Rabbis," Skumansky said, "are we all in agreement that this is sufficient?"

They nodded their approval and Fogal handed it back to Skumansky.

"Well then, my friend. I think we can now assume you will not pursue this matter nor cooperate with the authorities regarding this nonsense. Let this be a warning to you. I believe this ends our little discussion."

Jake panicked, thinking, "*That's it?*"

Skumansky hadn't admitted anything and hadn't committed any incriminating acts.

Without either of those, there was no way to get them on anything. That meant there was no way to force them to reveal where the kids were hidden.

The three rabbis stood and Jake followed their lead. He needed an idea to get this back on track. He never imagined they'd let him walk.

Suddenly, Skumansky raised his finger high in the air, and said, "Oh yes, my friend. There is one more little *detail*. We see that you seriously repented and believe you will not repeat your offense. But the act of *moser* you *already* committed by informing the police, is not reversible. What's done is done-- there is no way to prevent sentencing on that."

He nodded to the other two and they nodded back in

agreement. "This *Beis Din* hereby finds you guilty of *moser* and sentences you to death."

"Ten minutes to three. Mort, where *are* you?"

Jake turned in response to footsteps he heard to see two gorillas emerging from behind the room-divider.

He immediately pegged the pug-nosed one as Harold Winke– the thug Rabbi Skumansky hired to stun-gun Pinky and hold a gun to his head until he authorized them to give his wife a *Get*.

He tried to run, but it was too late.

Each of his arms were gripped tightly, as if locked into vices.

He could feel each steel finger gripping his arm, nearly stopping the flow of blood like tourniquets.

The two apes lifted him straight off the ground. He squirmed, kicked, and yelled, but to no avail.

"For the act of *moser*, this *Beis Din* hereby finds you deserving of the death penalty by choking. We will carry out sentencing immediately."

Jake turned his head, anticipating mechanical fingers gripping his throat. But Skumansky had much grander plans.

The two gorillas held him up while Diamond slipped a chair underneath him.

Skumansky appeared with a long, coarse, rope prepared with a noose at one end. Flinging the noose over the garage's cross-beam, he held the other end tight, then secured it to a hook in the garage wall.

Skumansky slipped the noose over his head as the gorillas pushed his head forward. Then he pulled up the slack.

Jake squirmed, but their grip was ironclad tight. There would *be* no escape.

Skumansky motioned to Diamond and Fogal and they each took their position beside each of the Gorillas.

"You won't get away with this!" Jake shouted. "The police are on their way, *right now*." Diamond and Fogal exchanged odd glances.

Skumansky laughed and shoved aside the room divider revealing a full-sized pine casket, lid open. He waved the note Jake signed-- the *suicide* note. "No one will question a funeral procession led by a rabbi taking the body of a poor suicide victim to be buried."

He instructed the two apes, "When these rabbi's kick the chair from beneath this *moser*, let go of his arms."

Jake managed another glance at his watch. *Seven minutes* to Mort's scheduled arrival.

"*Now!*" Skumansky barked.

But before they could respond, a commotion at the front of the garage drew their attention.

A pile of *esrog* boxes tumbled.

Jake took advantage of the distraction and managed to wriggle free, but the apes quickly retook control of his arms, and one now held his hand over Jake's mouth.

Skumansky held his finger to his mouth, ordering complete silence and slid the room divider in front of them to hide them all.

Jake tried yelling from beneath the hairy iron hand now sealing his lips, but he couldn't manage a sound.

"Rabbi? *Rabbi*?" cried a familiar Russian-accented voice. "Have you any spare change for a poor disabled man?"

Jake immediately recognized the familiar wheelchair squeak as it drew near.

Skumansky responded in a raised voice, "Yes, my friend. But please come back later tonight. I'll have something for you then."

Jake managed to bite the giant hand sealing his mouth, causing that gorilla to briefly release his arm, while kicking the other in the ribs, causing him to also release his grip.

Seizing the split-second opportunity, Jake reached

as high as he could, lifting himself by the rope and then swung both knees square into the middle of pug-nose's face.

The beast fell to the ground, whimpering in pain. The other ape grabbed Jake's right leg.

Swinging his left shoe with all the strength he could muster, he whacked his heel into that ape's eye socket.

He joined his fellow ape on the ground.

Pulling himself even farther up the rope, Jake let out a scream for help that made his own ears ring. He had a clear shot to hit Skumansky from up there.

"Rabbi, is everything alright back there? *What's going on rabbi?*"

Jake located Diamond and Fogal, cowering in the opposite corner of the garage.

He swung back and forth like a child on a park swing, until he built up enough momentum.

Aiming both heels at the back of Skumansky's head, Jake threw all his weight into his next downswing.

Bullseye!

Skumansky's face flew right through a plate-glass window.

Jake struggled to free himself from the noose. But he was afraid to let go, for fear he'd drop and break his neck of his own accord.

By this time, the beggar had wheeled himself behind the room divider.

"*Quick!*" Jake yelled. "Hand me that knife, carefully-- it's razor sharp."

"Where?"

"The *chalif*, in the velvet case on the table."

"I can't reach it from here," he said, motioning to the wheelchair.

"C'mon-- *I know* you can walk. Remember *me*? From the alley behind Shalomski's? I'll owe you big-time. Just do it, *fast!*"

The beggar jumped to his feet, removed the surgically sharpened instrument from its case and gingerly handed it up to Jake.

As soon as it was within reach, Jake gripped the rope tightly with one hand, let the other go, and grasped the knife's handle.

Before he could cut the rope, pug-nose shoved the beggar aside like a toothpick, smashing him into his wheelchair, then growled and grabbed both of Jake's legs.

Jake swung the knife at the rope, which gave way like butter, sending his full weight down upon the ape.

He made a nice cushion for Jake's landing.

Jake searched for the *chalif* that dropped when he crash-landed, but stopped abruptly when he noticed the red stains on his shirt.

He poked at the hot red goo, tracing it up to his face.

He flinched as his finger ran across the raw, exposed flesh on his left cheek. It had been surgically sliced open.

The second gorilla located the knife.

Holding the weapon sideways above his head, the monster charged at Jake. Certain he was about to be butchered, he closed both eyes.

"*Police!*"

"*Freeze it right there!*"

"Put the knife down, *nice and slow*. I want to see *both* hands at all times."

Uniforms and suits of every size and color converged into the garage.

Mort looked down at Jake.

"A few stitches and you'll be fine-- have a nice scar to brag about."

"*Mort!* The kids! *Time's running out!*" Jake pleaded. "We've got to get their location and get them."

"You leave that to us now, we'll get 'em. Don't you

worry."

As a paramedic attended to Jake's wound, he watched Mort go to work on Fogal. Fishel bawled like a baby.

"*I'll tell you, I'll tell you.* Just let me go. *Everything* Jake said is *true*. I was *there*. I'll give you Skumansky– just let me go!"

From the back seat of a squad car Diamond yelled, "*Shut up!* You'll get us both–"

"That's enough outta you," Mort shouted, as an officer cupped his hand over Diamond's mouth.

"Now, Rabbi Fogal, tell me where the Stein children are."

Chapter Sixty-Two

Five-thirty.

Excellent.

It was all over.

Mindy would never see those kids again.

Despite her successful revenge, Marsha was disappointed. She still had nothing to show for her troubles and it seemed that nothing could squelch her feelings for Jake.

Hoping it would offer comfort, she swallowed her medication, then returned to the computer screen.

There it was.

Fortunately, she'd been quick enough to prevent Jake and Pinky from swiping Sender's computer diskette, moments later. She'd found it in the computer and replaced it with a blank seconds before their arrival.

She prided herself on her quick-witted line about being the children's guardian and looking for them at Sender's.

They didn't even question how she'd managed to get inside Sender's house.

Her mother had given her Sender's spare key. But there was no way she'd let Jake know that.

It was a close call to be sure, but everything turned out fine.

Better than fine.

That diskette was just the ammunition she needed. As if God himself had handed her a gift.

Returning to Chicago as a new person was scary enough, without having to deal with her brother.

She never really knew him-- he was an infant when she'd been sent to live with her aunt. But he was *definitely* Herman Stein junior.

Mr. Creep, son of Creep.

At least, she now knew he'd only been her half-brother.

Her first read through Sender's electronic manuscript had been an emotional roller coaster.

First, the relief that she hadn't been molested by her *real* father, immediately followed by the ugly revelation that her real father was none other than Rabbi Joseph Skumansky.

It was embarrassing.

She'd taken pains to distance herself from that community.

Sure, she used them when she needed to. But she wanted no part of that lifestyle. She now saw Skumansky's personal interest in her job search in a new context. While she appreciated the help, the thought of a father like that gave her the willies.

"*Skum*-ansky," she thought. "How poetic-- he really was scum. Where the hell *was* he all these years? What a coward!"

After Herman's death, she needed a father more than anything. But he was too embarrassed to be there for her.

As she continued through Sender's crudely written novelette, she learned that Herman's embarrassing suicide wasn't even true. He had not done himself in. Another big relief that quickly vanished as Sender unfolded the details of Herman's murder.

Her real father, Skumansky, killed Herman, although it was for her sake-- or so she desperately wanted to believe.

It didn't take Marsha long to cleverly fashion a plan to exact her revenge against them all.

One by one they'd tumble.

First, there was Laurie Smilow, who'd swiped her first love, and now Mindy Stein, who'd stolen the heart of her second love, Jake Cooper.

The emptiness in her heart kept her up at nights, and

distracted her at work. Everywhere she went something reminded her of Jake.

She could smell him, feel him. *God*, she missed him.

Mindy Stein would have to pay dearly.

Of course, there was Sender, her *own* brother who exploited their mother's unstable mental condition, getting her to spill the beans on Skumansky, and Marsha's new identity.

Sender had called her.

First, he'd congratulated her on her new, high-paying job.

Then, without skipping a beat, he'd blackmailed her for cash in exchange for keeping her identity secret.

Last, but not least, Rabbi Joseph Skumansky.

The man who chose to conceal his shame from a community she despised, rather than be the father she so desperately needed.

They'd all hurt her in their own way. Now they'd all paid dearly.

It was perfect.

She easily duped Laurie into committing adultery. One phone call to Skumansky put him hot on Laurie's trail. Informing him of Laurie's sleeping with another man before receiving her *Get,* waved that checkered-flag to make Laurie's life a living hell-- excommunicate her, harass her, force her to leave town.

Marsha had no idea that it was Sender whom Laurie had taken as a lover. But Skumansky and his aides were good little detectives. They sniffed him out. She couldn't have planned things better had she tried.

She was sure it was Skumansky who did Sender in. Seeing the material Sender had collected on Skumansky, it was no wonder he wanted him out of the way.

For once in her life, she actually found something she learned in Hebrew school useful. She remembered that day clearly.

The day they were reading the biblical passages dealing with forbidden sexual relations. Her daydreaming abruptly ended.

Her ears strained to catch her teacher's every word.

She felt like everyone was staring at her– that they all knew.

She tried not to be too obvious about paying attention. But she really wanted to know what they could do to her father, Herman, if he were caught taking liberties with her.

She fantasized about stoning him, strangling,

beheading and then burning him. He deserved all four.

Yes, she decided.

He deserved that.

Though she hadn't grasped the finer details of who got which death, she did recall that stoning was carried out by pushing the offender off a cliff-- surprisingly similar to Sender's fall.

Too coincidental *not* to be Skumansky's work.

That took care of Sender, and Laurie, who ran like the dickens, fearing Skumansky would get her next.

Good riddance to them both.

But Mindy Stein-- *she* deserved an extra something special for her crime. An eye for an eye.

Better yet, two eyes for an eye– *Sarah and Danny.* Mindy stole the man Marsha loved.

Now she'd pay with her own loved ones.

Taking all three children would have been grand. But Adam would have been too difficult to handle. Getting the younger two however, was a snap.

So was enlisting Skumansky's help, now that she had Sender's little tell-all book.

Despite Rabbi Skumansky robbing her of a father, in some small way she felt he'd reached out to her by stopping Herman.

For that, she'd let him off easy.

If he succeeded in sending Mindy's kids to a place she'd never find them, she'd let him off.

Otherwise, she'd make certain Sender's diskette wound up in the hands that could ruin him, permanently.

The police would be very interested to learn how Herman Stein really died. Naturally, Skumansky agreed to help.

The terrible stories Sender fed Skumansky about Mindy made it easy for him to justify it all on what he deemed to be religious grounds.

Hey, if that helped him, fine.

But Marsha knew his true motives.

When Skumansky's attempted testimony against Mindy didn't pan out, she devised a new plan.

A brilliant plan.

Even if she were questioned by the police, she had the perfect alibi. She presented herself at the school as the children's aunt-- *no lie*. Malke Stein a/k/a Marsha Rein. No one had caught on. The name change combined with her new look was enough to conceal her identity. And it was easy enough to dress the religious-lady part again and reassume her Malke Stein persona.

No one questioned her claim of being their aunt. It

was true, after all.

Her line to the police if they questioned her?

Simple.

She'd claim that Rabbi Skumansky called her and said *Mindy's been in a terrible accident. Can she bring the children to him so he could take them to their dying mother's bedside?* Naturally, she agreed and delivered the children to Skumansky, as requested.

And how would she explain why she didn't get Adam?

Also, simple.

She couldn't find him and time was of the essence.

She'd say she rushed the two children to Skumansky who said he would take them to their mother.

What did she know?

No, the police would have nothing on her.

Marsha scrolled through the computer file one last time.

At this point only, her mother and Uncle Marvin could be hurt by this information.

The two people who'd stood by her, who'd taken pains to protect her, helped her get a fresh start.

Now it was her turn to protect *them.*

She clicked the delete button just as the phone rang.

It was the doorman.

"Ms. Rein, a Detective Roberts from the Chicago Police Department is here to see you."

Chapter Sixty-Three

Jake brushed the snow off his coat and stomped his feet before entering the one-story building. Chanukah decorations lined the waiting room walls.

"*Jake!*" Rabbi Miklin said, responding as he entered the rabbi's office. "I'm *so glad* you're *here*. Please, sit down. You've really done the community an important service. Stopping Skumansky was something no one else had been able, or at least willing to do, myself included I'm sorry to say."

"Oh, I think he's *more* than just *stopped* now. He'll be spending *time* behind *bars*. Mort's pretty sure the murder charges for Sender's death and the charges for trying to have me hanged aren't going away. Even *Herman Stein's* suicide has been officially reclassified as a homicide, now that Fogal's singing. Mort says, once he started talking, they couldn't shut him up. Diamond's trying to spill the beans faster than Fogal, seeing how he needs something to leverage his way out of prison. Mort says Diamond's edge is that he'll make a better witness than Fogal. But they'll probably go easy on both of them, being they were the ones who told the police to find us in the garage and not upstairs in Skumansky's office. Seems they were setting up

Skumansky to take the fall all along, hoping to take over his *Beis Din* themselves. Skumansky issued an excommunication order against them from his prison cell. He just doesn't give up."

"Actually, I'm surprised you even *called* me," Jake said.

"Why?"

"Skumansky excommunicated *me* too."

They both chuckled.

He continued bringing the rabbi up to date.

"Fogal said Skumansky had always been angry at him for leaving Herman's manuscript behind. He had it in his hands but dropped it on their way out. Mort's not sure how they pulled it off without leaving a trail of blood. Eventually they'll get all the details, between Fogal and Diamond competing for blab-time.

"Fogal also claims Diamond has been after Skumansky's position for a long time. He promised Fogal a spot in the new regime if he helped get Skumansky out. Diamond plotted to force Skumansky to step down by having Fogal snoop for dirt against him. Fogal was good at that-- and he found plenty. But they couldn't reveal the dirt themselves for fear that Skumansky would retaliate by revealing *their* little secret from their *yeshiva* days. But if the threat came from *Sender*, Skumansky would have no idea they were behind it. He'd be discredited and have no choice but to step down. But, when Sender realized the potential goldmine he was sitting on, *he* didn't want to make it *public*– he had a *bigger* scheme in mind, and he didn't just stop with Skumansky. He learned Fogal was skimming *esrogim* from Skumansky's stock, selling them under the table. He hadn't claimed the income and Sender had the documentation to prove this to the IRS-- the infamous manila envelope that eventually turned up in the bottom of Mindy's purse. Sender manipulated Fogal into gathering dirt on more community members and compiled his little atomic bomb manuscript, seeing how much he could shake down from whom. He was no longer interested in requesting Skumansky to step down. He wanted *cash*.

"But Diamond was determined. So, he devised another plan to topple Skumansky and take over. He knew what Skumansky would eventually do to get rid of me. He had Fogal call the police ahead of time and told them the meeting would be in the garage instead of in the rabbi's study. But he must've forgotten to call them back when the timetable escalated. That's why I saw the weird glances between Diamond and Fogal when I told Skumansky the police were on their way. They probably wondered how *I* knew.

"Those two yo-yo's might get some time, but nothing serious. Skumansky's the one the prosecutor really wants to go after. The bottom line, of course, is that Mindy's kids are finally safe and sound with their mother. Skumansky tried to change things at the last minute. He knew I was dangerously close. But Mrs. Trevel, the safe-house lady, wouldn't budge. She held fast to their waiting period rule, intended to prevent incidents precisely like this one. She'll be doing some time as well, but her connections with the Public Guardian's office may get her a reduced sentence.

"The police arrived just in time to catch her with the children packed and ready to leave.
A few more minutes and it would have been too late."

"Well," Rabbi Miklin said. "It's been quite an escapade. At least Mindy and her children can start putting their lives back in order now. I imagine it'll take some time for them to heal emotionally. But you Jake, *you* are truly a *hero*. We could use a man like yourself on our staff. Perhaps now that you've retired from computers, we could interest you?"

"*Me*? What could *I* do for the Rabbinical Board? *No offense*, but I don't want to hold myself out as a rabbi of *any* sort."

"That's not quite what I had in mind. Jake, there are many cases that cross my desk crying out for help with skills we simply don't have. Our *Beis Din* could use the full-time services of an investigator."

"Rabbi, the yellow-pages are full of competent investigators you could hire. Why *me*?"

Jake really didn't want to be tied to another job now that his lottery winnings afforded him the freedom to choose.

"Jake, you know how it is. Outsiders don't get very far in our community. They don't understand the culture, the people, the ins and outs of Jewish customs and laws. *You*, on the other hand, are not only fully equipped with those skills, but have blossomed into a first-class investigator. Mort seems to agree. He started coming to our Wednesday evening *Talmud* classes, you know. He's excited about the idea of you helping us."

"You ran this by Mort? He never mentioned it."

"I asked him not to."

"What do you say? Will you help us?"

"Well, I was looking forward to doing nothing for a while, after all this excitement. I really don't want to be tied down to a job. And I did promise to spend more time with

Mindy-- we've been seeing a lot of each other."

Ignoring Jake's objections, the rabbi responded, "You could just work on our most pressing cases."

"No, I really don't think–"

But before Jake could get the words out, Rabbi Miklin had opened a file and was holding up a family photo of a young couple and their children.

"Look at these unfortunate children, Jake. Don't let them down. Their father has been missing for several years now. Their mother struggles to keep food on the table, work full time, and still give each child the attention they need. But they need a father, Jake. He disappeared without a trace. The police have no leads. They won't actively work the case without some new evidence or leads. You could really help her, Jake. She has no husband, yet she cannot remarry either. She is an–"

"Yes, I know. An *agunah*-- unable to marry because her husband may still be alive."

"*Exactly*. In fact, there is a very suitable gentleman with four children of his own, very well off financially, whose wife died of cancer. We keep putting him off. It wouldn't be right, introducing them, knowing there's nothing they can do. The police suspect he ran off to start a new life. If we could locate her husband, we could get him to give her a *Get*. And if we could prove he was dead, she could remarry."

Jake really wanted a break now, but the man presented a strong case. "How about giving me time to think it over."

"Well, I suppose if he's been missing this long waiting a little longer won't matter. So, you'll let me know?"

"Absolutely. I'll call you."

*****

If you enjoyed this book and would like to read more Jake Cooper Novels, please help me by leaving a review on Amazon.com.

To receive my free bonus material* and newsletter, visit my website at www.irvsegal.com.

* Includes a glossary of Hebrew and Yiddish words and phrases and an extra "something" I think you'll really enjoy reading!

Made in United States
Orlando, FL
16 July 2024